Books by **Jennife**

de Vincent Series

Moonlight Sins: A de Vincent Novel (January 30, 2018)

Wicked Trilogy

Wicked

Torn

Brave

The Prince: A Wicked Novella (August 14, 2018)

Covenant Series

(Full series completed- Young Adult Paranormal)

Daimon

Half-Blood

Pure

Deity

Elixir

Apollyon

Sentinel

Lux Series

(Full series completed- Young Adult Paranormal)

Shadows

Obsidian

Onyx

Opal

Origin

Opposition

Oblivion (Daemon's POV of Obsidian)

The Dark Elements

(Full series completed—Young Adult Paranormal)

Bitter Sweet Love

White Hot Kiss

Stone Cold Touch

Every Last Breath

Standalone Titles:
The Problem with Forever
(Young Adult Contemporary)
Don't Look Back
(Young Adult Romantic Suspense)
Cursed
(Young Adult Paranormal)
Obsession
(Adult spin-off the Lux Series)
Frigid
(New Adult Contemporary Romance)
Scorched
(New Adult Contemporary Romance)
Unchained
(Adult Paranormal Romance)
The Dead List
(Young Adult Contemperary)
Till Death
(Adult Contemporary Romance
If There's No Tomorrow
(Young Adult Contemporary)

Wait for You Series
(Read in any order, as standalones.
Contemporary New Adult)
Wait for You
Trust In Me (Cam's POV of Wait for You)
Be With Me
Believe in Me (short story in the anthology Fifty Firsts)
Stay With Me
Fall With Me
Forever With You

The Titan Series
(New Adult Paranormal)
The Return
The Power
The Struggle

The Gamble Brothers Series

(Full series complete- Adult Contemporary Romance)

Tempting the Best Man

Tempting the Player

Tempting the Bodyguard

For details about current and upcoming titles from

Jennifer L. Armentrout,

please visit *www.jenniferlarmentrout.com*

A

TRILOGY

#1 *NEW YORK TIMES* AND #1 *INTERNATIONAL* BESTSELLING AUTHOR

JENNIFER L.
ARMENTROUT

Brave
Published by Jennifer L. Armentrout

Library of Congress Cataloging-in-Publication Data
Brave/Jennifer L. Armentrout—First edition
ISBN 978-1-947591-70-7

Cover Design by Regina Wamba, Mae I Design
Formatting by Christine Borgford, Type A Formatting

Chapter 1

The room was so dark I couldn't make out anything beyond the faint, silvery moonlight seeping between the crack in the thick curtains. The air was still and stale.

But I knew I wasn't alone.

I was never alone *here.*

Straining forward, I peered into the darkness. The cool metal of the collar bit into my neck as I willed my heart to slow down, but the pounding against my ribs increased until pressure clamped down on my chest.

I can't breathe.

I can't breathe in this—

Something moved closer to the bed.

I didn't see anything, but I felt the slight stirring of air. My heart lurched into my throat as every muscle in my body tensed. There. A shadow blotted out the thin strip of moonlight.

He was here.

Oh God, he was *here,* and there was no way out of this. There was nothing I could do. This was my future, my fate.

My swollen stomach ached as I shifted, pressing my back against the headboard. The chain jerked suddenly, throwing me to the side. My hands flew out. I grabbed onto the bed, but it was no use. A scream erupted, quickly lost in the shadows of the room. Yanked forward, I was dragged across the bed, toward him. Toward the—

My eyes flew open as I jackknifed upward and over, nearly tumbling off the bed. I caught myself at the last moment, dragging in mouthfuls of air—fresh air that was slightly scented and reminded me of autumns in the north.

Immediately, I pushed the mess of curls out of my face and scanned the room, stopping at the window. The curtains were pulled back, just as I'd left them before I'd gone to sleep. Moonlight streamed in, flowing over the small couch and sitting area. The surroundings and the smell were familiar. Sweet relief pounded through my veins at the sight of them.

But I had to be sure that what I'd just experienced had been a nightmare and not my reality. That I wasn't still held captive by the Prince, who was hell-bent on impregnating me to fulfill some unbelievable prophecy that would throw open *all* the doorways to the Otherworld.

Slowly, I placed my hand on my stomach.

Definitely not swollen.

Definitely not pregnant.

So that meant I was *definitely* not in that house with the Prince.

I lifted a shaky hand, dragging it through my hair. It was just a nightmare—a stupid nightmare. At some point, I had to get used to them. I would eventually stop waking up in a panic.

I had to.

My stomach churned, gnawing at me as I took a deep,

even breath. *Hungry*. I was hungry, but I could ignore the hunger, because ignoring the burning emptiness in my gut had worked so far.

Exhaling roughly, I dropped my hands to the bed and swallowed hard. I was wide awake now. Just like the night before . . . and the night before that.

Behind me, the bed shifted and then a deep, sleepy voice rasped out, "Ivy?"

Muscles in my back locked up. I didn't look behind me as I wrestled my legs free from the blanket. Heat crept into my cheeks. "I'm sorry. I didn't mean to wake you."

"Don't apologize." The sleep cleared from his voice and the bed moved once more, and I knew without looking that Ren was sitting up. "Is everything okay?"

"Yeah." I cleared my throat. He'd asked me that a million times. *Is everything okay?* And the second most popular question—*are you okay?* "Yes. I just . . . woke up."

A moment passed. "I thought I heard you scream."

Dammit.

The warmth creeping along my face intensified. "I . . . I don't think that was me."

He didn't immediately respond. "Were you having a nightmare?"

I was sure he already knew the answer to that, which meant it should've been easy to admit. Plus, a nightmare was no big deal. Hell, Ren of all people would understand if I was experiencing a side order of PTSD to go along with the main dish of Things Were Kind of Screwed Up Right Now. Especially since he'd also spent some R&R time with the Prince and his merry band of psychotic fae.

But for some reason I couldn't admit to him that I was having nightmares, that sometimes when I woke up, I thought I was still in that house, chained to a bed.

Ren thought I was brave, and I *was* brave, but in moments like these, I . . . I didn't feel very brave at all.

"I was just sleeping," I whispered, letting out a shallow breath. "You should go back to sleep. You have stuff to do tomorrow."

Ren was leaving what I was now calling Hotel Good Fae to see if he could help locate the super special Crystal. Originally, this Crystal belonged to the Good Fae—the Summer fae. The Order had taken it from them and then Val had stolen it from the Order, and now the Prince had it. Without the Crystal, we couldn't lock the Prince back up in the Otherworld.

"Ivy. Sweetness." Ren's voice softened as he placed a hand on my arm. The contact shook me. "Talk to me."

"I'm talking to you." I pulled away, slipping off the bed. The minute my feet hit the floor, I started moving. The gnawing emptiness in my stomach grew. "I think I'm going to go work out."

"At three in the morning?" He sounded incredulous, and I couldn't blame him for that. Working out in the middle of the night did seem odd.

"Yeah. Feeling restless." Laying back down next to Ren right now, when my stomach felt the way that it did and with my head where it was, wasn't an option.

Faye's words from the night she helped me escape the Prince took the opportune moment to cycle through my thoughts. *And if you keep feeding you're going to get addicted. You probably already are.*

Ren knew about the feedings, about the fact that I might've killed someone, but he didn't blame me. He even believed that I wouldn't hurt him. That I wouldn't cave to the part of me that had awakened while being held captive—the part of me that was fae and now knew how to feed and how it could make me feel.

And how *easy* it was.

Ren trusted in me, but I didn't.

I couldn't afford *belief* right now, because I would never, ever forgive myself if I hurt Ren like I knew I'd hurt others. My mouth dried up as my hands opened and closed uselessly.

"Ivy?"

Realizing I'd got lost in my head, I blinked rapidly and refocused. "Have you seen the gym they have in the basement? It's motivating even me to get on a treadmill."

Of course, he'd seen the gym.

Ren didn't have the body he had without getting all up, close and personal with the inside of a gym.

"Instead of going to the gym at three in the morning, why don't you come back to bed?" he asked. "We can watch some shows. Pretty sure you've missed some episodes of *The Walking Dead.*"

I had missed a lot of episodes of my favorite zombie show, which sucked, because every time I saw Tink, he was seconds away from spoiling everything. The same with *Supernatural.*

A sweet, almost bitter wave of yearning sucker punched me in the stomach, temporarily overriding the shadows lingering in the back of my mind. I wanted to dive-bomb back into that bed, cuddle up with Ren, and fall asleep in his arms, listening to Rick Grimes turn back into the Rick-tator we all know and love. That would be the normal thing to do, and God knows I wanted normal so badly, for so long.

It was why I had enrolled in college even though I already had a career. Well, *did* have a career in the Order. Who knew now? But I longed to know what it was like to wake up and go to school or work without worrying about dying on the job or discovering that my coworkers had been killed. Normal meant going out to restaurants and the movies. Staying in and marathoning shows without worrying at the possible, impending end of the world. Normal meant that my best friend hadn't ended up being a traitorous bitch and dying because of her actions and choices.

Normal was so underrated.

The bedside lamp flipped on without warning. Light flooded the room, reaching to where I stood. Some bizarre instinct roared to life. I didn't know why, but I didn't want to be *seen* right now. I backed away from the light, but the moment my gaze met those leaf-green eyes, I froze.

Ren Owens was . . . goodness, he was beautiful in a wild sort of way. He reminded me of autumns in northern Virginia, all golden and copper. His hair was a tumbling russet mess, falling over his forehead and begging to be brushed back. Thick, heavy lashes I was admittedly envious of framed his stunning eyes. His cheekbones were broad and they were matched by a hard, chiseled jaw. Ren's nose was crooked, and somehow that added to the beauty of his face. He had a lush pair of lips that were usually tilted in a grin, and when he smiled, there were matching deep dimples.

Those corners were straight now, forming a somber line, and there were definitely no dimples.

Before everything with the Prince happened, Ren had slept shirtless or nude and we hadn't been able to keep our hands off each other. Seriously. Even when we were injured with our bodies aching, we couldn't ignore the chemistry sparking between us. But since I came back—since we were reunited—he wore a shirt to bed, along with boxers or sleep pants.

All we'd done was kiss.

Three times to be exact, and they were chaste, sweet

kisses that tasted of a deeper, restrained need.

I think the nightmares were why Ren was sleeping in clothes, because those nightmares started the first night and had occurred every night after that.

And those nightmares felt like premonitions. A warning of what was to come, and I couldn't shake that feeling, not even when the sun rose, and I was surrounded by people who hadn't given up on me—who cared enough to go back into hell and drag me out.

I suppressed a shudder.

"Please." He extended a hand toward me. My eyes tracked up the vibrant vines tattooed on his arm that disappeared under the white shirt he wore. "Come back to me and stay with me."

My breath caught around the expanding knot in my throat. I wanted to be there with him. Desperately. But I . . . I needed space and I needed . . . I don't know what I needed. I just couldn't be here.

"Maybe later," I said, finally moving. I made my way to the small dresser where some of my clothes had been stashed away. Guilt crawled up my throat like bile. "If you're still awake when I get back, we can watch something."

"You didn't come back last night."

I pulled out a pair of leggings. "I wasn't able to fall back asleep, so I didn't want to bother you."

"You know you're *never* a bother to me. Ever." There was a pause. "And I didn't go back to sleep. I waited for you." The kind of patience I didn't have kept his voice level. "I can go with you to the gym. Just give me—"

Whipping around, I saw that he already had his legs off the bed. "No!"

Ren froze, his eyes widening slightly. "No?"

I clenched the pants in my hands. "I mean, I don't want

you to get up and feel like you have to keep me company. I've already woke you. You should go back to sleep."

His shoulders rose on a deep breath. "It's not a big deal. I can go with you." He stood, lifting his arms above his head and stretching. "We can have a race on the treadmills." He dropped his arms. "Whoever loses has to go to the kitchen and steal the box of beignets they have shipped in every morning."

My heart was pounding as he took a step toward me and then another. The room wasn't very large, so it took no time for him to be right in front of me.

"I just need to get changed. Or I could go like this? What do you think?" he teased with a small grin. "Might not be the most comfortable run."

Blood buzzed in my ears as my gaze dropped to his mouth. My stomach dipped as Ren reached for one of my curls. He'd pull it straight and let go. It was a favorite pastime of his, and then, if things were normal, he'd lower his lips to mine. Anticipation swirled as a tight shiver curled its way down my spine. Pleasant warmth invaded my veins.

But did I want to kiss him? Or did I . . . did I want to feed from him?

The fact that I had to even ask myself was terrifying.

I took a step back and bumped into the dresser, rattling it.

Ren went still as a statue. Terse silence filled the space between us as I stared up at him with wide eyes. "I'm not going to hurt you, Ivy. You know that, right? You're safe with me. Always."

Oh God, did he think I was worried he'd hurt me? Of course, he would. How could I blame him for thinking that when I was as jittery as a coffee fiend when he was around me?

My face burned as I looked away. "I know you wouldn't hurt me. I'm sorry—"

"Stop apologizing, Ivy. *Dammit.* Just stop saying you're sorry."

I opened my mouth and closed it when I realized I was about to apologize again.

Ren stepped back, giving me space. "You have nothing to apologize for."

Didn't I, though? It sort of felt like there was a list as long as my arm to apologize for, starting with the fact that I hadn't recognized the Prince masquerading as Ren right off the bat. And there was more—God, there was so much more, and when my head was running in a million different places, it was hard to remember that Ren wasn't holding any of this against me.

But how could he not? How could he sleep like he did at night? I wanted to ask him how he was moving on from this, because he'd been captured too. He'd been fed on—fed on in the worst way, and there had been this female fae. Breena. She'd claimed that her and Ren . . . She claimed a lot of things, but I knew if any of it were true, Ren hadn't been a willing participant.

Rage replaced the warmth. I wanted to gouge her eyes out again, and I planned to. Right before I killed her. Slowly. Painfully.

Ren was watching me in a way that made me feel like he saw right into my head, and if that was the case, then he probably wouldn't like what he saw. His shoulders tensed and then he exhaled roughly. "Okay."

Relief swept through me.

His gaze flickered over me, and I thought that he may have seen the way my stance loosened in response to him backing off. His jaw tightened. "I'll be waiting up for you."

I knew he would be.

And I knew that deep down he realized there was no point.

Chapter 2

My sneakers pounded off the treadmill, shaking the whole thing like a herd of cows were trampling on the contraption, but I ignored the sound. My hands balled into tight fists pumped at my sides. The curls that had escaped my twist now clung to the nape of my neck and temples. Sweat ran down my throat and pooled in areas I didn't want to even acknowledge.

Running.

Ugh.

I hated running—hell, loathed all physical activity on most days, but being a member of the Order, destined at birth to hunt down the fae who were feeding off mankind, I kind of had to be in shape.

But I wasn't on this treadmill at the moment because I was some kind of predestined protector of mankind. I was just running, because there was nothing else for me to do. I was stuck here, basically on house arrest at Hotel Good Fae. Since the Prince of the freaking Otherworld could sniff me out like some kind of bloodhound, it was too risky for me to be out roaming the narrow streets of New Orleans.

My nails dug into my palms.

Faye, who had been working undercover at the Prince's mansion, had explained that the glamour surrounding Hotel Good Fae would hide my presence from the Prince. That was the kind of power the fae who had descended from the Summer Court had.

A court that the Order had told us didn't exist any longer.

My lips thinned as I picked up speed, literally going nowhere. The Order had lied about so much. They knew that there were good fae out there—fae who chose not to feed off humans, who lived normal lives, and aged and died like humans. The Order had worked alongside them at one time.

Had David known?

Being the leader of the New Orleans sect, David Cuvillier had to know the true history of the Order and the fae. So that meant he'd also lied, and for some reason, it stung like a bitch. David was the closest thing I had to a father since I was shipped off to New Orleans. He was an ornery SOB and spent more time criticizing me than he did complimenting me, but he was . . . he was David and I had trusted him.

All of us in the Order had trusted David—we trusted the Order itself.

I didn't even know why I was stressing about this, because at the end of the day, did it matter? I doubted I was still an Order member.

After being missing in action for the last month or so, and with the Elite—the super special and secretive group within the Order—scouting for the Halfling, I was sure they either thought I was dead or that I was the Halfling they'd been searching for.

That Ren had been sent here to find.

I swallowed past the sudden rise of nausea as I gave my head a little shake. Sweat flung out, dotting the control panel. The problem was that we needed the Order to open the doorways so we could send the Prince back. I had no idea how we would complete the act, the so-called blood and stone ritual. It had to be done in the Otherworld. How in the hell were we supposed to get the currently missing Crystal *inside* the Otherworld with the Prince's blood, along with mine, on it? Just thinking about that made my brain hurt and I wasn't about that kind of life right now. My brain simply didn't have space for any of that.

Last night, I found myself here after leaving Ren in the room. I was here again, a handful of hours later, because running usually made my brain shut down. When I ran like this, pushing my body until my calves burned, my thighs ached, and my heart raced, there was little room left to *think* and dwell on the weeks of my life I'd lost—the weeks I'd spent with the Prince.

I normally didn't think about the horrid dress he made me wear or the way I'd been chained to a bed. When I ran until my muscles felt like rubber about to snap, I could ignore the insidious hunger gnawing in my gut—the kind of hunger that no amount of beignets or crawfish would succor.

When I ran to the point that my thighs felt like blocks of cement, I didn't think about how the Prince had forced me to feed on innocent people. I didn't hear the whimpers they made when my sneakers were thundering off the treadmill. I didn't feel the euphoria that had come from feeding.

And when I ran until it felt like my chest was on fire, I didn't have the space left to think about what that bitch Breena had done with Ren. Or what the Prince had done to me . . . had tried to do to me.

Keeping my thoughts locked down was top priority at the moment, but running wasn't working for me now.

I needed to focus on something—anything.

My gaze flickered over the wall. There were several mounted TVs, but they were all turned off. I'd never actually seen a fae work out in here. I honestly didn't know if they needed to work out.

Did that mean they couldn't get things like heart disease?

Why was I even thinking—

The treadmill's belt suddenly stopped under my feet, pitching me forward. I slammed my hands down on the rails, catching myself seconds from knocking my head off the control panel.

"Jesus," I grunted, lifting my gaze.

Tink stood beside me, holding onto the emergency cord. "Good afternoon, Ivy-Divy. I'm happy to see your reflexes are still on point."

Standing, I let go of the rails and turned to him as I dragged in deep breaths.

"But your observation skills suck ass," he added, cradling the gray sling he wore over his shoulders with one hand. "I reached right in front of you and unplugged that thing."

"You're an asshole." My chest rose and fell heavily.

He smiled proudly. "I am many things. An asshole is one of them."

One of these days I was going to straight-up murder Tink. And I had a lot of reasons to act like it was time to *Purge* when it came to him. Starting off with the fact that up until recently, I thought Tink was about the size of a Ken doll. That's how I'd found the damn brownie in the St. Louis Cemetery No. 1 suffering from a broken leg and a tear in his fragile, gossamer wings. He'd been about a foot tall if that.

I'd made him a leg brace out of popsicle sticks and nursed the little punk-ass back to life even though harboring any creature from the Otherworld would've gotten me killed. I still really don't know why I'd saved him. I just felt so bad for him, but maybe the part of me that was fae had taken over, caring for another creature of the Otherworld. Who knows? And how did he thank me for it? Spent my money on bizarre, random shit he ordered off of Amazon Prime, hid from me that I was a halfling, and forgot to mention that he *chose* to be only twelve inches tall. That, in fact, Tink was very, *very* tall.

And totally anatomically correct.

Seeing Tink all man-sized never failed to wig me out, because I never thought of Tink in that way. Not only had he seen me in my undies a hundred times when he was miniature size, there was now a lot more of Tink, and. . . .

And adult size Tink was . . . hot.

Acknowledging that made me puke a little in my mouth, but it was true. When he was small, he had this cute, handsome little face and he was just *Tink*, and now that he was all big, that cute little face had broad cheekbones and his body was ripped and . . .

Yeah.

I screwed up my face. Seeing Tink like this still messed with my head, but I guess at the end of the day he was still Tink, and even though I wanted to bitch slap him into the Otherworld often, I sort of . . . I don't know . . . loved him.

Not that I'd ever tell him that.

Tink's hair was so blond it was almost white, and today he had it spiked. He was wearing jeans and a thermal. He must've grabbed one of the towels on the way in, because he held one in his free hand. I glanced at the bottom of the sling, where a little ball was curled up. He'd taken to carrying Dixon—his new pet kitten—around in a sling that I was pretty sure was designed for human babies—

Wait a second.

My eyes narrowed on the gray thermal Tink had on. "Are

you wearing Ren's shirt?"

"Yeah. I think it will endear me to him. Help us bond so we can be like brothers from a different mother."

"Uh. Doubtful." Ren was going to be pissed. "That's also a little weird."

"Why? Girls share clothing all the time."

"Yeah, the key word is share, Tink. You just took his shirt." I couldn't believe I had to explain this. "Is that towel for me?"

"Yeah. You look like you've been swimming in a swamp." He threw it at me. "But at least you don't look like you popped an eyeball anymore."

"Thanks," I muttered, wiping the towel over my face. When I made my escape from the mansion, one of the Prince's minions had tried to choke the ever-loving life out of me. I'd burst a blood vessel in my eye during the struggle. It was just as gross to think about as it was to look at.

Valor, the Prince's minion, was a goner though. Ren had taken him out. That was one Ancient we didn't need to worry about.

"I can't believe you're in the gym again," Tink went on, stepping aside. "Why are you in here running so much? Are you preparing for the impending zombie apocalypse that I know nothing about? Because if you are, we need to find the nearest redneck to become best friends with, one that is hot in a dirty, rugged way. You know, the kind that probably smells like sweat and man, one with a complex background that makes you hate him at first, but slowly, over time, you grow to love him."

I stared at him. "You've put a lot of thought into this."

"I have. I like to be prepared. Since we're in the south, it shouldn't be hard to find one. So, why are you in the gym so much?" he asked, not missing a beat.

"What else do I have to do?" I draped the towel around my neck as I watched the little ball at the bottom of the sling start to move around.

"I don't know." Tink patted the outside of the sling and got a tiny, muffled meow in return. "You could spend time with some of the peeps here. They're pretty cool."

"You think they're cool because they worship you."

His smile was so wide it could've cracked his face. "Well, yes, there's that. They're smart."

Most of the fae here had never seen a brownie. The Prince and the Winter Court basically killed off Tink's kind.

"You could also spend time with Merle or Brighton," he added. "Momma Merle is almost always out in the courtyard, digging up something or planting something. She's interesting. Weird. But weird can be entertaining, and Merle is entertaining. And I like Brighton." He paused. "I don't think she likes me. Actually, I'm pretty sure she's kind of scared of me."

I arched a brow. Tink sure did like to ramble.

"She sort of goes in the opposite direction of wherever I'm going." His lips pursed. "Just this morning, I was in the common room. You know, the room you never hang out in, but anyway, I digress. The room has all these cool games and couches and shit. I was in there, winning a mean game of air hockey, and Brighton walked in, made eye contact with me, and then walked right back out. I don't understand why. I'm super friendly and approachable. I also know that I'm damn good looking by human standards, too."

I decided not to point out all the ways he probably freaked out Brighton, because that was a rabbit hole I did not want to fall down. Besides, I needed a shower stat, because I did feel like I'd been swimming in a swamp. I stepped off the treadmill, and the moment my feet hit the ground, my entire world wobbled. “Whoa.”

Tink grabbed my arm, steadying me. The dizziness vanished as quickly as it came on. “Are you drunk?” he asked.

I snorted, slipping free. “I wish. I didn’t eat breakfast or lunch yet. That was dumb of me.”

Tink was quiet as he studied me. “Do you think you might be overdoing it?”

“Overdoing what? Sitting around on an unasked-for extended vacation?”

“You haven’t been sitting around. You’re working out. Nonstop.”

“I’m not overdoing anything.” I walked away, edging around the stationary bikes and past the lazy-man treadmills—the ellipticals.

Tink was right behind me. “Not that you need reminding, but you were held captive for weeks and—”

“You’re right.” I whirled on him as the ever-present anger erupted inside me. “I don’t need reminding. I know where I’ve been.”

“But do you know where you’re going?” he asked softly.

I opened my mouth, but I had no idea how to answer that question. Where *was* I going? The anger slipped away, swallowed by confusion and a nearly overwhelming sense of helplessness.

God, I hated that feeling, because the last time I’d felt this way was when the fae had killed my boyfriend Shaun all those years ago. I’d been helpless then. I’d been helpless when the Prince put a collar around my neck and led me around on a chain.

I was still helpless, trapped in Hotel Good Fae.

Little Dixon popped his gray head out of the sling and looked around with sleepy kitten eyes. Tink reached down and scratched at his ear. “Ren should be back soon.”

My stomach dipped like I was on a rollercoaster that was about to plummet down a steep hill. I hadn't seen him since I left in the middle of the night.

"I saw him leave with Faye."

A hot, suffocating feeling blanketed me, curling low in my stomach and mingling with every other crappy thing I was going through. The world tasted bitter in my throat, like I was suffering from indigestion.

I hadn't known he'd left with Faye. Had he said something to me about it? I couldn't recall. Not that it mattered. I mean, I didn't suspect something or anything like that. Ren said he loved me, that he was *in* love with me, and I believed that. Totally. I just . . .

I wasn't out *there* with him. Someone else was, and my head—my head wasn't right.

"They were going out, trying to see if they could locate the Crystal thing." Tink still scratched the little kitten's ear and Dixon was purring like an engine. "You being stuck here while your man is out there, working to fix this has got to suck for you."

I dragged my gaze to his. "Really? Are you trying to make me feel better?" I turned and started for the door. "Just so you know, it's not working and you suck."

"I'm not trying to make you feel better," he replied, following me. "I'm just pointing out the obvious."

"It's not necessary to point out the obvious when it's obvious, Tink."

There was barely a half a second of silence. "You didn't join us for dinner last night."

Thinking this had to be the longest exercise room ever, I hurried up.

"You didn't join us for dinner the night before or before that," he went on. "And that means I've been eating with

Ren. By myself. We just may kill each other."

"You'll be fine." I reached the door, thank God.

"Where have you been?" he asked. "You've been here, but you haven't been."

"I'm here, Tink. I've just . . ." I didn't know how to answer this because words failed me. How could I explain that every time I was around the fae, they stared at me with distrustful, almost fearful, eyes? They knew what I was. They knew why the Prince had held me captive. They knew what I symbolized. "You know how I am with a whole lot of people. You guys eat in the cafeteria. I'm not into group activity—"

Tink grabbed my arm, stopping me from opening the door. He turned me around, and for once, his expression was a hundred percent serious. "Eating in a cafeteria isn't a group activity." His gaze flickered over me. "And it doesn't look like you've been eating by yourself either."

I laughed at that. "Trust me, I've been eating. A lot. Constant, actually." And that was the truth. I had to, because if I didn't the *hunger* got to me. "I've just—"

"Been running ten miles a day, drinking tons of coffee, and not sleeping?"

My eyes widened. "Whoa. Are you stalking me?"

"I'm paying attention. So is Ren." His gaze remained latched to mine. "Your face looks different."

"What?"

"Your cheeks are sunken in, and you have these shadows under your eyes. They weren't there before."

"Wow. You're starting to give me a complex."

"Looks like you already have one."

Uncomfortable, I pulled my arm free and whipped the towel off my neck, tossing it into the nearby laundry basket. "There's no reason to pay attention to me. Okay?"

"Ivy—"

Before he could stop me, I opened the door and stepped into the hall. I was so not in the mood for this conversation. Just like I wasn't in the mood when Ren brought it up, which felt like every five seconds.

Ren wanted to talk about things—things that I didn't want to think about around anyone, but especially around him.

I hurried down the hall, knowing Tink was still right behind me. Picking up my pace, I reached the end and turned, immediately stopping short.

Tanner stood in front of me.

He was the leader of this place. I kind of thought of him as King Good Fae, but he wasn't a king. At least, I didn't think he was.

When I'd first seen him, I almost fell over in shock. He was the oldest looking fae I'd seen at the time. Faint lines etched into the silvery skin around his eyes and his hair was more salt than pepper.

He was living and aging proof that he hadn't been feeding, at least not regularly enough to stave off the aging process.

"There you are." Tanner smiled, clasping his hands in front of him. He was always dressed like he was going to a business lunch—dark trousers and a button-down white shirt. "I was looking for you."

"Awesome," I chirped, happy for the distraction. "What's up?"

Tanner glanced at Tink, his gaze dropping to where I knew Dixon had to be. "I've just received exciting news."

"Amazon Prime will deliver here now?" Tink asked.

I rolled my eyes.

Tanner continued to smile, apparently besotted with the overgrown brownie. "Not yet, but we're working on it."

They were seriously working on that? Good Lord.

"I was looking for you since I knew Ren was out with Faye," Tanner went on, and I tried to ignore the ugly, stupid twinge in my chest. "We've made contact with another group who we believe can help us locate the Crystal. That's great news, because when I checked in with Faye earlier, her and Ren weren't having any luck at Flux."

Flux was a club that we knew was run by Ancients, namely Marlon St. Cryers, a huge developer in the city. Flux could possibly be one of the spots where this super special Crystal was stashed away.

"Really?" Excitement hummed through me, a trill in my blood that hadn't been there in what felt like forever. "How?"

"They're going to be here in a few days," he said. "And they have a . . . unique talent for finding things that are missing."

"Unique talent?" Tink mused, and when I glanced over at him, I saw that Dixon had retreated into the belly of the sling. "I have some unique talents."

"And you think they can really help?" I cut Tink off before he went into detail that none of us wanted to hear.

Well, maybe Tanner did. What did I know?

Tanner nodded. "I really believe so." His pale gaze flickered over me. "I have some errands I need to get taken care of. I hope to see you at dinner tonight."

"Sure," I muttered.

He skedaddled at that point, leaving me with Tink. I turned to him, wondering if Tanner had help coming, then why were Ren and Faye still at Flux? Or out there in general? But the moment I saw Tink's expression, I stopped thinking about it.

He was serious again. "Where are you going?"

"To shower."

"And after that?"

I lifted a shoulder. "I don't know. Probably to grab something to eat."

"Okay." He extended a hand toward the lobby of Hotel Good Fae. "I can come with you."

"I'm just going to grab a snack and hang out in my room. I'm sure you have better things to do," I told him, backing up. "Like you have an entire audience of fae more than ready to stroke your ego and allow you to beguile them with stories."

There wasn't a flicker of change in his expression. No grin. No smug glint in the eyes. "Are you okay, Ivy?"

"Of course," I said with a laugh. "I already told you guys I was okay."

And I had said that to them. I'd told Tink and Ren I was going to be okay that day out on the swing—the day that felt like forever ago, but I wasn't okay.

I was far from it.

Chapter 3

Arms folded across my chest, I ambled down the long, narrow aisle of the Hotel Good Fae library. It was on the same level as the lobby and gym but way over in a different wing. I'd accidentally found it a few days ago while everyone was eating dinner.

And why did everyone eat dinner at the same time? Was that like some weird, Summer Court fae tradition? It was like being in high school, but with attractive, silvery-skinned people . . . who weren't even people.

Unfolding my arms, I reached out and trailed my fingers over the thick tomes. Some of these books had to be decades old, if not older. A lot were in languages I didn't understand. Further back were the newer books and a lot of genre fiction, like romance and suspense. They even had a decent, up to date, young adult section.

That was where I was heading while everyone in the entire, massive building was sitting down to eat dinner. From the aroma radiating from the cafeteria, I was thinking they were having pot roast. Normally that would have me salivating, but my stomach twisted uneasily.

Every day I was either starving or on the verge of vomiting, and there seemed to be no in-between. At what point would this stop? A week had passed since the last time I'd . . . I'd fed. The hunger had to go away.

I should probably ask someone about it. Faye knew what I'd been forced to do, but that would require me actually talking to her—to someone, which yeah, that wasn't how I wanted to spend my time.

Reaching the end of the aisle, I hung a right and moved further into the library. I liked it in here. It was quiet, and no one, not even Tink, thought to look for me here. I could grab a book, find a corner, and just sit and read.

And that was what I did.

I picked up an old historical romance, the kind that had a barrel-chested dude on it and a chick who looked seconds away from losing her dress. I found a little cubbyhole toward the back and curled up in a comfy, oversized chair.

It took a couple of chapters for me to get lost in the story about a young woman caught in a feud between Scottish warlords. I loved reading, but it was hard to concentrate when it felt like I should be out there, doing more—doing something.

Maybe that was what was wrong with me? Maybe I just wasn't used to sitting around and doing nothing for days with no end in sight. Because who knew? I could be sitting around for weeks. Maybe even *months*.

I wouldn't make it.

Exasperated with my thoughts, I refocused on what I was reading. Once I got my brain to shut down, I was engrossed. So caught up in picturing the rolling green hills and Highland mists that I didn't hear the approaching footsteps.

"Ivy."

Startled by the deep, smooth as sin voice, I nearly

dropped my book as I lifted my chin. Air punched out of my lungs the moment my gaze connected with eyes the color of spring leaves.

Ren.

I had not been expecting him to find me.

"Hey," I said, finding my voice as I closed the old paperback. My hidey-hole was no longer a hidey-place. "What are you doing in here?"

His brows lifted at my question, and I immediately wished I hadn't asked that. It came across as if I didn't want to be found, and well, I didn't, but I also didn't want Ren to know that.

"I mean, isn't it dinner time?" I quickly added, feeling my cheeks heat. It was another dumb question I regretted at once.

"Yeah, it is dinner." Moving closer, he sat down on my chair and stretched out his long legs. "That's why I'm looking for you."

I'd done the whole dinner thing the first two nights here, forced myself to eat through the stares of curiosity and distrust. I don't know how Ren did it, but this was the first night he had actually come looking for me. Well, as far as I knew. If he had and just couldn't find me, he didn't bring it up at night.

"I just got caught up reading this book," I lied. "I hope you didn't interrupt your dinner to find me."

A weird look I couldn't quite decipher flickered over his face, but was gone before I could figure out what it was. He glanced down at the book. "Have you been here all day?"

"Um, I've been here for a while."

He bit down on his lower lip. A moment passed in strained silence, and . . . well, things were just weird between us. And it was all because of me. I knew that. I was making things weird. The day out on the swing—the day I felt like I had this, that with Ren and Tink by my side, everything would be handled—now felt like a different life.

Letting out a long, slow breath, he leaned forward, resting his elbows on his knees. "I got back a couple of hours ago and looked for you. First thing I did, actually."

My heart squeezed as a wave of guilt washed over me. His unspoken question hung in the air between us. *Where were you?* Good question. I should've been available, waiting for him. Anything could've happened while he was out there. The Prince, the Order—*anything*, and I had worried, but I hadn't waited for him.

I found a place to hide away and that's what I did.

Ren looked away, focusing on one of the shelves. "I checked the gym, the common rooms, and the courtyard. Should've known to look here, you little book nerd." His grin was brief. Still no dimples. "I thought . . . I thought you'd be in the room or somewhere, you know, easily findable."

The guilt surged, coursing through my veins like battery acid. "I'm sorry. The time just kind of got away from me." I curled my fingers around the book. "So, what happened at Flux?"

"We were able to sneak in." The line of his jaw softened a little. "Faye used glamour on the humans. Can't believe the damn place is open. There was staff there and a few lower level fae we took care of."

I was kind of surprised Flux was open and running. The last time I'd been there, it had been a massacre. Bodies hanging from the ceiling and all. A sight I would not easily forget.

"We didn't find anything," he continued. Faye had never seen the Crystal at the house the Prince was holed up in, so it had to be stashed away somewhere. "While we were out, we decided to check out some of the cemeteries. Nothing suspicious there."

"Did Tanner get a hold of you guys?" I dropped my gaze when he looked over at me.

"Yeah." There was a beat of silence. "Said someone or something was coming to help us locate the Crystal, but I'll believe it when I see it, you know? If that Crystal wasn't at the mansion, then it's got to be somewhere here."

I nodded. "How is it working with Faye?"

"Weird," he answered, and thankfully, there wasn't a twinge of jealousy. "Whoever thought we'd be working alongside the fae?"

"It had never crossed my mind." I didn't point out that technically he was dating someone who could be considered fae since I was a halfling. "Do you think the Elite knew?"

Ren had been raised in the secretive sect with the Order, destined to be a member. "I never heard anything like that, but the Elite had to know." His voice hardened, and I peeked up. He was focused on a bookshelf again. His lip was curled in disgust when he continued, "Kyle had to have known."

I felt the same disgust. Kyle Clare ran the group of Elite that Ren had come from, and he was a dick. A giant, flaming dickhead who had killed Ren's best friend, Noah.

Noah had turned out to be a halfling, leaving Ren torn between his duty and someone he cared about. The same exact position he found himself in with me.

"That's the thing that keeps getting to me." Ren tipped his head back, working his neck from side to side. "Why would they keep the fact that there were fae out there who were good a secret? That they worked side by side with them?"

"I don't know," I whispered. That was the question of the year it seemed.

Ren's gaze found mine. "We've had Order members dying

in the fucking streets every week fighting the fae. How many died the night the doorway was opened?"

"Sixteen," I answered, a number I'd never forget.

"And the whole time there was this place full of fae that could fight by our side, who want the same thing as we do. It's bullshit."

It was a lot of things. Bullshit was only one of them. "I've been thinking about it. I just can't believe there isn't a reason. I'm not saying it's a justifiable one, but why did the Order take the Crystal from these fae, and why did they hide their old alliance from all of us? It *has* to be something big." I glanced down the silent aisles. "And I can't believe it was just the Order. Especially since Tanner hasn't been exactly forthcoming on the hows and whys of what happened."

"Yeah, whenever I've brought it up, he's dodged the question. So has Faye." He leaned over, his arm brushing against my bent leg. "And you know what they always say. There are three sides to every story."

"The Order. The Summer Court. And the truth," I answered. "Do you . . . do you trust them—the fae here?"

When Ren's gaze found mine again, I didn't look away. "I do, or I wouldn't have given up the daggers to stay here."

Tanner had asked that our weapons be handed over, just in case. We had, but the thorn stake remained in our room, because those things were rare and were the only weapon that could take out an Ancient.

"We've been vulnerable, so they've had plenty of chances to take us out. They haven't. They've made sure we've been fed, have a roof over our heads, and we're somewhere safe. Plus, they helped get you here." He reached in, lightly touching my hand with the tips of his fingers. "Do you trust them?"

My gaze dropped to his fingers. Truthfully, there were

only two people in this entire world that I trusted a hundred percent right now. Ren and, as crazy as it sounded, Tink. I'd learned the hard way that no matter how well you thought you knew someone, that didn't mean you really did. Val was proof of that.

"I trust you," I said.

Ren quietly slipped his hand under my palm, threading his fingers through mine. My breath caught as a knot of emotion swelled in my chest. Slowly, I closed my fingers around his. He lifted our hands to his mouth, placing a kiss to the top of my hand. A whirling cyclone of yearning and hesitation formed a tangled mess inside me. I wanted to climb into his lap and I wanted to run away.

He lowered our hands to his thigh. "Let's go grab dinner."

Yes was on the tip of my tongue, but that wasn't what came out of my mouth as I pulled my hand free. "I already grabbed something to eat, but you can go ahead. I'm going to get back to men in kilts."

A muscle flexed along his jaw and then his expression smoothed out. "What did you eat?"

Recalling the conversation with Tink, I went into exaggerated detail on what I'd consumed today. Half of it was a lie. After I'd showered, I had eaten a giant bowl of Cheerios and a peanut butter sandwich. Both had settled in my stomach like lead and there had been a few terse moments where I thought I was going to spend the rest of the afternoon praying to the porcelain god.

When I was finished, I wasn't quite sure if Ren believed me or not. "Okay," he drew the word out. "Then come sit with me while I eat."

Tension seeped into my muscles. Knowing that the cafeteria would be jam-packed with fae—with fae that knew exactly what I was and what the Prince had wanted from me—turned my stomach.

I pressed back into the cushion of the chair. "I think I'm just going to chill here."

Disappointment flashed across his face, and I had to look away. "Ivy." There was a pause as I felt his intense gaze on me. "I miss you."

"I've been right here," I said, trying to suppress the sudden surge of irritation. Being irritated with him wasn't right. Ren was doing nothing wrong. I drew in a deep breath and forced a smile. "I have no other place to go."

"You're here, Sweetness." His voice was soft, but I flinched nonetheless at the use of the nickname. *I should've known.* When the Prince was masquerading as Ren, he never called me that. "Physically, you're here, but that's about it."

I opened my mouth, but I didn't know how to respond to that because he was speaking the truth. No one had to be observant to see that.

He waited for me to respond, and when I didn't, his shoulders lifted with a deep breath. He rose, and when he spoke, his tone made my chest ache, because there was this . . . immeasurable gulf between us and it just kept growing, expanding until I worried that there'd be no bridge big enough for either of us to cross. "I'm going to grab some food. You know where to find me."

Pressing my lips together, I nodded.

Ren stared down at me for a moment, and I thought he might say something, but he didn't. He turned and walked away, his back straight and stiff. And I sat there, staring at the space he'd stood in long after he'd gone.

I wanted him to stay.

I wanted him to pick me up and drag me to the cafeteria.

But I also wanted nothing more than what he'd just done, which was to leave me alone with the emptiness.

Chapter 4

As evening grew into night, I gave up on reading and left the library. I really didn't have a plan for where I was going. Antsy, I was just roaming the halls while avoiding, well, everyone.

I knew no matter how long I avoided going back to the room, Ren would be awake. He'd just be lying there, gaze glued to the TV, whether it was nine or two in the morning. Every night he waited for me while I got changed in the bathroom like I was sixteen again. The covers on my side of the bed were pulled back. I'd climb in and lay down, and a few seconds would pass, and then he'd curl around me, holding me tight against his chest.

That contact, his chest against my back, his arm around my waist, always frazzled me. It was too much and not nearly enough all at once, but it was the only thing that helped me fall asleep.

Ren was the only reason I fell asleep.

I slept the meager hours that I managed to get every night because of him, because he waited for me. Because he'd been nothing but patient, and God, he was such a good guy.

Perfect. For real. He could even fold fitted sheets, and who could do that? I was just being so . . . so freaking screwed up.

I stopped just outside the courtyard and stared up at the hundreds and hundreds of twinkling string lights.

When I first saw the old Power Plant off Peters Street, it had looked like one of the many rundown, abandoned buildings, but that was some powerful glamour. Now I saw it for what it truly was: a beautifully renovated building that rivaled any of the swanky hotels in New Orleans. Faye had said they could house hundreds of fae who were looking for a safe place to hide out. The courtyard was beautiful—peaceful. That was why I often found myself out here. I could just sit and be alone.

I could think—think about all the things I didn't want to think about around other people.

As I walked under the paper lanterns and twinkling string lights, I wondered if this was what parts of the Otherworld looked like.

That was something I'd never thought about before.

I followed the path toward what I now considered my swing. There was an unseasonable chill in the air, and locals probably thought it was too cold. I would've been loving it except I knew it was because the Winter Court was spilling into New Orleans.

That kind of took the fun right out of the cold snap.

Stopping at the pathway, I folded my arms around my waist and listened. It was strange. There was the distant sound of laughter and conversation coming from the inside of Hotel Good Fae. But there were no sirens. No blaring horns. New Orleans never slept and it was never quiet. Not like this. It had to be the fae. They had magical sound-blocking talents or something.

Damn, if they could bottle and sell that?

I found my way to the swing and sat, using my toes to push myself. Unfolding my arms, I placed my hands on my thighs and closed my eyes. My stomach churned, causing me to suck in a sharp breath.

I was so damn hun—

Nope.

Opening my eyes, I exhaled long and slow. I looked around, taking in the fully bloomed irises while I ignored the tremor rolling up and down my arms. Then I did what I did every night.

Drake.

Every muscle in my body locked up, squeezing my chest and throat until I thought I might vomit.

Drake. Drake. Drake.

I repeated the Prince's name over and over in my head. I kept saying it until some of the tension eased up and the pressure receded from my chest. I said his name until I didn't want to hurl any longer.

These mental gymnastics were harder than running on a treadmill. Desensitization. Because how would I face Drake if the mere thought of his name made me want to puke?

Shivering as sharp wind picked up, I looked around the courtyard. The flowers stirred and the lights swayed. The place was as empty as I felt, and dammit, I hated that—hated this.

Because *this* wasn't me.

It wasn't who I was.

So what in the hell was I doing out here? I should be inside—I should be talking to Ren. We were a team. Partners. Lovers. Friends. I needed to talk to him. Tell him what I was feeling, because if I just got those words out, I knew he'd help me make sense of them. I needed to tell him about the incessant hunger.

I could talk to him about it. I could talk to someone, tell them—tell Ren—that I didn't feel like myself. That somehow, I'd lost who Ivy Morgan was.

Because I couldn't keep doing what I'd been doing, roaming aimlessly and hiding. That wasn't brave at all, but most importantly, it wasn't smart.

I knew enough from the Psych 101 class I'd taken at Loyola that sometimes talking to someone was the best medicine out there. It might not fix all the messiness in my head, but it had to help. It was the first step in the whole healing and dealing with trauma thing. Putting what I was feeling into words was like cutting out that darkness inside me.

I would find Ren and I would talk. I would definitely say something of freaking value.

Standing up from the swing, I hurried inside and back down the hall, walking by several closed doors while I kept my gaze off the fae that passed me. None of them ever approached me when we crossed paths. Most didn't even look in my direction. I wondered if they treated Ren the same—if it was because we were Order members or if it was because I was the Halfling.

That was a question probably best left unanswered.

As I neared one of the large common areas, I heard something that brought me to a complete stop.

I heard Ren's laughter.

Drawn to it in a way that was almost uncontrollable, I inched along the wall like a total creeper. Stopping just before the wide archway that led into the room, I leveled up on the whole creeper thing and peered inside.

Tink was the first person I saw, and I was kind of shocked that he was in the room with a laughing and non-murderous Ren.

Tink was sitting on the arm of the couch, near a very

uncomfortable Brighton. Her blonde hair was pulled back in a ponytail, like always. Brighton was in her mid-thirties, but she looked like she was a decade younger, having this ageless quality about her, much like her mother.

Sitting beside Brighton was a fae I'd met on the night I'd escaped the Prince. He had fair hair, so I knew it was Kalen. Tink claimed he couldn't tell Kalen apart from Dane, the other fae that had been part of Rescue Ivy Operation, but Dane had dark hair, so I had no idea why he had so much difficulty.

Ren was sitting in a chair, his profile to the doorway. He was leaning back, an ankle resting on his knee, a cheek planted on a fist. He was smiling and his shoulders were loose. His entire body appeared that way. Ren looked . . . relaxed.

I hadn't seen him look like that since . . . since I told him I was the Halfling. Of course, the next time I'd seen him it hadn't been him but the Prince pretending to be him. Ren had been captured the same night I broke the news to him. I didn't see the 'real' Ren again until the Prince took me to the cell where they'd been holding him.

Biting my lip, my gaze slipped from him to Faye. She was in her human form. Dark hair. Rich brown skin. Beautiful. She was perched on the arm of Ren's chair.

I started to taste blood in my mouth.

Letting go of my lip, I crossed my arms as Faye smiled down at Ren like they were all buddy-buddy.

I mean, not that I was jealous, but I guessed scouting together was a great way to bond. That was how Ren and I grew close—okay, I stopped that line of thought before I ran into the common room, grabbed Faye by her hair, and ripped her off the arm of the chair.

Tink would totally approve since he loved drama of all kinds.

There were other fae in the room with them, ones I didn't recognize, but my gaze crawled its way back to Tink and Ren.

They looked so . . . well-adjusted, like this was a normal night, any day of the week. Happy even, and most importantly, they were at ease. Neither of them were that way around me. Not even Tink. Sure, he was Tink, but even he sometimes seemed like he was walking on eggshells around me.

Talking to Ren about everything took a back seat. The last thing he needed at the moment was to deal with my emo bullshit, because he'd been through some nasty stuff too and he needed moments like this. Moments where he could just relax and be normal and not dwell on what happened to him—to us.

I didn't want to take that from him.

I stepped back and turned around, starting toward the elevators when I stopped. Where was I going? Sighing, I pivoted and made my way back to the courtyard. After being held in that damn room at the Prince's mansion for weeks, I didn't want to be cooped up in yet another room. It was chilly outside, but I preferred goosebumps over four walls and a door.

Following the pathway once more, I let my fingers trail across the leafy vines that all but covered the archway. Outside of this place, the vines and flowers were starting to die because of the cold spell, but everything was alive here. Enchanted. Maybe that was why I found it so peaceful? I moved further into the garden, further away from Hotel Good Fae.

"Hey."

Startled by the voice, I turned with a slight frown. A male fae stood several feet from me. I hadn't seen him before, but he appeared to be around my age. I glanced over my shoulder. Of course, no one stood there. I faced the fae, surprised since none of them ever spoke to me. "Me?"

The fae's hands opened and closed at his sides. "You're the only person standing here, right?"

Wow. Okay, that was some unnecessary attitude. "Yeah, but I have a name and it's not 'hey.'"

His jaw tightened and those pale blue eyes were practically on fire as he stepped forward. "I know what your name is, but it doesn't matter. Your name is irrelevant."

"Whoa." I barked out a short laugh. "Aren't you warm and fuzzy?"

He ignored the comment. "Why are you here?"

That seemed like a stupid question. "Well, it's kind of a long story, but I can give you the version for dummies if you'd like?"

The fae sneered. "We all know what you are and what that means. That's all we need to know."

Inwardly, my entire body cringed, but I kept my expression blank as I moved toward him. No way was I going to let him know that bothered me. "I knew I shouldn't have updated my Facebook status to halfling."

His lips peeled back. "You stand there as if this is all a joke, in a place sacred to us, while putting all of our lives in danger? I'm glad you can find the humor in this."

All the snappy responses died on the tip of my tongue. "How am I putting your lives in danger? Look, just because I belonged to the Order doesn't mean I'm seconds away from killing you all."

"It has nothing to do with you belonging to the Order or your *indiscriminate* killing of our kind."

Sounded an awful lot like it had to do with the Order.

The fae's eyes narrowed. "It has everything to do with you being the Halfling. The Prince will eventually find you here. We all know it. It's just a matter of time, and when he does, he won't just take you and leave. He'll slaughter all of us," the fae shot back, chilling my blood. "Is it so funny now, Halfling?"

My body went cold. "I was told that this place was protected—"

"It is, but not for long. The glamour will fail." The sneer slipped from his face. "And that is why we have no other option. As long as you're here, we are all in danger. My family. My friends. They'll all die because Tanner gave you shelter."

I didn't get the chance to ask him to explain the whole option thing. A footstep snapped a twig behind me. In the very back of my mind, I cursed myself for not being observant—for not scoping out the location, no matter how serene it seemed.

I was trained in the Order since birth. I should have known better.

But it was too late.

Before I could even fully register what was happening, red-hot pain erupted along my back, radiating through my side and down my legs, dropping me to my knees.

Chapter 5

Time slowed down to an infinite crawl as sticky, wet warmth cascaded down my back. Shocking pain robbed my lungs of breath as I planted a steadying hand on the pavement. In a stunned state of disbelief, I placed my palm to my back.

Gasping out a sharp cry, I immediately regretted the decision. Jerking my hand back, I could see it was covered in inky darkness. Blood. Lots of blood. It made the air smell metallic.

I'd been . . . stabbed.

Holy shit, I'd been stabbed!

Snapping out of the shock, I lurched to my feet and spun just in time to see the moonlight reflect off a gnarly looking blade arcing high above me.

Instinct took over.

I caught the attacker by the arm and twisted. The crack of bone didn't fill me with glee like it normally would, because the movement tore at my side, sending another wave of blistering pain through my body. I stumbled in its wake just as the fae fell forward, dropping the blade as it cradled its broken arm to a chest—a *large* chest.

The fae was female.

"You *stabbed* me!" I gasped out.

She lifted her head just as I slammed my knee into her chin, snapping her head back. She toppled backward, either knocked out or dead by the time she landed on her back.

I reached to my waist for a dagger, only remembering quickly that I had no weapons. We'd promised not to carry them. Dammit, all to—

A body slammed into my back, taking me down into the nearby bush. Landing on my back, a scream punched out of me, ripping through the night air. My entire body went stiff with pain, and for a second, only a damn second, I was immobile.

And it was a second too long.

I was flipped onto my stomach. Weight landed on me. Knees dug into my back as I crashed through thick leaves and flowers. Dirt and branches dug into my face as hands forced my head down. Mouth open, I dragged in dirt and God knows what else as I screamed in rage.

I knew better. I knew better. The words kept recycling. There were two fae, maybe more, and I turned my damn back on at least one of them. Twice. So stupid—deadly stupid. *I knew better.*

I struggled to lift my head out of the dirt, managing to take in a gulp of clean air a moment before my face was slammed down once more with excessive force. Wet warmth exploded across my face, filling my mouth as I reached around, trying to grab one of the hands that were bound and determined to smother me in a damn butterfly bush.

"Just let go," the voice said into my ear. "Just let go and make this easier on yourself."

Letting go meant being suffocated in a bush and that

was just not how I wanted to leave this world, so that was going to be a big fat nope.

"I can't let you live," he continued. "I have my family to think about. We have this community to protect."

Lifting my legs up, I slammed my hands into the bush—*through* the bush—and pushed myself up with every ounce of strength I had in me. Space between the ground and me grew. Digging in, I grunted as I flipped my body.

The fae went along for the ride until he slid off my back, taking me with him. I landed on his chest. Both of us were stunned for a moment. Then I sprang into action. Lifting my right arm, I brought my elbow down, jabbing the bastard in the side. A rib gave way. Maybe two.

He grunted, arms falling to his sides. Rolling off him, I scrambled sideways, leaping to my feet as I lifted my hands.

Oh shit.

My eyes widened as I stared at my left hand. There was a branch—a mother-loving *branch*—imbedded clean through the center of my hand!

"Oh my God!" I shouted as I reached with my good hand, gripping one bloody end. "Holy shit, there's a branch *in* my hand!"

"Should've been in your head," the fae muttered.

"Rude," I gasped.

The fae whirled to his feet, moving insanely fast. I didn't get a chance to pull the branch out, so I stepped to the side and swung my hand out without thinking. My branch-hand slammed into the fae's face. He fell to the side, taking me with him. I landed on my knees. The fae howled as blood poured out of his gaping mouth.

"Sweet Jesus," I groaned. My branch-hand had missed his eye, but my hand was now attached to his cheek. The branch had gone *through* his cheek.

So freaking gross.

Tearing my branch-hand free, I climbed to my feet and grabbed one end of the branch. Dizziness rolled through me as I stepped back. I yanked the branch free, screaming as the burn spread all the way up my arm. Nausea twisted up my stomach.

Once I had the branch out, I tossed it aside. A moment later, the damn fae was on his feet, his face bloody. "Good God," I exclaimed, lowering my ruined hand. "Your face is disgusting."

The fae let out a roar and charged me. I darted to the side. Or thought I did, but my reflexes were dull. He caught my left hand and squeezed. Rage and pain powered through me. I drew him forward, bringing my knee up at the same time. I caught him in the midsection, but it barely winded him. With his free arm, he backhanded me straight into next week.

I fell, cracking down on one knee. "Shit."

When was the last time a normal fae had knocked me around like that? I couldn't remember. It had to be *years*.

The next blow almost put me flat on my back, but I pushed through it, regaining my footing. The fae and I went toe to toe, and with no true weapon like an iron dagger, it was going to require creativity and strength to outlast the fae.

But my steps were too slow. The kicks I delivered lacked any real power. Even my punches were weak and off. The time out of training and combat had taken its toll. I wasn't prepared. My head wasn't in the right place.

That was why I was getting my ass kicked by a normal fae.

Each hit I took either broke skin or my will. Each new burst of pain seemed shockingly too real. Each time I got knocked down, it was harder to get back up.

But I did.

I kept getting back up.

Dragging myself to my feet, I wiped the blood out of my eyes. Well, one eye. The other was swelling and blurring. Only a handful of minutes had passed since I literally got stabbed in the back, but my muscles felt like lead and my bones felt brittle.

And I was still bleeding.

Whatever noise we were making was lost in whatever damn enchantment the fae had on the courtyard. My feet were heavy as I shuffled off the pathway, closer to the entrance.

Ren and Tink were just mere yards away, but they could be in another city for all it mattered.

Breathing heavy, I whirled around, searching for some weapon. The knife was lost in the darkness, beside the still prone female fae.

"You grow tired." Blood and spittle dripped from the fae's mouth. "You grow weaker with every passing second. How you've fought our kind and survived all these years is beyond me."

"Screw you," I bit out, swaying. Or maybe it was the courtyard that was moving. I had no idea. That statement just pissed me off, but he was right. *Focus, Ivy.* I had to be smart. I was weak and tired, and backup was currently chilling, having a lovely evening. I wasn't going to win this. No way.

I was going to have to tuck tail and run.

"You have to die." The fae's words were mushy. "It's nothing personal. You just need to die and then the Prince won't come for you."

"Dying sounds pretty personal to me." The back of my neck tickled. I thought I heard movement in the courtyard.

The fae attacked.

Dipping to avoid a mean uppercut, I shifted my weight and kicked out with my foot. I landed the maneuver, swiping the bastard's legs right out from underneath him. He went down in a fleshy smack, and I didn't waste time.

I snatched up a heavy river rock and brought it down on the side of his head with everything I had in me. The sickening crunch rattled my entire body. Falling onto my side, I dropped the bloodied rock.

Breathing heavy, I squeezed my eyes against the topsy-turvey the courtyard was currently doing as I sat back—fell back—onto my butt. In my chest, it felt like my heart was . . . stuttering.

Okay.

I needed to get up.

I needed to get inside and find . . . I needed to find Ren. I had to tell him . . . What did I have to tell him? Everything. I had to tell him *everything*.

My head was swimming, and I was lying flat on my back. How did that happen? I wasn't sure, but I knew if I kept lying here, I wasn't getting back up.

I would die.

You are dying. The voice that whispered in my thoughts was a shock to my system. I was . . . I was dying. All the sticky blood covered my entire body. There couldn't be much left.

Blinking slowly, I drew in a shuddering breath. This was my own doing. I hadn't been in any shape to fight. Not eating right. Not sleeping. I should've been paying attention. I should've *known*. That was an amateurish mistake, just like all those years ago when I killed the fae before I'd been authorized to. I'd gotten everyone killed and now . . . now I'd gotten myself killed.

No.

I wasn't dying. I was just . . . sleepy.

I could sleep. Ren would find me. I would wake up and he'd be here. So, I did sleep. I think I did. At least for a little while.

But then air caught in my throat and my eyes fluttered open. The stars shone brightly. I was still here. I was alone. No Ren, no Tink. My head lolled to the right. The fae was still here, though, and by the looks of it, he was super dead.

I was alive.

Relief gave way to a keen sense of disappointment I didn't understand, but couldn't focus on at the moment, because I needed to get up. If I didn't, who would watch out for Tink? Ren would, but he'd blame himself.

I couldn't let that happen.

Lurching to my feet, I teetered unsteadily until I got myself turned around. I walked back toward the doors, except it felt like I was wading through quicksand and I wasn't making much progress at all. No, it was slow and uneven, and the entire world kept blinking in and out. I tripped over stones, gritting my teeth as I forced one leg in front of the other. If I could just get to the doors, get inside, and get to Ren . . .

Rounding the corner, I stumbled onto the pathway and reached out, gripping the vine-covered trellis. The soft glow of the lobby lights seeped over the pathway. The doors were right there. I swallowed down the taste of blood and kept going, my steps turning sluggish.

Ren. Ren. Ren. I chanted his name. I was almost there. Just a little bit more to go. My hands were numb. I'd lost feeling in them, but that was okay, because my feet were still working. Just a little bit further. . . .

A shadow appeared in the double doors and it grew

closer. The shadow became a more distinctive shape and then the shape became a person.

"Ren," I called out, but it was only a wet whisper. I tried again, but now there was no sound.

He appeared as if he'd been summoned by my chants, and maybe he had, because the doors were opening and he was walking outside, his gaze sweeping over the courtyard.

I knew the moment he saw me.

He drew up short. "Ivy?"

And I knew the moment the light from inside reached me.

I opened my mouth, but my tongue didn't work.

"Ivy!" Panic filled his voice as Ren broke into a run, his feet pounding off the pavement.

Something landed on my back, between my shoulder blades. Something sharp and hot and it took whatever air was left in my lungs. Stole what strength I had left.

I went down, but I didn't feel the impact. The fury rolled off Ren in waves, filling the courtyard and overshadowing everything else. He was a blur, shooting past me.

My cheek was suddenly resting against the cool stone. I couldn't feel my feet any longer. That was probably bad, but I wasn't thinking about that anymore anyway. There was a sharp cry, and a body landed next to mine, the head twisted at an unnatural angle. It was her—the female fae.

I hadn't killed her.

Stupid, stupid me.

Another ridiculous, amateurish error.

"Ivy. Come on, Ivy." Gentle hands turned me over, onto my back. "Jesus Christ."

The tone of his voice told me I should be worried, but I couldn't find it in me to dredge up those emotions.

A hand cradled the back of my head. "Sweetness, look at me. *Please.*" He lifted me, and I was weightless. Floating.

"Dammit, open your eyes and look at me."

WI wasn't looking at him?

Forcing my eyes open, I found myself staring into Ren's striking face. Those vibrant eyes were dark in the moonlight, wide and endless. He was so very pale and there was so much darkness crowding his features. "I'm . . ."

"Don't try to talk," he said, and he was moving fast, practically flying. "Just hang in there, Ivy. Keep your eyes open and on me, okay? Stay with me."

But I had to. I had to say it. "I'm . . . sorry."

Chapter 6

The world flickered in and out, like a fading light bulb. I tried to keep track of what was happening. I knew Ren was carrying me inside. I could feel his hard shoulder against my cheek. I felt every step he took. Darkness gave way to warmth and brightness.

"I need a doctor!" Ren was shouting, his voice edged with wild panic. "Jesus Christ, someone! I need a damn doctor!"

It was getting hard to keep my eyes open, and I thought that maybe . . . maybe it was too late for a doctor. The world faded out again.

The next thing I knew I was lying on a soft surface that didn't have much give to it and the room was extraordinarily bright—too bright. It took me a couple of seconds to realize I was in the infirmary, a place in the basement of Hotel Good Fae that I was sure saw little action.

"Ren." His name bubbled up from my lips.

"I'm here." He carefully touched my cheek with his fingertips, drawing my attention. "Fuck, Ivy."

There were other voices. A woman's I didn't recognize. "You're going to feel a big pinch," she said, holding my right arm.

I didn't feel anything as I stared into Ren's eyes, wondering why his face seemed fuzzy.

But then Tink was suddenly there, standing beside Ren. "What happened to you? Ivy?" His eyes were wide with horror as he scanned me. "Who did this? The Prince?"

Someone gasped in the room. The cool hand on my arm stilled.

"No," Ren growled, and the one word echoed in the room like a gunshot. "It was fae that lived here."

"Two," I managed to whisper.

"That cannot be." That was Tanner, but I couldn't see him. "Those who live here would not harm you—harm any of you."

The fact that I was bleeding out from multiple stab wounds proved differently.

The air in the room filled with static, and Ren's fingers left my cheek. I couldn't see his face or his eyes anymore. He pulled back, and I didn't see him move, but I heard a body hit a wall.

"No!" someone shouted, and Tink whirled. There was a scream.

What the hell was happening? It was a struggle to lift my head and clear my vision, but I managed just in time to see that Ren had Tanner pinned to the wall with a hand around the older fae's throat.

"You said we were safe here." Ren's voice was too flat, too cold. "We trusted you."

"You are safe here," Tanner denied, his tone remaining calm even though Ren was seconds from choking the life out of him. "We would never—"

"That's obvious bullshit." Ren cut him off. The muscles under his dark shirt strained as he lifted Tanner up. "Look at her." A moment passed and Ren shouted, "Look at her!"

Tanner must've looked at me, but I couldn't see past Ren's shoulder.

"Does she look like she's safe?" Ren demanded.

Tink stepped away from where I lay.

"She doesn't," Tanner replied. "I understand you're upset. I am, too. I'm also shocked—" His words were cut off when Ren slammed him back against the wall.

"Tink," Faye cried out from the doorway. When did she get here? "You've got to get Ren away from Tanner. He had nothing to do with what happened to her!"

Tink shook his head. "I ain't stopping shit, lady. He's just lucky it's Ren who had his hand around his neck."

That was true. I'd seen what Tink was capable of.

I sucked in a sharp breath when Tink turned to me. He had never looked more Otherworldly than he did at this moment. His features were sharp and brutal—animalistic. But when he picked up my ruined hand by the wrist, he was gentle. "There's a hole in your hand."

Tink. Even in the direst of moments, he was still Captain Obvious.

"Ren," Tanner began, clearing his throat. "You need to understand—"

"What I *need* is for you to shut the fuck up and listen," Ren snarled. "I'm going to make two things painfully clear. First off, you will find out who did this, who was involved and knew about this, and why. Then you will tell me exactly who those dead motherfuckers are. And the second thing you better understand all the way down to your bones is, if Ivy doesn't come out of this, laughing her laugh, smiling up at me as she's walking out of this damn room, I will burn this motherfucker down with all of you in it."

Damn.

"Ren," gasped Faye.

"You understand?" Ren asked. "Tell me you understand."

"I understand," was Tanner's quiet response.

My head was now too heavy to keep up. I was flat on my back, staring up at a drop ceiling and ultra-bright lights.

"I feel funny," I whispered, or at least I thought I said it out loud. My lips moved, but I didn't hear my words. My heart tripped up in my chest. Yeah, I didn't feel right.

Ignoring the wave of nausea following the burst of pain, I called out. "Ren."

He was there in an instant, by my head. The tips of his fingers were on my chin, slowly turning my face to his.

A kernel of panic blossomed in my gut. "I . . . I don't feel right."

"What do you mean, Sweetness?" His gaze flicked over to the other side of the bed. "What does she mean?"

My tongue felt heavy. "I can't . . . feel my legs."

Ren cursed and started to pull away.

"Don't!" The panic spread as I tried to lift my hand. If he left, I didn't think I'd see him again. "Don't leave . . . me."

His hand brushed over my forehead. "I'm right here with you. I'm not leaving. Ever. You know that, right?" His voice thickened. "Never leaving you."

"There's a damn hole in her hand," Tink pointed out again.

"The hand is the least of my worries," the female's voice clipped back. There was pressure on my side. "I need you to help roll her. I have to look at this back."

My mouth dried. Rolling me sounded bad. "No," I groaned. "I don't—"

"I'm sorry, Sweetness, but we have to." Ren leaned in. Those beautiful green eyes of his made up my entire world. "We'll make it quick. I promise. But we have to do this."

I wasn't given much of an option. Ren gingerly gripped my right shoulder as he cupped my cheek with his other hand. "Hold on, Sweetness. Just hold on."

I didn't want to hold on. I knew this was going to hurt—hurt bad, and I didn't think I could deal with any more pain. I was at my limit, between the burning in my upper body and the numbness in my legs.

Hands landed on my hip. Tink. It was Tink. My wild gaze met his. "I have to," he said as if he were pleading. "You can punch me in the throat for it later. Okay?"

They rolled me onto my side.

Someone screamed, and it sounded like a wounded animal getting run over by a tank. It took me a moment to realize it was *me*—I was making the horrible, ragged sound, and that was about when the world wanted to fade away again, but Ren wouldn't let it.

"Keep those beautiful eyes open for me, Ivy. I know. I'm sorry, Sweetness. I'm so sorry. I know it hurts," he said, and he kept talking as hands and fingers moved along my back, from my shoulders all the way down to the base of my spine. "It's not too much longer. Okay? The doc is going to look at you and make you better."

My back and stomach were on fire, burning through my chest. "We . . . have . . . a doctor?"

"We do." His gaze flicked over my shoulder for the briefest second and then returned to mine. "She's almost done. Just a few more seconds." His lips pressed against my forehead. "You hanging in there, Sweetness?"

I thought I said yes. I know my lips moved, but I didn't hear it. I didn't think Ren did either, but then I was being laid back down and some of the hellfire was easing off—everything was easing off.

I faded out again, maybe for seconds, and when I came

to, I thought I heard Ren saying, "Out there, she said she was sorry. Why would she say that?"

"I don't know." I thought that was Tink.

I felt Ren brushing the hair back from my cheek and then his face was directly in mine. He looked like he was screaming, but he sounded so very far away, like he was standing at the end of a tunnel.

"I'm here," I rasped. "I'm still here."

"Yeah, you are, Sweetness." His smile was weak. "You're here."

"It's not good," the female said, the one who I guessed was a doctor. "None of this is good."

"No shit, Sherlock. What do we need to do?" Tink demanded.

"I don't think you're understanding me," she replied. "The lacerations in the back are deep—too deep. There are definitely internal injuries, and that's what I can account for just from the stab wounds."

"Okay. Then fix her," Ren ordered.

The fae was hooking something up to an IV. "I'm not a surgeon. I have no experience with these types of wounds—"

"Then find a surgeon," Ren snapped, his hand stilling along the crown of my head.

"We don't have surgeons here," Faye answered quietly. "We rarely have injuries like these. And when we do, we don't use a doctor to heal. The fae will feed so they can heal themselves."

"I'll go get one." Tink stepped back from the bed. "Just give me half an hour."

Wait. What was he doing?

"You can't just go get a doctor," Faye argued. "I'm pretty sure that's called kidnapping."

"Do I look like I care?" Tink threw back. "Besides, I'll get a doctor and then you can glamour them."

"We don't believe in doing that," she stated. "We—"

"Are you kidding me?" Ren cut in. "I don't care what you believe in. If we need to get a surgeon, then we're going to get a fucking surgeon."

"There isn't time," the female fae said, and the entire room quieted. "We don't have time for that."

"What?" breathed Ren, his gaze frantic.

Refusing to even blink, I stared at Ren's face, letting my one good eye etch the hard line of his jaw and the curve of his cheekbone into my memories.

He was so beautiful, inside and out, and sometimes I didn't think I deserved him and his—his *goodness*. Not when I wasted such precious time. This last week we could've done so much, filled up a lifetime worth of memories.

"I can give her blood. We have some of that here, but she's a halfling," she continued. "I have no idea what that will do to her—if it will help or hurt her."

"Give her the blood," Tink decided.

"Giving her blood is only going to give us a little more time, but not enough," the female said. "Her blood pressure is dropping with every second. Her heart rate is too high. She's lost too much blood and is still losing blood. She wouldn't be stable enough for surgery. If she didn't have fae blood in her, you wouldn't even have a chance to say goodbye."

Ren stared across the bed, the muscle along his jaw flexing. "What are you saying?"

I stopped listening at that point, because I think I already knew what she was going to try to explain to Ren. I didn't hear her words, but I knew I was right. It was in Ren's wide gaze when it swung to mine. I knew what she had said because of the denial that crept into his face and in the way his hand spasmed against my cool forehead. I didn't have to hear her, because I heard Tink's sudden shout of objection.

I was dying.

Not in a couple of days. Not in a few hours. I was dying right now.

"No. No. God, no." Ren's voice came back to me as he moved in, his hand splaying across my cheek. He pressed his forehead against mine. His voice was a ragged whisper. "This is not happening."

I wanted to touch him. To wrap an arm around him, to comfort him, but I was too tired and my arms were too heavy.

"I'm not going to let you die. Hell no." Ren kissed my brow, and when he pulled back, his lips were smeared with red—with my blood. His jaw tightened as he looked across the bed. "Keep her alive until I get back with a doctor."

A doctor wasn't going to help.

Voices erupted around me. There was pleading for Ren to be realistic and there were threats, most of them coming from Ren. Tink had grown quiet.

Drawing in a shuddering breath, I dragged my gaze from Ren's, because I couldn't deal with the pain crowding his face. I glanced around the room, snagging on a figure standing far back, against the wall, where Tanner had stood.

Merle.

She was staring at us, her face devoid of emotion, and for some reason I had the hardest time looking away, but then I couldn't see her anymore. My eyelids were too heavy, but I heard Tink say softly, "There is another way."

Chapter 7

My lashes fluttered and soft light crept through the darkness. I was still in the room Ren had carried me into, but the overhead lights had been turned down. Everything was softer.

"Hey there, you're back." Ren touched my chin, tilting my head just the slightest to the left. I saw him then and my chest split wide open. His eyes were damp, thick lashes wet as he smoothed his thumb under my lip. Was he crying? I don't think I'd ever seen him cry.

His smile didn't reach his eyes. "I was getting a little worried. I thought—" His voice cracked. "I thought I'd lost you."

I thought he had, too. I didn't remember fading out again. The last thing I recalled was Tink saying something about there being another way and then there was just nothing but inky, consuming darkness. No dreams. No thoughts. But I had the feeling only minutes had passed.

In that short time, the room had all but emptied out. Only Tink and Faye remained with Ren. The two stood at the foot of the bed, and Tink was gripping Faye's shoulder. She looked like she was seconds from bolting from the room.

My gaze slowly moved back to Ren.

Ren's faint smile weakened as his thumb trembled against my lip. "I need you to hang in there just a little longer, okay? I need you to do that for me. Can you?"

My mouth moved around the word yes, but I wasn't sure if the word took flight or not.

He shifted in closer, his bright green gaze capturing mine. "I love you, Ivy. You know that? There's only been you. There will only be you. I love you so fucking much and that's why I have to do this." His voice broke again, thick and hoarse. "I'm sorry, Sweetness. Forgive me."

What was he sorry for? Confusion swept through my foggy thoughts. Forgive him?

Tink all but shoved Faye forward. The fae, normally graceful and nimble, stumbled. Stopping by my head, she shot a glare over her shoulder. "I don't agree with this. If you knew what he'd done to her and how it—"

"I know," barked Ren, lifting his gaze from mine. "I know, but I'd rather her pissed off and hating me than dead. Do it now."

Confusion gave way to unease. What was happening? I tried to get my tongue to work. I wanted to know what was happening, but then Ren shifted down, kissing my forehead. He lingered, his lips hovering just above mine.

Something . . . something dark and silky stirred in the pit of my stomach.

"Tink," Faye began. "You don't want to do this. We don't know what it will do to—"

"If you don't do this, I can promise you it will be a very unwise life choice." Tink had moved closer, speaking in a hard voice I'd never heard him use before. "I mean it, Faye. I like you, but I like Ivy more. You let her die, you're doing so with the last moments of your life. So, don't get it twisted."

"You two may regret this." Faye then placed a hand on my head. "You're going to need to restrain her when she's done," she said to Tink, and when she spoke again, there was something thick and seductive about her tone. "Look at me, Ivy."

I couldn't help but obey.

My head shifted and my nose brushed against Ren's. Faye's stare snagged mine. Her lips moved and then I was falling, slipping, and I wasn't resurfacing. The one word she spoke echoed over and over.

Feed.

In the small part of my brain that was still functioning normally, I knew what had happened. Faye had used a compulsion. It didn't matter that I knew this. It was like resisting the lure of a shot of morphine. No chance to fight it. There was a burst of panic that came from the fear of losing control but it fizzled out before it fully formed.

"Ivy," Ren whispered in the space between our mouths, and then he lightly kissed my torn, bleeding lip, and I . . . I didn't kiss him back even though my lips touched his.

No, I didn't kiss Ren at all.

A brutal hunger erupted from deep inside me, a gnawing atrocity that blazed a fire through my blood.

I *inhaled.*

The first taste of his essence was like stepping out into the winter wind after a long, endless summer. A refreshing coolness slipped over my tongue and splashed down my throat.

Yes.

I inhaled again. Deeply. Relentlessly.

Ren jerked and a hand punched down into the thin mattress beside my head. The fingers around my jaw spasmed, but I was latched on and he wasn't pulling away. Ren tasted . . .

He was like a jolt of caffeine that woke up every part of my being. He was like diving head first into an icy lake. He tasted of life.

There was a flash of pain and then wonderful, languid coolness waking up my senses. I lifted my ruined hand from the table, gripping the back of Ren's neck, holding him to me.

He groaned into my mouth, the sound a mixture of pain and something warmer, hotter. Something that tasted like summer and sun. *Pleasure.*

I kept taking from him, pulling his essence into me until I had no idea where I ended and he began. I was surrounded by his fresh scent that always reminded me of the outdoors. I was surrounded by him. Electricity poured into my veins. The air crackled . . . or maybe it was my skin. *Yes,* it was my skin sparking to life. Strength filled my weak muscles. Tissues knitted back together. My once stuttering heart now beat strongly in my chest.

Ren's hand dropped to my shoulder. His fingers dug in, tearing at my shirt and pressing into my skin. It didn't hurt. Oh God no, it felt wonderful. Everything did. The ever-present thirst was slaked, but I . . .

I wanted more.

Power flowed through me, the purest kind. My body was in full control. *I* was in control and nothing and no one could change that. Like a cobra striking, I flip Ren under me. His hand still clenched my shoulder as I straddled his hips. The sweetest fire consumed my body. My mouth was fused to his, as were our hips. A moan rumbled through Ren, shaking me, and I answered it with my own. A different kind of need roared to life. At once, my entire body felt tight and swollen.

I wanted *all* of him in me.

Reaching between us, I found the button on his jeans. It took nothing to open them. My hand flew to my own.

Ren's entire body jerked under me, but he held on, his fingers clenching and unclenching on my shoulder.

"Get her," someone ordered harshly. "Get her before she kills him."

Kill him? I didn't want to kill him. I just wanted him, all of him, in every way, because he was mine. I wanted to fuck and to feed, and I wanted nothing between us—

Ren's hand lifted from my shoulder and curled around the back of my neck. I could feel his arm trembling as his mouth moved against mine, weak at first but still distracting me. Ren kissed me—kissed me as I inhaled. His hand tightened, tugging at my hair. The tip of his tongue against mine changed everything.

I stopped inhaling as a blast of desire scorched my skin. Kissing. Kissing was just as good as feeding, so I touched my tongue to his as his chest swelled. Sharp desire pounded through me. I ached for him. Throbbed. My skin tingled with lust as my hips rolled against him, trembling when I felt him, hard and thick—

"Ren."

An animalistic sound erupted from deep within me, reverberating throughout the room. Someone was close, too close to us. I broke contact, lifting my head.

"Leave," Ren gasped out, holding my head to his with flagging strength. "She won't kill me."

"Are you out of your mind?"

I growled a low purr of warning as I turned my head to the side. I didn't care who was getting close, but I would rip them to shreds if they tried to get between us.

"I got her." Ren's lips dragged across mine, snagging

my attention. I gripped the front of his pants, tearing the zipper. "Goddammit, leave *now*."

There was a curse and then a voice I vaguely recognized. "It's your death wish."

"Go," Ren groaned as I found what I was searching for, wrapping my hands around the heated length.

Someone responded, but it was lost in the need pounding through my veins. I heard a door slam shut and then Ren was pulling at my bottoms with shaking hands.

"Take from me." His voice was hoarse and rough, a whip against my sensitive skin. "Take whatever you need from me."

Things became a blur of trembling hands and slippery skin. Ren wasn't holding me as tight. His hand had fallen to the bare skin of my hip but he was burning through me, his hips rising as I ground down to meet him. The air smelled of blood and sex. A great and terrible tension was building inside of me as I devoured Ren, nipping at his lips, sucking and licking. Bursts of energy entered me as I lifted myself up and slammed myself down on him.

"Kiss me, Sweetness," Ren groaned, sounding ragged. "Kiss me, Ivy."

I wasn't kissing him? No. I'd been feeding again, lost in the dueling sensations as I chased after another high, another release.

Ren's hand spasmed on my hip. "Ivy. *Please*." He shuddered under me. "I love you."

I love you.

Those three words cycled over and over, poking holes in the red haze clouding my thoughts. *I love you*. My heart squeezed. *I love you*. Wrenching my mouth from his, I sat up and kicked my head back. The tension in me became unbearable. I cried out as a wildness took over. Under me, Ren shook and groaned as he punched his hips up one last time, wringing a gasp out of me. His release sent me careening over the edge. The most intense sensation washed over me, like every nerve was firing at once all along every part of my body. Nothing had ever felt like that. I collapsed against Ren's chest, my body trembling.

The last thing I remember before slipping into the waiting nothingness was Ren's hand running up the center of my back and him whispering those three words over and over.

"I love you."

WHEN I OPENED my eyes again, I was quick to realize I was in that room and I was lying on top of a warm, hard body.

Shifting slightly, I lifted my head and looked down. Ren's face was turned toward mine. His eyes were closed and there were dark shadows under them. They looked like bruises, and there was a gauntness to his cheekbones that had never been there before.

Mouth dry, I lifted my hand and touched his cheek. Dry blood caked my fingers. "Ren."

There was movement behind his eyelids, but those lashes didn't lift. My gaze dropped to his chest. It rose with shallow, uneven breaths. I rolled onto the little space on the table.

I . . . I didn't feel right.

Swinging my legs off the table, I stood on weak legs. My hands were clammy as I reached down and pulled my pants up. The band was torn, but they stayed up. Ren still hadn't moved.

What had I done?

In the back of my mind, I knew, but my head felt like it was full of smoke, my muscles made out of something weaker, and my bones felt brittle.

And my skin . . . my skin felt numb.

"I don't feel right," I whispered to the quiet room.

My gaze darted around and my breath got stuck in my throat when the windowless walls seemed to shrink in, constricting. Pressure clamped down on my lungs. I stumbled toward the door.

It swung open before I reached it. Tink stood in the doorway, his white-blond hair looking like he'd spent hours running his hands through it.

"Ivy." He looked at Ren. "He's still alive."

A tremor started at the base of my spine. Of course, Ren was still alive. I didn't want to kill him. I wanted—

"And I'm still traumatized by the fact you were about to become a live-action porno right in front of me." Tink stepped into the room. "I forgot how that happens after—"

"I don't feel good," I whispered as my stomach cramped. I placed my hand on it, drawing in a shallow breath.

"To be honest, you don't look good."

I tried to step to the side, but my legs gave out. Tink moved quick as lightning, catching me. Somehow we ended up on the floor, Tink holding on to my chin. His eyes were wide with worry.

"Ivy, what's wrong?" he asked.

Everything was wrong.

The numbness in my skin spread, seeping into my bones and organs. "I can't . . . I can't feel myself."

His brows knitted. "That doesn't make sense."

"I can't—" The numbness suddenly turned on me. It started as a humming feeling, but then it began to burn.

"My skin—it *hurts*."

Tink stared, and I thought I saw understanding creeping into his face, but the burn intensified. I lifted my hand, half expecting to see it on fire as a scream burst out of me.

"Shit," Tink muttered. "Shit. Shit."

My entire body jerked against his as the fire spread all over my skin, starting from the base of my spine and rolling down my legs, then up my torso and over my arms. Screaming, my muscles turned rigid as my back bowed.

"Ivy." A weak, rough voice broke through the haze of pain.

Wide-eyed, my gaze swung to the right. Ren was sliding off the table. He took one step but fell to his knees, crawling the rest of the distance. His shadowed eyes widened with surprise. "Ivy—"

Pain I'd never experienced or knew was possible consumed every part of my body. I jerked away from Tink, but he caught me around the waist as Ren grabbed the sides of my face. His lips were moving, but I couldn't hear a single thing he was saying. Nothing made sense beyond the way my body was tearing itself apart from the inside.

A screeching noise erupted from me, the kind that would've normally raised the hairs all over my body, because it sounded so fae-like. The stiffness went out of me and I curled my legs up, panting as some of the burn eased off.

Then, just as I thought it was over, the most intense craving exploded in my gut. It was almost as bad as the fire. My gaze moved from Tink to Ren.

Need filled me.

Baring my teeth, I jerked toward him, but Tink caught me as Ren fell back on his ass.

"What is happening to her?" Panic filled his voice. "I thought we'd healed her?"

"We did," Tink groaned, twisting as I railed against him—against Ren. "Now she's paying the consequences."

HOURS BLURRED TOGETHER, a twisted kaleidoscope of razor-sharp need and all-consuming desire—lust for Ren and for what was inside him. Then the pain would return, burning through the cravings, turning me inside out.

The world around me faded in and out. There was Tink holding me to him as I felt Ren holding sweat-soaked hair back from my face. He was whispering to me, but there was nothing other than the cool, pleasant abyss where I floated.

Then it happened.

Without warning, intense cold washed over me. So brutally cold, my skin felt like it was set afire. A prickling sensation hit each inch of my body, as if every part of my skin was being pierced to the marrow. Pain enveloped me once more, becoming my world, but this time it was an icy fire.

"What's . . . what's happening?" I gasped, unable to see through the pain. The room—the world was white.

"You took too much." Tink's voice was strained. "You went too far. I'm sorry, Ivy. I'm sorry."

His words made no sense. Words, in general, were of no use to me as the icy fire heightened. Screams tore from my throat, a far different sound from the screeching.

I became aware of being moved, and I only knew that Tink was no longer holding me. I recognized Ren's scent. He held me throughout, wrapping trembling arms around my waist, his shaking legs hooked over mine. My back bowed and I stretched his embrace until it almost broke.

Then . . . then it was like a raging fire being doused with water. The pain barely eased in the beginning, but slowly, after time, it disappeared like smoke in the wind. After the burn, I fell into a familiar deep sleep. I wasn't sure how long I was out, but waking up was difficult. My eyelids felt like they'd been sewed together, and it was a struggle to pry them open.

The first thing I saw was the low ceiling. Infirmary. I was in the infirmary. Why? I searched my memories but they were cloudy and I was too tired to wade through the dark and shadowy pieces to figure out what the hell was going on.

But I knew I wasn't alone.

It took effort, but I managed to turn my head to the left.

Tink sat beside my bed in one of those metal chairs. He had an ankle resting on a knee. Curled in his lap was Dixon. The little kitten was doing what it always did. Napping. That kitten had the best life ever.

The last time I'd seen Tink, he hadn't had Dixon with him. And he hadn't been alone. Ren had been with him—Ren had been holding me.

"Ren," I croaked out.

Tink's gaze lifted to mine. He didn't say anything as he stared at me, and the first kernels of unease stirred.

I tried to speak again, but my mouth rivaled the Sahara Desert. I cleared my throat. "What . . . what's going on?"

Tink looked back at me, stare solemn. "'*The night is dark and full of terror.*'"

I frowned. "What?"

He lifted a shoulder. "I've always wanted to say that to someone. All I'm missing is my Lady Melisandre red gown and hood."

I stared at him.

"You know," he said, leaning back in his chair, "there's another thing I've wanted to say. Like when people have bad news? My car just broke down, and I'll be like, bam! '*The Lannisters send their regards*,' or I just got fired from my job and bam! '*The North remembers.*' That probably makes me a shitty brownie, but I don't care."

Having no idea why he was so stuck on *Game of Thrones* references at the moment, I tried to sit and realized right then that I couldn't move. Confused, I peered down at my body. There was a thin white blanket tucked in at my waist, but that wasn't what was keeping me in place.

White bands, some kind of cloth, circled my wrists and ankles. My stomach dropped. I was *tied* down. "T-Tink, why . . . am I—"

"Tied up like you're engaged in some freaking BDSM shit?" He leaned forward, mindful of Dixon. "'*The Lannisters send their regards.*'"

"Tink!" Panic sparked.

His gaze flickered away and then settled on me. "You don't remember?"

I had the sinking suspicion I didn't want to remember.

"You were attacked," he supplied.

Yes. I remember that. Walking in the courtyard, minding my own business. Two fae had attacked me. "They stabbed me," I whispered, filled with anger and horror. "They actually stabbed me."

"Yeah, they did. Put some decent sized holes in you, too. You also had a hole in your hand, and let me tell you, that was gnarly. I could look right through it and see the other side of the room."

I tried to see my hand.

"You're all healed up now." Reaching over, he tapped my left hand. "No gaping hole. No fatal stab wounds. You're good as new." He paused. "Better."

"How . . . ?" I trailed off. More memories surfaced. I'd been dying. Like legit bleeding out with internal wounds dying, but I hadn't.

I suddenly remembered Ren leaning over me. He'd been telling me that he loved me and that there had only been me, only would be me, and he . . .

I'm sorry, Sweetness. Forgive me.

Forgive him?

My heart started thundering in my chest. Pieces of the night started to fall together.

"You've actually been asleep for like forever," Tink continued. "Well, not forever, but like four days."

Four days? Holy shit.

"I was kind of worried that you were dead and you'd start stinking soon."

Images flashed of me on top of Ren, moving against him in a bloody, wild joining of our bodies. Had we . . . ?

"Where is Ren?" I demanded, trying to sit up. "And why am I tied up?"

"Well, you see, that's kind of a long story full of plot twists and probably a plot hole or two."

"Tink!"

His gaze met mine, and I remembered him yelling at Ren, because—oh, God, I'd been feeding on Ren. I'd fed on him.

The unease unexploded into full-blown dread. "Where is Ren?" I shouted. "Where is he, Tink?"

Little Dixon stirred in Tink's lap. He folded his hand over the kitten's head. "Calm down. Dixon needs his fifth nap of the day."

My eyes narrowed. "I swear to God, Tink, if you do not answer me, I will straight-up murder you."

"See, that's the problem, and why you're tried up. It's just precautionary. Now that you're awake, Tanner will be up here—"

"Why is it precautionary?"

He didn't answer for a moment. "You've changed, Ivy. We

didn't think that would happen. We had no way of knowing."

My pulse skyrocketed. "What in the hell does that mean, Tink?"

The brownie cringed. "Well, let's just say your skin kind of shimmers now."

My mouth dropped open.

"Like a fae," he added.

Chapter 8

It took several moments for me to process what Tink was saying because there was no way I had heard him correctly. "My skin is shimmering?"

"Yes. Like a fae," he repeated. "You're not full on silver or anything like that, it just looks like you've used the same kind of lotion I imagine strippers use."

I stared at him and then my gaze darted to what I could see of my skin. I was wearing long sleeves—a shirt that wasn't mine, but I wasn't going to focus on that fuckery at this moment—and with my damn wrists secured, all I could glimpse was the top of my hand. The skin looked normal. I squinted as I managed to lift my hand an inch. The light caught—

"Holy fuck!" I gasped, eyes widening. My skin did shimmer like I'd lubed myself up with glittery lotion. "Holy shit, my skin is—"

"Kind of shimmery, yes, but hey, it could be worse. You could look like Edward in the sunlight, all glittery and shit."

My gaze shot to him.

"It's barely noticeable. So is the thing with the ears."

"My ears?" I shrieked.

"Yeah." He drew the word out. "They're a little pointy now. Like mine." He tiled his head to the side, showing off his ears. "Nothing anyone would really bat an eye at. Plus, you have all that hair to cover them if you're feeling insecure."

Oh my God, I couldn't even process what he was saying. I liked my normal, rounded human ears and he was now telling me I had pointy, fae-like ears?

And my skin was shimmering?

Tink snapped his fingers, getting my attention. "Look, there is more good news. Since you've been out for a couple of days, you've slept off the worst effects."

I took a deep, even breath but it did nothing to stamp out the building panic. "What are the worst effects that somehow don't include my skin shimmering or my ears becoming pointy?"

Dixon took that moment to stretch his little legs out in front of him. Tink reached down, scratching him behind the ear. "Well, while you were asleep, you weren't always asleep. Sometimes you were awake."

Vague memories surfaced, flashes of rage and desire, of the need to—

I sucked in a sharp breath, squeezing my eyes tight.

"There were times when you were hungry, like zombie craving brains kind of hungry," Tink said softly. "That's why you're tied down. Faye seems to think the worst has passed. Sort of like you've done the detox part and now you just have to deal with a few cravings."

I remembered.

Knots formed in my stomach. I remembered Faye whispering her compulsion. *Feed.* That one word had echoed over and over and I had fed.

My eyes flew open. "Is Ren okay?"

"Well, you know—"

"Is Ren okay?" I demanded, breathing heavy.

Tink lifted his hand from Dixon's head. "Ren is fine. He's alive. He'd be here, but Tanner and Faye were worried that you being around a human right now wouldn't help with the getting over the whole wanting to suck them dry thing."

Relief crashed through me, but a raw emotion built behind it when what happened truly processed. "You . . . you all made me feed on Ren."

"We didn't have a choice, Ivy. You were dying and there was nothing else we could—"

"You should've let me die!" I shouted, and Dixon jerked in Tink's lap. I tried to calm down, but my heart was lodged somewhere in my throat.

His brows furrowed. "That's a fucked up thing to say, Ivy."

"It's fucked up that you made me feed on Ren!"

"He was down for it, Ivy. Ren would do anything to save you."

"Even force me to do something so horrible?" I asked, eyes blurring. "Ren volunteering for this doesn't make it right. He could've been killed."

His expression smoothed out. "But he's okay and you're going to be okay."

"Except apparently my skin and ears have changed. I'm not okay." And that wasn't all. I'd fed on Ren and then we had sex—bloody, crazy sex.

"Well, there is that. We didn't know that would happen, but—"

"The Prince did that to me. He made me—" My voice caught. Anger burned through my bone and tissue. "What have you all done to me?"

"We saved you—"

"What have you done to me?" I screamed.

His eyes widened. "We don't . . . we don't know, Ivy."

I couldn't believe it. Dying sucked. Yeah. Duh. But they forced me to feed against my will—feed on Ren, and it changed me into God knows what? Nausea crept up my throat. How would I ever look at Ren again?

How would I ever look at myself again? Dealing with being the Halfling wasn't something I'd fully accepted and now this? I couldn't. I couldn't deal with this.

"It'll be okay."

"Get away from me," I whispered.

"Ivy," he gasped.

Violent rage and bitter fear swirled like a storm inside me, feeding strength I didn't realize I had. I lifted my left arm, tearing the binding in half.

"Whoa." Tink shot up, holding Dixon close to his chest as he stepped back from the bed. "Ivy . . ."

Snapping the cloth around my other wrist, I sat up and turned to Tink. "You need to get the fuck out of my face right now."

Tink was still for only a moment, and then he got out of my face and left the room.

I COULDN'T SIT or lay in this bed. My thoughts were racing along with my heart.

What did they do to me?

Hands shaking, I broke the restraints around my ankles and swung my legs off the bed. I stood on bare feet, surprised to find that I wasn't dizzy. Raising my left hand, I first noticed the red, angry scar on top. The same scar was on my palm. Squeezing my hand closed, I could easily remember the stabbing pain of the branch shooting through my hand.

Now it barely even hurt.

There was no ignoring the glimmer when I twisted my hand and caught the soft glow of light. My heart dropped. A thousand questions erupted, but I already knew what the answers were going to be.

Had I fed too much and it had changed me?

Who knew that was possible? No one. Or maybe everyone, and they just failed to tell me.

A riot of emotions crept up, sealing off my throat. I squeezed my eyes shut. I couldn't believe this. On top of everything else, I was now . . .

I didn't know what I was.

Drawing in a shuddering breath, I opened my eyes. My gaze flicked over the room. The walls were bare, but there was a bathroom to my right. I hurried over to it, flipping the light on.

I stopped in front of the oval mirror above the porcelain basin, ignoring the mess of tangled, red curls.

"Oh God," I whispered.

The light was brighter in here, and as I tilted my chin up, the sheen of my skin intensified. My face looked like I'd taken one of those high-end highlighters and smeared it all over my face.

Which was what I normally looked like when I tried to contour.

Tink was right though. It wasn't that noticeable, not to a stranger or a normal human who had no idea fae were a very real thing, but to me?

I noticed.

But that wasn't all. My features were . . . sharper. More refined. Again, not entirely noticeable but my face *was* different.

Clutching the basin, I leaned in and stared at my reflection. There were only faint bruises where I'd taken punches I should've been able to deflect. There was a tiny red mark on my lower lip. A barely-there purplish bruise along my jaw.

It was almost like weeks had passed since the fight where I got my ass handed to me. A fight I should've been able to handle with one arm tied behind my back, but I had to be honest with myself.

My head hadn't been in the right place—it still wasn't, and I hadn't been eating or sleeping right. I'd been weak, and look at what it got me?

Two stab wounds and more.

Were my eyes paler? They'd always been a light blue, but they were almost . . . iridescent now, the pale blue so stark against the blackness of my pupils.

Lifting one trembling hand, I pushed my hair back as I turned my head to the side.

I gasped.

The tips of my ears were definitely pointy. Nothing extreme, and again, a normal person probably wouldn't notice it, but these were not ears.

This was not my skin.

Dropping my hair, I faced the mirror and bared my teeth. Normal. A sigh of relief shuddered through me. At least they didn't look oddly sharp like most fae, so there was that I guessed.

The door to the room opened, and I whipped around. What if it was Ren? My stomach tied up. I wasn't ready to see him. I didn't know if I'd ever be ready to see him, but I—

"Ivy?" Faye's voice rang out.

Definitely not Ren. A wave of disappointment washed over me. I didn't want to see him and yet there was a part of me somewhere deep inside that wanted it to be him. The same part of me that had wanted it to be Ren sitting there, waiting for me to wake up.

Things had been weird between us before. Now, it would be hella awkward . . . if there was anything left.

Sighing, I stepped out of the bathroom. Faye was alone, staring at the bed and probably at the broken restraints.

The anger resurfaced. "You used a compulsion on me."

Faye lifted her chin. "I hadn't wanted to. Trust me. I know what was done to you while you were with the Prince. I told them that. They didn't want to let you die."

I remembered her reluctance and Tink's threat. "Maybe letting me die was the right thing."

"Ivy, you can't feel that way. Truly."

"You don't know how I feel," I shot back. "You have no freaking clue."

She was quiet for a moment. "You're right. Allowing you to die would've been easier. It would've definitely solved the problem with the Prince. At least, temporarily."

My lip curled. "I thought you said all human life is valuable."

"It is." She walked over to the chair and sat down. "But what I made you do wasn't natural. What you've become isn't natural."

I sucked in a sharp breath. "Well, that makes me feel so much better about everything."

"I'm not trying to make you feel worse."

"Then you should try harder," I snapped.

Her shoulders tensed. "I know you're upset. I get it. I sympathize with it, but what's done is done. You're alive."

"At what cost?" I asked, stepping toward her. "You don't even know what I am."

Her gaze flickered over me. "I'm guessing the feedings while you were with the Prince and this last one triggered the part of you that's fae, making it more dominant. That must be why you have more fae-like characteristics. Whatever fae genes you have in you now are simply stronger. I don't know what that makes you, but you're not completely fae. You're still Ivy."

Seeing my skin shimmer and having pointy ears didn't make me feel like Ivy. "And this is something you knew would happen?"

"I've never seen it, but I knew it could. I wasn't thinking about that at the moment. I was saving you, like Ren and Tink demanded." She paused. "How are you feeling? Hungry?"

I ignored the question. "Where is Ren?"

Her lashes lowered. "He's currently interrogating every fae in this building to see if they had anything to do with the attack. He's not here with you because we wanted to make sure it was safe for him. Something that took an absurd amount of time to convince him of."

Turning away, I thrust a hand through my greasy, nasty hair. "He . . ."

"He's okay," she said, a lot quieter. "And it doesn't appear like you'll attack him, so he'll be here the minute I tell him it's okay."

I closed my eyes, sucking in a deep breath and holding it.

Faye was quiet for a moment. "I know you're mad at him—at all of us, but he did it because he loves you."

But would he still love me once he saw me? Once he realized I was turning more and more into a fae? Once he really thought about what he'd done, allowing me to feed off him like the bitch Breena had?

"Ivy?"

Exhaling, I opened my eyes. A knot of fear crept up my throat. "I've changed. That's obvious. But you all don't know how much. Like, am I going to need to feed now?"

"No fae needs to feed to survive, Ivy. It's a choice. You should live a normal lifespan, but you may be stronger than before. There may be other things that have changed. The thing is, we really don't have a precedent for this. It's not like there has ever been a huge population of halflings in the first place. I only know of one or two who'd fed on humans and those halflings had been in the Otherworld. We only have records of their existence. They changed, like you."

I turned, facing her as one thing she said took center stage. "What other things?"

Faye glanced at the empty bed and then her pale gaze met mine. "Do you remember when I talked to you about being . . . addicted?"

Everything in me stilled. I'd planned on talking to her about that, but well, I kind of got stabbed to death. "Yes. I remember."

"I hope you slept off the worst of it—the craving that comes after feeding, but it'll linger for a while. You'll have this need."

I totally understood what she was saying, but acid poured into my stomach nonetheless. That need had been there before I'd fed off Ren.

"You'll have to be careful," she advised. "When you're with Ren."

She didn't need to elaborate on where she was going with that. Folding my arms over my waist, I paced in a small circle. "You talk like glimmering skin and pointy ears aren't a big deal."

"To me, they aren't."

I shot her a dark look. "Well, no shit."

"You can barely notice," she added. "Things may seem overwhelming now, but it could've been worse."

For a moment, I was dumbfounded. "Yeah, I could be dead, and maybe that was meant to happen."

Shock splashed across Faye's face. "You don't mean that."

Did I? I wasn't so sure. It's not like I had a death wish, but I . . . I just didn't feel like *me* anymore and I had no control. Not over my life, my fate, my purpose, or even my body.

And I remembered that moment of disappointment when I came to out in the courtyard and realized I hadn't died.

The knots in my stomach expanded. I picked up my pace. "I almost died in a fight I should've won. I was forced to feed on my *boyfriend*." My voice rose a notch as I thought about what I'd done to him afterward, what we did. "And I woke up days later to find out that my actual body has changed. Not to mention, the fact that I was held against my will by a psychotic fae prince. Don't act like what has happened to me is just a normal Tuesday. My entire world changed the moment I found out I was a halfling. Almost everything I knew up until that part was a fucking lie, but when I looked in the mirror, I still looked like me. I was still Ivy. When I look in the mirror now, I don't recognize myself, and that isn't just because of the physical stuff."

Sympathy crept into her face, and that was possibly the worst thing to see. Taking a deep breath, I looked away and refocused. "How long do you think this whole wanting to suck people dry thing will last?"

Faye was quiet for a moment. "I don't know. Maybe a few days. A couple of weeks."

Weeks? Muscles in my shoulders tightened. I couldn't deal with weeks. "Have you never fed?"

"Never."

Stopping, I looked over my shoulder at her. "And Drake never noticed that? He didn't think it was suspicious?"

She twisted toward me. "Drake never really paid attention

to me. Breena and Valor usually kept him occupied when he wasn't trying to convince you to come to the dark side."

I frowned, thinking something about that didn't sound right.

"I know you've been through a lot, Ivy, and finding the Crystal is the last thing on your mind, but I wanted to tell you that we are expecting the fae we were waiting for to arrive tomorrow. There was a delay in them getting here. They've had to be careful to not arise the suspicion of the Prince." She rose, smoothing her hands on her denim jeans. "I hope you can join us."

In other words, she meant she hoped I pulled my shit together long enough to be there. I nodded absently, my thoughts stuck on what Faye had just said.

How in the world did the Prince never realize she hadn't fed around him? Wouldn't someone on Team Dark Prince think that was suspicious?

Because I sure as hell thought the fact they *hadn't* noticed was crazy suspicious.

Chapter 9

I guessed Faye deemed me not a risk, so I was allowed to leave the infirmary. She walked with me though the hotel, and I figured it wasn't because she was worried I was going to start attacking fae. Faye was with me because I got my ass handed to me. She was like the bodyguard I didn't want and shouldn't need.

Luckily, she left me at the elevator, but my steps slowed as I walked toward the room I'd been sharing with Ren. My heart was tripping over itself as I stopped in front of the door. Was he inside? Trepidation filled me as I reached for the handle.

God, when did I become such a chicken shit? It was ridiculous. Taking a deep breath, I threw open the door and stepped into the cool room.

The bed was made perfectly, but empty and quiet. It looked the way I'd left it, plain and neat.

I missed my apartment.

I missed me.

Exhaling roughly, I headed to the bathroom. Days' worth of grossness had built up on my skin and hair, and I had to believe that once I showered, things would be clearer, they'd make more sense, and maybe—just maybe—I would feel like me, despite everything.

I kept my mind purposely blank as I stripped off the clothing, avoiding the mirror as I walked past it to the shower.

The last thing I wanted to know was if my boobs also shimmered.

I scrubbed and scrubbed like I could somehow rub off the stupid glimmer. By the time I was done, my skin felt pristine and actually kind of hurt. I'd just finished slipping on a pair of leggings and a shirt Tink had gotten me for my birthday last year—zombie troll dolls, because of course—when the door opened. I whipped around, the air lodging firmly in my throat when I saw it was Ren.

He came to a complete stop, his eyes widening slightly as his gaze roamed over me from head to toe, notably getting more hung up on the shirt than anything else, but still, the shock was there. And I didn't know if it was because he wasn't expecting me to be in the room or it was due to my new glittery appearance.

But he . . . he looked good. Healthy and beautiful in that wild way of his. Looking at him now, I could almost imagine that I hadn't fed on him. That I hadn't seen him with those wretched shadows under his eyes or his sunken cheekbones.

I remembered what I'd done to him, though. That memory fueled the words that parted my lips. "Like the new look?" My voice dripped with acid. "I look like a vampire from Twilight." Turning my head, I yanked back the wet curls. "And look! Don't need a costume for Halloween now that I got these super awesome pointy ears."

His head tilted to the side as he stared at me. "You look beautiful as always."

A harsh laugh burst out of me. "Seriously?"

"Seriously," he said. "Beautiful and hot. The shirt is a little weird though."

"A gift from Tink," I explained, wondering if Ren was for real. How could he think I was beautiful when I truly looked like I had fae blood in me now?

"Figured." A wry grin tugged at his full mouth. "God, you have no idea how I feel seeing you standing in front of me. Alive. Talking. Sexy even in a shirt that shouldn't have ever been made."

I stared at him. "My skin is shimmering and my ears are pointy now."

"I didn't even notice. All I was paying attention to was the fact you were standing and breathing." His gaze flickered over me again. "But now that you mention it, I'm kind of digging it."

My mouth dropped open. "How in the world could you be digging that I look more like the creatures we were born to hunt and kill? That doesn't make sense."

Ren looked taken aback. "You don't get it. Your skin could be green and your ears the size of UFOs and I'd still think you're absolutely stunning."

At that point, I started wondering if Ren was high.

"I'm about to sound cheesy as fuck and I'm kind of surprised that I even have to say this, but it's not just about how you look. Don't get me wrong, that's a way nice bonus, but it's *you*, Ivy. What's on the inside, Sweetness."

Whoa.

That wasn't cheesy at all. It was . . . it was actually a beautiful thing to say and something I so desperately needed to hear and *wanted* to believe.

Silence stretched out between us and then Ren moved. Kicking the door shut behind him, he started toward me, intent tensing the lines of his mouth. Ren was such a shower and not a teller. He was going to prove that he still thought I was beautiful. He was going to take me in his arms. He would kiss me, and I didn't know what I would do, what I was capable of.

I locked up. "Don't."

Ren immediately stopped, his brows pinching together.

"I mean, I don't know if you should come near me right now." The next part killed me to admit. "I . . . I don't know what I'll do."

Understanding flared. "I trust you."

"You shouldn't." I looked away. "You shouldn't have trusted me before."

"I did, and you didn't hurt me."

"Didn't hurt you?" I gasped. "I fed on you. I saw what you looked like afterwards—"

"I was fine—I am fine. I was just tired. That was all."

"But that wasn't all I did." My cheeks burned as the memory of ripping open his pants resurfaced.

"What came after you fed?" His voice deepened. "I didn't have a single problem with it. That was—"

"It was messed up," I said, shaking my head. "I was out of my mind. I fed on you and I—"

"I told you to take from me what you needed and I meant that. I gave you what you needed, no matter what that was."

"You didn't think it was wrong?" My voice dropped to a whisper.

"I think how we got to that moment was wrong, but what we did on that table wasn't. It never is between us."

As I watched him, I knew that he believed that, but I still felt like I'd done something wrong. I folded my arms over my waist, looking away.

He was quiet for a moment. "I ran into Faye. She told

me you'd woken up and were fine. That you went up to our room. I came as soon as I heard. Would've been there. I wanted to be there, but—"

"I know. They wanted to make sure I wasn't going to suck the life out of you." My lips twisted into a gross reflection of a smile.

"I never once believed you'd do that." His gaze was steady as he reached to his side. That was when I realized he was carrying the thorn stake. He unhooked it, laying it on the small table by the door. I guessed the whole not carrying weapons thing was now off the table. "Not once, Ivy."

"Really?" I looked at him again and welcomed the same razor-sharp anger I'd felt toward Tink despite how good their intentions were. Being angry was sure as hell a lot easier than the roaring confusion and nearly overwhelming anxiety.

"You could've done it, but you didn't. You stopped." Ren stepped forward before stopping again. "I know that you will always stop."

He may have believed that, but I didn't. "You're an idiot if you believe that. You should've never agreed to me feeding off you. It was too dangerous—"

"I would risk it again." Another step forward. "A hundred percent, I would risk all of it again to save you."

Disbelief thundered through me, as did fury. "You know what can happen to humans when they've been fed on. We've had to put them down. You have!"

"Like I said, I would risk it all over again." He held my gaze. "That was my choice."

"It was never your choice, Ren! It was mine, and it was taken away from me."

"What choice did you have?" He stopped, nostrils flaring. "You were dying, Ivy. There was no time to get a surgeon or take you to the hospital. You were bleeding out right in front of me. There was no choice, because allowing you to die was never an option."

"If you'd done that at least then I wouldn't have been forced to feed on you just like the Prince made me do!" The moment those words came out of my mouth, I wished I hadn't said them.

Ren's face paled. "You'd rather be dead, Ivy?"

I sucked in a breath. "I'm not saying that."

"Then what are you saying exactly, and Sweetness, I need you to be real detailed, because I'm thinking the worst."

I turned away, thrusting my hands through my hair. I wasn't stupid. If Tink and Ren hadn't forced Faye to do the compulsion, I would be dead. And I didn't want to be dead.

But I didn't want to be *this*.

God, I just didn't want *any* of this.

"Ivy."

He'd spoken my name so softly that I reacted to him without thought. I faced him, lowering my hands.

"When I found you outside, I thought I was too late. When I carried you into that damn room, I was covered in your blood. Drenched in it." As he spoke, his gaze never left mine. "And when that fae doctor said that you were dying, it felt like a piece of me died right then and there."

I opened my mouth.

"Let me get this out and you can yell at me and be pissed all you want," he insisted, and I snapped my mouth shut. "I have never been more afraid than I was right then and there. I was going to lose you before I even got to have you. And when Tink said there may be another way, it was the only choice I had and I made that choice knowing you could hate me for it. I made that choice knowing that it could hurt me. I made that choice knowing that you may never forgive me for it."

Ren's voice thickened. "I'd rather have you pissed off at me for the rest of your very long life than to allow the world's brightest fucking star to go out. You can hate me today and tomorrow, but at least you'll have a tomorrow, and I'll make damn sure you have a whole bunch of them to be angry with me."

Oh God.

I didn't know how to respond to that. Emotion crawled up my throat. Tears filled my eyes. I stepped back and then to the side. Sitting down on the edge of the bed, I leaned forward, dropping my arms into my lap.

Ren didn't make a sound, but I felt him move closer. He dropped down to his knees in front of me, surprising me. Looking up, he placed his hands on either side of my hips, close but not touching me. "I'm sorry that I took part in making you feed. I hated doing that, knowing what you'd been through. I hated the fact that I wasn't with you when you were attacked. Fuck," he bit out. "I wish I hadn't walked away from you the night you told me you were a halfling. I could've stopped all of this."

I stiffened. "Ren—"

"Yeah, you're going to say that wasn't my fault, but if I hadn't acted like a dick and gotten myself captured, the Prince would've never been able to masquerade as me. None of this bad shit would've happened."

That wasn't true. Even if Ren had fully accepted what I was the moment I'd told him, Drake would've found another way.

He was creepy and psychotic like that.

"And I have to live with that for the rest of my life," Ren added, slowly lifting his hands. He found mine, threading his fingers through them. "And I'll have to live with the choice

I made and the choice I took from you. I am more than willing to do that, but I do not regret one second making that choice to save you, even if it means that you hate me."

Deep down, I knew the truth and how messed up it was. If the shoes were on different feet, and Ren was a halfling and dying, I would've done the same to save him.

I would've taken his choice from him.

I would've taken his will away.

I would've saved him even if it cost me his love.

My chest squeezed and I whispered the truest thing I could say in that moment. "I don't hate you."

Ren's grip tightened on my hands as he bowed his head. His curls fell forward and when he spoke, his voice was rough. "I can't lose you."

"You haven't."

He brought my hands to his mouth, kissing the top of both of them. "Then why does it feel like I already have?"

Startled, I pulled on my hands, but he held on. "Why do you think that?"

He looked up at me, his eyes the color of dewy grass. "Do you really have to ask that, Sweetness?"

I started to say yes, but the word died on my tongue. My thoughts raced to find a way to deny why he'd feel that way, but I came up empty. Not because he was right. Not in the way he thought.

Because it wasn't him losing me.

It was me losing myself.

Chapter 10

Ren and I didn't talk much after that, but he convinced me to go down with him to have dinner, and I didn't have it in me to make up an excuse.

I discovered then that Ren had confiscated the iron daggers at some point, and we armed ourselves up just in case someone wanted to go for a round two with me.

"Was there anyone else involved in the attack?" I asked as I hooked the dagger to my hip. It felt good to have it back. I tugged my shirt over the belt and dagger.

"Not as far as I can tell." Ren opened the door, and we started down the hall. "And trust me, I've been very convincing on when it comes to how important it is to tell the truth."

I glanced at him. His jaw was set in a hard line. "So, you think it was only those two?"

Ren nodded as he hit the button to bring up the elevator. "I've interviewed nearly eighty percent of the fae here. So far, none of them were involved."

Eighty percent? "Damn, you've been busy."

The elevator doors slid open, and he stepped aside, allowing me to enter. "Had to keep busy since I was banned from your room. It was either that or go crazy."

I folded my arms over my waist, focusing on the brown paneled walls. I couldn't imagine what it would be like if Ren had been injured and I hadn't been able to see him.

"I do have some questions." Ren leaned against the wall, drawing my gaze. "Did the fae say anything to you?"

Exhaling slowly, I nodded. "They didn't come after me because I'm an Order member." I paused. "Or was. Who knows at this point. Anyway, they did it because I was a halfling and . . ."

What the fae had said to me came roaring back. Holy crap, I'd forgotten that the fae had said the Prince would find me here, that he'd eventually break through the glamour.

My stomach bottomed out just as the elevator opened on the main floor.

"And what?" Ren stepped out.

I followed, my skin feeling like ice. "They were just scared. That was all." My gaze lifted to his. "They were just scared."

"I don't give a fuck if they were terrified or not." His eyes hardened. "You were supposed to be safe here. You weren't."

The doors closed behind us, but neither of us moved. "And I should've been able to defend myself."

"You didn't have a dagger, something that won't happen again."

"With or without the dagger, I should've easily taken them down or gotten away," I pointed out, still disgusted over how easy it had been for the fae. "I was unprepared and hadn't been paying attention."

Ren stepped into me. "You took one of them down, Ivy. Without a weapon. After being stabbed. Give yourself some credit."

My lips twitched but it didn't spread into a real smile.

Not when the fae's words were echoing in my head. "I need to talk to Tanner real quick. I'll join you in the cafeteria."

His head cocked. "I can go with you."

"You don't need to." I quickly stepped around him. "It's only going to take a couple of minutes. I'll be right there."

Ren opened his mouth, but I didn't give him the chance to say anything. I jogged off down the other corridor, relieved when I looked over my shoulder and didn't see him.

It took no amount of time for me to find Tanner. He was in his office, and when I burst into the room, he was sitting in a wingback chair across from Merle, engaging in some tea time.

Merle had been ostracized from the Order ages ago, something that always irritated me since she had given her life and then some to them. Rumor was she'd been caught by a fae without the protection of a clover and her mind had been a few screws short since then, but who even knew if that was true? Merle may be odd, but she was sharp as a tack whenever I was around her.

And I couldn't help but remember her standing in the back of the room Ren had brought my bleeding body into. Her face had been void of all emotion. Could she have had something to do with it?

She could be odd, but she always seemed to like me.

"Ivy." Tanner put his itty-bitty cup on a platter and smiled even though it was obvious he was surprised to see me. "I'm so glad to see you up and moving about."

"Are you really?" I asked, staring pointedly at Merle's back. She didn't turn around.

"Of course." He looked and sounded surprised by the question. "What happened to you was inexcusable and you have my most sincere apologies that it occurred. I promised you sanctuary. You did not receive that."

Before I could respond, Merle did. "Ivy is a trained member of the Order. Two ordinary fae should not have been difficult for her to handle. Back in my heyday, I could take four out in the blink of an eye."

Wow.

My eyes narrowed on her back. "Well, thank you for making it sound like getting stabbed was my fault."

"It was not your fault," Tanner was quick to add. "I am glad to hear that so far Ren has not found any conspirators." His gaze dropped to where the dagger created a slight bulge along my hip. "Though I do understand why you feel the need to arm yourselves."

"I'm not here to talk about getting stabbed."

"Then what are you here for?" Merle glanced over her shoulder at me as I stalked to where they sat. "I imagine it's something quite urgent since you forgot that it was polite to knock."

As much as I liked Merle, I had to ignore her at this point. "Can the Prince find me here?"

Tanner's brows lifted as he leaned forward in his chair. "Outside of what happened, you're safe here, Ivy. I can assure you—"

"I'm not asking if I'm safe," I cut him off. "Because no matter what you claim, that's obviously not true. I'm asking if the Prince can sniff me out here?"

He glanced at Merle, who calmly took a drink from her tiny tea cup, and a moment passed before he answered. "Our presence here is heavily glamoured, even from other fae. Unless they know to look and see, they will not find us."

I wasn't stupid. "That doesn't answer the question, Tanner."

Clasping his hands together, he tilted his head to the side. "The glamour isn't infinite. Everything has a limit, Ivy. The

Prince wasn't looking for us before, but by now, I am sure he knows that we exist in New Orleans. He'll be searching and he's powerful."

My heart turned over in my chest. "What does that mean, exactly?"

Merle lowered her cup. "What he's saying, dear, is that the Prince could poke a hole through the glamour. It would not hold against his will."

Oh my God. "So you're basically saying that if he somehow figured out that Hotel Good Fae was here, he could rip away the glamour and enter?"

The smile slipped from Tanner's face as he nodded. "He could, but we have no reason to believe that he would become aware of us."

"And why is that?" I demanded. "You have hundreds of fae here. Any number of them could say the wrong thing to the wrong fae."

"They know what is at stake," Tanner replied. "None of them want to be found by the Prince. They know what would happen to them."

Even if that was the case, that still didn't mean it was unlikely that the Prince would ever find this place. "Did it ever occur to you that he could have someone like Faye on his team playing spy?"

Tanner's lips thinned. Merle didn't answer, and I seriously wondered if that had crossed their minds. If not, they were utter idiots.

Pressure clamped down on my chest. "What would happen if the Prince got in here?"

"Besides him taking you?" Merle lifted her chin, her unlined face hiding her true age. "The fae here, without feeding, are no match for the Prince and his warriors." Merle's gaze was sharp. "If he comes, they will not survive any attack he may launch."

I closed my eyes. So the fae who attacked me was right. "Me being here is a danger to all of them."

"The Prince being in this world is a danger to every living creature," Tanner said, and when I opened my eyes, he had sat back in his chair. "The fae who consider this place a haven know this."

"I am thinking a few are not happy about that," I pointed out.

There was nothing Tanner could say in return to that.

"So, let me get this straight. The fae here are basically safe as long as the Prince doesn't catch wind of this place? But if he does, he'll find a way to get in and he will kill every fae in here for shits and giggles?"

Tanner paled. "That is an *unlikely* yes."

Unlikely? Yeah. Right. I felt like I knew Drake well enough to know he'd eventually, sooner than later, find this place. "I think you forgot to mention all this in your stay at Hotel Good Fae pitch when I first arrived."

"He didn't fail to mention it, dear. He chose not to." Merle held my gaze. "The safety of those here is irrelevant to the mission of keeping your belly empty of the Prince's seed."

I vomited a little in my mouth. "Can you never say it like that again? Please?"

"It's the truth," she replied. "These fae would be dead if the Prince discovered the location whether you were here or not. Keeping you out of his hands is the top priority."

That was hard to swallow. I didn't like knowing that my life—or, well, my womb—had a higher value than other lives. "Or I could, you know, just die. That would fix the problem."

She held my gaze. "It would, however, it appears you're hard to kill when you can feed and heal yourself."

I sucked in a sharp breath. "I didn't choose to do that."

"I know." Something flickered over her face. Sympathy? Compassion? Constipation? Who knew? "I know you would not have made that call, but there are people here who will make that call for you. And they will continue to do so, to save you."

She was right. "But me being here means that the unlikely chance of him discovering this place moves closer to the likely territory."

"It's irrelevant, sweetie," Merle repeated.

I blinked at her and then turned to Tanner. "Every time someone goes out there—out in the world beyond the glamour of this building, they run the risk of being seen by one of the Prince's minions." My heart lurched in my chest. "Just like when Ren and Faye went out there looking for the Crystal. They could've been seen and followed."

"Faye is careful and she's aware of the risk," Tanner stated.

"And what about Ren?"

Tanner didn't reply and a horrible thought occurred. Did Ren know about the danger of me staying here? No. There was no way he would've signed off on putting the fae here in danger. But then I thought about what he'd done for me. I obviously didn't know what extent he'd go to keep me safe. "You said that me being here was no problem."

"And it isn't, Ivy." Tanner picked up his cup. "We have survived here longer than you realize without being discovered by those we wish to remain hidden too. We shall continue that way."

"Things are different now. That was before the Prince arrived."

He shook his head. "Things are just more complicated." A faint smile appeared, one of approval. "I appreciate your concern for my brothers and sisters, more than you know, especially after what was done to you, but we are willing to shoulder the risk to make sure the Prince does not open those doors, destroying the mortal realm just like his court did to our world."

Not every fae here was obviously willing to shoulder that risk.

"I don't appreciate your concern," Merle retorted. "It's misguided and will lead to foolish decisions."

"Do you not care about the fae here?" I demanded.

A small smile appeared, the kind that reminded me of a grandmother's. "You wouldn't want me to answer that question."

"And we wouldn't ask her to answer that question," Tanner added.

I couldn't believe they could be so dismissive of the risk involved or the fact that they thought I'd be okay with this. The inhabitants of this place were fae, but they weren't hurting humans. Like Tink, they were just trying to scratch out some sort of life. And Tink and Ren were also here. Them staying safe was of the utmost priority to me. "I'm not okay with this."

"We don't expect you to be," Merle answered. "We just expect you to *deal* with it. You grew up in the Order. You know sometimes you have to sacrifice the many to protect the few. You've lived that life every day you've breathed. Get with the program, Ivy. It hasn't changed."

I sucked in air and turned to Tanner. "You all have to realize that it's only a matter of time before the Prince realizes you're harboring me here. It's not *if* he does, it's *when* he does. What do you do then? How long would the glamour hold against him?"

Tanner took a sip of his tea. "We'd hopefully have weeks." There was a pause as his pale gaze met mine. "But if we're lucky, we'll have days. Hours if we aren't."

Chapter 11

Get with the program?

Oh, I was so going to get with the program. Throwing the door shut behind me, I flipped on the light and stalked toward the narrow closet next to the dresser.

Spying the weekender bag Tink had used to pack some of my stuff in, I grabbed it from the floor of the closet and tossed it onto the bed.

Days? Hours? Weeks? They had no idea how long we had before the Prince found this place and broke through the glamour. It wasn't an unlikely event. It was *inevitable.* There were too may fae here, too many unknown variables at play. With me here, the Prince would discover Hotel Good Fae, and there was no doubt in my mind that the very first person he'd take out was Ren.

Panic unfurled in the pit of my stomach as I stared at the bag. With sudden clarity, I knew I couldn't tell Ren or Tink what I was planning to do. Neither of them would want me to leave. They'd stop me, and the whole point was to keep them safe.

That meant I had to leave without them.

Raw pain punched my chest as I turned to the dresser. Could I do that? Could I walk out of here without saying goodbye? Without one more kiss? One more I love you?

And what about Tink?

He would be so pissed, and would probably annoy Ren to the point of getting himself murdered in cold blood, but Tink had to understand. He knew what the Prince was capable of.

"Oh God," I whispered, pressing the heel of my palm to my forehead. The back of my throat burned as I closed my eyes.

What was I doing?

The panic turned into the kind of hurting that sucked away at the soul. I had to leave them. I knew that. It was the only way they'd be safe until they found that damned Crystal, or I . . . found a way to weaken the Prince so he could be killed.

Lowering my hand, I opened my eyes. They were damp as I stared at the dresser. Everyone was focused on putting the Prince back in the Otherworld because killing him was virtually impossible, but nothing was truly impossible.

Someone out there had to know how to weaken him enough that cutting off his head was feasible.

Steely resolve filled me as I stepped forward, opening the drawer. Since the Prince could sense me, he had to know I was still in New Orleans. If I left, then he'd follow. I'd just have to keep moving until I figured out a way to weaken the bastard long enough to kill him. While I was gone, Ren and Tink could work with Tanner to find the Crystal. They'd be safe, and that was all that mattered.

The door opened just as I yanked several pants out of the drawer. Spinning around, I saw Ren standing in the open doorway.

Crap.

I guessed I wouldn't know if I could walk out of here without seeing him or saying goodbye. This just got a hell of a lot harder.

Nothing about him looked relaxed as his gaze moved from my hands to the open bag on the bed. "You didn't come to the cafeteria." There was a pause. "What are you doing, Ivy?"

What I was doing at that exact moment was being frozen between the bed and dresser, cradling pants to my boobs. "I . . . I'm packing."

Stepping into the room, he closed the door behind him. "Packing to go where?"

I opened my mouth, but I had no idea what to say. I hadn't planned to see him before I left.

His brows lowered as he came closer. "What are you doing, Sweetness?"

Swallowing, I glanced down at the bag. A huge part of me wished I could lie, but I'd already lied too many times to him. As much as this was going to suck, I had to tell the truth. "I . . . I need to leave."

"Leave?" He stopped beside me. "Okay. I feel like I'm missing a vital part of some story. Did something else happen?" His eyes flared a vivid green. "Did someone try to attack you again?"

"There wasn't an attack between the time I left you in the hallway and now." I placed the pants in the bag and looked up at him. "Did you know that the Prince can get through the glamour here?"

His expression smoothed out. "You're safe here, Ivy. No matter what. I'm going to make it so—"

"I'm not worried about me being safe!" My frustration

rose. "Why does everyone keep bringing that up like I need to be taken care of? I got my ass kicked. I almost died, but I'm alive and I'm not scared."

Confusion filled his striking eyes. "I'm not saying that you're scared, but it would be okay if you were, Ivy. No one could blame you for that."

Cursing under my breath, I spun and grabbed a handful of underwear. The thing was, I wasn't scared. I was *angry*. Furious. Enraged all the time, but I wasn't scared. Not for myself. "I'm not afraid."

There was a pause while I shoved my underwear into the bag. "Ivy—"

I whirled on him. "Do you guys even realize that I'm the only one here that the Prince won't kill? Unless he finds another halfling somewhere in the world, spoiler alert, I'm surviving this story. I can't say the same for all of you."

"Yeah, and what he wants from you isn't a walk in the park, Ivy."

My hands tightened. "I know exactly what he wants from me. Trust me. I got front row tickets for that."

Ren drew back, wincing. "I'm sorry. That was callous of me to throw that out there like that."

"It doesn't matter." I waved him off. "I can't be here. Not when the Prince knows damn well I'm still in New Orleans. He has to be out there looking for me. It's only a matter of time before he follows a fae here."

"So you're . . . leaving the one place that could protect you from him to protect the fae here?"

"Yep." I moved to the dresser, searching for tops. "That sums it up quite nicely. And let's not forget, it's not like everyone is happy to have me here. Not that I can blame them for not wanting me here. If I go, they're safe."

"That's absurd."

"I don't think you really believe that."

"I'm going to get real with you. I don't give a fuck about the fae here."

I gasped as I faced him. "Wow, Ren."

"What?" His chest rose with a heavy breath as he met my wide eyes. "It's the truth. I'm not wishing ill on them. Except for the very dead bastards who went after you, the rest seem cool, but there is no choice when it comes to you and them."

That kind of made me feel all warm and fuzzy in my chest for all the wrong reasons. "It's not just the fae that are in danger because of me. Tink is. You are." Panic spread in my stomach, reaching my chest. "The Prince would love nothing more than to kill you. You know that."

A muscle ticked in his jaw. "I would love nothing more than to come face to face with that fucker."

Horror seized me. The mere thought of Ren going toe to toe with the Prince made me want to scream until my voice gave out. "Are you serious? You know what he's capable of. It's not like fighting a normal fae or even an Ancient. The Prince—"

"I know what he's capable of," Ren growled, eyes glimmering. "Do not underestimate the strength of my hatred for that son of a bitch."

"I don't, but—"

"I can take care of myself. So can Tink. You're not doing us any favors by leaving."

Grabbing shirts, I walked them over to the bed. "I don't think I'm doing you a favor. I'm. . . ." Squeezing my eyes shut, I shook my head and tried again. "I couldn't live with myself if something happened to you or Tink. Do you understand that? I couldn't deal with that."

"And we feel the same way about you. I think you know

that already."

I did.

Look what they'd already done to save me. Ren would live with the guilt of forcing me to feed for the rest of his life. Tink probably didn't feel all that bad about it, but whatever. They were already making sacrifices and horrifying choices because of me.

It stopped now.

His voice was closer, more even. "I get that you don't want to put these people in danger. That you want to protect Tink and me, but Sweetness, you're just . . . you're reacting because of what happened to you. Knee-jerk. You're not thinking this through."

I dropped my shirts into the bag. "I'm reacting because I have to do something. I can't sit around and just wait for him to storm this place or wait for one of the other twenty percent you haven't talked to that may or may not want to kill me to protect their families. I'm not going to do that."

Ren placed a gentle hand on my shoulder, but I still jumped at the contact. This time, though, he didn't pull his hand away like he normally would when I was jumpy. Instead, he carefully turned me to him.

I drew in a deep breath. "I can't stay here, Ren. You know that I can't do that. I can't be okay with putting other lives in danger, and I know you're not okay with that either."

He looked like he was about to disagree with the last statement. "We have help coming. Fae that can find the Crystal. Tomorrow."

"But what if it doesn't work?" I asked. "What if they can't find the Crystal in time? And if we get this Crystal, how in the hell are we going to trap the Prince, and get his blood and my blood on it in the Otherworld?"

His jaw tightened. "We haven't exactly crossed that

bridge—"

"That's the point. I don't even think that bridge has been built yet, so what if we never cross it?"

"We will," he said, voice hard. "Even if I have to build that fucking bridge myself with my own two damn hands."

I sighed. "We should be focusing on finding a way to weaken him. There has to be something out there, someone who knows."

There was a pause. "And that's what you want to do out there? Find out if it's possible?"

"It has to be possible. He has to have a weakness, and even as hard as killing him will be, it has to be easier than completing the ritual of blood and stone."

And I knew exactly where I was going to start.

The Order and the Elite. If any two groups out there had any idea, it would be them, and it was far past time for them to start talking.

A long moment passed. "Okay." His shoulders squared as if he had come to some kind of conclusion. "Where would we go?"

"I haven't exactly thought that far ahead," I admitted, leaving out the whole paying a visit to the Order thing. I wouldn't be able to stay in New Orleans long. My visit with them would have to be quick and I had a feeling it would be bloody. This time I wouldn't be unprepared. Oh hell no. "But I think I'd have to get as far away as possible. Maybe Europe? I have money saved up. I think I can get out before he realizes where I am."

"And then what?" he asked, cupping my cheeks in his broad hands. He brought me to him, against his chest. One arm circled my waist. "Tell me what the next step is."

Relaxing into his touch, I let out a little sigh. Weariness invaded my bones and muscles. I didn't want to leave him.

God, that was the last thing I truly wanted to do. "I don't know. Keep moving until . . . we figure out how to put him back in his world or can kill him, but I'll be wherever and you—you and Tink will be safe."

Everything about Ren changed in an instant. A small tremor went through him and then his entire body stiffened. "Wait. You're planning to leave without me?"

A slight frown turned the corners of my lips down. "I don't want to, but if I'm not around you, then you're not in danger—well, you'd be in less danger. The Prince will go where I go. You'll just be in . . . normal danger, which is a lot better than psycho Prince danger."

Ren pulled back, tilting my head up so our gazes met. His lips parted on a sharp inhale. "You were in here packing your stuff to leave without me. That's what you were doing." Understanding seeped into his features. "Holy shit. If I hadn't walked into this room, would you have even stopped to say goodbye? Or were you planning to sneak out of here without saying a word?"

Crap.

I didn't want to answer that because he wouldn't understand my answer.

Ren dropped his hand and took a step back and then another. "Shit, Ivy."

Oh, this was not good. "I don't know what to say."

"I think that says it all," he replied, voice rough.

"No—no, that doesn't say *anything*." A different kind of panic blossomed in the center of my chest. None of this was going how I'd planned. Then again, I didn't have much of a plan. Ren had been right about the whole knee-jerk thing. "You don't understand. If I had—"

"You're right. I don't understand, Ivy. I cannot even comprehend how you could walk out of here without saying anything to me." His gaze drifted over me in a way that made me think he wasn't sure who he was staring at. "After everything that has happened, you'd do that to me?"

My spine stiffened. "I'd do anything to protect you. Just like you'd do anything to protect me, right?"

"Are you fucking shitting me right now?" he exploded. "Does protecting me include stressing me the fuck out?"

I folded my arms over my chest. "Well, no—"

"Okay. How about having me go insane with worry?" He stepped forward, chin dipped. "Does protecting me also mean leaving me to think the goddamn worst thing has happened to you *again*? That another fae got to you or worse?"

I jolted. "I would've left a letter. I wouldn't—"

"A letter? You have got to be shitting me." Lifting a hand, he thrust his fingers through his messy hair. "I should've known." Dropping his hand, he laughed harshly. "You've already done this before."

"What do you mean I've done this before? Last I checked, this is the first time we've found ourselves in this predicament."

His eyes widened in disbelief. "It's not. Back at that damn mansion you made a deal with that son of a bitch to free me."

My arms fell to my sides. "That is not like this at all."

"It's not? You put yourself in danger needlessly," he argued.

"What was I supposed to do?" I shouted, fighting back tears. "He was going to kill you, Ren. Do you not get that? What else was I supposed to do?"

"Anything but agree to give yourself to that monster to free me!" he yelled back, body tense.

Air lodged in my throat as I stumbled back a step.

"Did you think I forgot about that?" He shook his head.

"The hell I'm letting you walk out of here to do that again."

"Are you going to stop me?" I shot back. "Lock me up in this room? Chain me to the bed?"

One side of his lips curved up into a humorless smile. "Don't tempt me, Ivy, because you're obviously in need of someone to make better life choices for you."

My heart thundered in my chest. The ever-present fury that had been simmering inside long before I escaped the Prince erupted like a super volcano. "Really?"

"Really." He crossed his arms. "At least then I know I won't find you in a bloody heap somewhere, or you won't be running around, getting yourself captured."

I lost it. "Then that makes you no better than the Prince!"

Blood drained from Ren's face. Immediately, I knew I'd gone too far. Holding anyone anywhere wasn't cool, but Jesus, Ren was *nothing* like the Prince.

What was wrong with me?

Something had to be for me to say that to him. Something horrible. But I didn't get a chance for some deep self-discovery to figure out exactly how much my head was messed up.

Ren's expression locked down. "Tanner said that the fae should be here tomorrow. Can you wait until then before you run off and do—" He looked away for a moment and then refocused on me. "Do whatever it is you're going to do?"

I flinched. His tone was so incredibly distant—cold. I'd never heard him sound like that to me. Ever.

"Will you stay?" he demanded, emerald eyes blazing. "Stay until the ones Tanner thinks can locate the Crystal come? If that's a bust, then I won't say a word. Promise me you will stay at least until then. Please."

Part of me didn't want to risk waiting another hour. Who knew when these magical Crystal sniffing fae were actually going to show up. I had no doubt in my mind that the Prince would discover this place, but we probably had a couple of days before that happened. Maybe even a week, but when the Prince did come, I knew there wouldn't even be hours before he broke through.

Ren . . . Ren had said *please*, and all I could think of was him saying that same word to me, begging me to hang on when I'd been injured.

I exhaled raggedly, plopping down on the bed. "Fine. I'll stay until they get here, but if they can't help—"

"You're out," he growled. "Got it."

My gaze flickered to his. "Ren—"

"Don't," he cut me off, and my stomach soured. "I don't want to hear whatever is about to come out of your mouth."

I stiffened. There was no mistaking the fury etched onto his face or in his tone. It was restrained but there, like the eye of the storm in the middle of a hurricane.

"I know you've been through hell and you're trying to deal. Damn, I know that there's a huge part of you still stuck in that hell, especially after the attack and what we did to save you—what happened between us afterward. I know there's a huge part of you still there, back at that house. That's what wakes you up every night and that's why you spend your day hiding from me—from everyone. That's why you don't talk to me."

"I-I talk to you," I said, feeling my throat squeeze shut.

"Bullshit," he shot back. "Seeing you hurting and having no clue how to help you *kills* me—eats away at me every damn day. That pain is worse than anything I went through at that damn house."

"You haven't talked to me!" I reminded him. "It's not like you've done the whole caring and sharing thing."

"You haven't *asked*, Ivy."

Air lodged in my throat. Oh God, he was right. I

hadn't . . . I hadn't asked.

"But you want to know now? Fine. As you already know, I got my ass captured the night you told me you were the Halfling. I was caught up in my head and walked right into a damn trap that bitch had set. I got knocked out, and when I woke up, I was in that pitch-black cell, chained to a damn wall. I saw the Prince first and that's how I knew what he was going to do. After feeding and beating the shit out of me, he became me. Then he left me to Breena."

My stomach twisted.

"That bitch knows how to use her nails and teeth."

The image of his bare chest surfaced. His skin had been shredded and bitten. I could taste the fury I'd felt upon seeing him and I wanted to draw blood all over again. "Did she . . . ?"

"Did she force herself on me?" His eyes flashed. "Would it change things if she had?"

"God. No." Everything inside of me was twisted up. "It wouldn't be your fault. I wouldn't think differently about you or anything like that."

Ren was quiet for a long moment. "She messed with me, but she was more interested in fucking with my head than my body. Pretty confident she's actually disgusted by humans and wouldn't lower herself to screw one. Did she say something different?"

A bit of relief swept through me, but it was bittersweet. Knowing that what Breena claimed had happened between them was false didn't lessen the horrific things that were done to Ren. "She did, and I was never sure if I believed her. Faye said Breena hadn't, but Faye would lie to keep me from attacking Breena." Memories of Breena's taunts returned. "She knew where your Order tattoo was."

The three interlocking spirals were in the same place as

mine, near my hipbone.

"Their favorite pastime was to strip me naked and leave me to freeze my balls off."

"Jesus." Exhaling raggedly, I sat back down on the bed. The weariness returned, dampening the anger until it returned to a simmer.

The silence was broken when Ren said, "I know that I'm only aware of about one-tenth of the shit you went through there, and I've wanted to know all of it. Every single damn horrible thing so that I can be there for you, but I've waited, because I wanted you to be ready—to be at the point where you can talk to me. So it shocks the shit out of me that you were going to run without me, without even telling me. That you didn't want me beside you, no matter what."

Anything I was about to say turned to ash on my tongue. That wasn't how I meant for it to come across. Not at all.

He swallowed hard. "And you know what I just now realized? You've been running without me this whole time, haven't you? There's never been an us. There's been you and then there's been me chasing you."

Tears crawled up the back of my throat as I rose on shaky knees. "That's not how it's been. Ren, that's—"

"It's not? You might want to think about that." He stepped back, opening the door. "The fucked up thing, Ivy? You were willing to stay, but not for me—not for us. And that's not because you're trying to protect me. You were bailing on me. You were bailing on us—if there ever really was an *us*."

Chapter 12

I did a lot of thinking that night.

It was all I did.

And for once, I didn't spend the night thinking about what had happened or what could've happened while the Prince held me captive. I wasn't even thinking about getting stabbed. Instead, I lay there, my thoughts consumed by what Ren had said as I stared at the bland white ceiling.

Ren had left and hadn't come back to our room, and I didn't sleep, nor did I put *all* my clothes back in the dresser. Instead, I'd created myself a little bug-out bag, stashing about two days' worth of clothing in the bag and placing it back in the closet just in case we ran out of time.

Then I'd waited.

Part of me had expected Ren to return, but the other half knew that what I had planned cut him deep and a few hours wasn't going to stitch the hole I dug open in him back together. I hadn't meant for everything to turn out the way it did. I just wasn't . . .

God, I just wasn't thinking straight.

Now that I was here, all alone, with nothing but my

own stupid head to keep myself company, I realized that the whole take off running with no idea where to go was incredibly stupid and cruel. So damn cruel, not just to Ren but also to Tink.

Ren had been right about what my leaving would've done to them. It would've been terrible, and even though I'd had the best of intentions, in all honestly, they were panicked intentions.

I gave way to panic, and the idea of running was at least doing *something* other than sitting around and twiddling my thumbs.

Or getting stabbed.

You've been running without me this entire time.

It took several hours for me to work through the denial of that statement. Had I been running from him this entire time? I didn't want to believe it, because it was so terrible.

God, it sucked ass to admit it to myself, but it was true. Even from the beginning, I'd made everything exceptionally difficult for Ren. It wasn't because I wanted to be a challenge. When I met Ren, he was the first guy I was interested in after the death of Shaun. I'd been so closed off, so awkward at being interested in a guy. Things had been easier between us when I finally opened up to him—when I finally allowed myself to fall in love with Ren.

But then I found out I was the Halfling.

That was when I started lying to him—when I started *running*. Maybe not physically but definitely mentally. I hadn't told him about seeing the Prince outside Cafe Du Monde. I'd hid the truth of what I was until I virtually blurted it out to him on the damn street. Ren had been trained since birth and he was a member of the Elite. He knew how to take care of himself, but I'd blindsided him, bringing his biggest fear to life. Not only that, but I'd constantly cut him out of decisions. It wasn't like I had to include him in everything. Lord knows Ren never expected that from me or anyone, but when you are with someone, when you love them, you include them.

You're a team.

You don't hide things from them. You sure as hell don't lie, and you don't compare them to a monster.

I'd screwed up, more than once, and long before the Prince had dug his claws into me.

Now the gulf between us truly seemed unsurpassable.

No wonder Ren felt the way he did. We never really got the chance to have normalcy in our relationship. To go out on dates and spend lazy weekends at home, exploring each other and inevitably getting on each other's nerves. We hadn't gotten the chance to have normal fights, about what to eat or if we wanted more in the future. We didn't get the chance to build any amount of trust, which was why I was amazed by how accepting and patient he'd been up until a few hours ago. We were still . . . new at us, and we never got a chance to fully take off and become anything.

Everything had been rocky in the beginning, ragged in the middle, and now . . . at possibly the end . . . it was a catastrophe waiting to happen.

We were broken.

It wasn't all on me. Ren taking part in that compulsion and allowing me to feed on him wasn't a small misdeed. I got why he did it. I even understood it, but it still happened and it was still between us. But other than that? I was woman enough to know it was on me.

And I had no idea if it was fixable or if Ren wanted to repair the damage, but I did know that it wouldn't matter if Ren ended up killed or if the Prince was somehow successful when it came to getting himself a bouncing baby.

Our relationship was the least of our worries. Not that it didn't feel like my chest was being cracked open and my heart spooned out of me. It did. It hurt just as bad as getting stabbed in the back.

I needed to focus, though. I needed to get my shit straight before I could even think about getting my house in order.

The Prince was going to find me. Eventually. Because at the moment, I was an easier target for him than to find another halfling somewhere in the world, especially since the Elite made it their duty to straight-up murder any they came across.

For the whole baby Armageddon to work, the baby-making between the Prince and I had to be consensual. He had to know that was never, ever going to happen, so what could the Prince hope to accomplish? The only reason he'd gotten me to agree to stay with him, to be with him, was to free Ren.

He had collateral.

And *Drake* still did.

It was in the wee hours of the morning when it struck me that I'd been wrong about the Prince killing Ren on sight, and that realization was what had me pacing the room until the sun began to rise.

The Prince wouldn't kill Ren. Oh no, he would use him against me, just like he'd done before. The Prince would do the same with Tink if he discovered his presence. He still had the means to control me. All he needed was to get his hands on one of them.

Stopping at the window, I lifted my gaze to the fading stars.

I was back to square one.

Even if I left here, the Prince would still go after Ren, because he knew it would draw me back from the ends of the Earth. He'd do what he did before, use Ren, and even though I knew what was at stake, I *loved* Ren. I couldn't be the reason he was hurt. Not again. Never again after Shaun. That was my weakness.

Not Ren, but my past.

Shivering, I saw that there were only three options before me, and as the last of the stars twinkled out, I knew running wasn't one of them.

Find the Crystal and complete the ritual.

Figure out how to weaken the Prince and kill him.

Or go down the path that had stopped Tink from telling me from day one that I was the Halfling. The same path Ren and Tink had yanked me from a few days ago, which was to permanently remove myself from the equation.

I LOOKED LIKE crap as I stared in the mirror, having had only a few hours of sleep and still no sign of Ren. The healthy glow from sucking the essence out of him was lost in the dark shadows under my eyes and the, well, slightly shimmery skin that wasn't actually a shimmer. Tink had been wrong about that. So had I.

It was a very faint silvery sheen that only looked shimmery. I knew this because I was standing in front of the long mirror attached to the back of the bathroom door, buckass naked for a while now.

Before my skin started to look like I had covered myself in Urban Decay eye shadow, staring at myself completely naked wasn't something I did often. I mean, I really didn't need to check out the many different scars and stretch marks, but here I was.

Why? Because I had a new life motto. It was simple.

Get my shit together.

Since offing myself wasn't exactly my top choice of

options and I couldn't help find the Crystal, the only next thing for me to do was find a way to weaken the Prince.

I was forcing myself to realize that my body had changed. It was definitely a new skin tone, my features were sharper, more defined, and my ears were pointy, and yeah, my eyes were . . . well, they were kind of cool. I mean, the contrast between the irises and pupils was kind of striking. People would probably think they were fake. I could deal with this. My body had changed but it was still mine.

My gaze dropped below my navel.

I *really* needed to find a razor. Or a waxer.

But I could deal with this, because I had to deal with this. My appearance may have changed a little. I may have gotten my ass handed to me a few days ago. I may have lost a little of myself when Drake was holding me captive. I may have lost myself along the way, but I was still Ivy.

I twisted to the side and sighed.

And my ass was still not the most attractive thing in the world naked. You'd think the extra fae-ness would've given me a nice heart-shaped bottom or something. *That* I wouldn't have complained about.

Whatever.

Turning to the other side, I ran *my* hands over *my* sides and back, *my* fingers skating over the rough ridge of a new scar.

I swallowed hard, facing the mirror once more. I kept my eyes open as I smoothed my hands over my waist and then up, over my breasts. My hands stayed there, cupping them.

All of this was . . . it was mine.

My body didn't belong to the Prince. Or Ren. My body sure as hell didn't belong to some whacked out prophecy. It was *mine*—silvery skin, pointy ears, and all the scars were *mine*.

Realizing that I was basically fondling my own breasts, I rolled my eyes and dropped my hands. I quickly changed, leaving my hair pulled up because I didn't care about my ears. Nope. Not at all.

Now I was off to find Tink, which wasn't hard. I just had to look for the largest and loudest table in the cafeteria.

He was practically holding court. All I could see was his shockingly white hair in the center of a dozen or so fairer heads.

Ignoring the way my stomach acids decided to get all bubbly at the scent of cooked meat, I strode into the cafeteria. I was also going to need to invest in some Tums because the not being able to eat thing was stupid. It was one of the reasons I'd gotten my ass kicked.

Heads looked up and followed my progress. Conversations stopped. Whispers started.

My shoulders started to curve inward under the weight of their stares, but I caught myself. Old Ivy would not bow her chin. She would not care.

So new Ivy didn't care.

Fixing the kind of smirk on my face that always annoyed the piss out of David, I lifted my chin and approached Tink's table. It wasn't until I was right there that I realized two things.

Tink was Dixon-less.

Aaand Ren was at the table.

How in the world I hadn't seen him until then showed that I also really needed to work on my observation skills, but there he was, his russet head bent over a plate of egg whites and what was probably turkey bacon and whole wheat toast.

Because Ren was healthy like that.

Seeing him threw me completely for a loop. He hadn't

gone back to the room when I'd been there, but he was freshly showered. His hair was still damp and he'd changed. He was wearing a black thermal, pushed up to his elbows. I had no idea where he'd showered since he hadn't returned to the room.

A thousand words rose to the tip of my tongue. I wanted to apologize. I wanted to tell him that he'd been right. I wanted to ask him to help me fix things.

But I said none of those things, because those were things neither of us needed an audience for. Certainly not me, because I would probably break down in ugly, horrible tears.

I had a feeling he knew I was there without looking up. Maybe it was the way the chatter at the table eased off, or it was his weird sixth sense kicking in, but his shoulders tensed and he stopped chewing.

Tink, on the other hand, had no idea I was there . . . or alive, because it looked like he was eye-screwing the male fae across from him. An impressive level of eyeball fuckery that I could've taken lessons from. But when I saw Tink's lips part and he looked like he was a second away from licking his bottom lip, I intervened.

I cleared my throat. "Tink."

"Ivy!" Tink beamed up at me. Three empty plates were in front of him, the fae across from him forgotten. "You here to eat with us?"

"Uh, no. I already ate." I managed to scarf down a banana on my way downstairs, so that wasn't a lie. Turning over a new leaf and all. "I need to talk to you."

He sighed heavily. "Look, the fire last night was small. I put it out before it spread, and I already apologized for it. The room needs remodeling anyway."

I forced my gaze from Ren. He still hadn't acknowledged I was here. "No, it's not—wait, there was a fire last night?"

“Oh.” Tink sat back, crossing his arms. “Forget about that. What do you want to talk about?”

I opened my mouth and then decided not to question the whole fire thing, because I probably didn’t want to know. “I want to talk to you.” I peeked at Ren. He’d stopped eating, fork down, hands flat on the table. “In private, Tink.”

“Oh, secret squirrel stuff.” Tink started to rise. “I’m here for this.”

Ren looked up just then, his gaze snagging mine. “Hey.”

That one word was flat, emotionless. Empty. “Hi,” I managed to croak out.

He stared at me for a moment, and I worked up the courage to ask him to join us. But then his jaw tightened. Picking up his plate, he rose and stepped away from the table. “See you guys later.”

“Wait . . .” I trailed off, because it was no use. Ren was already halfway across the cafeteria. Watching him leave made it feel like my chest split right open.

“What the hell?” Tink asked.

I turned to him, blinking back the sudden rush of hot, stupid tears. I cursed myself. I hadn’t planned to exclude Ren from this conversation. I just hadn’t expected to see him so I’d wasted precious moments standing there like an idiot.

Operation Get Your Shit Together was off to a wonderful start.

I took a deep breath. “Can we step out into the hall?”

“Yeah.” A frown marred Tink’s features. “Sure.”

I took the few seconds to put myself back together. I needed to focus and not be on the verge of crying.

“What’s up with you and Ren?” he asked the moment we were out in the hallway. “Are you the reason he nearly knocked my head off this morning when I told him he looked like shit? Because the boy did look like he was rode hard and put away wet."

I stopped, crossing my arms. "I don't even want to know what that means."

"Well, it means getting fu—"

"Tink," I snapped. "I didn't ask you to come out here to talk about Ren."

"But I want to talk about him. You guys barely spoke to each other in there. That's weird."

I took a deep breath. "I know. We had a fight last night, but it'll be okay. It'll be fine."

"What?" Concern flashed across his face. "Like a big fight? Or a small one? Oh my God, are you two breaking up? Who will I live with?"

"Who will you live with?" I gaped up at him. "You're not twelve and you're not our kid."

"But I need to be taken care of. Loved. I need access to Amazon Prime."

"Then get a job, Tink. You look human enough to do it."

"A job?" Absolute horror filled his face. "The loss of blood must've done something to your brain because you're out of your mind."

"Okay. This conversation has veered off into very pointless territory. Everything is fine. Moving on." I struggled to remain patient. "Look, I have a couple of questions I want to ask you about the Prince."

A fae walking near us stopped and gasped. Her silvery skin turned a paler shade of gray.

Grabbing Tink's arm, I pulled him into a nearby room. It was small, with just a round table and two chairs. "Take a seat."

Tink sauntered over to the one furthest from the door and dropped down, stretching out his long legs. "Being in here with you feels naughty."

I shook my head as I closed the door behind me. "There's something wrong with you."

He grinned. "I could say the same thing about you."

"Touche," I muttered, sitting down across from him. "But let's analyze each other later. You once told me that killing the Prince was impossible, but nothing is impossible."

Tink tossed an arm over the back of his chair. "Well, yeah technically it's not impossible."

"Right." I rested my arms on the table. "We know a thorn stake will weaken an Ancient—"

"So you can chop their head off," he finished for me. "You can do the same with the Prince, but as you know firsthand, even cutting him with a stake isn't easy."

"No, it's not." The Prince had whipped my ass each time we'd fought, and the last time I'd had a thorn stake. "So the only way to kill the Prince is to weaken him enough to fight him."

Tink nodded slowly.

"Okay, so there has to be something out there that weakens him, right? That will make it easier to kill him."

"Yeah. A thorn stake." He squinted. "But you already know that."

I tapped my fingers on the table. "There has to be something else that doesn't require going toe to toe with him. I need you to think about this, Tink."

His head tilted. "I have thought about this."

"Think hard," I insisted. "I need you to really think about it. Maybe it's something small. Maybe not. You were in the Otherworld while the Prince was there. Maybe you saw something—heard something."

His nose wrinkled. "The only thing I saw was him feeding and screwing. A lot. I heard a lot of moans and screams. Not pain-filled screams. You know, the Prince was always a dick, but not as big of a dick as he is now. Oh! Maybe sex is a weakness for him."

My brows lifted.

He raised a shoulder. "Probably not. I mean, as much as he was doing it, I doubted it weakened him. Probably gave him strength. Like every time he came, he powered up like Mario—"

"All right, let's move on from the whole sex thing." I was going to need a Brillo Pad for my brain later.

He kicked a huge foot up on the table. "Why are you even asking about this? I thought some fae were coming that could help locate the Crystal?"

"They are, but I'm trying to plan ahead in case they don't find the Crystal," I explained. "Plus, we're going to have to get his blood. None of that is going to be easy when fighting him in combat is nearly impossible."

Before Tink could respond, the door swung open without warning, revealing Faye. "Our visitors are here."

Chapter 13

Tink and I followed Faye down the hall, toward Tanner's office, which I was guessing was now the official meeting place. I had no idea where Ren was, if he was already in the room, or coming. I didn't like how separate we were, but I tabled that problem to deal with later.

My hand brushed the dagger at my hip as Faye stopped in front of Tanner's office. Her gaze followed my hand. "Our guest means you no harm."

Noting how guests went from plural to singular, I glanced at the door. "I'll be the judge of that."

"Can't blame her for that," Tink chimed in, folding his long arms over his chest.

Her lashes lowered. "No. I cannot." There was a small pause. "How are you feeling, Ivy?"

"Fine."

The look on her face said she didn't quite believe me, but she didn't push it. Turning, she opened the door, and having no idea what to expect, I slowly followed her in.

"Holy yummy in my tummy," Tink murmured, stopping behind me.

I knew immediately what had provoked his reaction.

Sitting in one of the wingback chairs was a stranger who looked like a . . . well, a Viking. Not the historically accurate kind, but like the ones that graced the old romance covers I read. He was tall and broad, his thighs wide and like tree trunks. His hair was a glorious mane of blonde waves, reaching far past shoulders that stretched the plain white T-shirt he wore.

The stranger was stunningly beautiful and he was definitely no ordinary fae. The fae had the air of an Ancient, one of the most dangerous fae. Up until recently, we'd believed that there were no Ancient fae left in our world.

We must have been wrong.

I had a feeling we'd been lied to by the Order.

But there was something uncomfortably familiar about this fae's features—about the angular cheekbones and expressive mouth. It was the brow, too. Something about his face and his shape reminded me . . .

A chill ran down my spine.

He looked like Drake—a warmer version of the Winter Prince. I glanced at Faye, but she looked unperturbed as she took a seat on the couch by the window. She had to see the similarities. A warning that the stranger could pass for the cousin of Drake would've been nice.

Air stirred around my left arm. My head whipped to the side. Ren was there, as quiet as a damn ghost. Our gazes met, and my heart stuttered. Breaking contact, he focused on the stranger. The only emotion he showed was the tightening of his jaw.

Did he see what I saw?

"Who is this?" the stranger demanded, staring at me like an insect under a microscope.

Tanner rose from behind the desk, but before he could

introduce me, Tink stepped forward, coming to stand next to me. "She's Buffy with the bad hair."

Slowly, I turned and looked up at him. "*Buffy with the bad hair?*"

He nodded eagerly, glancing at the stranger. "Yeah, like it's a combination of Buffy and Beyonce, the two greatest females of all time. You're like Buffy. Bad ass. But you're not Becky with the good hair. You have bad hair. We all know that."

I stared at him. "My hair isn't that bad."

"Oh, it's bad." Tink's eyes glimmered. "You definitely aren't a Becky."

"I think it's a compliment to not be a Becky," Ren chimed in, and when I looked over at him, amusement danced in his eyes. "But I'm pretty sure that being a Becky isn't just about hair."

I hated all of them. Seriously.

The stranger lifted his chin and then rose, his nostrils flaring. "You're the one who belongs to the Winter Prince."

Wait.

What?

Ren tensed.

Did he really just say that?

Hearing that ranked right up there with hearing you had air cabin pressure issues while on a plane, thirty-some-thousand feet in the sky.

"I don't belong to him."

One blond eyebrow rose. "You are the Halfling."

"And you are a fae five seconds away from getting throat punched."

He chuckled a low, soft, almost sensual sound. "Is that how you greet someone who is here to help you?"

"You demand to know who I am and then tell me that I

belong to Drake—"

The fae hissed—bared sharp teeth and actually hissed. My brows lifted as his lip curled in distaste. "Do not speak his name."

"Why? He's not Voldemort."

"Voldemort?" Confusion filled his expression.

I stared at him for a moment and then shook my head. "Never mind. Who are you?"

The fae inclined his head. "I am Fabian." The air around him shimmered like a hundred fireflies had taken flight. "*Prince* Fabian of the Summer Court."

My mouth dropped open. Prince Fabian? Faye and Tanner sure as hell hadn't mentioned that one of our guests was a *prince*.

A prince.

A prince that could impregnate a halfling.

I sucked in a sharp breath.

Ren realized the same time I did, because he was suddenly beside me.

"Relax," Fabian said. "I have no interesting in impregnating you."

I blinked.

Well then, that was one blunt way of putting it.

"I am happy to hear that." Tink's smile reminded me of when it was Prime Day on Amazon.

Tanner cleared his throat. "I'm sorry. I know this must come as a shock that our guest is a prince."

"Damn right it's a shock," Ren growled. "You never once mentioned that we were waiting on another damn prince."

"Or that our guests were really just *a* guest," I added.

"I did not travel alone," Fabian explained, sitting down. "My consuls are not needed at this meeting. They are resting."

"Consuls. How fancy," I muttered.

The Summer Prince cocked his head.

Faye shifted in the beam of sunlight streaming in through the window. "We did not know Fabian would come. We assumed he would send—"

"His consul. Got it," I cut in. "I didn't know that there was still a prince of the Summer Court, alive and well."

"Up until recently, you didn't know the Summer Court still existed," Tanner gently reminded me, his tone level. He was right. We'd believed that the fae courts had been dismantled. Obviously, we'd been wrong or lied to. "Our Court had all been destroyed in the war with Winter. The safety and location of the remaining royals is not something we take lightly. Forgive us for not telling you such, but our Prince has no interest in fulfilling the prophecy."

"Even if I was, you wouldn't be my type." Fabian leaned back, folding one leg over the other. "Unlike the Winter Prince, my obligation to our world is not worth lowering myself to breed with a halfling."

Wow.

I was relieved to hear that, but I was also kind of offended. He made it sound like I was a stinky, single-celled organism.

"That's good to know." Ren leaned against the wall, appearing relaxed, but I knew better. He was coiled tight. "Forgive us for not rolling out the red carpet. We don't exactly have the best impression of Otherworld princes, especially since you look like the Winter Prince."

There. Thank God I wasn't the only one seeing it.

Fabian frowned. "I look nothing like that bastard."

"Well," I drew the word out, "yes, you kind of do. Doesn't he, Faye?"

She nodded. "I see a resemblance."

"I've seen the Winter Prince." Tink frowned. "He doesn't look like him."

I shook my head. "The hair color is different. Some of the face is, but yeah . . . he does."

"I don't know," Tink mused, his brow knitted together.

The Summer Prince's gaze landed on Tink, the look appraising. "A brownie. I haven't seen one of your kind in over a hundred years."

Tink smiled widely. "And you've never seen a brownie like me."

I rolled my eyes. "You'll have plenty of time to stroke Tink's ego later—"

"And hopefully other parts," Fabian replied smoothly.

Oh dear.

Ren choked on what sounded like a laugh.

"Yeah, sure. Um, okay. So, you're a prince. How many of the royal court are here, in our world, and do all of them feel the same way as you?"

"As in having no interest in ever seeing you naked enough to have intercourse?" he asked.

My eyes narrowed. Jesus. "Yeah. That. Thanks for putting it so kindly."

"Those of the court that are still alive, and there are few, have no desire to fulfill the prophecy. Just as Tanner stated. We came here to escape Winter's rule, to live out our lives. We understand what his presence will do to this world. He will destroy it, just like he and his Queen have done to our world."

"Queen?" Ren asked.

"Mab?" I turned to Tink, recalling how he always said her name.

Tink's eyes widened. "Mab picked no sides. She's neither Winter nor Summer. She's not as petty as Titania or

Morgana."

"Wait. I thought they were all the same person with just different names?" Ren said.

I thought the same, because that was what the Order had taught us. Plus, I was pretty sure Morgana was completely fictional, a part of the King Arthur tales.

Fabian snickered. "If you believe that, then who are we to correct you?"

God, he was *so* helpful.

"Their names have been interchangeable throughout the years, replacing one another in various myths." Tanner sat down, resting one arm on the desk. "But those are myths. The truth is that they are not one and the same. Our politics have never been represented accurately in the legends mortals have spun."

Ren gave a little shake of his head. "Do you think a Queen is also here?"

"We do not know if any Queen has come to this world," Faye answered. "Let us hope that one hasn't. That is a complication that none of us need."

My head was spinning. "But what if one of them has?"

"Queen Morgana sided with Winter during the war. She became their Queen." Fabian's lip curled in disgust. "If she has crossed over to this world, I will personally rip the spine from her back."

I lifted my brows.

"She killed my brother during the Great War and refused us the honor of burying his body." The Prince's eyes burned with unholy light from within. "She is, how do you humans put it? The worst?"

"Sounds about right." Ren unfolded his arms. "Do we have any evidence that she or any Queen is involved in this?"

"No," Faye answered. "I've been with the Prince. I have

not seen Morgana or any other Queen."

"Would you even know what Morgana looks like?" Fabian twisted in his chair. "She is the queen of many faces and has perfected the art of treachery. It would take a royal to recognize that bitch." He paused. "Or coincidentally, a brownie. Their ability to see through even the strongest glamour was one of the reasons the Winter Court hunted them down."

In her human form, a sheen of dullness settled over Faye's dark skin and she looked down.

"How would we kill her if she were here?" I asked.

"The same way you would kill any of us," the Summer Prince answered. "Decapitation."

The line of questioning brought me back to my earlier conversation with Tink. "But she would obviously need to be weakened. The same with *Drake*." I ignored the way his lips thinned. "How do we weaken one of you enough to go toe to toe?"

The room quieted as Fabian eyed me from where he sat. "And why would you want to know how to weaken a royal?"

I met his burning gaze. "To kill Drake. Duh."

"I thought you needed help finding the Crystal?" Fabian leaned forward, placing both feet on the floor. It was then that I realized he wore no shoes. Odd. "Not with killing the Winter Prince."

"We do need help finding the Crystal." Tanner's gaze bounced between us. "Ivy was captured by the Prince at one point. She's understandably a little . . . murderous when it comes to him."

"She's not the only one," Ren threw out.

"I'm not a little murderous," I clarified. "I'm a lot murderous."

"You think I would tell you how to weaken the Winter

Prince? Which would mean you'd know how to weaken me?" Fabian chuckled. "You're foolish."

Steel dripped into my spine as I stepped forward. "You want us to trust you blindly and yet you will not do the same? We have no reason to use this knowledge against you. I only want to kill the Prince, because I'll be damned if I spend weeks or months or the rest of my life looking over my shoulder for him, wondering if anyone I know is safe because he'll use them to get to me."

Fabian smirked as his icy gaze landed on me. "You silly little girl. You speak as if you're a special snowflake, unique and one of a kind."

Ren snorted from where he stood.

I shot Ren a death glare before glaring at Fabian. "You don't know who Voldemort is, but you know what special snowflake means? I call bullshit on that."

Fabian cocked his head to the side. "One always knows when they meet a special snowflake."

"Yeah, and those calling others snowflakes are historically the actual snowflake."

"Sticks and stones," Fabian murmured. "Or I am rubber and you are glue. Whatever you say bounces off me and sticks to you."

My mouth dropped open. Oh my God, it was like having a conversation with a ruder Tink.

Who, by the way, was practically shimmying with excitement as he leaned in, whispering into my ear. "I like this guy. I *really* like him. Can I keep him?"

The Summer Prince heard him, and interest sparked in his pale blue eyes. "I've never been kept by a brownie before, but . . . I've heard things. Interesting things."

I so needed an adult right now, but the *adults* were all staring at the ceiling, pretending like a live version of Fae

Tinder wasn't going down right in front of us.

Tink straightened. "Do tell."

Fabian stepped toward us. "Is it true that a brownie's co—"

"Okay," Ren stepped in, apparently to Tanner's relief by the look on his face. "Let's get back on topic. You were talking about how Ivy isn't a special snowflake."

Dear mountain momma, I was two seconds from launching my dagger across the room and stabbing the Summer Prince in his eye, punching Tink, and throwing Ren out the window.

"All right, *Fabio*," I snapped. "Can you get past the insulting me part to saying something actually helpful? For once?"

His fair brows knitted. "Are you dense? My name is not Fabio. It's Fabian."

I rolled my eyes. "Whatever." I didn't have the patience to explain who Fabio was. "Just say what you need to say."

The Summer Prince's smirk grew. "The Prince has found another halfling and he's left New Orleans, taking the Crystal with him."

Chapter 14

All hell broke loose around me while I just stood there, in the center of the room staring at the Summer Prince. Faye was standing and so was Tanner. Ren had moved forward, asking questions, but I didn't hear what he was saying. Tink was calm, though. Sort of. He was eyeballing Fabio again, in the way Ren looked at me when he actually liked me.

But I . . . I was just so shocked I couldn't think past my roiling emotions. One stood out. Relief. It coursed through me in waves, leaving me dizzy.

The Prince wouldn't be looking for me.

Ren was safe.

So was Tink.

I was safe.

Well, as safe as any of us were, but Drake wasn't gunning for me anymore.

My throat thickened as tears rushed my eyes.

All of that probably meant something was wrong with me. I mean, Drake was still out there bound and determined to knock up some poor, random halfling, but he wasn't coming after me.

A laugh bubbled up my throat, but I squelched it before it escaped as I blinked back tears of relief. No one would understand.

I was such a terrible person, but I couldn't help it. Weight lifted from my shoulders. We still had to deal with Drake, but I . . . I felt *free*.

"I thought the Elite had killed all the halflings?" Tanner's voice rose above the noise, drawing my attention.

"The Elite has hunted down every halfling they've been able to discover," Ren answered, and I flinched, knowing that I was one of them. "That doesn't mean they got all the halflings in the whole world. The Prince is obviously better at finding them than we were."

"I don't know if that's true since you guys probably killed a whole crapton of them," Tink pointed out.

Ren shot him a dark glare before turning to Fabian. "How do you know this?"

"Just as the Winter Prince has had scouts out looking for possible halflings, we've had our own eyes on them." Fabian yawned, appearing bored with this whole conversation. "He and his consul left two days ago."

Two days ago? While I was passed out because some fae tried to murder me because they thought the Prince was here? Another near hysterical laugh started deep in my belly.

"You had no idea that they were scouting for other halflings?" Ren asked Faye.

"I know Valor wanted the Prince to look for another, but as far as I know, they weren't actively seeking one." Disbelief colored her tone. At some point, she'd lost her human form. "Where did he go?"

Fabian stretched out his legs, crossing them at the ankles. "That we don't know."

"You apparently know everything else, but you don't know this?" I demanded.

"Yes." His gaze flickered to me. "That is exactly what I'm saying. It was too much of a risk for my spies to follow."

Whatever relief I'd felt when I discovered that Drake wouldn't be looking for me began to fade. "Then he and this Halfling could be anywhere."

He lifted a shoulder in an elegant shrug.

"This changes everything," Faye said, sitting back down heavily, lacking her normal grace. "I knew nothing of the scouts or that he'd be able to find another halfling this quickly."

"It doesn't change anything." All eyes focused on me. What I said was true. Everything changed for me, but we still had the same mission—a more urgent, desperate one now. "We need to find him, put him back where he belongs, or kill him."

Ren whirled on me. "Are you out of your mind?"

"Excuse me?"

"You don't need to do anything but keep your pretty little ass here," he announced like he didn't have a death wish. "The Prince might be on the hunt for another halfling, but you're still a halfling, Ivy."

"No shit," I spat back. "But only I get to say where my ass gets to go and doesn't go."

His eyes flared a deep shade of green. "If he's not here, there's no reason for you to go after him. The smartest and safest thing is for you to stay here."

"And what? You're going to go after him?"

His jaw tightened. "That *is* my job."

"And it's *my* job too!"

Tink lightly touched my arm. "He has a point, Ivy." He narrowed his eyes at Ren. "He's really bad at making said point, but he does have a point."

"Thanks," Ren bit out before taking a deep breath. "Look, I get that it's your duty too, but you're still at risk. He could turn his attention back to you."

Folding my arms, I cocked my hip out, moving into the standard pissed off stance. "And I get it's your duty, but you do realize the only way the Prince controls me is through *your* ass, right?"

Ren stepped back, his spine going rigid.

"Yeah. Let *that* sink in, buddy." I was on a roll. No stopping now. "You go out there, and if he doesn't kill you, he'll capture you. Using you to get me to agree to things is probably a lot easier than convincing some random halfling to have sex with him."

"Actually," Faye cut in, "if the Halfling doesn't know what she is and what he is, it wouldn't be hard at all. One-night stands happen all the time."

Tanner sat down heavily. "This is bad."

"It's still too risky for you to go." Ren ignored them. "Not trying to be an ass about it, but the further away you are, the better."

"So, I'm supposed to sit around and do what exactly? Tend to the garden outside? Maybe take up knitting classes?"

"At least then you're doing something." One side of his lips kicked up. "Idle hands are the devil's playground, or so they say."

I was going to hit him.

Seriously.

"I'm about to shove these idle hands so far up your ass, you'll think you've become a puppet."

"You know what?" Ren leaned forward, lowering his voice. "I might actually enjoy that."

My body flushed out of anger and something totally

different. I ignored the latter, getting right up in Ren's face. "I'm not staying behind, Ren. Not going to happen."

"You're impossible to reason with." Shaking his head, he thrust his hand through his hair. "I swear to God."

"Stop fighting," Tink said, dancing back and forth between us. "It makes me anxious."

"It makes me wish I had popcorn," Fabian added.

I spun on the Summer Prince. "Why are you even here? You came from who knows where—"

"Florida," he supplied.

"Figures," Ren muttered under his breath.

"You came here just to tell us that Drake had left? You couldn't, I don't know, phone that piece of knowledge in?"

Tanner sighed from behind the desk.

"You still need me." He threaded his fingers together. "After all, how do you plan to find the Crystal? Or the Winter Prince when we don't know where he's gone? Even if we do discover that, he will be smarter, hiding his presence. We will be able to sense one another, but he will not know I'm working with you."

"Would he truly think that a prince of a court he's helped eradicate is in the same city as him to join him for dinner?" Ren demanded, bringing up a good point.

A muscle thrummed along Fabian's jaw. "The Winter Prince will not see me as a threat. If anything, he'll just be curious." His gaze slid to me. "That will be his weakness."

Meeting the Summer Prince's gaze head-on, I had a feeling that wasn't the only weakness to learn.

"None of that truly matters if we don't know where the Prince has gone." Faye lifted her hands. "We can sit here and argue over who is leaving and who is staying, but none of that matters. We have no idea where he went."

"That's another good point," Tink chimed in.

Those around me started speculating, but that was all they could do. Speculate. Which meant nothing. We couldn't chase false leads or suspicions. We didn't have the time. We needed to find someone who'd know—

Then it hit me.

"I know who would probably know where Drake has gone," I said, and all eyes turned to me. "Marlon—Marlon St. Cyers. The developer in the city?" I added when everyone continued to stare at me. "He's an Ancient who was working closely with Drake. He may know where he went."

Tanner turned to Faye. "Do you think that's possible? That Drake would've trusted him enough with that information?"

"They were close, so it's possible." Excitement sparked in her pale eyes. "It's worth checking out."

"Then that's what we'll do." Resolve filled me. "We'll find Marlon and we'll make sure he talks."

Chapter 15

The meeting sort of fell apart after that. Tanner wanted everyone to 'calm down and gain perspective' before we spoke of leaving to search down Marlon. Ren shot me a look that told me our conversation—er, argument—wasn't over before he stalked out of the room. Prince Fabian rose fluidly, and when I saw he'd zeroed in on Tink, I made my way out into the hallway. Ren had already disappeared.

Faye followed, and when I glanced over at her, there was no missing the tension lining her face. "Are you okay?"

"Yeah." Faye nodded, but she still looked a little ill. "It's just something Fabian said about Queen Morgana. How I wouldn't recognize her if I'd seen her." Drawing in a deep breath, she reached up, tucking her hair behind an ear. "Just the possibility of being near her without knowing makes me feel as if someone has walked over my grave."

My brows lifted. "She's that bad?"

Faye stopped, facing me. "What has been told about her spun in tales to entertain children are just that. Tales." She gave a little shake of her head. "Stories of her brutality are only whispered among the oldest of our kind, her cruelty most horrendous. She has committed such grievous crimes, her ability to create life was stripped from her. In a way, she's our boogeyman, something we all fear. Her hatred of the Summer Court is only surpassed by her hatred of humans." Faye looked away, swallowing hard. "If she is involved, the doorways to the Otherworld opening would be the least of our worries."

AFTER THE SOMEWHAT creepy conversation with Faye, I tried to find Ren because I was more than ready for round two of our argument. I knew I'd hurt him the night before, but that didn't change the fact he had absolutely no right to try to tell me what I could do.

Unfortunately, he was missing in action, which was disappointing because it made me want to yell at him more.

I liked yelling at him, actually. It made me feel . . . normal. And that was kind of messed up, but whatever.

Since he was nowhere to be found, I did the next best thing. I headed to the gym, but I didn't go into the room with the treadmills. I went for the smaller room, the one with thick mats covering the floor and a punching bag.

That's where I spent the rest of the day, going through old training sessions with myself, like I was sixteen again. A few months ago, I would've balked at the notion that I needed to practice evasive techniques or groundwork, but I knew better now. I needed all the practice I could get, especially if I planned on facing the Winter Prince again.

It would've been nice to have a partner though.

I moved on to the punching bag, working with the iron dagger. I didn't jab as hard as I could, because I doubted the fae here would've appreciated a bag full of cuts, but I picked up speed as the now too familiar sensation simmered to life in my stomach. It reminded me of gnawing hunger, but it was a craving, the same kind I imagined an addict went through. It was nowhere near as bad as it had been before, but it was still there, a shadow inside me.

Sweat was dripping into my eyes when the door opened and a burst of fresh air entered the room. Yanking the blade out of the bag, I spun around and saw Brighton.

She was standing just inside the door, one hand curled around the ends of her ponytail. "Sorry. I didn't mean to interrupt."

"It's okay." Swiping an arm over my forehead, I sheathed the dagger. "What's up?"

"I was just roaming around. Saw that you were in here." She nodded at the small window in the door. "I haven't seen you since . . . well, since you were attacked. You seem to be doing well."

"I am. I would say I'm lucky, but I guess being part fae is why I'm okay." Those words rolled off my tongue easier than I thought they ever would. "The whole feeding thing saved my life."

"That's what I heard. Mind if I sit or is it a distraction?"

"Sit." I shrugged. "I'm done anyway."

She pulled out one of the middle chairs and unfolded it. "How are you handling everything? The whole feeding thing?"

I started to tell her that I was doing fine, but that's not what I said. "I honestly don't know." I walked over to where she sat. "I mean, I'm happy to be alive, but knowing what I did to be here doesn't sit right."

She looked up at me. "I can understand that."

Looking away, I bit down on my lip. "Do you know what Ren and Tink did?"

There was a beat of silence. "I heard they made Faye use a compulsion on you."

"They did. I was so angry with them, but. . . ."

"You're not anymore?"

"I still am." Exhaling roughly, I sat down on the mat in front of her. "And I'm also not. I get why they did it. I appreciate it, but I'm not okay with it."

She folded her arms in her lap. "I guess the question is, can you forgive them?"

"I already have," I said, and that was the God's honest truth. "I kind of had to, you know? Because I would've done the same thing to save them."

A faint smile pulled at Brighton's lips. "Well, I'm glad you're still alive."

I wondered if her mom truly felt the same. Then again, it really didn't matter. "Me too. Anyway." I leaned back on my hands. "Did you hear anything about our visitors?"

Brighton widened her eyes as she nodded. "Yeah. Freaking unbelievable. Another prince? And halfling?" Her shoulders tightened. "The fucking Order has lied to us from day one."

I couldn't help it. I squelched a laugh, but she cursed, and I couldn't remember hearing her curse before.

"I mean, nearly everything we thought to be true turned out not to be." Her lips thinned. "What else do we think we know that isn't true?"

"God. It could be anything. But there has to be a reason why they didn't tell us about the Summer fae or the royal courts." I stretched out my legs. "And does the Order even know the Prince has left?"

"I have no clue, and at this point, it's a risk to even reach out to them and find out." She sat back. "But we're going to have to. Once we get the Crystal, we'll need their help opening the gates."

"Or we kill the Prince." I ignored her gasp of surprise. "We'd probably need the Order for that too, considering we'd need all the help we can get."

Brighton then pointed out the obvious. "Killing the Prince is almost impossible."

"*Almost* impossible," I stressed. "He has to have a weakness other than having an ego, and the Summer Prince knows what weakens them." I wrinkled my nose. "I kind of understand why he wouldn't be so forthcoming with that info, but if we can weaken him, we can probably kill him."

She appeared to consider that. 'Then we just have the other princes and princesses to worry about, right? Because who knows how many from the Summer Court are here?"

I snorted. "Right? We're just supposed to believe that all of them are live and let live hippie fae?" Something occurred to me. "And I seriously doubt the Summer Prince isn't feeding. The power practically dripped off him."

"I think—" The door to the room opened, revealing Tink. He had company.

"Merle and crew were looking for you." He stepped aside. "Told them you were probably here or the library, so I decided to be their escort because I'm cool like that." He glanced at Brighton and then waved at her. "Hi!"

Brighton seemed to sink into the chair as she murmured, "Hello."

He turned away from us. "I also found your daughter. I am so helpful."

I arched a brow as I looked around him. Standing behind Merle was Tanner. Neither looked happy.

I pushed off my hands, sitting up straight. I figured they were ready to discuss the plans to find and question Marlon. "What's up?"

Merle stormed into the room. Something metal dangled from her hand. Wait. Were those . . . *handcuffs*? "Ren told us."

A chill swept through me.

"Told you what?" Tink frowned as his gaze swept over us.

Merle's eyes were like glaciers of ice. "Ivy's planning to run."

Chapter 16

For a good, long second, I was too shocked by the fact that Ren had actually ratted me out to have much of a reaction.

Holy crap, he'd actually gone to Merle and Tanner?

I was going to punt kick him into next week!

"What?" Tink shouted, his voice echoing off the walls of the small room. "You're going to run?"

"Not anymore." Merle lifted the handcuffs.

The purpose of the handcuffs registered with sudden clarity. I launched off the floor. "You're going to handcuff me? Are you out of your mind?"

Merle's grip tightened on the handcuffs. "My mind is as sharp as a fiddle, girl."

Sharp as a fiddle? That didn't even make sense. Whatever. She took a step toward me, and my hand flew to my dagger. "If you come one inch closer to me, you'll find out that this dagger is sharper than a fiddle."

"Ivy," Brighton gasped, rising from her chair.

Merle held still. "You were planning to run off—"

"I *was* planning to leave when I thought the Prince was

still here, which is totally my choice." My fingers tightened around the handle of the dagger. "But all of that is a moot point now, isn't it?"

"That's what I tried to explain to Merle." Tanner, ever the mediator, stood to my right.

"It's still dangerous. Doesn't matter if he's found another halfling to impregnate or not." Merle lifted her chin. "We don't need Ivy running around out there, too. Like Ren said earlier, she needs to stay here, where the Prince isn't."

I struggled to keep my voice even. "First off, if I want to leave here, I will. No one is going to keep me here against my will. I've already been down that road and have the baggage to prove it. I'm not going for a round two."

Merle opened her mouth, but Tanner placed a hand on her arm, silencing her. "That is true. We are not holding her against her will. She can walk out of here whenever she pleases."

I appreciated his support, but I wasn't done. "Secondly, you're seriously overreacting at this point." Muscles in my neck tensed up. "When I learned that the Prince could get through the glamour here, I did plan on leaving. My presence here was too much of a risk for me to live with, and I don't give a *fuck* if you agree with that or not."

Merle's eyes widened slightly.

"But I agreed to stay until the guests got here. None of that matters now. Drake has found another halfling, and while that's a hell of a relief, that doesn't mean my duty has ceased to exist." When she started to speak again, I cut her off. "You really do not want to have that argument with me. Seriously. Because you aren't going to win."

She clamped her jaw shut.

"Mom," Brighton began quietly. "You cannot seriously handcuff Ivy. That's not right."

"Sometimes what is necessary isn't always what is right," she replied coldly.

I ignored that deep statement of the day, because boy did I ever have bigger fish to fry at the moment. I zeroed in on Tanner. "When will we discuss finding Marlon?"

Still focused on Merle, he said, "We've already discussed it."

A hot flush swept over me. "You have?"

Only then did he look at me. "A few hours ago. A team leaves at nine in the morning to scout for him."

I saw red. "And I'm guessing I was conveniently left out of this meeting?"

Tanner's gaze dropped away.

A bitter laugh punched out of me. "But I bet Ren wasn't. During this meeting did he tell you about my plan to leave?"

"He did before Fabian and his consul arrived," Tanner answered. "I do believe he didn't mean for *this* to happen." He glanced wryly at Merle. "I made the error of mentioning it to Merle, who as you can see, had a strong reaction."

I was about to have a strong reaction.

"I will be with whatever team leaves tomorrow." I stepped around Tanner and Merle, silently daring her to get those handcuffs near me. "I am done with this conversation."

I didn't give them the chance to respond, stalking out into the hallway. I made it about five feet.

"Ivy. Wait." It was Tink.

Inhaling deeply, I turned to tell him that whatever he had to say had to wait, but I saw the look on his face.

His expression was stricken. "You were going to leave me?"

Oh God. "I—"

"You really were going to do that?" Tink crept closer, his eyes welling with emotion. "Why would you do that?"

Running my hands down my face, I shook my head. "It doesn't matter. The Prince—"

"Found a new halfling and doesn't care about you anymore. Yeah, I was there for that." His hands opened and closed at his sides. "But before? You were planning to leave me—leave us. That's why Ren is so upset."

"Well, there are a lot of reasons why he's upset, but yes, that's one of them."

Tink stared at me for so long that unease filled me. "So, you were going to leave without telling me."

I shifted my weight, uncomfortable. "I learned that the Prince could get through the glamour. I . . . I panicked. All I could think about was him using you or Ren. I thought that if I left, then you guys wouldn't be at risk."

"Did you not think that we would've freaked out and left, looking for you?" he demanded.

"I didn't really think it through."

"No." Hurt filled his eyes. "You didn't."

Shame settled over me like a coarse blanket. "I know, and I'm sorry. I would do . . . I would do anything to protect you two."

"And we'd do anything to protect you," he said quietly. "You saved my life, Ivy."

"You saved mine," I reminded him.

"And you yelled at me for it." When I started to respond, he continued on. "I get why. I do."

I rubbed the heel of my palm against my hip. "Can we . . . I don't know? Start over? I really am sorry. It was a stupid plan—"

"A cruel and stupid plan."

"Yes." I sighed. "It was."

He lifted his chin. "I already lost my family once. I do not want to lose my family again, Ivy."

My breath caught.

"And that's what you are to me—you and even Ren," he said, and I sort of wished Ren was here to hear that. "You two are all that I have. If you had left me, it would've killed me."

Guilt was a knot in my throat, one I needed to live with. I stepped forward, placing my hand on his arm. "I'm sorry, Tink. I just panicked, and I know that's not a good excuse, but it's the truth. I panicked and I didn't think about what it would do to you and Ren. And that was wrong, because you two are all I have left. You are . . ." I drew in a deep breath. "You're my family."

Tink studied me a moment and then sprang forward, wrapping his long arms around me. He hugged me—hugged me tight, and I reacted without thought, folding my arms around him. Squeezing my eyes closed against the sudden rush of tears, I planted my face against his chest.

I was learning Tink gave great hugs.

"All is forgiven," Tink murmured into my ear. "But if you ever think about doing something like that again, I will not forgive you."

"Okay," I whispered thickly.

"And I will go onto Amazon and order some weird shit. Not only that, I'll make my wish list public, which means it will be your wish list," he continued. "You don't want that."

My lips twitched as I pulled back. "I don't want that."

"Good."

Drawing in a deep breath, I glanced at the closed door to the gym. "I need to find Ren. Do you have any idea where he's at?"

"I think he's at the pool."

Surprise filled me. "There's a pool?"

Tink looked at me like I was half stupid. "All the roaming

around you've done and you haven't found the pool yet? You are not living your best life."

TINK WAS RIGHT.

I wasn't living my best life if I didn't know there was a damn pool in this building, and there apparently was one on the second floor. The faint scent of chlorine led the way, and with each step, my earlier anger resurfaced with the vengeance of a thousand burning suns.

I knew I'd made a mistake with the whole leaving thing. Ren had been right. It had been a knee-jerk reaction, but him running to Tanner was going too far.

It was time to have that strong reaction that didn't include crying and feeling like a douche.

Slamming my hands into the double doors, I burst into the room and immediately came to an abrupt halt. My eyes widened. The room was large and bright due to the floor-to-ceiling windows all along the furthest side. The pool was one of those huge ones, Olympic size, but it wasn't the pool that had rendered me completely incapable of moving.

It was Ren.

"Holy crap," I whispered.

He didn't hear me, because he was currently gliding under the water like some kind of sea God, his body sleek and quick as he swam. He was only wearing what appeared to be black boxer briefs. There was a pile of neatly folded clothing on a nearby bench, and I could almost picture him standing there, folding the jeans and shirt. His shoes were tucked under the bench.

The panther tattoo on his back moved with him, an absolutely stunning piece of artwork somehow highlighted by the glistening water. Lean muscles along his back flexed as he broke the surface in the deep end. He didn't see me at first, which was great because it gave me more time to creep on him as he lifted his powerful arms, pushing the water and hair from his face.

My mouth dried as a zing shot from my chest to my core. He was. . . .

Ren's head swung sharply in my direction. Those eyes were like polished emerald jewels, placed perfectly behind thick, wet lashes.

Tense silence filled the room as we stared at one another. He was the one to break it.

"Hey," he said, wading away from the middle of the pool, toward the edge where I stood.

I blinked slowly and then got my hormones in check. Okay. Ren was hot and he looked like some kind of God. Whatever. I was not that easily distracted.

"I am so pissed at you right now," I told him.

"Really," he replied dryly, dropping a heavy arm on the cement. One side of his lips kicked up. "Is that any different from this morning when you were pissed at me?"

"Oh." I laughed harshly. "You think this is funny?"

The smirk didn't fade. "I always think you're funny, Sweetness."

Did he now? "Okay. I'll show you something that's really funny."

His other arm came up and landed on the cement. "You have a riveted audience for it."

Spinning around, I stalked toward the bench and picked up his clothing.

"Ivy—"

I whirled and engaged full-bitch mode, darting to the end of the pool.

"Don't you dare. I swear to God, Ivy!" Muscles in his

arms pumped as he lifted himself straight out the pool. He was on his feet within seconds. "Ivy—"

"Too late." I threw his clothing into the pool.

Ren spun, but there was no saving his stuff. His shirt and tactical pants landed with a satisfying splash. He stared at them for a moment.

"Fuck," he spat.

I faced him, grinning like the Mad Hatter. "That was real funny, wasn't it?"

His narrowed gaze landed on me. "Are you out of your mind?"

"Nah, but I'm thinking you are."

"I'm the crazy one? You just threw my clothes into the pool!"

"And I wish I could do it again!" I stalked up to him. Since he was a good foot taller than me, I had to lean my head back to glare at him. "You ratted me out to Tanner!"

Understanding flared in his face and then he rolled his eyes. "That's why you threw my stuff in the pool? Jesus, Ivy." He coughed out a short laugh. "I told Tanner this morning before that Summer Prince showed up."

"Oh, so because you ratted me out before it became irrelevant makes it okay?"

His brows furrowed. "He needed to know in case you didn't hold to your promise and made a run for it."

I gaped at him. "Are you serious?"

Shoving his wet hair off his face, he stepped back. "As serious as you throwing my shit into the pool."

"I'm about to throw *you* into the pool," I snapped, struggling to not let my gaze wander from his face, because he was wet and had a lot of hard skin on display. "You didn't have to tell him."

A muscle ticked in his jaw as he looked away, and

dammit, my gaze dropped. His chest was all wet and hard, and water still coursed down those taut abs. The band on his briefs hung indecently low and they left little to the imagination. Soaking wet, they clung to every long, hard inch. . . .

Wait. Was he hard?

My eyes widened.

Yes. Yes, he was.

"My face is up here," Ren mocked.

I flushed as my gaze jerked to his. "Asshole."

"Not that I mind you staring at me like you want to take a bite out of me, but right now, I'm kind of worried you might actually bite."

I folded my arms over my chest. "I promised you that I'd stay until we learned about the Crystal, and I would have." My hands curled into fists. "You could've trusted me."

Shaking his head, he looked up at the ceiling. "I trust you, Ivy. I trust you to always do what I least expect."

My head tilted to the side. "Do you have a death wish right now?"

Ren looked away again, frowning as his pants floated past us. "I'm sorry that you didn't like that I told Tanner, but I felt he needed to know since he'd sheltered us—not the greatest shelter, but a place nonetheless. Who knows what would've happened if you'd left, what effect could've rippled back on this place? But no, that's not something you thought about." His hard gaze found mine. "You know, with your great escape plan and all."

Dammit, he had a bit of a point there, but I sure as hell wasn't telling him that. "Do you know what Merle did?"

"I didn't tell Merle shit."

"But Tanner did," I said. "She showed up just a few minutes ago with a pair of handcuffs. Yes. Handcuffs."

"What?" He laughed, this time the sound lighter, more

genuine. "I would've paid money to see that."

"Are you for real?"

He said something and laughed again, and I swear my vision went white with rage. Storming forward, I slammed my hands into his chest.

His laugh was cut off as he lost his balance, falling backward.

I don't even know how what happened next went down. Ren's arms flailed out and he must've grabbed my arm, because the next thing I knew I was falling sideways into the pool.

My shriek was silenced by the rush of water swallowing me whole. I sank nearly to the bottom, eyes squeezed tight, mouth full of air.

Holy shit, the water was cooold.

Using my feet against the bottom, I pushed my way to the top, breaking the surface and gasping for air. I could hear splashing next to me, alerting me to Ren doing the same thing. The impact had knocked my hair down, and it covered my face like a red, tangled veil. Using one arm to swim to the side, I used the other hand to push it out of my face.

Ren turned in the water toward me, his eyes wide with surprise. "You pushed me into the pool."

"You pulled me into the pool!" My feet reached the stairs.

He stared at me for a moment and then did the craziest thing. Ren started laughing—laughing deep, belly laughs as he held on to the other side of the pool.

Something about his laugh was . . . infectious.

My lips twitched and then a giggle escaped. It was like a levee breaking. One soft laugh and I lost it. Our laughter reached the high ceiling, and my stomach cramped from the force of it, because this—*us*—was ridiculous.

I was gasping for air by the time I made it to the shallow end where I could stand with the water reaching my chest. "We are so stupid . . ." I trailed off because I'd looked over at Ren. He was just staring at me, mouth slightly open like he'd just witnessed a total solar eclipse. "What?"

"I . . ." He shook his head, his cheeks flushing pink. "I just haven't heard you laugh like that in a long, long time."

I frowned, my arms floating at my sides. Our gazes connected over the distance. "It . . . feels like it's been a long time. It's nice to laugh like that." I felt like a fool for admitting that, so my cheeks flamed to life.

Ren pushed away from the wall, wading out into the center of the pool. "It was beautiful."

I bit down on my lip as I watched him come closer. "Really?"

"Yeah." He reached the end where his feet could hit the bottom. A moment passed as his chest rose and fell sharply. "I just wish I heard it more often."

My breath caught as a bubble of emotion swelled inside me.

Ren stopped moving. "And all I want is for you to feel it more often. At the end of the day . . . that's what I wish."

I opened my mouth to tell him there were so many more important things to wish for, but the words got stuck in my throat because I wanted that too. I wished for that, too.

I could feel my face start to crumple.

"Talk to me," Ren pleaded quietly, like he always did. "Talk to me, Ivy."

It was like the sharp edge of a dagger taken to an overinflated balloon. I burst wide open, every thought and feeling on the outside of me, drenching my skin and threatening to pull me back under.

There was no hiding, no pretending. There was no room left to lie. I closed my eyes. "I don't . . . I don't know who I am anymore."

Chapter 17

There.

I'd said it.

I'd said it out loud and I'd said it to Ren. There was no taking it back, not when it was out there in the open like that. No way.

"Ivy." He said my name like it broke him. Like he was a balloon that had burst, too.

I kept my eyes closed because I didn't want to see his face. "Ever since the . . . the Prince, I haven't felt like myself. I did things and I know—I know he made me do those things, but it made me feel like I wasn't me." I lifted my hands from the water, squeezing them into fists. "Now I don't even look like me, and I have this thing inside me—this need that was never there before—this hunger. I just . . ."

Pressing my lips together, I inhaled roughly through my nose and opened my eyes. Ren hadn't come any closer. He was as still as a statue, but he was watching me, and I knew he hadn't looked away. Not once. "And I've been stuck in my head, you know? Just trying to make sense of every damn thing that happened so it's hard to get *out* of my head.

That's why I got my ass kicked by those fae. I wasn't paying attention, and I haven't been eating right, and—and that night I told myself I'd finally talk to you. I would tell you what's going on, but you . . . I saw you with Tink and Faye in one of the common rooms, and you looked so relaxed. So relaxed and normal that I didn't want to ruin that. I didn't want to take that from you."

Ren closed his eyes, face tense.

"I really did plan on talking to you that night, but then . . . then the whole stabbing thing happened." I drew in a shuddering breath. "Then I fed and we—you know what happened. Then I learned about the Prince being able to get through the glamour, and I just panicked. I flipped out and yes—*yes*! My plan was stupid. It was a knee-jerk reaction. You're right. And Tink is right, because it was also cruel. And I'm sorry for not telling you. I was running, and it was wrong, but I just wanted to make sure you two were safe, because you and Tink are all I have. I wanted to be in control, but I just didn't think it through."

His eyes were open again, his expression strained. Pale. It was hard looking at him, because he looked like how I felt.

"And I . . . I woke up this morning and told myself that I was going to be okay. I was going to get my shit together. That I was in control of me. I could ignore the hunger. That my body was mine, my thoughts were mine. That I could be okay with having slightly silvery skin and pointy ears. I even wore my hair up to prove that." I was rambling now and I couldn't seem to stop myself. "I woke up this morning telling myself I was in control, and then I . . . I really wasn't."

A tremor coursed through me as I stepped back, bumping into the pool wall. "You telling me I had to stay here, then Merle trying to handcuff me to God knows what, and all *I* want is for things to be the way they were before."

Ren's jaw tensed, and a too-long moment passed. "I'm sorry."

Not expecting that response, I blinked.

His chest rose with what appeared to be a heavy breath. "I didn't mean to take that from you today. Fuck." He lifted a hand, running it over his head, pushing locks of wet hair back. "I just wanted you safe, and if the Prince had left New Orleans, then you would be safe here."

"I know," I whispered, wiping at the tears on my cheek. "But I have to be there when you go to find Marlon. I have to . . ."

"Take back control. I know." He dropped his hand as he stepped forward, stirring the water. "I've made this harder for you while I'm thinking I'm making it easier, doing the right thing."

"We both have," I admitted quietly, and that was the truth. We both thought we were doing what was best for each other, but in the end, we were doing more harm than good.

Ren looked away, his jaw flexing. "Yeah, but I gave you shit for planning to leave without me, and then I turned around and planned to do the same thing."

"But you probably meant to actually tell me first," I pointed out.

"That doesn't matter." The muscles in his shoulders tensed. "We fucked up, didn't we?"

My breath hitched again. He wasn't looking at me, and I felt my stomach drop like I was on a rollercoaster. "I know you probably don't want to do this with me anymore. I know I hurt you and—hell, you were right when you said I've always been running. You don't have to keep chasing me. That's not right." I swallowed hard when his head swiveled toward me. "We never even got the chance to have a normal relationship. Can't be surprised that this isn't working out. We can't—"

"What?" Ren cut through the water like he was born in it. Within a heartbeat, he was right in front of me and then his hands were touching my cheeks, cupping them. "Let's hit pause for a second, because I want to make something real clear."

Our gazes locked, and I couldn't even formulate a response.

"I was pissed at you. You're probably still pissed at me. We're fighting and we got some shit to work through, but that's normal. What we're dealing with outside of us isn't, but we are still an us." His gaze searched mine. "I still love you. I'm still right here with you. Has that changed for you?"

My heart all but exploded in my chest. I didn't know until this very moment how badly I needed to hear that—to remember that this was normal. Couples fought. Sometimes they said things they wish they hadn't. Sometimes they didn't agree and did things that could hurt each other. It wasn't like Shaun and I never argued. There'd been calls that ended abruptly. Doors slammed in faces. I'd just . . . I'd just forgotten that.

I'd forgotten that there could still be an us through the storm.

And that's what made this different, made *this* special, because I knew out there in the *normal* world, there were people who never made it past the first hurdle, who gave up the moment it got hard or required them to admit they'd been wrong. And our hurdles had been high. They were still there, the size of skyscrapers, looming over us like the shadow of winter when you're desperately clinging to summer.

"I'm still here," I said, my voice shaky, my entire body trembling. "I'm still with you. I still love you. I never stopped. I can't."

I don't know who made the first move. It could've been me. Maybe Ren. But whatever distance that was between us evaporated and I don't know if it was him who kissed me or me who kissed him. We were both grabbing at one another. Ren holding my cheeks. Me clutching at his shoulders, rising up onto the tips of my toes.

And when our lips met, it was the sweetest, softest kiss. A touch of our mouths that turned into a slow exploration as if we were getting reacquainted with each other, and . . . we really were.

His bare skin against my hands was hot and wet as one of his hands slipped back, his fingers brushing my ear and tangling in my hair. My lips parted as I whispered his name, and the kiss deepened as he shuddered against me.

God, I missed this—the closeness, the intimacy. What had happened between us after I fed wasn't intimate. It was just ferocious need driving both of us. This was different.

My hands slid down his chest, to where his heart beat as wildly as mine.

Ren pulled away to ask, "Is this okay?"

Was it? We were in the pool and we'd been fighting *minutes* ago. Anyone could walk in on us, but there was still an us, and I didn't care. I wanted him. I needed him in a way that was like nothing I'd ever experienced before, and we were kissing without me trying to suck out his essence.

I needed this.

"Yes," I told him, and I thought I ought to show him too.

Hooking an arm over his neck and leaning in, I brought my mouth to his. This kiss was nothing like the one before it. It didn't start off sweet and slow.

Oh, no.

Ren made this sound in the back of his throat that curled

my toes and turned my blood into molten lava. The hand at the back of my head tightened and his other dropped, his arm circling my waist, sealing our hips together. The kiss deepened and the first touch of his tongue against mine was like striking a match to gasoline.

Ren pushed in, trapping me between his body and the pool wall. I tilted my head as the hand at my hip slid down my thigh. He lifted my leg, curving it around his waist, and I moaned into the kiss.

With him wearing nothing but boxer briefs and me in thin leggings, it almost felt as if there was nothing between us. *Almost.* I could feel his hard length against my core, and when he pushed his hips in, I thought I might have an orgasm right then.

My body reacted without thought. I wasn't thinking about us fighting, about how I'd changed, or what the Prince had done to me. There was no room for that. We were kissing like we'd been in a drought and we had just been given water. Each time I rolled my hips, he answered and gave it back. Our bodies were moving, stirring the water, and our hands were exploring, slipping over wet skin. His were under my shirt, skimming over my ribs and up and up until my heart was slamming in my chest.

Then Ren stopped.

Breaking the kiss, he placed his forehead against mine as he dragged in deep breaths. His hand splayed across my cheek now. "Maybe . . . maybe we should slow it down?" His warm breath danced over my lips. "I want to make sure you're ready for this."

My heart squeezed in my chest in the most wonderful way. I touched his jaw as I opened my eyes, seeking out his gaze. I found it. "I'm ready. More than ready, and I . . . I don't want to wait."

Ren growled something that sounded a lot like 'thank God' and then he kissed me again. Our hands fumbled in the water. I managed to slip him free, and somehow he got my soaking leggings down below my knees. It was a slippery job, and we were both laughing, because holy crap, wet leggings were not easy to work with, but then the laughter died.

Ren's gaze held mine with an all-consuming intensity as he lifted me up just enough until I felt him between my thighs. Then his lips moved over mine and along my jaw as I felt his hand against me. One finger and I nearly went off like a firecracker.

"God," I gasped against his mouth as I clutched his arm.

He worked his hand, pressing his palm right against the most sensitive spot. He added another finger, and we both groaned out loud. It was too much, and when he hooked that finger deep inside me, the first orgasm hit me so hard I dropped my head to his shoulder to smother my cry.

"I've missed you." His voice was husky and ragged. "Fuck, I've missed you so much."

Raw emotion swelled as my body shook. He kissed his way down my throat, coaxing my head back. "I missed you," I said. "I've missed all of this."

"Not anymore," he promised. "Never again."

Then he was inside me, in the way I wanted, *always* wanted. At first it was a shock. Ren was not small and I couldn't spread my legs with leggings down at my knees, and for some reason that made it all so much more . . . *wow*. The friction, the tightness was incredible.

He started moving, one hand clamped around the back of my neck, his other arm wrapped around my waist as he pumped into me—one deep, long thrust after another.

What we were doing, knowing we could be caught at any moment, was crazy but that didn't stop us. It was just us, our bodies moving together until it became frenzied, sending the water lapping over the side.

"Hell, Sweetness," he groaned, and I felt it building inside me all over, that terrible tension, a mess of longing and lust.

He launched us backward, and then the rough cement was digging into my back as he pressed into me as far as he could go, grinding against me until he pushed me to the edge of bliss again and then threw me right over it. I came, crying out as he buried his head in my neck, thrusting once and then twice before he followed me right over the edge, my name a harsh burst of air at that oddly sensitive spot below my pulse.

I was limp in his arms, my cheek slipping to his chest, vaguely aware of him pulling out and lowering me so my feet hit the bottom of the pool. He didn't pull away though, still holding me tight to him.

His breathing slowed as he dropped his chin to the top of my head. For a little while, we stayed like that, neither of us talking. It was just us and the rippling of the water.

It was Ren who broke the silence. His hand tightened around the back of my neck. "Are we okay?"

For the first time in days, I didn't have to think about how to answer that question. I knew the answer immediately. "We're going to be."

Chapter 18

Having non-feeding related sex didn't fix all the problems we had and were facing, but it sure as hell chilled me out enough to be able to talk about them.

"I don't know how to do relationships," I admitted from where my cheek was plastered to Ren's chest. After the pool, we'd come back to our room and changed into dry clothes. Well, mostly. Ren threw on a pair of sweats and I'd stolen one of his shirts. It was long enough to cover all the interesting parts. Then we hit the bed, him on his back and me on my side, pressed up against him. His arm was curled around my waist, his hand resting on my hip. "I mean, I think I used to. I did with Shaun. I guess I just forgot how."

"I don't think there's one way to do relationships." His hand was still, but his thumb moved in a slow, continuous sweeping motion. "And you know what I think?"

"What?"

Ren shifted onto his side, and the next thing I knew, we were face to face. "We've got to cut ourselves a break."

My gaze wandered over his face. "I like the sound of that."

His lips quirked up on one side as he dragged his hand

up my side. "Seriously though. Both of us have been through some shit. We're both getting over that. We're not going to be perfect."

Folding my hands between us, I smiled a little. "You're pretty close to perfect."

He caught the edges of my hair and tugged on a curl, pulling it straight. "No, I'm not. I should've kept my mouth shut this morning." He let go of the curl, watching it bounce back. "You have every right to be pissed over that."

Yeah, I did. "And you have every right to be pissed at me for trying to bail on you guys."

"True." His grin spread as he touched a finger to my cheek. "Look at us, agreeing on something."

"So, you're not going to flip out when I get up in the morning and get ready to go find Marlon?"

"No." He let out a sigh. "It's not going to be easy, but I'll deal with it."

"Good."

He trailed his finger along my cheekbone. "And you're going to keep talking to me, right? Especially when you feel like you don't know who you are anymore? You're going to let me help remind you, right?"

Tears immediately blurred my vision. Ren saw them, because his hand stilled with his thumb just below my lip.

"Right?" he persisted.

"Right," I rasped, choked up.

Lowering his hand, he skated his thumb over my lip. "Promise me that, Ivy."

I swallowed down the sudden knot in my throat. "I promise."

He leaned in, his lips replacing his thumb, kissing me softly. When he pulled back, his gaze was a little less heavy. "When we were in the pool and you were letting me make your dreams come true—"

"Wow."

He smiled broadly then, and my heart skipped a beat. There was one of those dimples! And I bet if I could see his whole face, both would be out in all their glory. "How were you feeling? Besides being blissed out of your mind?"

I rolled my eyes. "I felt . . . normal. Like I wasn't thinking about . . ." Heat crept into my cheeks, but I didn't allow myself to shut down. "I wasn't thinking about him or anything like that."

If Ren had been worried about that, he didn't show it. "And what about the whole sucking out my essence thing?"

The warmth in my cheeks deepened, but I pushed through the uncomfortableness. "I didn't want to feed. It never crossed my mind."

"That's good, right?"

"Yeah, it's just that . . . I don't know if it will always be like that or if it'll hit me again—the cravings." I forced myself to keep going. "I mean, it's there. Not all the time, but it's like . . . indigestion."

He lifted a brow.

"But more serious than heartburn," I added.

Ren was quiet for a moment. "You've got to trust yourself, Ivy. I know that's easier said than done, but even when you were . . . dying, you didn't want to feed. And when you were feeding, you stopped. That part of you is not gone. I never once worried about you jumping on me like the face-clinger thing from those *Alien* movies."

I laughed softly. "Good to know."

"I trust you." His eyes met and held mine. "I'm going to make sure you start trusting yourself."

My vision blurred again, and it didn't help when he kissed the tip of my nose.

"Now, on to a much more serious conversation."

Oh dear.

He rose onto one elbow. "I'm not sure if you realized this or not, but you're pretty strong."

"Of course I am," I murmured.

He dropped his hand to the curve of my waist. "No, Ivy. Stronger than you realize."

I frowned up at him.

"When you pushed me into the pool, I wasn't off-balance. You shouldn't have been able to do that so easily."

Unsure if I should be annoyed by that statement or not, my frown increased. "I've been training since I can remember. Knocking you over isn't that hard."

He grinned down at me. "And I've been training since I can remember. Plus, I have a good hundred pounds on you. When you pushed me, it felt like a truck was slamming into me."

"Wow," I muttered. "That's not flattering."

Chuckling under his breath, he raised his brows at me. "I want to try something, okay? I want you to hold me down."

I stared at him. "Seriously?"

He nodded. "I want to see if you—"

Ren didn't need to ask twice. Sitting up, I placed my hands on his shoulders and pushed him back, into the bed. I moved, straddling him.

"Okay." He laughed. "You're down for this."

I grinned. "I'm always here to knock you down a peg or two."

He blew a kiss at me, and then I felt his muscles flex under my palms. He started to rise up, but I pushed down, keeping him relatively pinned.

"That's the best you got? Come on, Ren. Stop messing with me."

"I'm not messing with you." His jaw locked down as his body coiled tight under mine. He lifted his shoulders up, but I exerted more pressure, keeping him from sitting up. "Jesus," he grunted, falling back and losing the inches he'd gained. "That's what I'm talking about."

I blinked and then jerked my head back. "You're really not fooling around? You can't sit up?"

"No."

I didn't believe him. "Try it again."

"Whatever." Ren did an ab curl, and I could feel the power and strength in his body. He wasn't holding back, but he wasn't getting very far. His muscles trembled. "See?"

Shocked, I let go and then he shot up like a rocket, snagging an arm around my waist before I toppled off of him. "Holy crap."

"Yeah." Once he had me steady, he fell back onto the bed. "That's what I'm talking about. You're stronger than me."

All I could do was stare at him. I'd always been fast and strong. Years and years of training did that, but Ren had more muscle mass. I shouldn't have been able to overpower him.

The dimple appeared in his cheek. "And it's kind of hot as hell."

I cocked my head to the side and sighed.

"What? Remember that night when you flipped me?"

"Yeah, I remember. You had broken into my apartment," I replied dryly.

"I didn't break it. The balcony doors were unlocked."

I rolled my eyes. "You still entered without permission, Ren."

He skated right over that. "Anyway, I think you've got some fae strength in you."

Sitting back, I let my hands rest on his abs. "You know,

being a halfling and all? I never really got sick growing up. I never broke a bone, but I've never been *this* strong."

"Probably the feeding." His hands landed lightly on my hips.

I thought back to when I first woke up. "Faye did say there may be other . . . changes in me, and I . . . I broke the restraints they had on me. I'd forgotten all about that."

"Restraints?" The grin faded from his face.

"Yeah. You didn't know? Apparently, they were worried I'd do something terrible." I blew out a long breath, thinking about when I was training earlier. I hadn't gone full beast mode on the dummy, so I wouldn't have noticed if I was stronger than before. "Maybe it'll fade."

"Maybe." He tilted his head to the side. "But look at Faye or Kalen and Dane. They don't feed and they're strong."

And I had changed, physically. There was no denying that. Being stronger wasn't bad. Not at all. Considering my line of work and what we had facing us, it was a blessing.

Odd.

I wasn't sure how to feel about being okay with that change. Then I realized that I could be okay with it. I just had to let myself be okay.

Could it be that easy?

I shifted and then stilled, pulled completely out of my head. I felt him hardening under me. My brows lifted. "Really?"

A lopsided grin appeared. "I don't know if you remember this or not, but you're not wearing anything under *my* shirt and you're straddling *me*."

A sharp tingle radiated from where I could feel him straining up against me. "Good point."

"And like I said, you overpowering me is hot as hell."

I laughed as I tipped forward, marveling at the way his

abs tightened in response and how his eyes deepened to a forest green. "It must be nice being a guy."

His eyes became hooded as his fingers tiptoed along the edges of the shirt I was wearing. "It is when I have you sitting on my dick."

A laugh burst out of me, and I got blessed with two dimples appearing on his face.

His fingers curled under the hem of the shirt. "I want to see you."

My breath caught, because I knew what he meant. Immediately, my pulse pounded. I was seriously naked under his shirt.

"May I?"

Biting down on my lip, I nodded.

Ren lifted the shirt, sliding it up my sides and over my head. When he tossed it onto the bed beside him, I was completely bare and there was no hiding the fact that every part of me had a silvery tint to it.

And Ren was taking it all in.

His gaze locked with mine and then slid south, the intensity almost a physical caress. I felt his stare as it slipped over my shoulders. My breasts grew heavy, nipples tightening, and it was hard to sit still as his gaze continued to move, over the apex of my thighs, all the way to where my knees were bent.

"Thank you," he said finally, his voice a husky drawl.

My mouth dried.

The very tips of his fingers dragged over my sides and hips, down my outer thighs and then back up, over my lower stomach. His hands stopped just below my breasts. "You're beautiful, Ivy. I've told you that, right?"

I found my voice. "Yes."

A half grin appeared as his fingers brushed over the swell

of my breasts. "I don't think I tell you that nearly enough."

I drew in a shallow breath. "You can keep telling me that." My voice hitched as his fingers grew very close to my nipples before skating away. "I don't mind."

He bit down on his lower lip, sucking it between his teeth. Parts of me clenched in response. His fingers circled the very center of my breasts, and the torture of him getting close and then pulling away was possibly the most wicked thing he could do.

"We're going to have to get up early tomorrow." His gaze followed his fingers now.

"What's . . ." I shivered as he drew close yet again. "What's the plan?"

"Faye is in the process of finding out where Marlon lives since I don't think he's staying at that hotel any longer." His hands slipped to my ribs, and at this point, I was panting with anticipation. "And since he's not usually at Flux until the evenings, we really don't have the time to wait on that."

"Agreed." I swallowed, trying to focus. "Who's going with us?"

Ren's hands stayed at my waist, much to my disappointment. "Not exactly sure yet."

I started to respond, but Ren suddenly sat up. Circling an arm around my waist, he tilted his head just the slightest as he kissed me. It was brief, too brief, and then he leaned away, his gaze snagging mine.

At first I had no idea what he was up to. I could tell he wanted to take this further. Besides the fact he stripped me naked, he was still hard under me, and there was no mistaking the intent in his gaze, but he wasn't making any move.

And then . . . then I realized what he was doing, and I thought I might fall apart.

Ren wasn't just waiting.

He was handing me the reins in this, giving me complete control.

"I love you," I whispered, and then I took it, showing him what I wanted with his hands first and then his mouth.

"TOOK A LOT of digging, but I think I found where Marlon lives," Faye announced the following morning while we sat around a small table in the cafeteria.

There'd been stares, but I wasn't letting them get to me. Right now, I couldn't afford to allow myself to get caught up in stupid distractions, and I wasn't. The fact that Tink sat on my left and Ren on my right helped.

"Since his new house was completed about a month ago, he hasn't been staying at the hotel," she explained as I picked up a piece of bacon. My appetite still wasn't back to normal, but I needed to eat. "He actually bought an older home over in Lake Vista. Renovations were complete a few weeks ago."

"Lake Vista?" My eyes widened. Holy crap, that was one of the richest, most exclusive neighborhoods in New Orleans. Being an evil, Ancient fae must be working out well for him.

"Yep. His house is on Flamingo Street." Turning the laptop she had in front of her around to face us, we got a view of the massive home. "Nice, isn't it?"

"I'm jealous," I whispered, eyeing the beautiful two-story home with a balcony. Faye had it pulled up on some real estate website.

Tink leaned over, squinting. "Why don't we live in a place like that?"

I looked at him. "If you want to live in a place like that, you're really going to need to get a job."

"I don't think there is any job I'd be qualified for that would help you afford that house."

Ren snorted.

"*Anyway.*" I munched down on the piece of bacon. "Pretty sure that neighborhood is gated."

"With security," Faye said.

"Shouldn't be a problem." Ren picked up a slice of wheat bread and dropped it onto my plate.

Faye closed the laptop. "We don't hurt humans."

"Not planning to." Ren glanced to where Dane and Kalen sat next to Faye. "We need to get into that neighborhood with as little trouble as possible."

"And that means you want us to use compulsion." Dane leaned forward, crossing his arms on the table. "I have no problem with that."

Faye sighed.

I hid my grin as I bit into the bread and immediately regretted it. No butter. No jam. Tasted like cardboard. I dropped it onto the plate and reached for my coffee to wash the blandness away. How in the world did Ren eat that?

"I don't either," Kalen chimed in. "But I doubt whoever is working the gate is human. Marlon would have to be a fool if that's the case."

"Good point." Ren eyed my discarded bread. "Either way, we're going to have to be quick and hope like hell he's home."

"And then what?" Tink asked.

"We have transportation that won't raise suspicions immediately," Dane answered, tilting his dark head to the side.

"And then what?" Tink repeated.

I ignored Ren as he poked at the thing he called bread, nudging it closer to me. "Then we get inside his house."

Tink tilted his head as I grabbed the other slice of bacon.

"That's not exactly going to be easy."

"No." Ren sighed heavily when he realized there was no way in hell I was putting that bread in my mouth again. He picked it up from my plate. "That's why we need to be fast, because there's no way they won't know who we are."

"But they don't know me," Tink pointed out. "I could blitz attack them."

I slid him a long look. "Besides you. You are staying here where you'll be nice and safe."

Tink frowned. "But I—"

"You should stay and keep Prince Fabian company," Faye suggested. "He's not coming with us."

The corners of Tink's lips tipped up. "That I can do. When are you guys leaving?"

Kalen checked the time on his phone. "As soon as our wee little halfling finishes her breakfast."

I stopped with the piece of bacon halfway to my mouth. "Wee little halfling?"

The fae grinned.

"Are you ready for this?" Dane asked, not at all smiling. "Not trying to be a dick by asking, but you've been out of commission for a while and—"

"And I got my ass kicked by two fae not too long ago," I finished for him. I glanced at Ren. He'd asked the same question this morning, and it hadn't been an easy one to answer. "I'm as ready as I will ever be."

That response didn't seem to satisfy Dane. "If he's there, there's going to be a lot of fae with him, and he's not a normal fae—"

"He's an Ancient. I know." My shoulders tensed. "But I'm not the same Ivy who got jumped in the courtyard."

"She's ready." Ren met Dane's stare.

Dane was quiet and then he said, "She'd better be."

My eyes narrowed, but then Ren draped his arm over my shoulders as he leaned over, kissing my temple, and I was thoroughly distracted. "Finish up," he whispered, brushing his nose along the curve of my cheekbone. "And then hopefully we'll know exactly where that bastard is before lunch."

Chapter 19

The mode of transportation was a surprisingly smart one. A florist van, except there weren't any flowers. Just a bench running along one side and the other side contained chains bolted to the side.

This was a true kidnappers' van.

Kalen and Dane were up front. Faye stayed behind out of concern for her being recognized since we didn't know if there'd be fae working the gates or if the fae would possibly recognize her right off the bat. The thing was, if there were fae at the gate, they would sense what Kalen and Dane were immediately. The van was to not attract any attention leading up to the gate, but it wasn't going to get us through it.

Being outside of Hotel Good Fae was . . . God, it was hard to put into words, but it hadn't been easy for me. While Faye and the guys walked out of the opening in the wall beyond the courtyard as if it were no big deal, my stomach twisted like it was full of vipers. Everyone had been talking, but I hadn't been listening. I'd stopped at the opening, my feet unable to move.

Ren had placed his hand on the center of my back. He

hadn't spoken, but I knew he'd sensed my wariness. It was probably etched onto my face. With him by my side, I'd stepped outside the protection of the courtyard and quickly realized it was warmer than the last time I'd been outside. More normal temps for October in New Orleans.

It had been strange walking out of the courtyard, into the world that existed beyond the glamour of Hotel Good Fae. Even though I knew that Drake and his minions were far away, I half-expected them to appear out of thin air.

They didn't.

A part of me still waited for there to be some kind of trap, for the Prince to suddenly appear and tell us we'd been played. The other half of me wanted to run around, breathing in all the good and bad scents of the city.

I didn't get to do the last part. There wasn't a lot of time to process that I was . . . *free.*

"We're nearing the gate." Kalen peered through the open window separating the front of the van.

Sitting beside me on the bench, Ren nodded. "Got it."

Kalen closed the door, and I exhaled roughly as I ran my hands over the knees of my tactical pants.

"You nervous?" Ren asked quietly.

I started to say no, but then nodded. "A little. Been a while since I even wore a pair of pants like this."

His gaze flickered over me. "You look damn good in them."

"Thanks." I shot him a grin. Truth be told, they were looser than they should've been this morning, but it felt good pulling them on.

I quieted when the van eased to a stop, hating that I couldn't see anything, but both Ren and I tensed. His hand went to the iron dagger at his waist and mine went to where I had one secured to my thigh. Ren had the thorn stake in the inside of his boot.

"Hi there," we heard Dane speak. "We have an order for—"

"What the hell?" exclaimed an unfamiliar voice. Crap.

Ren unhooked his dagger just as we heard a car door open, followed by a grunt of pain. Someone cursed and then there was silence.

We looked at each other, knowing it could mean one thing or a really bad thing.

We had our answer quickly.

The back door swung open, revealing Kalen with a man slung over his shoulder. Ren shot off the bench, reaching for him.

"One fae and this human," Kalen said as he and Ren laid the human male down in the back of the van. "He's out, but not dead. Glamoured. Figured we'd keep him in here just in case anyone comes along and sees him passed out in the building."

"Good call." Ren rolled the human onto his back. "And the fae?"

"Recognized us immediately." Kalen's jaw hardened. "Took him out." He looked over to where I sat. "We're heading up to the house now. You guys ready?"

I nodded. "Yeppers."

Kalen tilted his head and then shook it. Closing the door, the van rumbled to life once more as Ren took his seat beside me while I stared at the unconscious man.

He was lucky to be alive.

"You know what?" I said, blowing out a long breath. "If it were the Order conducting this mission, would they have knocked him out or killed him?"

Ren didn't answer for a long moment. "Guess it would depend on who it was."

"Yeah." That didn't sit well, because even though I knew we weren't supposed to kill humans, it happened. A lot. "I suppose."

As the van slowed to a stop once more, Ren reached over and curved his hand around the nape of my neck. "Hey."

I let him turn my gaze to his. "Yeah?"

"I love you." He kissed me then, moving his lips over mine in a way that had my toes curling inside my boots. "You're going to be careful?"

I rested my forehead against his. "Are you?"

"Yeah, because I want to get you in bed at least one more time before we have to hit the road." He nipped at my lower lip. "You like the sound of that?"

I did, so I kissed him back. "Then you better make sure you don't get yourself hurt."

He grinned against my mouth. "We got this."

"We do," I whispered, pulling away from him when I heard the driver's side door open and close.

Moving off the bench, we were careful not to step on the poor dude on the floor as we crouched at the back door. Seconds later, the door slid open and we hopped out into the sunlight.

There wasn't any time to waste or to think about what I had to do and what was going to be needed from me, because I knew already. It was ingrained in my bones and muscles. I'd fought and hunted a thousand times.

Today was no different.

I had *this*.

Ren and I rounded the back of the van, right behind Kalen, just in time to see a tall female fae run down the wide, stone steps. Dane met her there. I barely saw him move, but he got her. She stumbled back, shock registering on her face for a moment before her features crumpled into themselves.

I shot up the steps, my heart pounding with . . . actual anticipation for battle. It had been so long, but that mixture of fear and excitement could be a heady, dangerous mix. Or it could sharpen the senses.

And my senses were sharp.

Curling my hand into a fist, I banged it on the double bronze doors and then stepped back. I knew without looking behind me that the guys were right there.

The door inched open, and there was a glimpse of silvery skin. All I needed to see. I planted my booted foot into the center of the door, kicking it wide open. The fae behind the door slid back, losing his balance. He went down as Ren flew past me. The fae was dead before he could sound the alarm.

But the alarm didn't need to be sounded.

As I scanned the wide open foyer, I saw several fae—at least a dozen of them lounging about, standing and talking in the atrium style room, or watching TV from the rec room behind the spiral staircase.

With this many fae, Marlon had to be here.

"Oh, look." Ren rose with fluid grace. "A welcome party."

"Yay." Dane flipped a dagger—an iron dagger—in his *fae* hands. He, like Kalen, was wearing gloves since the mere touch of iron singed their skin.

The welcome party did that creepy hiss thing really pissed off fae were known for. Then they charged.

There was a tiny part of me that wondered if maybe I wasn't ready, but pure adrenaline coursed through my veins, years of training kicking in. Instinct took over.

Striding across the Spanish tile, I unsheathed the daggers at my thighs and spun, slamming the very sharp end into the chest of the fae on my right. Yanking the dagger out, I whirled and took out the fae on my left before the first one finished collapsing into itself.

Another charged me, and I dipped low, kicking out and knocking the fae's legs out from underneath them. I shifted, stabbing the fae in his stomach. Popping up, I darted to the right, just missing what would've been a mean uppercut. I caught that fae in the back, right between the shoulder blades. Then I spun, not even out of breath.

Ren caught a fae with his hand around its neck. Those bright green eyes of his were focused on me as I shoved the dagger deep into the gut of the fae he was holding. "So freaking hot."

Flushing, I grinned.

"If you guys are done screwing each other with your eyes, head up here," Kalen called from halfway up the stairs.

"Give us one more second." Ren winked at me as he pivoted, slamming his shoulder into the fae rushing him from behind.

Rolling my eyes, I took off for the steps, taking them two at a time. Kalen reached the second floor, coming face to face with a very tall, very bald fae. Unease powered down my spine. The fae looked like one of the Knights—

"Shit," he muttered, and a second later, the fae lifted a hand. The dagger ripped free from Kalen's grasp and slammed into the nearby wall, where the blade trembled from the impact.

An *Ancient.*

Yep. He was one of the Knights that had come through the gateway the night the Prince had entered our world.

"You picked the wrong side as usual, Summer fae." The Ancient stalked forward just as footsteps pounded up the stairs behind me. "And you will die for it."

The Ancient swung his arm to the side, and without even touching Kalen, he threw him into the wall. Drywall cracked and plumes of plaster flew into the air. Kalen dropped to his knees, obviously stunned.

The Ancient turned to me, cocking his head to the side. Curiosity marked his features at first, and then, understanding. "Halfling?"

"Hi!" I chirped, launching into the air. I spun, kicking out and catching the Ancient in his stomach. I landed in a crouch as the Ancient stumbled and lost his balance, going down on one knee. The surprise that filled his gaze mirrored what I felt.

A normal kick like that would've taken down a human for hours. It would have stunned a normal fae, maybe knocked it to the ground, but an Ancient? It would've made them stumble.

It had knocked the Ancient down.

I *was* stronger.

Rising, I smiled widely as my grip tightened on the daggers. "Surprise. I'm not your normal halfling."

"You'll be a dead halfling soon." He shot to his feet.

"Oh, I don't know about that." Catching Ren's gaze out of the corner of my eye, I nodded. We had to get past the Ancient before Marlon escaped. "Sort of already did that. It didn't stick."

The Ancient started to lift his arm, and I knew what he was capable of. I shot forward, spinning as Ren darted past us. I caught sight of Dane grabbing Kalen by the arm, lifting him up as the Ancient caught my leg. He threw me to the side. I rolled, bracing myself for the impact. I hit the floor hard, but I held on to the daggers and breathed through the jarring pain.

"Not going to fall for that again." The Ancient started toward me.

I sprang up. "But you already did."

He drew up short and then whipped around, but it was too late. Ren shot forward, and the Ancient let out a guttural groan. Yanking the thorn stake out of the Ancient's chest, Ren smirked. "Guess you're going to do the dying thing."

The Ancient's mouth dropped open as he stared down at his chest. I shot past him, flipping him off as we joined the Summer fae at the end of the hall. All the doors were open, the rooms empty. One remained shut at the end. Double doors. Obviously, the master bedroom.

Dane slammed his shoulder into the doors, and they gave way, flying open. I saw Marlon at once, standing before a large bed. He lifted his arm, and his hand wasn't empty. It held a gun.

A gun that was pointed directly at Ren.

"Shit." My heart lodged in my throat. I darted to my left, knocking Ren to the side as the gunshot echoed in the hall.

Ren caught himself and me, throwing an arm around my waist as his eyes widened slightly. He straightened as his gaze met mine. "Thanks, Sweetness."

Nodding, I pulled away as I heard the gunfire again. Dane and Kalen were on Marlon. The bullet had fired harmlessly into the ceiling.

"A gun?" Kalen chopped down on Marlon's arm. The gun fell to the floor as Dane twisted Marlon's other arm. "That's kind of tacky."

"I guess you've been relying too heavily on your guards, because this was far too easy." Dane smiles slightly. "Pathetic."

Marlon sneered as Dane moved behind him. "You're going to regret this. When the Prince—"

"The Prince isn't here, now is he?" I walked into the bedroom. "So, he's not going to do shit."

Marlon's gaze narrowed on me as Dane clicked iron

handcuffs around his wrist and Kalen forced Marlon's other arm back. "You're that fucking halfling."

"That's me." I smiled, sheathing the one dagger.

"Sit," Dane ordered, and then made sure the Ancient did just that, forcing him down onto the bench with a heavy push on his shoulder.

"Looking less like a halfling and more like a fae," Marlon spit out. "That's interesting."

"I am. That's a long story, but I'm not here to tell you all about that." I hooked the other dagger to my thigh. "Because frankly, I don't care enough to tell you."

Marlon smiled, baring his teeth. "He should've killed you. He should have went ahead and fucked you and then killed you."

I didn't get a chance to respond to that.

Ren moved like a cobra striking. His fist slammed into the side of Marlon's jaw, knocking him to the side. Kalen caught the Ancient as Ren knelt, getting his face right in Marlon's. "You really need to think wisely about what you say to her."

"I remember you." Marlon laughed, and bluish-red blood trickled out of the corner of his month. "You were her pet."

I stiffened. "I cannot wait to kill that bitch."

Marlon lifted a dark brow as his gaze flickered to me. "You think you're going to kill her?" He laughed again. "You're an idiot."

"I nearly gouged her eyes out once." Anger flowed as I stepped forward. "I'm going to do it again. Slowly."

"Is that so? She'll gouge yours out and dine on them as a snack."

I rolled said eyes. "Why would anyone want to eat eyeballs? That's gross."

Kalen grinned as he fisted Marlon's hair, yanking the

Ancient's head back. "Where did the Prince go?"

"He left?" Marlon replied.

"Don't play like you don't know." I folded my arms. "You know damn well he's not in the city. He left because he found another halfling. And you're going to tell us where he went."

"Is that why you've reappeared after your daring escape?" Marlon snorted. "You're so brave."

I smirked. "We're going to find out just how brave you are."

"I'm not going to tell you shit," Marlon said, growling when Kalen yanked on his hair. "You may as well kill me now."

"Oh, you're going to talk." Tilting his head to the side, Ren straightened, thorn stake in hand. "Do you know what this is?"

Marlon's gaze flickered over the stake. There was a tightening around his mouth. "I do."

"And you know what it can do to you? It can hurt you." Ren smiled as he placed the stake directly above the fae's heart. "It can kill you."

"So will the Prince if he knows I talked to you. I'll die either way." Marlon swallowed. "Killing me is not a threat."

I could see the cold smile grace Ren's lips as he drew the stake up over the center of the Ancient's throat. "Dying is the easy part. I'm not going to make this easy for you."

And Ren didn't.

It wasn't easy or clean. It was bloody and messy, and Marlon held out far longer than many would have. Hundreds of thin slits covered every inch of exposed skin, and a few times, I wanted to look away, but I forced myself not to. Not when Ren wielded the stake and didn't have the luxury of closing his eyes. So I made myself watch, and I didn't flinch when blood sprayed from a vital artery along the Ancient's throat, dotting Ren's face and the front of my shirt. I didn't look away once, and that's how I knew deep in my bones that when Marlon uttered the words we'd been waiting for, it was the truth.

"San Diego," Marlon gasped. "The Prince left for San Diego."

Those were his last words.

Chapter 20

We didn't have a lot of time alone once we returned to Hotel Good Fae and met with Tanner and crew.

San Diego.

It would take well over a day to get there, roughly twenty-seven hours, and we had to drive since we were carrying weapons and that would require way too many humans to be glamoured for us to travel by air.

Both Ren and I needed to shower since neither of us wanted to hit the road with blood on us, and we probably didn't get ready as quick as we could have, because it was someone's idea—Ren's—to shower together, not that I was complaining.

How could I when it was Ren who washed the smudges of blood off my face? Or when I did the same for him as we stood under the steady stream of water? I was thinking about how we needed to get on the road when he found his way behind me in the shower. And when he got his hand involved, and other parts of his body, complaining and strategizing and thinking in general was the furthest thing from my mind.

"We did good today," he whispered against the side of my neck.

"We did."

He kissed the space below my ear. "You were amazing, Ivy."

A small smile pulled at my lips. "So were you."

"Yeah." He lifted his mouth from my neck as his fingers skimmed on the most sensitive part of me. "It wasn't my . . ."

I placed my hand over his, stilling him. "Wasn't what?"

"Today wasn't one of my finer moments."

My smile started to fade. "What do you mean?"

He was quiet for a moment. "I knew what I had to do to make Marlon talk. I knew what he was. What he would've done to us if given the chance. But I still don't like that I had to do it."

My chest squeezed. "But you had to."

Ren didn't respond, so I started to turn to him but the hand curling around my neck stopped me. He guided my head back, turning it just the slightest, and then he kissed me, scattering my thoughts. The hand between my thighs slid up and his arm folded around my waist. He lifted me up onto the very tips of my toes.

I gasped into his mouth when he entered me from behind, thrusting so deep I thought at first I couldn't take it, but he proved that I could, again and again. We were a slippery, soapy mess as I threw my arms out, planting my hands on the wet tile in front of me as Ren kept one arm secured around my waist and then the other went between my thighs again. He worked me with his fingers and his cock, his breath hot on my neck, his words scorching my ears. When I came, I threw my head back against his shoulder, having a near out of body experience.

Two things surprised the hell out of me in that moment. One, I hadn't ended up on my ass, and two, even after the whole shower sex thing, Ren was ready to go again when we were getting changed.

Sometimes I wondered if Ren was even human, but I guessed we were just making up for lost time.

And we had a lot of making up to do.

We were ready with minutes to spare, and I used them, stopping at the door before we left, blocking it with my body.

Ren arched a brow, our bags in both hands. "What are you doing?"

"I want to say something and I want to have your full attention."

One side of his mouth kicked up. "You always have my full attention, Sweetness."

"I know, but I really want it right now." I took a deep breath. "What you did today to get Marlon to talk couldn't have been easy. I know that. I had a hard time watching, but I did. I watched. That's not the same as actually doing it."

"No." He exhaled roughly. "It's not."

"But you had to do it, Ren. We needed to know where the Prince went. You did what you had to do and you shouldn't lose a moment of yourself to that."

His chin dipped, and for a brief moment I wasn't sure he would respond. "I won't."

I wasn't sure I believed him. "You promise?"

Ren's gaze found mine. "I promise."

"I'll keep you to that promise," I swore. Springing forward, I stretched up and kissed the corner of his mouth. His arms swept around me and he held me tight to his chest. Several moments passed before I could force myself to pull away from him. "We better get going."

"Yeah." His voice roughened. "If we don't, we may never

leave this room, apocalypse baby or not."

I blushed as I turned, opening the door, knowing he'd make good on that rather pleasant warning. We arrived in the lobby to discover a rather decent size group waiting for us by the doors I'd never seen opened before. They appeared to lead out to the front of the building.

Dane and Kalen stood beside Faye, the three of them carrying black duffel bags, so I assumed they were part of our entourage. I scanned the group, relieved to see that Merle wasn't there but a little unnerved by the fae faces I didn't recognize.

Tink was there though, standing a little bit apart from the group. There was a rather large suitcase beside him. Slung over his shoulder was a . . . Wonder Woman backpack. I parted from Ren, walking up to him. "Where did you get that?"

"I stole it from a little fae girl." He paused. "Hashtag thug life."

"What?" My mouth dropped open.

"I'm kidding," he said, and I wasn't sure if I believed him or not. "Ordered it from Amazon a few months ago. Goes good with my leotard."

I eyed him as Ren joined me, holding two paper cups of coffee. He handed me one with a wink. "Thanks." Then I faced Tink again. "Why do you have your bags down here?"

"Why?" Tink wrinkled his nose. "We have no idea how long we're going to be gone and I'm not going to wear the same clothes."

"You're not going, Tink. You're staying—"

"I'm not staying here. Hell no. You're going to San Diego, and so am I. You need me."

Frustration snapped at me. "Tink—"

"Don't Tink me," he shot back. "I get that you want to

keep me safe and sound, but I can handle myself."

I knew he could handle himself, but I still didn't want him putting himself in danger. "What about Dixon? You can't bring him."

"I know that. Hunting down the Prince and possibly killing him is not the place for an adorable kitten," he said. "Brighton is watching him for me."

My brows lifted, and then I shook my head as I stepped closer to Tink. "I don't want you in danger."

Tink smiled. "Ivy-divy, I know that I'm fucking cute and adorable, but I think you forget what I'm capable of. You guys need me on this trip."

Ren lightly touched my arm, drawing my attention. "As much as this pains me to admit, Tink is right. We could use him."

"Don't take this from me." Tink lowered his voice. "You all are out there risking your lives. I've already spent enough time watching you leave and do that. It's time I step up."

I wanted to argue more, but Tink and Ren were right. We could use him. I couldn't take that from him. I sighed. "Okay."

"Good." Tink looked over at Ren. "Wait. Have you two stopped fighting? Oh my Queen Mab, you guys are in love again!"

My eyes widened as I glanced around, seeing that several of the strangers were watching us with detached interest. "Tink . . ."

"We were never not together," Ren said, dropping his arm over my shoulders.

The blue and red bag slipped to the floor as he clapped his hands like an overexcited seal. "You guys are! This is amazing."

"Tink," I said again, this time with a little more force

behind his name.

"Thank the faery lords and ladies, I will not be a product of a split home."

"For the last time, we are not your parents, Tink." I shook my head as I started to turn but stopped. "Pick up your bag."

Ren leaned in as Tink snatched the bag off the floor. "You sound like his mom."

"Shut up," I hissed.

"There you two are." Tanner stepped out of the huddle. He didn't look at me like I wasn't supposed to be there. "Let me introduce you to Fabian's consuls."

The strangers stepped forward, and after a blur of very fae-like sounding names except for the last dude who was introduced as Fred, I realized I would not remember a single name from this point on.

Each one smiled and nodded kindly, leagues more polite than their prince.

"We have three vehicles waiting for you outside," Tanner said, and Faye stepped forward, carrying several packages.

"Each of us will have a phone equipped with GPS that will be tracked from here in case something happens and we must separate," Faye explained, handing me the envelope.

Setting my coffee on the nearby table, I felt around the envelope, touching four separate phones. I figured Tink would be traveling with Ren and I. "Why are there four?"

"Because I will be joining you."

My jaw clenched as I turned around. Fabian had arrived, looking as dashing as a doorknob. "Yeah, you're going to need to find a different car to ride in."

"Ivy," Tink whined in a low voice. "He will be riding me."

Ren choked on his coffee and turned, wheezing softly.

I turned to Tink. "You want to maybe rethink what you just said?"

"Oh, no. I said that right."

"If he's going to be in the car with us, he will not be *riding* you while we're in there, okay?" I couldn't believe I actually had to speak those words. "I think I'm going to find who Faye is riding with—"

"Oh no." Ren caught the back of my shirt. "You are not leaving me with them."

Fabian moseyed on up to Tink, eyeing the suitcase. "What is in the suitcase? Seems rather . . . bulky for clothing."

Come to think of it, the Summer Prince was right.

Grabbing the handle of the large suitcase, Tink looked over at Fabian. "Our last resort. Meaning this suitcase is not to be opened unless the shit has gone so far south we're up to our necks in fuckery."

Ren nudged me. "Uh, what do you think is in the suitcase?"

"I have no idea, but I'm thinking I probably should find out." I started toward him, but the doors opened and sunlight poured in. Just like earlier today, I was startled for a second to know that I could just walk right out of here.

And that's what everyone was doing. I followed Ren outside to where Faye and her crew loaded up into one of the SUVs, Fabian's consul got in what appeared to be a fancy Porsche of some sort, which left us with an SUV that was the size of a small tank.

I didn't even attempt to take the keys from Ren.

After loading up the back with the bags Ren and I had hurriedly packed before we left the room, I walked around to the front passenger seat. Tink trailed after me. "Do you think the Prince has already found the Halfling?"

"I hope not." I opened up the door. "Because that sure as hell complicates things."

"It does more than complicate things." Fabian watched

me closely. "If the Winter Prince has found her and does what we've feared, we'll have to handle it."

I stiffened.

Ren's fingers coasted over my waist as he walked by. "We will."

Handle it.

I knew what that meant. I hated it. Because it could easily be me in that situation—it could be me being handled, just like Merle had said when I first arrived here. But if the Prince had found the Halfling and managed to do the deed, we had to stop the baby from being born, and I knew the crew we were traveling with wasn't going to be down with having a very uncomfortable conversation with this Halfling and hoping she volunteered to do what would be the right thing in this case.

I watched Fabian walk over to the other side of the SUV and then my gaze roamed over to the other cars.

I knew what they'd do. They'd take the woman out, no questions asked.

The idea of killing an innocent woman and her child sickened me. I didn't want to do that. I didn't want any of us to do that.

So that left us with only one option.

"We better find her first," I said, filling with steely resolve. "And make damn sure she doesn't get pregnant."

Chapter 21

We hadn't even gotten out of the state of Louisiana and I was already ready to duct tape both Tink and Fabian's mouths shut. A few hours into the trip and I'd learned two things.

Fabian could make everything sound like he was insulting me. And Ren had this magical ability to tune everyone out and focus on driving.

Rubbing my forehead, I stared out the window as we cruised on down I-10. The outside was a blur of buildings and trees, and somehow the conversation in the back seat had moved on to me and my hair.

"I don't think she can honestly brush it," Tink was saying. He'd leaned forward so he was halfway between the seats. "Because when she does, it just turns into a giant poof."

Counting to ten, I slid a glance over at Ren. A faint smile played across his lips, and if he hadn't been driving, I might've punched him.

"So she doesn't comb it all?" Fabian asked, sounding genuinely confused.

I looked over my shoulder. "I comb my hair, you

assholes."

Ren snorted. "I've seen her do it. When it's wet."

"Let's talk about something other than my hair, okay?" I suggested before I climbed into the back seat like a rabid spider monkey and strangled all of them.

"Like what?" Tink sat back. "I'm bored."

"You're bored already and we have like another twenty-some hours left," I reminded him.

Tink groaned. "I'm not going to make it."

"I could entertain you," Fabian suggested. "We could—"

"Yeah, no," I jumped in, because I had a feeling his version of entertaining Tink wasn't PG-13 and I didn't want to witness any of that. My gaze zeroed in on the Summer Prince. He was obviously into Tink, but the fae were pretty much into anything that walked and had a hole. A wave of protectiveness seized me. "Let's talk about you, Fabian."

The Summer Prince stretched an arm along the back of the seat and inclined his head. "I have no problem with that."

"Of course not," Ren muttered under his breath.

I fought a smile. "How old are you?"

The Summer Prince raised a fair brow. He looked like he was in his late twenties, but instinct told me that wasn't his real age. "Older than some of the trees planted along this road."

So my suspicions were correct. I glanced at Ren and saw that he was listening. "Then that means you feed, because you sure as hell aren't aging like Tanner."

"I am the Prince. All of the royal court feeds."

"Really?" I said, my hand balling in my lap. That was something else that Tanner had not disclosed.

"You don't like hearing that." A smirk appeared. "And yet you fed to save your life."

"It wasn't a choice I made," I said.

Tink leaned forward again. "What Fabian is leaving out is that they have people who volunteer to be fed on. They're not being forced."

My brows lifted. "Volunteered or under a compulsion? I remember the people Drake had in that house. Some looked like they wanted to be there, but I doubt any of them knew what they were getting themselves into."

A shadow crossed Fabian's expression. "Those who allow us the honor of feeding from them do so under no compulsion. They know what we are. They choose to help us as we help them."

I didn't believe that for a second. "And how do you help them?"

"In my community, we protect the mortals who allow us to feed. They want for nothing. Money. Healthcare. Security."

Sort of reminded me of escorts, but I figured I'd keep that part to myself. "And they know what you guys are capable of? How you can drain them to the point they turn into mindless, psychotic creatures?"

His eyes narrowed. "We never take more than we need. If any of my subjects were to, they'd be executed on the spot."

"Really?" Ren's gaze flicked to the rearview mirror. "That's pretty hardcore for a race of beings that have always put themselves first."

"As if you know anything about our race," Fabian replied. "We have been here far longer than you know. Think about that."

"I'm thinking about it," he replied dryly.

"You knew nothing of the Summer Court or that our courts have taken up residency here. There is a reason for that. We do not kill. We do not abuse mortals. Believe it or not, we view them as equals."

"I know it sounds hard to believe," Tink chimed in. "But he's telling the truth."

"How do you know?" I asked, eyeing Tink.

He met my gaze. "Because why would he lie?"

"Oh, I don't know. So we don't kill him?" I offered.

The Summer Prince snorted. "I am not easy to kill."

"Yeah, back to that. If you're the perfect example of a non-homicidal fae who loves and cherishes humans, then why won't you tell us how to weaken Drake?"

He laughed, and the sound was too cold for a Summer Prince. "You don't trust me. Why in the world would I trust you? You may be a halfling and he may be Boy Wonder—"

"Boy wonder?" Ren wrinkled his nose.

"But the Order has already betrayed us once," Fabian continued, his stare hard. "The fact that we are working with you now to stop the Winter Prince puts me and my people at an incredible disadvantage. Do you think I chose to ride with you just because of him?" He glanced at Tink. "Someone needs to keep an eye on you two and I will not risk any of my consul in doing so."

Tink didn't look at all bothered by that statement.

"How did the Order betray the Summer Court?" Ren asked, sliding a hand over the steering wheel. "Tanner mentioned it. Now you have. We're in the dark on what happened."

"You're in the dark about a lot of things," the Prince snarked, and then smiled when I swore I could feel steam coming out of my ears. "Do you ever think about that?" His gaze met Ren's in the mirror. "Really think about why the Order and your precious Elite kept so much from you—from the very people willing to kill and die for them without remorse or challenge? Did any of you question that perhaps you were killing innocents? That not every fae wants to rule the mortal world? Did any of you once, in your incredibly short lives, ever ask if you were fighting on the right side?"

Uncomfortable with all the truthiness he was speaking, I flipped around and faced the windshield. A moment passed, and I glanced at Ren. A muscle thrummed along his jaw as he stared straight ahead. What the Summer Prince questioned had struck a chord with him too.

How could it not? He'd been right. We'd killed and died for an organization that had lied to us. And here we were, judging Fabian and his kind.

"What did they do?" I asked quietly, unsure if I was ready to hear it or if I wanted to.

Fabian didn't answer for so long that I thought he might never, but then he did. "Everything you know is practically a lie."

Ren's knuckles were bleached white from how tightly he was clenching the steering wheel. "You going to fill us in?"

"We did not start this war with mortals," he said, looking at the window while Tink watched him quietly. "We were not the ones who broke the treaty between our kinds."

A frown pulled at my brow. "What treaty?"

He smiled in a way I imagined parents did right before they wished they could crate train their children. "We used to be able to travel more freely between our worlds. Some would grab humans and take them back, but trust me, when they did, it was usually people you would never miss. People who deserved their fate."

Tink arched a brow.

"Others came willingly." He raised a shoulder in an elegant shrug. "After all, we are beautiful and mortals are drawn to beautiful things. There used to be a lot more halflings."

I bit down on my lip. I still had no idea if it was my mother or my father who was the fae. I'd probably never know.

"The Order has been in creation since we first crossed over, and our treaty remained in effect for hundreds of years. They hunted the ones who killed mortals in this world and left ones alone who did not, and when our world began to falter, and more fae crossed over, we worked together with the Order to ensure what was happening to our world did not happen to yours. We confided in them our weakness. We shared our secrets and helped them seal the doorways, but in the end, everything we showed and taught them, they used against us. It was not the fact that they took the Crystal from us that created the rift between our two kinds. Did Tanner tell you that? I'm sure he did. He wouldn't want to overwhelm you with the truth."

The inside of the car felt icy. "And what is the truth?"

He turned from the window. "Once we sealed the gateways, the Order slaughtered every fae that had fought beside them, took the Crystal we used to close the doors, and then killed our King, ultimately weakening the entire Summer Court and forcing us into seclusion."

I gasped in surprise.

"We'd already been weakened, having lost our Queen and my brother many decades before in the fight with the Winter Court," he continued. "The Order knew that. We trusted them."

"Why?" I asked after a moment. "Why did they do it?"

Fabian tilted his head to the side. "That is a question we have waited many years to have answered. I have a feeling we'll have that answer sooner rather than later."

TALKING ABOUT COLD-BLOODED betrayal and what

was tantamount to murder sure killed the vibe in the car. The only blessing was that it shut Tink and Fabian up for the next several hours.

I spent most of the time mulling over what Fabian had said. Initially, I wanted to deny everything, because it was hard to let go of years and years of a different history, but I knew the Order had lied. We'd seen the evidence of that. The question was how much had they lied about and why had they turned on the fae that had been helping them?

I didn't have the answers, but when we stopped about eight hours into the drive, somewhere in the never-ending state known as Texas, to fuel up and get something to eat, I used the brief alone time with Ren to get his thoughts while he pumped gas. Tink and Fabian were in the convenience store that was attached to a fast food joint. Our convoy had joined them with the exception of the fae named Fred. He was just staring outside the glass windows of the convenience store, obviously taking watch.

"What do you think about everything Fabian was saying?" I leaned against the passenger door, squinting into the fading sunlight.

"Honest?" He shifted so he was facing me. "I don't know why he'd lie. What would the point be?"

"I know." I sighed as I reached up, pushing a curl out of my face. "What about the whole feeding thing?"

"You and I both know there are people who enjoy the feeding." He pulled the nozzle out. "It's quite possible that they have a harem of people willing to give away a little of themselves in exchange for money and protection."

I snorted. Harem of people? For some reason, I pictured a bunch of people barely clothed fanning the Summer Prince with palm fronds.

"And to be honest, I don't even know where I stand on

that. A couple of months ago? I would've been dead set against it, but now? Everything has changed." Placing the nozzle back, he brushed his hands on his pants. "I think we've got to let go of some of our beliefs."

I nodded slowly. "I think you're right."

"I'm always right, don't you know?"

I snorted. "Keep telling yourself that."

Grinning, he stopped in front of me. "Processing everything we're learning about the Order isn't easy. Makes you think about . . . about some of the stuff we've done."

My stomach shifted unsteadily. "Yeah, it does."

Namely, it made me think about how many innocent fae I might've killed in the past. It wasn't like every fae I'd hunted had been caught red-handed. Some had run from me.

And I chased them down like . . . like an animal and killed them.

"Hey," Ren said softly, drawing my attention. I looked up and saw concern pooling in his gaze. "Where is your head at right now?"

"Just thinking about who I've hunted. If they were innocent or not. Like I could've murdered—"

"Stop." He leaned in, eye to eye with me. "We can't go back and change what we did. We've got to live with that and deal with it. Doesn't mean it's easier to deal with. Just means we've got to."

I found myself nodding again, because he was right. We couldn't change what we did or didn't do. "We can only change what we're going to do."

"Exactly," he replied, looking over the roof of the SUV. "You want to head in with me or hang out here?"

"Hang out here."

Ren dipped his chin, kissing my temple and then the corner of my mouth. "What do you want me to grab you to eat? And don't say nothing. You haven't eaten in hours."

"That's bossy."

He kissed me then and when he pulled back, he nipped at my lower lip in a way that sent a jolt right to all the interesting parts. "What do you want me to get you?"

"A burger and some fries," I relented.

"'On it," he murmured before kissing me again, and then he was off, swaggering across the parking lot.

He did end up getting me a burger and fries, and I ate it—all of it—except the tomato, because ew. Ren had taken the limp slice from me, slapping it down on top of his burger.

The burger and fries sat weirdly in my stomach, and afterward, a brief craving for something more hit me. It was almost like wanting a smoke after dinner, but I focused on Ren, Tink, and Fabian, who were arguing about the speed limit of all things, until the craving passed.

Somewhere in the middle of the night, Tink fell asleep, and so did Fabian. I offered to take over driving, but Ren was insistent to keep going. I ended up dozing off with Ren's hand resting on my thigh.

It was the sudden pitching forward motion and Ren's arm smacking me in the chest that woke me hours later. I grunted, my eyes flying open.

All I saw at first was the dark road and the faint glow of red taillights. "What's going on?"

"Faye has stopped up ahead." Ren reached for the cellphone as Tink and Fabian stirred to life in the back seat. "She shouldn't be stopping."

I looked out the window and saw literally nothing but darkness. "Where are we?"

"About to cross into Arizona." He lifted the phone to his ear. "The other group is ahead of—"

Lights flipped on several yards ahead, the glaring

intensity blinding as it pierced the blackness.

Fabian was suddenly leaning between the two front seats. “What the—?”

The night air erupted in gunfire.

Chapter 22

At first, all of us were frozen, so shocked by the sound ripping apart the night sky. The gunfire hadn't reached us, but that meant nothing. Bullets could travel quite some distance.

"Someone is shooting at them!" Tink all but flailed behind me. "Let me out. Oh my Queen Mab, let me out!" He rattled the door handle. "I am so going to kill them shooting at my new friends! I'm going to go full Tink on them!"

"You hit the childproof locks?" I asked.

"Damn straight." Ren whipped around. "I need both of you to stay in this damn car until we know what the hell we are dealing with."

Fabian leaned forward. "I am a prince. I can—"

Ren slammed on the gas and jerked into the left lane a second before I saw the car gunning in our direction.

"Holy Christ," I shouted, grabbing the handle above the window.

The car came out of nowhere—out of the damn desert! The engine of the SUV roared as we gained speed, nearing where Faye was trapped.

"I don't give a fuck what you are," Ren said. "But if we're being shot at, then there's a good chance they know who is in these cars. Meaning, those aren't regular bullets in those guns."

Understanding hit me. "You think it's the Order?"

"Who else would be shooting at us in the middle of the night, in the middle of fucking nowhere?"

"If that's the case, then they knew we were coming." Right now, we didn't have time to really delve deep into that theory.

"We need you alive," Ren was telling Fabian. "Try to stay in this car and not get dead. Because pretty sure a bullet to the head is going to put you down long enough for them to take that big head off your shoulders."

"It would, but I am faster than a bullet."

"Can you both just stay where you are?" I demanded. "At least—"

Our back window exploded without warning. Glass shot through the car. Spinning in my seat, I saw the strangest damn thing ever.

Fabian had Tink pinned down on the seat, covering Tink's body with his.

Okay. Fabian had just earned some bonus points, but was Tink hurt?

"Tink?"

"I'm doing just dandy," he called out, voice muffled.

"Get down, Ivy." Ren reached for me with one hand, yanking me down so I was flattened on the center console.

"What about you?" I protested.

"I'll be fine."

"That's so—"

"There's a gun in the glove compartment." Ren rubbed my back. "Get it, but stay low."

Muttering under my breath, I inched over and yanked open the glove compartment. Reaching inside, I grabbed the Glock. It was heavy in my palm.

As Order members, we were trained in guns too, but we didn't use them often, usually preferring the quieter stab-you-to-death method. "I can shoot."

"Give me that."

"Screw that," I hissed. "You're driving."

"I can multi-task." He pushed down on my back just as my window shattered.

I gasped as glass pinged off my back. "Ren."

His hand fisted the back of my shirt. Tires squealed as he slammed on the brakes again. "I'm fine. Hand me the gun, Ivy."

Cursing under my breath, I broke Ren's hold and popped up in my seat. I whipped toward the broken window, ignoring the crunching glass. Extending my arm, I fired several shots at the sedan spinning out in front of us.

"Dammit!" Ren shouted, grabbing ahold of my shoulder again, pushing me back down. "Are you out of your mind?"

"Are you?" I demanded. "You can't drive and shoot at the same time. You're not James Bond."

"Let him be James Bond," Tink said from where he was plastered to the seat. "Let him—"

The back right-side window blew out, pelting Fabian as the shards of glass flew sideways.

I peered up through the seats, noticing that the sedan was now behind us as we blew past the car Faye was in. Ren cut between the two, leaving the road. The ride turned bumpy as he swerved to the left. I felt the SUV go up on two wheels as we spun out.

"They're behind us again," Fabian advised rather calmly. "I do believe they either intend on shooting us until we die or causing us to crash."

Dust poured through the shattered windows. Fabian was right. They were obviously trying to kill all of us.

Cursing again, I rose as Ren shouted at me. "Stay down!" I yelled at Fabian.

The fae's eyes widened as I leveled the gun over his head and pulled the trigger. The sedan behind us suddenly veered to the left, fishtailing until it skidded to a halt yards away.

"Holy crap," I whispered. "I think I got the driver."

"That's my girl," Ren murmured a second before yanking me back down.

Taking out the driver didn't stop this. There were probably more people in the car. Faye and crew were trapped, because their cars hadn't moved. Who knew if they were even alive? We needed to bring out the big guns. And we did have one—one we needed alive at the end of this, but one who could probably unleash the Kraken on these bastards.

"Stop the car."

"What?" Ren demanded.

I wiggled out from under his hand. "Stop the car!"

He glanced at me, and who knew what he saw in my face, but he strung together an impressive string of f-bombs before hitting the brakes.

I stared into the back seat. "Can you take out whoever else is in that car? And can you do it without getting killed?"

Fabian turned his head from Tink to me. He smiled. "I am capable."

"Then do it. I'll provide cover."

Before Ren could stop me, I threw the door open and slipped out, keeping low.

"What the hell are you doing?" demanded Ren as he climbed out of the SUV.

"Providing the necessary distraction." I crept along the

side of the vehicle. "Stop worrying about me. I can take care of myself. You need to do the same and that's to get a damn gun."

He glared at me for a moment, and then I like to think he realized he wasn't going to win this argument. "There's some guns in the back. Ivy—"

"I'd get one of them just in case this goes south." Rising, I headed toward the idling sedan and opened fire. "Now, Fabian!"

The back door blew up and out shot the Summer Prince. He stalked past me, his hair lifting in the sudden hot wind that swirled across the desert floor. I kept firing until I was out, tossing the gun aside as Fabian let out a roar that didn't even remotely sound human . . . or fae.

A yellowish glow rippled from his body, encasing him in light until he looked like the sun had risen in the night just for him. In the distance, I heard Ren opening the SUV, but I couldn't pull my eyes from Fabian.

Car doors on the sedan flew open. Two—no, three people flew out. I could see them lifting their hands. Guns. Shit.

The air around Fabian warped and then expanded. Hairs all over my body lifted as I took a step back, away from him just as a burst of unnatural power left his body, shooting across the clearing and slamming into the sedan.

The car shot up into the air, sending at least two people flying in different directions. They landed in fleshy thuds just as the car exploded in a thunderous crack, bursting into flames like a damn fireball had hit it.

"Holy crap," I stumbled back, reaching for my dagger. I'd never seen anything like that.

Fabian shot forward, a blur of speed, reaching the first person on the ground before I could even blink. He caught the first guy around the neck, snapping it within a heartbeat. He turned on the second man—a man I could see was dressed in all black. The Summer Prince placed his hand on the man's head.

And that was it.

The man dropped the gun, screaming as he lurched back. Flames erupted over his body like he was a victim of spontaneous combustion.

Fabian laughed as he whirled, zeroing in on the third man, who was still standing. He turned to run, but didn't make it very far. Fabian was on him in a second, and the smell of charred flesh reached me.

I kept walking backward until I bumped into the SUV. I turned, finding Ren standing there with a gun in his hand. "Maybe . . . maybe we should've let him out of the car earlier."

"Good God," he murmured, eyes wide.

The kind of power the Prince could wield was beyond frightening. A weapon of mass destruction with pointy ears, and apparently a hard-on for Tink. If he was capable of this, what exactly was the Winter Prince truly capable of?

Tink peeked his head up over the window. "That was kind of hot. Literally. Figuratively."

I turned to him. "I think you should be really, really careful with him."

"We need to get to the others." Ren handed me another gun. "There's still gunfire back there."

I turned just in time to see Fabian taking out the men that were thrown from the car. My stomach turned as I faced Ren. "Please be careful. Don't get shot."

Ren gave me a devilish smile. "Keep yourself in one piece, because when this is over I have a lot of ideas on how I want to work out some of the adrenaline this fight is going to give us."

Oh my.

That was definitely great motivation to stay alive.

Stretching up, I grabbed his chin and brought his mouth to mine. I kissed him with everything I had in me, and it was harsh and fierce. When I pulled back, I almost didn't want to let him go. "I love you."

His hand brushed over my hip. "Prove it to me later."

Then Ren was gone, rushing around the side of the SUV, toward the glaring headlights.

I spun to Tink. "Stay—"

"Don't." He opened the door, forcing me to take a step back. "I'm not a child, Ivy. I can take care of myself. Trust me."

"I know you're not a child, Tink." Another rapid succession of gunfire echoed across the highway. "But this is really dangerous."

"I know." He closed the door behind him. "But I can help. So, if you want to cancel Amazon Prime, then do so, but I'm not staying in this car while all of you risk your lives."

There was a shout, and I could hear footsteps pounding off the ground. Arguing with Tink was just going to get us both killed. "Stay close to Fabian."

A wild grin whipped across his face. "Don't have to tell me twice."

As Tink shot past me, I whipped around and saw a man racing toward me. I didn't recognize him, but he was definitely human. He lifted a hand, and the moonlight glinted off a dagger.

An Order member.

Crap.

He charged forward, and I dipped low. Springing up, I spun and slammed my foot into his back. There was a sickening crunch that startled me.

The man went down, twitching and spasming.

"What the . . . ?" I stumbled back, shocked that a simple kick to the back would . . . oh God.

I was stronger now. How could I keep forgetting that?

A kick to the back had broken the man's spine. My stomach churned as I spun, and I didn't have time to really process that. A second man raced at me, and I sidestepped his attack. He whirled, but I caught his arm. Twisting sharply, I winced at the crack and desperately ignored the man's yelp of pain. He dropped the dagger.

"I don't want to kill you," I said, putting pressure on the man until he went down on his knees. I seriously didn't want to. Killing humans, well, it was nothing like killing fae. They didn't cave into themselves like fae did. Instead, it was bloody and messy and stuck with you long after the deed was done. "So, if I let go, you're going to behave, right?"

The man gasped out a harsh laugh. "You better go ahead and kill me, because if you let me up, I'm going to take you out, you bitch."

"Wow." I increased pressure out of spite. "I'm holding your broken arm, dude."

"Kill me," he gasped out. "Go ahead and do it, you traitorous whore!"

My jaw clenched as someone in the distance shouted. There was a flare of orange light, and I assumed Fabian was lighting some people up in the worst possible way. "You're an Order member."

"Just like you were," he said, twisting his head to the side. "But you betrayed us."

"I didn't betray shit. How did you know we were out here?"

"How do you think? You—" He lurched, grabbing the dagger.

I cursed as he swiped behind him. Letting go, I jumped out of the way. He stumbled to his feet.

"Whatever you think about me is wrong. I haven't betrayed the Order. I'm trying to stop—"

He came at me like a freight train, and instinct took over. I didn't want to kill him, but I also didn't want to get stabbed to death either. I already knew how sucky that felt.

Shooting forward, I shoved my other dagger into his chest, between the ribs. I yanked it out as I whispered, "I'm sorry."

He didn't speak as he fell forward.

Swallowing hard, I shot around the SUV, back toward the headlights. I kept to the dark, racing toward the car the Prince's consul had been packed into.

Bullet holes lined the entire side. Windows were gone. My steps slowed, and the burger I ate earlier almost ended up on the ground.

All of them . . . they were slowly collapsing into themselves, their pale eyes wide with terror and pain, skin peeling and flaking away. Mouths gone. They couldn't make a sound.

"God," I gasped, looking away from the sight and then back. My gaze met Fred's. I didn't know what to say, but I saw it . . . I saw it in his gaze.

He was pleading with me.

I looked down at the dagger, knowing what he wanted—knowing that I could end this for them quickly. Everything inside me rebelled against the idea, which was so crazy. I could kill during battle, but I was having a hard time carrying out a mercy killing? It was different though.

Briefly squeezing my eyes shut, I forced myself to woman up and then I . . . I did it. I took care of all of them, and when I was done I wanted to be done with *all* of this, because their pain-stricken faces and knowledge in their eyes that I was sending them back to a world that was dying would haunt me for the rest of my days.

But it was far from over.

I turned, coming to an abrupt halt when I saw Fabian standing there, staring into the car. "I had to—"

"I know." His gaze shifted to me. "Thank you."

"Don't say—" I saw movement over his shoulder and reacted without thought, firing the gun. Fabian whirled with a gasp just as another Order member went down.

"Don't thank me for that," I said, then took off for the other car—to where I no longer heard gunfire.

Tink was up ahead, having not stayed close to Fabian. He was kneeling next to something—someone—and he was shirtless.

Faye—he was next to Faye.

"Is she . . . ?"

"I'm fine. Didn't get hit by a bullet, but a piece of glass nearly severed my arm," she answered, voice strained. It was then that I saw Tink was wrapping his shirt around her bicep. "I'll heal. Dane is . . . he's dead."

Pressure seized my throat. Shit. "Kalen?"

"He's with Ren," Tink answered, not looking up. "I'm staying with her."

I started forward, but I stopped. "I'm . . . I'm sorry about Dane."

Faye closed her eyes.

Drawing in a deep breath, I started running. Up ahead was a truck, the kind that had running lights on top. I was careful to be quiet, but it was pointless. There was another car in-between us, one that looked like it had just arrived on the scene. There wasn't even a part of me that hoped they were on Team Not Kill Us. I just knew better.

The doors opened up, and five climbed out. Five. Great.

I didn't see guns, so at least there was that. Fabian was suddenly behind me.

The odds starting looking a lot better.

A rush of adrenaline coiled tight as I shot forward, reaching the first Order member. She dove at me, but I shot under her arm, faster than she could track. I came up behind her, and I shut everything down inside me. I didn't think about her being a human or that we used to be on the same side. I didn't wonder if they'd still be fighting me if they knew how much the Order had lied. I had to for me to do this. I couldn't think about the fact that I was pulling the trigger and shooting her right in the chest.

Swinging around, I caught another in the back with my boot, and he went down on one knee. I brought the dagger down, wrenching it back out when I hit the target.

Hearing pounding footsteps coming from behind me, I spun and jumped to the side, narrowly missing a dagger to the chest. I started to twist, but the man's neck snapped to the side. He fell, revealing Fabian.

"Thanks," I gasped.

"I owed you."

Fabian made quick work of the remaining members, clearing a path for me to make it to where I hoped Ren was still standing. I neared the grill of the truck when a form stepped out. I lifted the gun, prepared to blow a hole straight through whoever it was.

Kalen lifted his hands. "It's me—just me."

"Crap." I lowered the gun. "I could've shot you. Where's Ren?"

The fae jerked his head. "He's got one of them."

Apparently, Ren was the only one who had the intelligence to leave one of them alive. I followed Kalen around the side of the truck, keeping an eye out for other Order members.

I saw Ren and wanted to tackle him out of relief. I managed not to do that, mainly because he had a gun pointed at someone, and I figured a tackle-hug wouldn't help the situation at the moment.

"Now that Ivy's joining us, I'm hoping you're going to change your mind and start talking." Ren's voice was as hard as granite. "She's got way less patience than I do."

I smirked as I reached his side. My gaze followed to where the gun pointed, and I had to look down because Ren had whoever it was on their knees. I gasped as I recognized the dark-haired man.

Every muscle in my body locked up as I stared down at the man who'd killed Ren's best friend. The man who oversaw the Elite and had come to New Orleans to hunt me down.

Kyle Clare.

Chapter 23

Kyle didn't change his mind. Not that I was entirely surprised. As Order members, we were practically bred to keep our mouths shut if we were captured by the enemy.

And to Kyle, we were the enemy.

So, we were going to have to make him talk, like we had with Marlon, and that wasn't exactly something I was looking forward to. Even if Kyle was a giant prick, who needed a healthy dose of karma.

Since it was only a matter of time before our little showdown along the interstate would be seen by some unsuspecting person with terrible luck, we had to get off the road and someplace safe where we could question Kyle and find out how they knew we'd been heading to San Diego.

Who was left of our group piled into the SUV, including a tied up and gagged Kyle. We made it to some creepy-ass roadside motel where I normally wouldn't even think twice about staying, but they had vacancies and looked like the type of place that was used to hearing screams in the middle of the night.

We paid cash for three rooms and stuck Kyle in the middle one, gagged and bound to one of those uncomfortable desk chairs. It was just Ren and I in the room with him. We figured having any of the fae there wouldn't entice him to play nice.

Besides, Kalen was out there somewhere dumping our damaged vehicles and getting us new rides, and Faye was resting so her arm would heal. I guessed Kalen was going to glamour someone into handing over their keys, and I really didn't have the brain space to decide if that was right or wrong.

Ren stood directly in front of him, arms folded over his chest. "I'm about to remove that gag and I'm hoping you're smart enough to not make a lot of noise."

Kyle glared up at Ren, and I had no idea if he was going to be smart enough or not.

"We want to talk to you and we need you to listen," Ren said, stepping closer. "We're on the same side."

A moment passed and then Kyle nodded. Ren removed the gag, and the first thing out of the older man's mouth was, "We aren't on the same side, boy. We stopped being on the same side the moment you realized what she was and you didn't put her down."

I arched a brow. "This is going to be a lovely conversation."

Kyle's dark gaze shot to me. "Should've listened to my gut the first time I met you. Hearing stories of you fighting the Prince and surviving? Bullshit."

"Contrary to what you believe, I did fight the Prince and I did survive. Not only that, I was then kidnapped against my will, and I still survived." I held his gaze. "I didn't know I was the Halfling."

He sneered. "Like that matters."

"I guess it doesn't," I mused, "because I'm sure you put

down a lot of halflings in your day, people who had no idea what they were or why you were killing them."

"Why don't you ask him how many he killed before he met you?"

Ren stiffened in front of me.

"He didn't have the balls to take out Noah. Or you, apparently." Kyle smiled. "But he's killed—"

"Shut up," I spat.

"Thought you wanted me to talk?" He leaned forward as far as the rope Ren found God knows where would let him. "How does it make you feel knowing that the very reason he came to New Orleans was to put a bullet between the eyes of the Halfling—to kill you. But I guess you've got a golden pussy, because—"

Ren moved so fast I barely saw his fist connect with Kyle's face, knocking his head back and the chair up on two legs. Ren's jaw was so hard it could crack stone as he stood there, staring down at Kyle.

I stepped forward. "Just so you know, I like the idea of my vagina being golden. That's not an insult."

"Yeah, you wouldn't." Kyle spit out a mouthful of blood. "The lighting is shit in here, but I see you."

I had a feeling I knew what he meant and I realized I didn't care. It hit me like a speeding train, but it was what it was. I knew I looked different. I knew what it meant, and I *didn't* care. "I don't give a shit what you see."

"How? How did you hide what you really looked like?" he demanded. "Because I know damn well if David saw you for what you really are, he still wouldn't be defending you."

My head cocked to the side as Ren glanced back at me. "David is defending me?"

For a moment, I didn't think Kyle was going to answer. "He didn't want to believe you betrayed the Order.

Obviously, he was wrong."

"I didn't betray the Order." I paused. David still believing in me was surprisingly great news. My lips pursed. "Well, killing those Order members who attacked us probably ranks up there in the betrayal department, but we were defending ourselves."

Kyle stared at me. His left eye was swelling, an injury I guessed had occurred out by the cars. "You look like a goddamn fae. You're disgusting."

Striking like lightning once more, Ren's fist connected with Kyle's stomach. The contact echoed throughout the room. He caught Kyle by the shoulder, stopping the chair from toppling backward. "I think you meant to say she's beautiful, but I understand. Words were never your forte."

"Doing your duty was never yours." Kyle looked up at Ren and laughed. "Now was it?"

They were eye to eye. "You know damn well I did my duty over and fucking over."

"But not when it counts."

"You're wrong. When it counts, I'm doing the right thing." Ren stepped back as the chair righted itself. "We're not here to talk about what I was supposed to do. How did you know where we were?"

Kyle spit out more blood. "Go fuck yourself."

"Language," Ren murmured, letting his arms hang at his sides.

The leader of the Elite laughed, and it sounded wet. "What information do you think you're going to get from me? You and I both know how this is going to end."

I glanced between the two. "How is this going to end?"

Kyle's upper lip curled. "He's going to kill me."

Looking at Ren, I waited for him to answer and when he didn't, I decided it was time to step in. "Okay. Let's get this train back on track. Do you know the Prince has found another halfling?"

A muscle flexed along Kyle's rapidly bruising jaw. "No shit."

"So, did it ever occur to you that if the Prince was en route to San Diego for another halfling, that maybe I wasn't on board with getting pregnant and ushering in the end of the world as we know it?"

Another moment passed. "Doesn't change what you are or the danger you present."

I exhaled noisily. "Okay. I'll give you that. But why do you think we are heading to San Diego? Don't you dare say to join up and meet with the Prince, because I might just punch you, and guess what? I hit a hell of a lot harder than Ren does."

"You're traveling with a bunch of fae," he replied. "Pretty sure it's obvious."

"We're trying to stop him, you dumb son of a bitch." Ren moved to stand behind Kyle's chair. "But you kind of got in the way, delaying us. You better hope he hasn't found her."

"The Order in San Diego has been watching for him. We aren't stupid."

Ren clapped his hands down on Kyle's shoulders, causing him to jump. "That's up for discussion."

A little bit of hope that we weren't too late sparked in my chest. "They haven't seen the Prince yet?"

Kyle said nothing.

"That doesn't mean the Prince isn't there, that he hasn't already found her." Ren's hands curled, digging into the man's shoulders. "And while you're here barking up the wrong damn tree, he's getting exactly what he wants."

"You know we have almost no time to stop him from succeeding," I tried again to reason with the man. "You don't have to like what I am. You can think whatever you want, but by now you have to have realized we're not working for the Prince."

"But you're working with the fae."

"And this isn't the first time the Order has worked with the fae." Ren smiled when Kyle winced. "You want to talk about that?"

Kyle fell silent.

"That's the interesting thing about all of this." Ren's hands slipped off his shoulders, nearing the man's throat. "You talk to me about duty, but you all are a bunch of damn liars. Did you ever think one of us wouldn't cross paths with the Summer Court and learn about how the Order and the Elite worked alongside them? How they helped close the gateways? How they don't kill humans or feed off them?"

Well, except for the Royals. They fed, but I thought it was best we kept that to ourselves at the moment.

His eyes flashed. "You all were trained to kill, not to ask questions with the fae while you share tea and biscuits."

My brows lifted. "The Order lied to us—all of us—and continue to do so, because they thought none of us would ever talk and listen to one of the Summer fae?"

"Worked so far."

I stared at him a moment, dumbfounded. "That is absolutely stupid."

Kyle gave me a bloody smirk. "Order members were never trained to *talk* and *listen* to the fae. You were trained to strike first. Always."

"Again," I said. "That is stupid and sloppy."

"You know what's stupid? You thinking you're going to make it out of this alive."

"Shaking in my boots." I rolled my eyes. "I'm guessing you put a bulletin out on us, and we were spotted. That's why you found us."

"Probably in Texas," Ren agreed, sliding one hand around Kyle's neck. "When we stopped to grab food. I'm also guessing the sect in Southern California is going to be looking out for us."

The man visibly swallowed. He may act like he was tough shit, but he was scared.

Kyle dragged in a deep breath as Ren let go and stepped back. "I've got nothing to say to you all."

"It's okay." I smiled. "Because you did tell us something we can use."

Kyle's eyes narrowed. "I haven't told you shit."

"Oh, you did." I laughed softly as Ren's gaze lifted to mine. "You told me exactly who we need to contact. David."

His gaze widened with understanding.

"So . . ." I lifted my hand, extending my middle finger. "Thanks for that."

There were no words to describe the satisfaction I felt when his face paled. "Go ahead and kill me."

"I'd love to do that for you." Ren walked past him, smacking him on the back of the head in the process. "But what does that do but prove you right that we're the enemy?"

I looked at him sharply, but managed to stay quiet. Based on the look on Kyle's face, he was just as surprised as I was.

Ren smiled down at Kyle. "Leaving you alive will hopefully get through that thick skull of yours that we're on the same side. I won't have your blood on my hands. Neither will Ivy."

Chapter 24

Smothering a yawn, I followed Ren into the room next door. We'd gagged Kyle before we left and turned the TV on just in case. He wasn't going anywhere though. Not unless he developed super special powers and managed to break free from where we left him . . .

Tied to the pipes in the bathroom.

"You really going to call David?" Ren asked, stopping in front of the bed that was sunken in the middle. I wondered how many people got pregnant and died on that bed.

Then I vomited a little in my mouth and decided I didn't need to think about that. "I think he's our best option if it gets down to having to open the doors to send the Prince back."

"It's a risk." He scanned the small, dingy hotel room, his brow raising as he took in the TV that looked like it came from the eighties. "He may not think you've betrayed him, but when. . . ."

As Ren trailed off, I watched him unstrap the dagger and the thorn stake. He placed them on the small nightstand closest to the door. A gun joined them.

"When he sees what I look like now?" I finished for him.

Ren turned to me. "It shouldn't change a damn thing, but it might."

I bit down on my lip. "I know. That's why it's best if I call him once we get to San Diego. Calling him now is too much of a risk. We could run into another roadblock along the way if I'm wrong about him."

"We could." He toed off his boots. "We can't stay here long. Other Elite members will be looking for Kyle. We've probably got a handful of hours. We need to rest and then get on the road."

"Agreed."

I think you're right," he said, running a hand over his messy hair. "We'll contact David when we get to San Diego and . . . go from there."

I nodded, watching him as he tugged the shirt off over his head, showing off those defined abs and pecs. Something was off about his tone, and his gaze skittered away from mine whenever they met.

"What are we going to do about Captain Dickhead? Do we really plan on leaving him alive?"

His lips twitched into a faint smile. "We should kill him. I want to. Badly. For a lot of different reasons." He sat down on the edge of the bed, and I was surprised when the thing didn't collapse. "But if you or I kill him, it just proves him right—proves what other members of the Order must believe."

"So, we're just going to leave him here?"

Thrusting his hand through his hair again, he nodded. "I think that's the right thing to do."

I didn't think that was the right thing to do at all. Leaving Kyle alive meant we'd be looking over our shoulder every single second while we dealt with Drake and everything else. We needed to talk about this.

"Kyle was right."

Blinking, I frowned. "Right about what?"

Ren leaned forward, resting his arms on his legs. "About me killing the halflings."

All thoughts about killing Kyle vanished. "Ren—"

"You know how many I killed?" He lowered his chin and gave a little shake of his head. "I do."

Oh, no. "That doesn't matter."

"It doesn't? I kind of think it does." He was quiet for a moment. "I would've killed you if I hadn't gotten to know you—if I had learned you were a halfling before I learned who you were."

That was hard to hear, but I walked toward him. "But that's not what happened."

"It could have." He lifted his head, his gaze so troubled that it made my heart ache. "They were like you, Ivy. Some weren't Order members, but others were, and they had no idea what they were. No idea why they were seconds away from dying. They never even knew what hit them."

My breath caught, and I found myself at a loss for words.

"Sometimes I don't know how you can be with me," he said, and those words broke my heart. "How you can look at me, love me, knowing why I came to New Orleans."

I swallowed down the lump in my throat. "Well, it helps that you didn't try to kill me."

Ren didn't smile like I thought he would. I knelt in front of him, placing one hand on his leg and cupping his chin with the other. "Look at me."

Slowly, his gaze lifted to mine. "I'm looking at you, Sweetness. Always am even when my eyes aren't on you."

My chest squeezed in response to those words. God, Ren was . . . he was too good for all of this. I saw that with sudden clarity. If he hadn't been born into this world, he'd probably be a doctor, saving lives, or a teacher ushering in a better youth for tomorrow.

And maybe if I wasn't born into this, I'd also be . . . too good.

"Who you were before and what you did is not who you are now and what you're going to do." I dragged my thumb under his lip. "Both of us have done things we wished we hadn't, and I like to think that we wouldn't have done those things if we had known differently. We are not who we used to be."

Ren's eyes closed as he turned his head, kissing my palm, but I could feel the tension rolling off him. "We killed people today—people I once worked with. I recognized at least three of them."

I sucked in a sharp breath.

"I know we had to. If we hadn't, they wouldn't think twice about killing us." A shudder rippled through him. "But that doesn't make it any easier."

"I'm so sorry," I whispered.

Ren didn't respond, and as I stared up at him, I knew right then that Kyle's blood couldn't be on Ren's hands. There was no way I could push the issue of killing Kyle.

The stress continued to pour off him, and I decided I had to do something. Anything to ease his troubles. Sleep would help, and we both needed that, but all I wanted in that moment was to take his pain and self-loathing away, and there was only one way I knew how.

I didn't think about the thin, dirty carpet as I dropped to my knees between his legs and reached for the button on his pants.

He straightened, lifting his head as he caught my wrist. "Ivy—"

I shushed him as I stretched up, kissing him softly as I worked on his zipper. I felt him then, already hard and straining. I broke the kiss and lowered back down as my gaze moved to his.

"Please?" I whispered.

Ren let go of my wrist, lifting one finger at a time.

Tugging the zipper down the rest of the way, I grabbed ahold of his pants and boxers. He lifted his hips and I was able to drag them past his knees and off. Then I took him in my hand, marveling at how he could feel as smooth as silk and yet hard as steel.

He exhaled harshly as I moved my hand from the tip to the base and back up. A bead of liquid glistened. His entire body jerked as I moved my thumb along the tip, and my gaze flew to his. He watched me intently, his lips slightly parted as he reached behind my head, finding the pin in my hair and tugging it out. Curls fell past my shoulders in a tangled mess, and then his hand was threading through them, curling around the back of my head. He used the slightest pressure to show me what he wanted.

The salty taste of him danced over my tongue, and my ears blistered at the ragged sound he made. I didn't drag it out. This wasn't about playing and teasing. This was all about taking his mind out of the dark places it had gone. It was about easing him. I took him in my mouth, and even though I didn't have a ton of experience with blow jobs, I quickly learned that when a guy was into you, there really wasn't a wrong way of doing this.

Well, except for probably using the teeth in a not so seductive manner, but whatever.

"Ivy," he growled, his entire body flexing as I sucked and moved up, swirling my tongue along the head. He swore and his body tightened.

Heat swamped me, slipping down my body. I ached for him in a different way than moments before.

I took him as far as I could, and that seemed to be enough based on the way his hand tightened around my head and the deep sounds he was making. Then his hand slipped to my neck and his thumb found my pulse, that oddly sensitive spot for me, and he gently massaged the skin until I was squeezing my thighs together. He swelled against my tongue a second before he tried to pull me away, but I didn't let him, not as he pulsed and growled my name.

When it was over, I sat back, rather proud of myself. Or, I tried to sit back. That wasn't what happened though. Ren moved fast, grabbing me under the arms and lifting me onto my feet. I gasped as his fingers made quick work of my pants, and before I could even say 'yum' he had my pants, my underwear, and my boots off of me.

Jesus, he was talented.

And strong—really strong.

Ren lifted me up onto the bed as he sat down, holding me up so that a very private part of me was lined up with his mouth.

He said nothing as I looked down at him. My heart thundered at the fierce, raw intensity etched into his striking features. Stunned, I locked my legs to stay balanced as he gripped my hips—my ass, his fingers digging into my flesh.

And then his mouth was on me.

With no warning. No slow build-up. Lips. Tongue. Sucking. Dragging. I gasped, holding on to his head for support. He devoured me, his mouth hot and wet and all-consuming.

I tried to say his name, but I lost all control as my body coiled tight. I was beyond coherent speech, beyond anything other than what his mouth was doing between my thighs. I felt like I was going to die, that I was dying, and then it happened. I cried out, my body liquefying as release pounded through me, throbbing and pulsing and never-ending. It took my legs right out from underneath me.

And Ren caught me.

I collapsed in his arms—limp, sated, and exhausted. I barely processed him twisting so we were both lying on our sides, my cheek plastered to his chest. Not a word passed between us, and that was how he fell asleep, holding me close as if he feared I was going to float away from him.

I didn't sleep though.

I couldn't as the pleasant haze of release faded away and I thought about what I had to do.

What I had to do for him.

Chapter 25

Ren was still in the shower when I slipped out of the room. I told him that I would check on Kyle and make sure he was fine before we hit the road. I insisted on it, because I didn't want Ren anywhere near that bastard.

It was early and the morning sun caused me to wince as it burned up the parking lot. I wasn't alone when I stepped outside.

Fabian stood in front of the door Kyle was being kept in.

"Have you been out here all night?" I asked.

"On and off," he replied, face expressionless. "Wanted to make sure he stayed where he needed to be."

"He's not going anywhere. Trust me."

"He won't."

The coldness in his voice sent a chill down my spine. I looked around, not seeing anyone else. "Where's Tink?"

"Asleep in the room at the end. He's with Faye." He inclined his head. "Why do you call him that? Tink?"

I lifted my brows as I shoved a limp curl back from my face. The question surprised me. "I just . . . well, he never told me his real name and he reminded me of Tinkerbell."

Fabian's mouth twitched. "Interesting." There was a pause. "I heard you guys last night."

My eyes widened as heat poured into my face. Oh my God, we barely made any noise! Well, there was moaning—definite moaning of the sexual variety. The walls in this place had to be as thin as the damn carpet. "I don't know what you think you heard, but it wasn't us."

He frowned as he watched me. "I heard you and Ren talking to the man inside there."

"Oh. *Oh*." I let out a choked laugh. God. Now I was just embarrassing myself. "Carry on then."

His frown faded, but his stare was still heavy. "That is why I am waiting."

My gaze flew to him. A terse moment passed, one full of understanding, and then Fabian stepped aside. I reached for the door.

"I did hear you moaning also," Fabian added. "You sounded like a wild moose grazing."

My mouth dropped open. "A wild moose grazing?"

"Yes. That is correct. It was quite . . . disturbing."

Oh my God, I didn't sound like a wild moose.

Face flaming, I flipped him off and then opened up the motel door. The room was quiet, but we'd left the bathroom light on and I could see him from the entryway.

He was dozing, his chin resting against his chest, wrists secured to the pipe. The man had senses of a cat though, because I took one step toward him and he woke right up.

"Good morning," I said, making my way toward him. "I would've brought you coffee and a doughnut, but then I remembered I don't like you."

He snorted, looking away. "If you're here to finally kill me, just get it over with, because you're fucking annoying."

"I'm not here to do that." Walking into the bathroom, I

sat down on the closed toilet seat. “I want to talk.”

“And I want to use that toilet, so if you’re not going to, how about you move your ass and untie me.”

I laughed. “Not going to happen. Not yet.”

His gaze slowly slid to me. “You know they’re coming for me. They already have to be out there, closing in on all of you.”

“I know.” I crossed one leg over the other. “So, we don’t have a lot of time.”

“You’re almost out of time.”

“Almost.” My gaze flickered over him, and I saw the fine tremor that coursed through him. “You may not believe this, but I was kidnapped by the Prince. I was taken against my will. I fought to stay alive and to not give in. You have no idea what I had to do to do that.” My throat thickened, but I kept going. “You can hate me. You can hate Ren. But we’re the world’s best chance right now. We were on the same side.”

A muscle ticked along his jaw. “Were?”

I didn’t address that. Not yet.

“Are you married? Have children?” I asked.

“What?” he snapped.

“Just curious. A lot of Order members marry one another. Have children. Did you?” I rested my chin on my palm. “You don’t look like you did. No wedding band. You’re all about the job. Duty.”

“Yes,” he seethed. “Eradicating the fae is my duty.”

“Even the ones that helped the Order? The Summer Court?”

Kyle didn’t answer.

“What happened? Why can’t you tell me that? I’ve heard their side, but I know there has to be more. There has to be for the Order to have turned on them.”

Pressing his lips into a thin line, he tipped his head back against the bottom of the sink.

Clenching my jaw, I shook my head. I wanted to kick him in the face, but I doubted that would get him to talk. "It can't be just because they were fae."

His head whipped toward me. "It can't be?"

I stilled.

"It doesn't matter if they weren't feeding or not or if they helped the Order. They're a damn abomination infecting our world—a fucking disease. The Order couldn't see that, but we could." His eyes flashed. "We did what we needed to do, like we always do."

Was he being for real? "You—the Elite turned on the Summer fae because they were fae?"

"Is there another reason I am unaware of?"

"Holy shit," I whispered, shocked to my core. "That's all? You betrayed them. Killed them. Took their Crystal. You did all of this because they were fae. Wow. I'm really out of words."

He cursed and called me an idiot, but all I could do was stare at him. There was no deep motivation, no hidden agenda. Just . . . bigotry and fear. If this was what the Elite were then they were . . . they were no better than the fae that wanted to take over the mortal world.

I was nothing like him. Neither was Ren. The moment we learned that there were fae out there just trying to live their best lives without harming others, we called a truce. It wasn't easy, but we were . . .

We were good human beings.

On most days.

Just not today, though. Today I was not a good person. I was the worst of the worst.

And I was okay with that.

Kyle sighed heavily. "He's going to have to kill me, you know that? Sooner or later. Because I will find you and I will kill you. Then he'll come after me, and if he doesn't kill me, I'll kill him. He's a traitor."

I unfolded my arms. This conversation was over. "He's not going to kill you."

Kyle smirked. "You're a dumb bitch if you think that's a smart move."

"Guess what? I'm a bitch, but I am not dumb." I rose from the toilet. "I get why he thinks letting you live will help build a bridge with the Order again. He's just that kind of a person. A *good* person. He's better than you."

"He's fucking a halfling," Kyle spat.

I let out a cold laugh as I backed out of the bathroom. "And he enjoys it. A lot."

A look of disgust crept into his expression. "He'll do it. I promise you that. He and I will see each other again."

"You're wrong, so very wrong about that." I stopped in front of the main door. "Ren's not going to kill you later. I'm not going to allow that."

He laughed. "What? You're going to do it? Then lie to him about it later? Kind of hard to kill me when you're all the way over there."

"No." I waited until he was looking at me and then I smiled. "I'm not going to do it either, because I made a promise not to lie to him anymore."

"Isn't that sweet," he spat, shaking his head.

"It is." I wrapped my hand around the door and started to open it. "But I didn't say no one was going to kill you, Kyle."

I stepped aside.

And the Summer Prince walked in.

Chapter 26

Kalen had found us one of the large SUVs that could seat a damn soccer team, so we were all in one car now.

All of us that were left.

One day on the road and we'd already lost five people. That was hard to think about or even acknowledge.

I think that was why Faye and Kalen were quiet in the furthest back row. I hadn't known Dane well, but I liked him even if he had called me a wee little halfling.

Fabian was also quiet, and I was sure that had to do with him losing his entire consul. Every last one of them had died in that car, riddled with iron laced bullets.

I bit down on my lip, glancing over at Ren. He had no idea what I'd done. As planned, we left without Ren checking in on Kyle and he hadn't asked me how Kyle was. And I didn't ask Fabian what he'd done to Kyle, but the Summer Prince was noticeably more relaxed when we left.

I was sure he made Kyle pay for every death that had taken place.

Part of me was still in a state of disbelief over what Kyle

had told me. The Elite were the ones who betrayed the Summer Court simply because they were fae. I didn't want to believe it. I wanted there to be some reason that would help me understand why the Elite had done what they had. But there was nothing except bigotry and fear.

And all I could hope was that bigotry and fear didn't extend far into the Order. I knew it probably did, but Kyle had said that David hadn't wanted to believe that I would betray him. We had a chance.

My fingers curled around the burner phone. I didn't even remember pulling it out of my pocket, but I'd been holding it for hours now, the device hot in my hands.

Calling David was a huge risk, but one we were going to have to take. He was our only hope when it came to opening the gateways to send the Prince back.

"Hey." Tink leaned forward, between the seats, his voice low. "I was thinking about something."

With Tink, it was anyone's guess about what it could've been. I turned to him. "What?"

"Do you think it's possible that the Order has already discovered who the Halfling is and has them in, I don't know, protective custody?" he asked.

A muscle thrummed along Ren's jaw. "The Elite is in San Diego, that much is obvious. If they've discovered who the Halfling is, then they wouldn't be in protective custody."

Ren was right. The Elite would've killed them immediately. They wouldn't try to keep her safe.

"That's kind of screwed up," Tink commented.

"You're just now realizing this?"

He looked at me. "It's just wrong."

Yeah.

Yeah, it was.

Tink sat back, and when I glanced over at Fabian, my

gaze met his. "If the Halfling is still alive and not compromised, she will be under the protection of the Summer Court," he said. "We will not allow harm to come to her."

"And if she is compromised?"

"Then we'll cross that bridge when we come to it—if we come to it," Fabian replied, looking out the window. That was a very different answer than when we started this trip. "Let us hope that is not the case."

I wasn't sure how much hoping had worked out for us in the past, but I was willing to give it a try. It couldn't hurt. We spent the rest of the trip discussing our game plan for once we got to San Diego. According to Faye, Tanner had taken care of lodging. We'd be staying at a rather secluded home, just outside of San Diego, in Del Mar. I had no idea if he knew the owner or if this was some kind of Airbnb thing which made me want to laugh. Faye knew where to retrieve the keys on the property, and despite how serious our visit was, I was excited to learn that it was on a beach. I wanted to walk barefoot in the sand just once.

Priorities.

From there, I'd call David on the burner phone. The kind of phone Tanner provided us was encrypted and untraceable, connecting to wifi instead of cellular towers. That didn't mean that David couldn't trace us via the internet if we were using a static IP, so that meant we needed public wifi just to be sure.

And from there, well, all we had was hope.

Hope that David would hear me out and agree to meet with us. Hope that they had some idea of where the Prince was, and hope that we weren't too late.

WE REACHED SAN Diego around dinnertime and stopped

at a fast food restaurant that had free wifi to make the call and grab something to eat.

Parked in the back of the lot, I stayed in the car with Ren while the rest went into the restaurant. Tink was going to grab me, not one but two, orders of chicken fries, and I was happy to report that I was really, really looking forward to devouring them.

I hadn't had any cravings since the last one, so that was good, I thought.

"You ready to do this?" Ren's gaze met mine. He was leaning back in the driver's seat, his arm resting along the back of my seat.

Nodding, I drew in a shallow breath. "Ready as I'll ever be." My fingers hovered over the number pad. I knew Tanner's number by heart. "What if he doesn't answer?"

"Then you keep calling until he does."

I nodded again. My stomach was full of knots. What if Kyle lied? What if David wasn't even in San Diego? There were so many risks.

Ren touched my cheek, drawing my attention. His gaze searched mine. "You got this."

"I do." I tried to smile, but it felt weird. "David's like . . ."

"What?"

I gave a little shake of my head. "He's like a father to me. I know that sounds stupid—"

"It doesn't." He smoothed his thumb over my cheek. "Not at all."

The smile came easier this time. "It's just that when Kyle said that David didn't believe that I'd betrayed the Order, it really meant something to me, but what if he does think that? I mean, David can be a big prick, but it would be . . . it would hurt."

Ren leaned toward me, kissing the center of my forehead.

"I wish I could say something that would make it better if that's the case, but there isn't anything I can say except if he thinks that about you then he doesn't know you at all."

Shifting my head, I kissed his lips, and when I pulled back, I had to swallow the sudden knot in my throat. "I need to call him."

"You do."

And that's what I did. Punching in his number, I hit the speaker button and then waited. It rang once, twice, and by the fourth ring, I started to worry that he wasn't going to answer.

But then he did, on the fifth ring. "What?"

My stomach dropped as I stared at the phone. That was definitely David. Only he would answer an unknown number like that.

I glanced at Ren, and he nodded.

"David?" I said, wincing when my voice cracked. "It's Ivy."

My introduction was met with a long beat of silence and then, "You're alive."

I blinked. "Yeah, I am. So is Ren."

"You gonna tell me where you've been, what you've been doing?" he asked.

"I want to. That's why I'm calling you. Hoping you're where I am."

"And where is that?"

"San Diego." The phone was going to crack from how tight I was clutching it.

There was another stretch of silence. "Funny. That's where I am."

Well, at least that was good news. I guessed. "I know you probably don't trust me, because God only knows what you think, but I didn't betray the Order. I'm here to stop the Prince. So is Ren."

"You don't know what I'm thinking. That's probably a good thing, but you better start talking and telling me where in the hell you've been." David paused. "I'm figuring there's a lot of things you need to tell me, girl."

There were a lot of things that I needed to tell him, but I started with the most obvious. "I'm the Halfling."

David was quiet.

"You probably already know that," I continued, a little breathless. "But I didn't know, not until the Prince came—well, I actually figured it out right before that. I cut myself with the thorn stake, but I didn't know until then. I had no idea. Neither did Ren."

I closed my eyes, hating to say what I had to. "The Prince kidnapped Ren and then me. He held me for a while, but I escaped—we escaped. And if you followed the Prince here then you have to know he didn't get what he wanted from me."

"Maybe I know that." There was a pause. "Maybe not."

Instinct told me that David knew that the Prince was after another Halfling. "I want to meet with you—just Ren and I. We need to talk."

"That we do."

"And by talk I mean we don't want to walk into a trap, David. We're on the same side."

"Why would you think there'd be a trap?"

"Oh, I don't know." I opened my eyes and stared at the leafy palms moving in the breeze. "Maybe because an entire convoy of Order and Elite members tried to kill us in Arizona."

"What?" he exclaimed.

I looked at Ren, unsure if his reaction was genuine. That was when Ren spoke up. "You didn't know about that,

David?"

"Well, hello, Mr. Owens. Glad to know I'm on a speaker. Anyone else there that wants to say hi?"

"No one else is with us right now," I stressed that last part. "But we didn't come alone. We came with backup."

"For what?"

"To take out the Prince, what the hell else?"

"Girl, you and that tone. Watch it," David warned.

For some reason, the scolding made me grin, because it was so . . . so David. "Sorry."

There was a heavy sigh on the other end. "I didn't know about the Arizona thing. I'm guessing that was Kyle. And I'm guessing that's why I haven't heard from him."

I could feel Ren's stare on me. "We want to meet and talk."

"Why should I think this isn't a trap on your end?"

"Because if I was working for the Prince, I wouldn't be worried about trapping the Order. I'd be pregnant and staying as far away from you people as possible."

"You people?" He barked out a laugh. "Thought you were one of us?"

"I will always be a part of the Order, but I figured after everything, that wasn't an option anymore," I admitted. "We're on the same side, David. It doesn't matter that I'm a halfling. That, I swear."

David was quiet for so long that I started to worry that he'd hung up, but then he said, "Fine. We'll meet at eleven tonight, down in the Gaslamp Quarter, across from the Convention Center. I'll be by the sign."

He hung up then, and I stared at the phone for several seconds before I spoke. "Well, I guess that went okay?"

THE HOUSE IN Del Mar wasn't really a house.

It was a freaking mansion—a sandstone, palatial mansion that sat on a cliff overlooking the Pacific Ocean, smack dab in the Torrey Pines State Reserve.

I'd never seen anything like it. Ever.

"Why don't we live in something like *this*?" Tink asked, lugging his suitcase up the wide steps.

Before I could answer, Fabian was by Tink's side. "Where I live, it would put this place to shame."

Tink's eyes widened. "Do you have Amazon Prime?"

"Of course." Fabian smiled.

Tink looked over at me. "I'm moving."

"Uh-huh," I murmured, way too distracted by the house and the upcoming meeting.

Faye was up ahead, opening the double doors. The inside was just as stunning. A large atrium and an elegant spiral staircase greeted us.

"I'm calling dibs on the bedroom!" Tink raced past us, carrying his luggage against his chest. His Wonder Woman backpack thumped off his side.

"Is he always like that?" Fabian asked, staring up at where Tink was already disappearing down the hall.

Kalen snorted as he walked by with his black duffel bag in hand. It was the first noise he'd made since we'd gotten in the car.

"Pretty much," I said to the Summer Prince.

"I like it." He tilted his head to the side. "His thirst for life is . . . infectious."

"You call it a thirst for life, I call it a hyperactivity disorder." Ren stepped in, carrying our bags.

Fabian lifted a shoulder in response.

I eyed him closely. "Are you into Tink—like, really into him?"

The Summer Prince twisted at the waist, facing me. "If you are worried that I will somehow harm or hurt him, you have nothing to fear."

That wasn't exactly the answer I was looking for. "Tink is like a brother to me—a really weird, often annoying, brother. I know you said you won't hurt him, but if you do, I will find a way to end you. And it won't be pleasant."

Fabian grinned. "Oddly, I am starting to like you."

I frowned, thinking that was a weird response. "All righty then."

Ren was smiling when I turned to him. I had no idea what to say about Fabian, who was climbing the staircase, in search of a room or Tink or both.

Walking over to us, Faye worked a key off the ring and handed it over to me. "You have a few hours before you have to leave for your meeting."

Ren nodded. "I need a shower and a power nap."

"I still don't like the idea of you guys going there by yourselves," Faye said, crossing her arms. "I don't like it at all."

"We're not going by ourselves," I reminded her. "You and Kalen are going to come, but you're not going to be seen."

Ren and I were not foolish enough to go without any backup. Just like I knew David wouldn't.

"I know, but not being seen means we may not have a lot of time to react," she argued.

Kalen joined us, his eyes shadowed. "If any Order member even looks at you two in a way I don't like, they're done for."

"Well, David is probably going to look at me in a way you don't like. He looks at everyone in a bad kind of way," I explained. "I really don't think David is going to do anything."

At least, I hoped not.

"He better not," Kalen said.

Maybe Kalen should stay behind, but he'd pivoted around and stalked off, disappearing into the massive house.

"You think he's going to be okay with this?" Ren asked, thinking along the same lines as me. "This is going to be risky enough without either side jumping the gun."

Faye sighed as she pushed her hair back from her face. "He will be."

"He was really close to Dane, wasn't he?" I asked.

She nodded. "He was, but we . . . we all knew what we were signing up for when we left." She lifted her chin, but her lower lip trembled. "There is no greater honor than dying for what is right, for the Summer Court, and for mankind." Her voice cracked a little. "Now if you'll excuse me."

"Yeah," I whispered, wishing there was more I could say.

Ren nudged me with his arm. "Let's go find a room."

That's what we did, and it was a nice room at the end of the hall on the second floor. One whole wall was glass and faced the ocean. In an hour, the sun would set over the ocean, and I . . . I wanted to see that.

I needed to see that.

"Wow." Ren dropped our bags on the bench in front of the bed. "This room is insane—the house is insane."

"It is." My gaze got snagged on the huge king size bed. "Do you think Tanner knows who lives here?"

"I would have to think so. I mean, renting a place like this would cost a fortune." Ren eyed the huge TV mounted directly across from the bed. "Did Fabian say he had a place like this? I might try to move in with him, too."

"Shut up." I actually missed my apartment. Tink had told me the rent had been paid, so my place was still there. Thank God.

"I'm going to hop in the shower." Ren grinned. "Want to join me?"

I'd love nothing more than to do that, but my head was in way too many places. "I think I'm going to check out the beach."

One side of his lips kicked up. "I'll miss you."

I laughed. "Well, at least I won't be hogging all the water."

"True." He extended a hand toward me. "Come here for a sec."

I went to him, putting my hand into his. He pulled me to his chest, folding his arms around me as he held me tight to his chest. Ren didn't say anything as he tilted his head down and I lifted mine up. He didn't need to. Everything he felt was in that kiss, and it was probably a good thing that I wasn't joining him for the shower, because he would definitely not be getting any rest afterward.

"I won't be long," I promised him.

He brushed his lips over my forehead. "Be careful."

"Always."

Leaving the room, I backtracked my way downstairs and managed to find the back door that led out onto a veranda . . . that led to a massive pool. Like bigger than the one at Hotel Good Fae.

My cheeks flushed, because I immediately thought about what Ren and I had done in that pool.

I was probably never going to be able to look at a pool the same again.

Reaching the end of the patio, I saw the path that led down to the beach. I toed my boots and socks off and then rolled up my pant legs. It didn't take very long to make my way down the steep trail. I stopped, exhaling roughly as my toes sank into the cool sand.

The temps were chillier than I expected and it probably had to do with the Winter Prince being here, but the golden tipped waves and sand were still absolutely beautiful.

I walked out across the beach, nearing the lapping shoreline I reached up and tugged my hair down, letting the wind sift through the curls.

The cool water teased my toes, and for a moment, I let my head empty of all the stresses, the worries, and the fears. I didn't want to think about or feel anything other than what I was witnessing.

The water turned a fiery orange as the sun kissed the ocean. There was a moment where it looked like the world was about to be set ablaze, where the water and sky was a stunning array of reds and blues, and then the sun was gone, slipping far beyond where the eye could see.

The breath I took was shaky and the back of my eyes burned. I never thought I'd see the sunset on the Pacific Coast, and it was truly a sight.

I stepped back, making my way until I was sure the waves wouldn't touch me, and then I sat down in the sand, mindful of the daggers still attached to my thighs.

I had no idea how much time had passed as I sat there, but stars blanketed the sky and it was so quiet, so peaceful with the only sound the crashing waves and distant traffic.

Tonight could go well. David could believe us, and together we could find the Prince, hopefully stopping him before he got ahold of the Halfling, and then we would either kill Drake or send him back to the Otherworld. Or tonight could go extraordinarily bad. Ren and I could be walking into a trap, one that no matter how fast Kalen and Faye moved, they wouldn't be able to stop.

But tonight had to happen.

A sharp swirl of tingles danced along the nape of my neck. I twisted at the waist, not surprised to see Ren's tall form making his way across the sand.

"You should be resting."

"I was." He neared me. "For about fifteen minutes, and then I looked out the windows and saw you sitting out here."

I'd forgotten there was a view from the bedroom. "Ren, we have a long night ahead of us. I got to sleep on and off on the road."

"I know." He sat behind me, spreading his legs on either side of me. Circling his arms around my waist, he pulled me back against his chest. "When I saw you out here, I thought to myself, I could leave her alone, but then I was like, I don't want to."

I laughed as I relaxed into his embrace.

Ren was quiet for a few moments. "It's beautiful out here."

"It is. You should've seen the sunset. It was . . . amazing."

"Would you live out here?"

I started to respond like I would've a handful of months ago, but I realized that mine, that our, circumstances weren't the same. "I really like New Orleans, but there's something about this that's just as good. I could live out here."

"Me too," he replied. "Then again, I'd be willing to live wherever you went, even if it was Alaska."

"Really? Alaska?"

"Even Alaska."

I laughed again. "You don't have to worry about me ever picking Alaska."

Ren kissed my cheek. "Thank God."

My smile faded from my lips. "Are you nervous about tonight?"

"Be stupid not to be."

"True."

Ren was quiet for a very long time and then he said, "I know."

My breath caught. Instinct told me what I needed to

know without asking. He was talking about Kyle, and I didn't know what to say. It wasn't like I thought Ren would never find out, but I hoped I'd make it twenty-four hours before he did.

"I'm sorry," I said finally. "I couldn't let you do it. I couldn't do it, but he could not live. He would come after you—"

"Don't apologize."

I started to turn in his embrace. "But I should, because I didn't tell you. I should've—'"

"I know why you didn't tell me." His voice held a rough edge. "Wanting to leave him alive was foolish."

"It wasn't." I drew in a shallow breath. "And it was. I mean, I get why you wanted to let him live. Maybe it would prove to the other members we hadn't betrayed them, but he would've kept coming after us. He would get more of us killed."

"You're right. And it would've been me to put him down. That son of a bitch would've made sure of it, because he knew—yeah, he knew it would get to me."

"That's why I couldn't let that happen," I admitted quietly.

He was silent for a moment. "You made sure that I didn't . . . I didn't have to carry his death on my shoulders. Thank you." He curled a hand around my chin, tipping my head back. He kissed me. "Thank you, Sweetness."

I really had no idea what to say to that. None whatsoever. But then Ren tightened his arms around me again and held me tight, blocking out the coolness in the air.

Right then and there, I sent a prayer up to whatever god or gods were listening that this meeting with David went the way we needed it to and that it wasn't a trap.

Because if it was, I didn't plan on dying tonight. I didn't

plan on seeing Ren or Faye or Kalen die tonight. That meant we'd be doing the killing, and I didn't want that either.

But I would if I had to.

Chapter 27

Ren and I arrived in the Gaslamp District of San Diego thirty minutes before we were scheduled to arrive so we could scope out the area. Faye and Kalen were also with us. We couldn't see them, but we knew they were there. All of us were armed, but our weapons were well hidden.

I immediately understood why David had picked this place. It was out in the open and teeming with people. The bar and restaurant-lined streets reminded me of the French Quarter.

"Would've been cool to check some of these places out," I said, happy when I smelled charbroiled hamburgers and my stomach didn't revolt.

Ren's hand tightened around mine. "We should come back when this is all over. We could use a vacation."

I smiled, liking the sound of that—the idea of making plans. It made me feel like there was a future to look forward to. I started to tell him that, but Ren spoke again.

"There." He cursed under his breath as he pulled me to the side, out of the middle of the sidewalk. "David is already here. And he's not alone."

"What?" I was not at all surprised that David had done just what we had, which was to arrive early as an attempt to control the situation. I followed Ren's gaze, and it took me a moment to find David.

He was sitting in the center of a bench, his arms hooked around the back and his long legs stretched out, crossed at the ankles. To a stranger, he looked like a normal guy, out enjoying the cool night. Behind him was Miles Daily, the man in charge if David was to go down.

My shoulders tightened. I never knew where I stood with Miles. He was older than me, maybe in his thirties, and completely unreadable.

"Can't blame him for not coming alone," Ren said. "And I doubt they are the only two here."

I scanned the little park area, but just because I didn't see any familiar faces didn't mean that every person and every couple I saw wasn't an Order member. They could have us surrounded by the dozens, and we wouldn't know since we didn't know any of the San Diego members.

Looking up at Ren, I squeezed his hand. "You ready?" I asked.

My gaze trained on where David sat as he nodded. I stretched up and kissed his lips. "Let's do this."

Ren let go of my hand as we crossed the street. My heart was thumping in my chest. I doubted that they'd try something in such a public spot, but I'd been wrong before.

"Hey," Ren spoke first, hopping up on the sidewalk. "Long time no see."

David and Miles looked up and over, but I knew that they had been aware of our approach before that moment. "You guys are early," David said.

"So are you," I replied.

"Thought you were coming by yourself." Ren's gaze

flickered over David's second in command. "How are you doing, Miles?"

Miles lifted his chin. "Can't complain."

If both of them were here, I wondered who was running the New Orleans branch. I was about to ask that when I stepped under the street lamp, but I didn't get the chance.

The men saw me, like, really saw me.

David's lazy sprawl changed in an instant. He pulled his legs up and sat straight, his eyes widening. For the first time in my life, I saw a reaction in Miles. His mouth dropped open as his gaze flicked over my face.

"You should see the ears," I said, having left my hair down.

Miles snapped his jaw shut.

"What in the hell?" David exclaimed. He looked like he was about to stand, but couldn't move.

Ren started to step in front of me, but I lifted my arm, stopping him.

"I look different. I know. It's a long story."

David stood then and took a step toward me. I could feel Ren tensing. "How?" David asked, voice gruff. "How is this possible? You couldn't have gotten—"

"It's more of a recent thing." I was starting to feel a little uncomfortable with their intense scrutiny. "And I will tell you everything, but I think . . ." I glanced over at Ren, who looked like he was seconds from making sure they were staring at someone or something else. "I think we should start at the beginning."

"Yeah." Miles' expression smoothed out, becoming unreadable. "I think you need to do that."

So that's what Ren and I did. We told them everything, starting with how I figured out I was the Halfling, how the Prince was able to capture Ren and me, and how we escaped.

I even told them about the forced feedings and that it was a fae who had helped me escape. We told them how I had been attacked and how I had been healed.

It was Ren who explained that in a low voice. "I made the choice. It wasn't Ivy's. If it was, she would've never agreed to it and she wouldn't be here right now."

David looked somewhat awed when he sat back down while Miles had no change in his expression at all.

"He saved my life—feeding saved my life." I shifted my weight from one foot to the other. "I wasn't okay with it. Ren was right. I wouldn't have agreed to it, and I was pissed at him, but I would've done the same thing to save his life. That's why I . . . I look the way I do now. It made the part of me that is halfling stronger, but I'm still Ivy." I lifted my chin as I said the last words. "Who I am hasn't changed."

"Kind of hard to believe that when I'm looking at you, seeing that you've changed," Miles said.

"Just because she looks more beautiful than she did before, doesn't mean she isn't still the kickass Ivy out there fighting the good fight," Ren interjected.

There was a good chance I fell in love with him even more in that moment.

Miles tilted his head to the side, his brows snapping together.

"You all have no idea what we've been through to get where we are standing right now. No idea," Ren continued, his voice hardening. "And if we were really working with the Prince or against the Order, we wouldn't be standing here. Do not question my loyalty and you better not question hers."

"Is that everything?" David asked, sounding wary.

"It is," Ren answered.

Kind of. We'd told them everything—everything except

for where the Summer Court was and that they had come with us. I also hadn't told them about Tink.

"Why didn't you contact me—contact us?" Anger seeped into David's voice. "We had people out there looking for you. Both of you. For weeks, until we assumed you were both dead—"

"Or that we had betrayed the Order," I finished for him. "We did neither of those things, but it was too risky to contact you. I was still healing and my head . . ." Drawing in a shuddering breath, I tried again. "I wasn't ready to talk to you, or to anyone."

David's gaze met mine for a brief moment and then he looked away.

"What about Kyle?" Miles asked. "David mentioned that you ran into him on the way here. We haven't heard from him."

"He's dead." I was the one who answered. "He tried to kill us, and if he was alive, he'd have kept trying to kill us. So, he's dead—a dead liar."

"Bold words," David murmured.

"True words." I waited until a young couple passed us. "Do you know how the Elite and the Order once closed the gates?"

Miles didn't answer. Neither did David. "I know that the Order once worked with the fae to close the gates. That was how you all got your hands on the Crystal, and I know that the Elite betrayed those fae—the fae who did not hunt mortals—the fae who hunted others of their kind that did." I didn't mistake the sharp inhale. "Kyle said it was the Elite that turned on them, but there was no way that the Order didn't know. I know that was before all of our time and the stories have changed over the years, but I'm alive because of good fae."

"It's hard to think that such a creature exists," Miles commented.

"You'd be surprised"—Ren pinned him with a stare—"by what you once thought was true. I was trained in the Elite. I know I was trained with a lot of lies."

"And that statement is damn near treasonous." Miles stepped around the bench. "You do realize that."

"Still the truth." I kept an eye on him. "The Order knew that there were good fae before—that the fae had helped us. Why were we never told that?"

"The treaty between our kinds was so long ago it no longer mattered how it used to be," David said. "If I remember correctly, it was the Summer Court who helped us once upon a time, and after the gates were closed, there was no more Summer Court. It would've been too dangerous for our members if they knew that maybe—just maybe—there were fae out there that didn't want to harm them or other mortals. Each time they'd hesitate to determine if the fae they were dealing with meant them harm, they'd be vulnerable to attack."

"I understand that, but we should've known." My hands closed into fists. "They were there, always there. They could've been helping us this entire time."

"They could've. And many more of our members would've died trying to decipher which fae were good and which were bad," David reasoned. "And you're forgetting that we had no reason to believe that these Summer fae were still here. We were told that they were all killed."

"Slaughtered would've been a better word." I got what David was saying. It even made sense, but it didn't make it okay, and we were all going to have to move past it if we had any hope of defeating the Prince. "We can stand here all night and argue about who are the bigger betrayers, and while we do that, I'm guessing the Prince gets one step closer to the Halfling that's in San Diego."

"Because that's why you're still here, right? If you all had found the Halfling, you would have killed her and then we wouldn't be having this conversation." Ren lifted his chin. "We're here to stop the Prince, just like you are."

"We know how to send him back to the Otherworld," I said, and that got their attention. "He has the Crystal. We know there is a ritual that will seal him back in the Otherworld. And if we can't get the Crystal and complete the ritual, then we'll kill him. Since we have no idea how to weaken the bastard enough to get him with the thorn stake or to, you know, decapitate him, we're going to need the Order's help."

"We're going to need all the help we can get," Ren affirmed. "We need to work together, and then afterward, you can kick us out of the Order. Exile us. Whatever. But right now, we need to get past all of that."

"I know it's asking a lot," I said. "But I'm asking you to believe what we're telling you."

David's mouth tightened and then he exhaled heavily as his gaze met mine. "I've known you for years, girl. Known that you've made a lot of bad and dumb decisions."

Um.

"You're often reckless and impulsive," he continued, and I really wasn't sure where this list of my glaring flaws was leading. "But I've never known you to be a traitor. I believe you."

Relief hit me so hard I almost fell over. I looked over at Ren and saw that his shoulders had loosened. "Thank you," I said, because it was all I could say. "And you?"

"The jury is still out on that," Miles answered after a heartbeat. "But you two are right. We need everyone we can get to stop the Prince. We need to work together. All of us."

"Then what's next?" Ren placed a hand on my lower back.

David stood. "We plan."

"Now is not the time. Out in the open like this." Miles crossed his arms. "The San Diego branch has us set up in one of their homes on the harbor. We can meet—all of us. That means whoever you've come with."

"We've come with fae," Ren answered. "Are you sure these Order members are going to be cool with that? The Elite?"

"Cool with seeing me?" I pushed.

"We will make them okay," David promised. "We all need to set a lot of things aside if we hope to stop the Prince from succeeding."

I glanced at Ren.

He nodded. "Tell us when and where."

Chapter 28

The house in Del Mar was quiet when we returned to it. We'd already filled Faye and Kalen in on everything, but we couldn't find Fabian or Tink. Well, we really didn't look that hard, figuring they were holed up in one of the many bedrooms.

Ren had stopped me when I headed for the stairs, grabbing ahold of my hand and pulling me toward the back of the house, stopping to grab a soft looking blanket off the back of the couch. He'd led me out onto the veranda surrounding the pool, to one of the comfy looking chaise lounges.

So that's where we found ourselves after our meeting with David and Miles, our daggers on the table, within reach, and our shoes tucked under the chair. I was lying on my side, between his legs, and nestled against his chest. The blanket was draped over us, and we both were staring up at the stars blanketing the night sky, the low whoosh of moving waves a comforting, lulling sound.

I was glad that he'd brought me out here. There was something so normal about this that I wished I had the ability to slow down time and make the time out here last forever.

"Yeah," Ren said finally, his fingers idly moving through my hair. "I think I could live here."

A grin tugged at my lips. "Especially if we had this house and view."

"True," he murmured. "But all I'd need is to be able to see the stars and have you right here, like you are right now."

The grin turned into a smile. "There you go, always saying the right thing."

His arm tightened around me. "I don't always say the right thing. I think you know that."

"But when you do, you make up for the stupid stuff that comes out of your mouth."

Ren chuckled as he tugged on a curl. A moment passed. "I think tonight went good."

I closed my eyes. "Yeah."

"You don't sound like you really believe that."

I bit down on my lip as my stomach twisted with nervous energy and something else. The . . . hunger was there, but it was manageable.

He let go of my curl and his fingers drifted over my cheek. "What are you thinking?"

Impulse almost had me saying nothing, but I stopped myself before that bad habit took over. "I . . . I'm wondering if tonight was, you know, too easy. Do you know what I mean? I could just be paranoid—"

"No. You're not being paranoid. All things considered, it was easy."

I tilted my head so I could look up at him. "Do you think it's a trap?"

Silvery moonlight cut across his cheekbones. "It could be, but we're going to be prepared if so."

We would be, but I kept replaying David's reaction to

me over and over in my head. Both him and Miles had been shocked, but I'd expected more of a fight to convince them that we hadn't betrayed them.

But David knew me. He might not know Ren all that well, but he knew who I was at the core. "Thank God David is still here. If he wasn't, I don't think we'd be able to convince Miles."

"I have no idea how to read that guy," he admitted.

"Don't feel bad. I've known him for years and I still can't." Snuggling back down against his chest, I folded my hand against his side. My stomach started to settle, but my mind was nowhere near that. "I'm . . . I'm hungry."

"I'm sure there's food. . . ." Ren trailed off. "You're not talking about food, are you?"

"No," I whispered, my hand curling around his shirt. Shame burned at the back of my throat.

Ren's fingers kept moving along my cheek. "Is there anything I can do to help?"

I swallowed down the sudden knot in my throat and closed my eyes again. "I don't think so. It's really not that bad. The . . . feeling is fading. I just—I don't know. I just wanted to say it out loud."

The arm at my waist somehow got tighter. "I'm glad you did. I just wish there was something I could do to make it easier for you."

Some of the tension eased out of my muscles as the shame faded off. Ren wasn't bothered by it. At least not enough to have any measurable reaction to it. I don't know how I was expecting Ren to respond, but him not freaking out and just being, well, Ren did more than he knew. "You're doing it right now. Helping me."

"I'm glad to hear that even though it doesn't feel like I'm doing much."

"You're doing everything." I squeezed his side, letting out a sigh. I needed to refocus. "So, let's say that our next meeting isn't a trap. We find the Halfling before the Prince does, we still need to find the Crystal or we need to figure out how to weaken him enough to kill him. Finding the Halfling before he does is just a small step in the right direction."

"But it's a step." Ren fell quiet and several minutes past before he spoke again. "There's something none of us have really talked about."

"What?"

"The ritual." Tension crept into his body. "I'd asked Tanner and Faye about it. Even Merle. None of them had any details on exactly how we're supposed to complete the ritual safely."

"You mean, how I'm supposed to get the Prince's blood and mine on the Crystal while in the Otherworld?" I placed my hand on his arm.

"Yeah. I don't like the idea of this ritual, Ivy. No one is talking about it, and you have to be in the Otherworld to complete it?" His hand curled around the back of my head, his fingers tangling in my hair. "I don't need to know a lot to know that there is a metric shit ton that can go wrong with that."

A shudder worked its way through me. "Yeah, like . . . getting trapped in the Otherworld."

"That will not happen." His voice was hard.

I wanted to believe that. I had to believe that, because if I didn't, the mere idea of being trapped in the Otherworld with a very pissed off Prince terrified me. But we didn't have enough information on this ritual, like how much time I'd have between starting it and getting back through the doorway.

There was a tiny part of me, though, that was curious

about the possibility of seeing the Otherworld, even if it was only for a handful of seconds.

"I think you're onto something about finding out a way to weaken the Prince," Ren said. "Fighting him will be dangerous, but it's not as big of a risk as the ritual. We just need to find out how."

Unless Fabian was going to start talking, I wasn't sure how we would find out. It was beginning to feel like we didn't have a choice on how this was going to go down.

That was if we even made it to the point where we did have one.

"AND YOU THINK this is wise?" Fabian asked the following morning over breakfast. We were sitting at an island large enough to seat ten people. "That they can be trusted?"

"As much as we can be trusted." I peeled the skin from a banana. "They're taking a risk meeting us, too."

"But there are more of them than us," Kalen said, repeating what he'd said last night.

"But we have a Summer Prince." Ren dropped onto the bar stool beside me. "Pretty sure that he can take out a dozen of them in about five seconds if things go south."

I arched a brow as I munched down on my banana. "Let's hope it doesn't come to that."

Fabian inclined his head. "Did they tell you anything about the Winter Prince or the Halfling?"

"Not yet. I'm hoping they fill us in today with good—" Something out of the corner of my eye caught my attention. I turned.

Holy crap.

I lowered the banana as Tink buzzed into the room—twelve-inch-tall Tink with gossamer wings. My mouth dropped open. Ren followed my gaze, and he made a choked sound. It had been so long since I'd seen him in this form that I forgot whatever it was I had been talking about.

He flew across the kitchen, his wings moving silently, but everyone was staring. Faye looked like she was going to slip off the stool while Kalen was actually—wow, he was actually starting to grin.

The brownie was wearing dark trousers, but he was shirtless and shoeless as he buzzed up around the pocket light then came back down.

"Tink." My eyes widened as he hovered over Fabian's shoulder. "You're . . . Tink sized."

"Heard we'd be taking a field trip this morning. Figured I'm too cute to kill in this form." He landed on the Summer Prince's broad shoulder. "Plus, I'm less intimidating this way. That's why Ren didn't kill me at first."

"That is not why I didn't kill you at first," Ren replied dryly.

I watched Tink sit down on Fabian's shoulder.

Kalen looked over at Faye and then back to Tink again. "I've never seen a brownie in this form."

"You've never seen a brownie before me at all," Tink pointed out as he kicked his feet off Fabian's upper chest. "So which way do you like me better? Big or small?"

My brows furrowed.

"I think . . . this way," Kalen answered. "Yeah. Like this."

"Not me," murmured the Summer Prince.

Tink leaned over and grabbed a chunk of the Prince's hair. He pulled it back and whispered something in Fabian's ear that earned him a deep laugh.

I really didn't want to know what it was.

I finished off the banana, and then it was time to leave. Sliding off the stool, I followed Ren out into the foyer. Tink left Fabian's shoulder and flew over to mine. He landed, balancing himself with a hand against my head.

"I'm excited to meet these Order members." He shifted closer to my head.

"Why?"

"Because I cannot wait to see their faces when they get a look at me!" His laugh was more of a childish giggle. "They are going to freak."

A grin tugged at my lips. "They probably will. So, I want you to stay close to either me or Fabian, okay? At least, at first."

"Of course—oh!" He turned on my shoulder, yelling as I neared the door. I winced. "Fabian, don't forget my suitcase!"

Ren pivoted around. "Your suitcase?"

"Yes. It's Plan B."

"We have a Plan B that involves your suitcase?" he asked.

"We do." Tink launched off my shoulder and landed on the suitcase Fabian was not rolling out.

I stopped as Faye and Kalen headed outside. "Uh, maybe you should tell us what's in the suitcase, Tink?"

"My stuff." He held on to the handle as Fabian rolled him and the suitcase out the front door. Tink waved a little hand at me. "My *friends*."

"What do you mean by your friends?" I hurried after them, into the bright sun. "Tink!"

"It's okay." He flew off the luggage, and the Prince lifted it, placing it into the back of the SUV. "Don't worry about it, Ivy-divy."

But I was worried, really worried, because I had no idea what in the hell he had in that suitcase. I started after him, but Faye stepped in front of me.

Her pale blue eyes were full of restrained worry. "I know

you trust these people, but if we're walking into a trap—"

"If we're walking into a trap, then we fight. I hope that's not the case, but we don't have any other options. We need their help."

Sighing, she looked away. "We do."

I really hoped Ren and I were correct. That we weren't going to regret this, but we were already in too deep and there was no stopping now.

Kalen got behind the wheel with Faye in the passenger seat. Ren and I took the middle row, and the Summer Prince took the back seat. Tink buzzed back and forth between our row and Fabian's, serving as a complete distraction as we made our way toward the harbor and to the home.

"I think this is it," Kalen announced. "But it's not a house."

I leaned over Ren to peer out the side window. Kalen was right. The address had led us to what was either a condo or an apartment building on Ocean Front Walk. The building was three stories tall.

"It's the right place." Ren tapped his finger off the window, pointing out what appeared to be a fenced patio around the lower level.

Several men were standing outside. They weren't dressed like they were about to walk to the sandy dunes. Sunglasses shielded their eyes, and their jeans and loose shirts did nothing to hide the daggers I knew they were carrying.

I was willing to bet that railing and fence was all iron.

My heart rate sped up as I sat back. Was this whole apartment building Order controlled?

Ren reached over, squeezing my knee as Kalen pulled into one of the parking spots. "Let's do this."

I turned to where Tink was, which was now on the seat beside the Prince. "Is your backpack still in here? The

Wonder Woman one?"

His little brow puckered. "Yes, actually. It's in the back."

"Okay. I want you to get into it."

Tink's nose wrinkled. "But I'll suffocate!"

I rolled my eyes. "I'm not going to zip it all the way closed. I think it's just smart if you stay unseen at first."

"Fine. Whatever. But if I suffocate, I'll come back and haunt you for the rest of your life."

Ignoring that, I looked at Fabian. "Can you grab the backpack for me? Please?"

"Wow. You said please." The Summer Prince twisted at the waist. "That must've hurt your soul."

"It did," I muttered and waited for Tink to get in the bag. He made a show of it, of course. Stomping the whole way and moaning as Fabian zipped it up, leaving a couple inch gap at the top.

I took the bag, surprised by how heavy it was.

"There's David." Ren nodded toward the window. "We'll get out first and then the rest of you, okay?"

They agreed, and when I looked back at Fabian, he nodded. Ren climbed out, and I followed, slipping out the same door. Once standing, I slipped the bag onto my back.

A second later a tiny fist landed in the center of my back. I grunted and turned my head, whispering, "Knock it off, Tink."

"It's hot in heeereee," whined Tink.

"Shut up," I hissed, wondering if we should've left him back at the house as David stepped away from the glass patio doors.

David nodded at Ren, but like the other Order members standing on the patio, they were still staring at the SUV. "Who's in the car?" he asked.

"They are fae." I ignored the swift kick in my kidney.

"Our friends. They are taking a huge risk by coming here."

"And we're taking a huge risk by receiving them."

I scanned the Order members, seeing the exact moment they realized my skin had a silvery tint to it. I ignored it.

Ren turned, motioning for the rest to join us. "This is Kalen and Faye, of the Summer Court. They helped us—have been helping us."

A muscle thrummed along David's jaw as the two fae slowly approached us. He didn't speak. They got a curt nod from him, which was returned by the two fae.

"Hol-lee shit," another Order member whispered, and that was when I knew that Fabian was now visible.

Fabian strolled toward them like he was out for an early morning walk. The breeze lifted his blond hair as he stepped around the iron railing.

"This is Fabian," I said. "*Prince* Fabian of the Summer Court."

The audible gasp wasn't lost on me. Neither was the stiffening of the Order members. Or the way some reached for their hidden daggers. Ren stepped closer to Fabian, but the Summer Prince simply smiled.

"You were not expecting royalty, were you?" Fabian tilted his head.

David slid me a long look. "No, we were not."

I lifted a shoulder in a shrug.

"You should understand one thing, and one thing only." Fabian stepped closer, and I swore you couldn't even hear the traffic in that moment. "If you threaten any of us, I can kill every single one of you before you even know what hit you. I do not want that to happen. I want us to work together, like we did before, but test me and you will not survive the consequences."

Tink banged his fist off my back in what I guessed was

agreement.

Well, that probably wasn't what David wanted to hear, but he clipped out, "Duly noted." David stepped forward, going toe to toe with the Summer Prince. "And if any of you harm any of our members, we will spend our dying breaths killing every single one of you."

Fabian's smile spread. "*Duly noted.*"

"All right then." Ren clapped his hands together. "Now that we have that settled, can we get on with this?"

David smirked. "Follow me."

The Summer Prince arched a brow at the men and then trailed after David, following him through the patio doors. Ren went next, and then Faye and Kalen. I took up the back.

"Nice backpack," one of the Order members snorted as I walked by.

I turned. "It is, isn't it?"

I got another kick in the back, and I swore when this was over, I was going to flush Tink down a toilet.

Stepping through the patio, I immediately realized this was no normal apartment building. It only looked that way from the outside.

A narrow hall led to a wide-open space that I assumed was a large meeting room, one that reminded me of the headquarters in the Quarter. A large map of what I was guessing was San Diego and the surrounding cities was hanging on the wall. There were several cafeteria style tables with benches, and at least three dozen Order members.

All of them were standing, staring at the five of us.

Most of their stares showed open hostility. Only a few appeared curious. I saw Miles standing beside a tall, dark-skinned woman, whose expression was almost as unreadable as his.

"These people look friendly," Ren said under his breath.

"Right?" I whispered back.

David made a quick round of introductions, and when he got to the woman, I learned that her name was Liz, and she ran the San Diego branch of the Order.

"We've been told that we are all fighting on the same side," she said, crossing her arms. "As you can imagine, it is hard for us to accept that."

"Just as it's hard for us to accept the same from the Order," Faye replied, standing beside Kalen. "But we're all here."

"We are." Liz lifted a hand. The Order members sat as her gaze found me. "So, you're the Halfling?"

I lifted my chin. "I am. Most call me Ivy, though."

She ignored that. "And you're the one the Prince held captive but escaped?"

I nodded.

She inclined her head, and I guessed that was some kind of 'good job' nod. "What is in your backpack?"

Tink stopped shimmying around, and Fabian turned to me. "My . . . my friend is in this bag."

David lifted his brows. "Your friend?"

"Yes."

"You have a friend in a backpack?" he persisted.

Ren pressed his lips together.

"Yeah." Carefully, I let the bag slide off my arm. I knelt and placed it on the floor. I reached for the space between the zippers, and felt a nip of pain. I jerked my hand back.

Tink bit my finger!

That little bastard!

"Behave," I warned, shaking the sting out of my hand.

A soft laugh came from inside the bag.

"What in the hell?" David stepped forward. "What's in your bag, Ivy?"

"A pain in my ass," I muttered as I unzipped it. "Come on out."

Several Order members stood while others tried to see over those standing. Sighing, I straightened as one tiny hand came out of the bag, curling around the material and then another.

Liz's eyes narrowed. "What is . . . ?"

Spiky, icy blond hair appeared, and then a forehead, followed by two big round eyes. Then, because Tink knew everyone was watching, he slowly lifted his wings so they became visible.

Someone cursed.

Liz's mouth dropped open, but she didn't speak.

"Is that . . ." David trailed off as Tink lifted a hand and wiggled his fingers.

"Such a showboat." Ren sighed, folding his arms.

I fought a grin. "This is Tink. He is a . . . well, he's a brownie."

"A brownie?" Liz shook her head. "They're in our world?"

"No. Just Tink."

Tink took that moment to fly out of the bag and zip up to my shoulder. He landed there, picking up my hair and . . . hiding behind it.

I resisted the urge to roll my eyes. "Anyway, he was in my bag. He's a . . . shy little guy."

Ren made a choking sound.

"You have a brownie?" Miles blinked rapidly. "I thought they were—"

"All killed off by the Winter Court?" Fabian answered for him. "Nearly all of them were. Tink is the only one of his kind in this world."

Tink peeked around my head as he balled his fists into my hair and whispered, "I look adorable, don't I?"

"Something like that." I cleared my throat. "I'd like to tell you one day about how I met Tink."

A glimpse of wonder snuck into Liz's expression. "I would very much like to hear that story."

I smiled at that. "But we need to talk about the Prince and the Halfling."

"That we do." Liz watched Tink move to my other shoulder, the look of incredulity still filling her expression. She gave a little shake of her head. "We have not been able to discover who the Halfling is, but we know where the Prince is. As far as we know, he has not made contact with the Halfling."

I was too realistic to let hope take flight. Just because they didn't think the Prince had gotten with the Halfling yet didn't mean it hadn't happened. "And where is the Prince?"

"He's been holed up in one of the resorts," Miles answered. "The Valencia."

Never heard of it, but I was betting it was nice. Sounded like it was.

"And how many fae does he have with him?" Kalen asked.

"About a dozen that came with him," Liz answered. "But he has more. The fae here have been gathering at the resort."

"The Order has not gone after him?" Fabian frowned.

"There are humans at the resort. Too many who would get caught in the crossfire. It would draw a lot of attention. And the twelve fae he brought with him are Knights." Liz's jaw hardened. "The Order is brave and we are willing to die for our cause, but not foolishly."

"And why do you believe he hasn't met with the Halfling?" Ren asked.

"We lucked out when he left New Orleans. He was seen and we were able to follow," Miles explained.

One of the Order members who was over by the tables

answered. He'd been introduced when we first walked in. Pretty sure his name was Rob. "We were able to track him once he entered the city from the license plates of those who traveled with him. He arrived at the resort, and we've had eyes on him the entire time. He hasn't left once."

Something . . . something about this wasn't making sense.

"Two of his Knights have come and gone, appearing to be running errands." Liz walked up to the map, pointing to a black pushpin. "This is where the resort is. We're thinking that the Halfling is somewhere in this area."

A weird chill curled its way down my spine as I looked over at Ren and then Fabian while Tink hung on to my hair. The Summer Prince had said his people became aware that Drake had left New Orleans. Marlon had told us where Drake had gone, and meanwhile, the Order had seen the Prince leave.

That was . . . that was too many coincidences or sloppy work on the Prince's behalf. The latter was hard to believe since Drake had managed to go unseen this entire time, setting up a base camp just outside of New Orleans without the Order ever discovering his location. But now? Everyone in their mother had seen him.

I didn't like this—didn't like this at all.

I took a step back.

"What's wrong?" Tink asked, speaking directly into my ear. "Your shoulders are suddenly as tense as a turkey around Thanksgiving."

My brow puckered. "I . . . I don't know."

"They must be aware that you know they are here," Faye spoke, her expression pinched. "And they have to be wondering why you haven't attacked yet."

David nodded as he widened his stance. "I think they believe we are too afraid to do so."

"Is that not the case?" Fabian asked.

"Oooh," Tink murmured.

The New Orleans sect leader narrowed his eyes. "We are not afraid. We're smart. We've been planning."

"What does the plan entail exactly?" Ren asked.

"We know the Prince has the Crystal." Liz turned away from the map. "With the Halfling here, we can complete the ritual and send him back."

Ren stiffened, and suddenly, the fact the Order members were so willing to accept our presence made sense. They had realized they needed us—needed me to send the Prince back, but there was something else that picked away at me.

"This ritual," Miles said. "What is it called?

"Blood and stone," Fabian answered.

"That's right. I've done a bit of reading up on it." Miles' gaze found mine. "Do you know what the ritual is?"

"I know that my blood and the blood of the Prince's must be on the Crystal," I said, wincing as Tink stepped on my hair, pulling it. "And I know it needs to be completed in the Otherworld."

Miles lifted his brows. "But do you know what happens after you complete the ritual?"

"I get the hell out the Otherworld?" I surmised.

Someone snorted, but Miles stepped forward, a slight frown marring his features. "I may not be reading the ritual correctly, but from what I can gather, whosever blood is on that Crystal is trapped in the Otherworld."

Dread exploded in my gut. "What?"

"It will trap both of you in the Otherworld. Not just the Prince." Miles glanced at Fabian. "I'm guessing whomever told you about the ritual forgot to tell you that."

Chapter 29

Stunned, I let my arms fall to my sides. He couldn't be telling the truth. A huge part of me went into denial, because that would mean that they all . . . they all had lied to me.

"No," whispered Tink, and then louder, "that cannot be true." He walked out onto the end of my shoulder. "*No.*"

I couldn't move as things began to click into place. No one had been forthcoming with information about the ritual with Ren. Those who knew about the ritual were readily accepting of the change I'd gone through and trusting me—trusting us.

"What the fuck?" Anger filled Ren's tone as he turned toward Faye and the other Summer fae. "Is that true? Ivy would be trapped in the Otherworld?"

Faye blanched, and I knew right then it was true, and it was like the floor had opened under my feet. My chest hollowed. "It makes sense now."

Ren turned to me. "This isn't making any damn sense."

"But it is." My throat thickened, and I couldn't take my eyes off Faye. "That's why you guys helped me escape and made sure I was safe. It wasn't out of the kindness of your hearts. You needed me—needed me alive unless you found another halfling. One that had a chance of making it to the Otherworld with the Prince and completing the ritual."

David and Miles, along with the San Diego branch looked on in silence. I had no idea what they were thinking.

"You knew that you were needed alive to complete the ritual." Fabian turned toward me. "It has to be the blood of a halfling and the Winter Prince. You must be alive for that to happen."

"No shit," snapped Ren. "We know that. We also know that the ritual has to be completed in the Otherworld. At no point did anyone mention that it would trap her there."

"That *is* a pretty big thing to forget to tell someone," Miles chimed in.

"We didn't forget." Faye faced us, her eyes pleading with us to understand. "We had hoped to find a way to ensure that you would not be trapped there."

A choked laugh escaped me. "You hoped?"

"This is awkward," Liz murmured under her breath.

"That's it." Ren stalked toward me. "We're out."

"What?" I turned to him, and Tink walked back up my shoulder, placing a hand on the side of my head to steady himself.

"We're done with this shit." His bright green gaze met mine. "So fucking done."

Kalen started toward him. "Ren—"

"Fuck no." He shot the male fae a dangerous look of warning, one Kalen heeded by stopping. "We didn't sign up for this. *Ivy* didn't sign up for this. She's not going to sacrifice herself. Fuck that shit."

Do I have a choice?

That question caused a shiver to course down my spine.

Just as I feared last night, we were left with only one other option. Find a way to weaken the Prince long enough to kill him.

Betrayal mixed with anger as I lifted my chin and stared at the Order members. "Do you all know how to kill the Prince?"

David and Liz exchanged looks. It was her that spoke up. "A thorn stake—"

"We know that a thorn stake will kill him—kill any prince." I looked at Fabian, who arched a brow. "But have you fought a prince? A Knight or an Ancient?"

Liz's lips thinned. "We haven't—"

"Then you don't realize how incredibly hard it is to even fight an Ancient, and that's nothing like facing a prince," I told them. "So, I'm guessing you have no idea how to weaken the Prince."

"We have one standing right in front of us that could answer that question," David pointed out.

"Ivy," Ren said, frustration biting at his tone. "Let's—"

Someone from outside shouted, and I whipped around so fast that Tink left my shoulder and hovered beside me.

The door we'd come through exploded off the hinges. A body flew through the air, hitting the floor with a fleshy smack. It was an Order member, one of the men who'd been outside. His throat . . . God, it was ripped out, exposing tissue.

"Shit." I reached for my daggers. Order members shot from their chairs, and everything I'd just learned faded to the background.

The feeling from earlier came back, the one that screamed all of this, from the moment the Prince left New Orleans to now had been too easy. I knew deep in my bones that this was a trap and all of us had walked right into it.

Another body landed near the other, thrown from deep in the hall.

"We're under siege!" Liz shouted, brandishing weapons. "Prepare!"

"Get back, Tink." My grip tightened on the daggers, and I prayed to God he listened as icy air rolled into the large meeting room, seeping over the floors.

Ren appeared at my side, thorn stake in hand. "This is not good."

"No. It's not."

A roar that shook the walls filled my stomach with knots. A stuttered heartbeat later, they came through the doorway. Kalen cocked his arm, letting the dagger he held fly. It smacked into the chest of the first fae, taking it down, but then another and another came through the narrow opening, until dozens of fae were in the room with us. Most were not normal fae. Most were Ancients—Knights of the Prince.

"Crap," I whispered, stamping down on the bite of fear.

We met them head-on.

Instinct took over as stakes whizzed through the air, some falling, clattering off the dusty floor, and others striking true. Screams and shouts mixed with the wet sound of tearing flesh and cracking bones. It was a whirl of mayhem, and I quickly lost sight of Tink in the crowd of fast-moving bodies.

Ren brought down the nearest fae, moving as fluid and graceful as a dancer. I whipped around, shoving my stake deep into the chest of a fae as Fabian began to glow like the sun. I caught sight of him stalking forward, lifting an arm. A fiery ball of light formed in his hand as David squared off with a Knight.

I started toward them, cut off by a fae who charged me. I danced to the side, my booted foot slipping in something wet—blood. Straightening, I lifted my gaze and saw the female fae coming my way. She darted toward me, but didn't engage. Then it clicked into place. She was *keeping* me from engaging. They weren't trying to fight me. They knew I was the Halfling and that I . . . I needed to be alive, but if there was another halfling, I was disposable.

None of that mattered at the moment.

Rushing toward her, I caught her arm as she tried to sidestep me. She screamed as I twisted, spinning her around. Stabbing the dagger down into her chest, I jerked it back out as I let go of her. She was already folding into herself by the time she hit the floor.

The temperature dropped again and I spun toward the opening as a tall, slender woman stalked into the room. *Breena*. That fucking bitch was here. Every part of my brain clicked off as I prowled toward her. If anyone died today, it would be her. I swore to God and baby llamas everywhere, that bitch was going down.

Another Order member reached her first. It was Rob. He lifted his arm, but she was fast—wicked fast. Her hand flew out and went straight through the man's chest.

My steps skidded to a halt as my mouth dropped open in horror. Wait. That didn't make sense. That wasn't possible.

Breena yanked her hand back, and it was a bloody mess. His heart—she held Rob's *heart*. But Breena wasn't an Ancient. She was just a normal fae. How was that—

My heart lurched into my throat as I saw the Prince. He walked through the door as Breena dropped the mangled organ. Fear and rage spiraled inside me as I stared at the Prince.

His gaze swept the room until those expressive lips curled into a smirk. He had found me.

Drake smiled. "Hello, Ivy. It's been too long."

My body turned to ice as a roar of red-hot rage erupted behind me. Ren. That was Ren causing the tiny hairs all over my body to raise.

Fabian whipped around, shock etched into the one word he spoke, in a language I didn't understand.

The Prince's shoulders tensed as his gaze snapped from mine to the Summer Prince. Some kind of emotion flickered over Drake's face as he stared at the other Prince.

Dear God, they looked so much alike. Like they could be—

"No." Fabian lowered his arm, and a bright glow faded from him as he stumbled—actually stumbled back a step. "No. My eyes are lying to me. It is not you. You're dead."

What in the hell was going on? What was Fabian talking about, and why were they staring at each other like that?

"Ivy! Ivy!" Tink flew near the ceiling, his wings moving frantically as he shrieked my name in a way that caused panic to explode within me. "She's here! She's—"

It happened so fast.

That bitch Breena's head snapped around, her gaze following Tink's flight. A flicker of surprise showed in her expression and she threw out her arms.

A shockwave rippled through the room. It caught me by the knees, lifting me up in the air and flipping me backward. There was a glimpse of Tink flying backward as I landed hard on my back. Icy fog poured into the room as I rolled onto my side. I'd lost one of my daggers.

That kind of power—it was not normal.

"Ren!" I shouted as I rose to my knees. "Ren—"

"Here," he grunted, and from the thick white smoke, I saw his hand. His knuckles were bloodied as they wrapped around mine. Ren squeezed my hand and then let go.

A soft laugh carried through the fog—a laugh that sent a bolt of dread straight down my spine.

I stood slowly, breathing heavy as I clutched the one dagger I had left. The icy mist rolled back, revealing those who were still standing.

There weren't many, but I saw David and Miles standing near Kalen and Faye. I also saw Liz. I didn't see Tink. My stomach plummeted.

But there was the Prince, his chest rising and falling sharply.

He wasn't alone. Something rose like a wraith, tall and slender, and as the mist slipped away, I saw a crown of bone, and I knew what Breena was.

Ren groaned. "Oh, *hell.*"

Behind the Winter Prince stood a Queen smiling a blood-soaked smile.

Chapter 30

"Shit," I whispered, rooted to where I stood.

Tink's screeching warning made sense. A brownie would've seen Breena—seen through whatever facade she was wearing. He'd seen the Queen and tried to warn us.

But it was too late.

A damn Queen stood before us, and she looked like Breena, but not. Her hair was now a frosted silver, nearly reaching her waist. She wore Breena's face, but her chin was sharper, her eyes wider and lips fuller. Her blue eyes were luminous against the color of molten silver.

And that crown . . .

It really looked like it was made of bone curved into a half circle and sharpened to rise into three single points, the middle the tallest.

She brushed her hand over Drake's shoulder, drawing his gaze from the Summer Prince. "Focus, my love," she murmured. "Focus."

The Prince went still.

Flanked behind them were three Knights and two more

fae. We'd taken down a lot, but not enough—not nearly enough with the Queen here.

Someone, some brave fool, rushed her, brandishing what appeared to be a thorn stake. An Elite member. She caught the man's arm, and with a flick of her wrist, snapped the bone. The man screamed as she jerked him to her. She was like a cobra striking, burying her mouth in his throat. The man's scream ended in a gurgle as blood spurted into the mist. She lifted her head and let the man go. He fell to the floor, throat torn out as she faced us.

"Holy fuck," Miles gasped behind me.

Blood coursed down her chin as she tilted her head. "Surprise?"

I sucked in a breath. A knot of fear formed in my throat. Breena had been the Queen all along?

"The brownie?" she spoke. "Where is it?"

I had no idea where Tink was, but wherever he'd gone, I prayed it was far from here.

"You bitch," Fabian growled. "You lying, traitorous bitch."

"Careful," she said, wiping the back of her hand across her mouth. "I do believe you're the last of your court? Well . . ." She laughed as she glanced over to the still and silent Drake. She placed a hand on his chest. "The last who *knows* that he is."

Fabian's nostrils flared.

Wait. Was Drake—?

The Queen's gaze flicked to me. "Look at you. I must say, the changes are an improvement. But not much." Those icy eyes found Ren. "And you? You're still as yummy as I remember."

Potent fury swept through me. "You know what I remember? Gouging your eyes out."

Her bloody smile spread. "Yes, I remember that too, and I do plan on repaying that favor very, very soon, but we still need you alive for the time being."

I stiffened as my hand tightened on the iron dagger. "There was never a halfling here, was there?"

"No, you silly little bitch. Perhaps there *might* be one here." She lifted a shoulder in an oddly dainty shrug. "I have no idea. You went into hiding and we needed to draw you out." The Queen laughed when Ren cursed under his breath. "After all, do you think we would've been so obvious about our moves?"

I knew it.

Dammit, I *knew* it.

We'd all been played, and we should've known better. Now we were trapped here, all of us, with Drake or whoever he was, and a damn Queen.

"Why San Diego?" Liz demanded. "Why here?"

"Because it has the largest number of Order members. No other city has more in one location," David answered. "You take out the San Diego branch, it will have a crippling ripple effect."

It happened so fast.

Several Order members stepped forward, brandishing their iron daggers. Kalen shouted a warning, but it was too late. They gripped the shoulders of other members as they dragged the blade across their throats.

Horror seized me as I spun around to see David drag a blade along Liz's throat. "No!" I screamed, and I didn't even know why. It was too late.

Liz's hands flew to her throat, trying to stanch the flow of blood as she stumbled and then dropped to her knees. Only a handful of seconds had passed and then she joined the other Order members on the floor.

My wide gaze swung to David as my heart broke. I couldn't believe it. David had betrayed us—all of us. My mouth opened, but I didn't have words as I stared at the man who was the closest thing to a father to me. This was like Val all over again, but worse, so much worse.

"Son of a bitch," croaked Miles, and for the first time in my life, I saw real emotion on his face as he stared at David in horror and disbelief. "How? How could you do this?"

"Because this is a war we will not win." David wiped his blade on his pants, cleaning it of blood. His gaze found mine. "Did you never once question why I was so accepting of what you had become? Or what you did to Kyle? I knew he'd gone after you. And I knew that one or both of you would kill him."

The next breath I took got stuck. I'd questioned it. We both did, but we wanted *hope*. Stupid. We'd all been so damn stupid.

"Right now, all across the city, Order members will be meeting the same fate. And back in New Orleans? The same, according to plan. But what I didn't plan on was a brownie." The Queen's lips curled, baring razor-sharp teeth. "Where is it?"

Drawing in a shallow breath, I pushed aside everything with David and met her gaze head-on. I'd have to deal with that fresh betrayal later—if there was a later. "I don't know what you're talking about."

"Okay. You want to play a game. I love games." She clasped her hands together. "This is a game I like to call, kill everyone. Except you. I still need you, but the rest are about to die." Her gaze found Faye. "Starting with you."

Faye's chest rose with a sharp breath, but she held her ground as Kalen stepped to stand next to her.

"Or maybe not you." The Queen drifted forward. "Maybe him."

My heart lurched. She was staring at Ren. "If you touch one hair on his head, you'll regret it."

"Somehow I doubt that." She moved faster than I could track. A second later she was standing behind Ren, her long fingers encircling his neck. "Do you like this game, Ivy?"

Ren's jaw locked down as he held very still, meeting my gaze. My heart was pounding fast, too fast as I lifted the dagger to my own throat. I didn't hesitate. Not for a second. "If you hurt him, I will slit my own throat and then you'll really have to find another halfling. How do you like that game?"

Her lips thinned as she tilted her head to the side. "You'd kill yourself to save him?"

"In a heartbeat."

"Ivy," Ren gasped out.

Disbelief crowded her face. "You wouldn't—"

The sound of plastic wheels gliding over wood floors drew all of our attention toward the door. I couldn't believe what I was seeing at first. I blinked, thinking I had to be seeing things, but my eyes weren't lying to me.

Tink's suitcase rolled across the floor, sliding past the Prince and stopping just short of Fabian. Then Tink zoomed into the room, flying as fast as a little missile, toward the suitcase. Gripping the zipper in his tiny hands, he dragged it along the seam. One side of the suitcase swung open and hundreds of troll dolls spilled out, scattering over the floor in a sea of neon blue and hot pink hair.

"What the . . . ?" I stumbled back a step.

The Queen cocked her head to the side as she held Ren.

Everyone stared, because there were hundreds of troll dolls rolling across the floor, through blood, and yeah, it was really bizarre.

Flying forward, Tink hovered above his sea of troll dolls and lifted his arms. “Rise up, my little babies.”

The dolls trembled on the floor and then shook. All of them. Their little plastic bodies rocking, and then their bodies . . . weren’t plastic anymore. Their legs bent. Their arms moved. Their heads turned, and their eyes were the palest blue, like all creatures from the Otherworld.

I had no words.

The troll dolls rose onto their stubby legs. Their mouths opened and a high keening screech erupted from them, raising the tiny hairs all along my arms.

Well, I was going to have a life’s worth of nightmares because of this.

“Holy crap,” I whispered. “Instead of being the Night King, he’s the *Troll* King.”

The dolls’ heads turned toward the Queen.

Letting out a shriek of rage, the Queen threw Ren aside, sending him sliding several feet across the floor. He went down on one knee as I shot to his side, grabbing his hand and hauling him up.

“We need to get out of here,” he said, his wide eyes on the dolls. “Now.”

“Agreed.”

Holding tight to his hand, I shouted for Tink as the dolls stomped across the floor, racing toward the Queen. Tink flew to my shoulder as I spun toward Faye and Kalen. The male fae met my gaze and nodded.

The dolls reached the Queen, their little hands clutching at her dress. They climbed up her legs, dozens of them.

She shrieked, plucking one off her thigh. Blood covered its little mouth. They bit? She crushed it in her hand as she screamed in rage. Dozens more were climbing up her, reaching her stomach, digging in with their hands and . . . mouths. The Knights started toward her, but were also overcome by dolls. They swallowed them whole, like a carpet of flesh-eating troll dolls.

I was going to need therapy—years of therapy.

Ren started toward the door and Tink hopped from my shoulder to his, but hands landed on my back, jerking me away from Ren. My hand slipped free as I was spun around. I came face to face with David.

"I can't let you go," he said, his grip digging in. "I'm sorry, Ivy."

I didn't stop to think about what I was doing, but my chest ached and my eyes burned as my grip tightened on the dagger.

"David," I said, my voice hoarse.

His gaze met mine a second before I slammed the dagger deep into the center of his chest. David's mouth opened, but there were no words. None. I saw his eyes dull over.

Exhaling roughly, I let go of the dagger as I blinked back hot tears. I jerked as another hand touched my arm. I turned to find Miles beside me. "We need to go," he said. "Now."

Unable to speak, I got my feet moving. We raced across the floor, our feet slipping and sliding in the blood. At the doorway, I realized Fabian wasn't with us. He was standing in front of Drake, speaking too fast for me to understand.

The Queen was in the center of the room, spinning as she sent evil troll dolls in every direction.

Fabian picked up a fallen dagger. I stopped, heart somewhere in my throat. It was iron. It wouldn't kill Drake at—

Fabian didn't stab the Winter Prince.

He sliced open his own palm, drawing blood, and he lifted that bloodied palm, dragging it down the center of Drake's face and pressing it against his mouth.

The Winter Prince's entire body jolted as what appeared to be a thousand fireflies surrounded him, encasing his entire body in a shimmering golden glow. Only a second or two passed and then the shimmering, dazzling lights receded.

The Winter Prince stood there, his luminous blue eyes wide and unseeing. It was like a layer of darkness seeped off and slid away. Black hair gave way to golden. Shadows peeled away from the hollows of his cheeks. His features were the same, but he was not of the Winter Court. He was . . .

What in the holy fu—?

"Ivy!" Ren was once again at my side.

"Look," I whispered. "Look at him."

Ren followed my gaze. "What the hell?"

The Prince fell back a step, his wide gaze darting over Fabian and us. His stare met mine, and his entire face contorted as if he were in pain.

I bumped into Ren as the Prince whipped around and let out a sound that was as terrifying as it was inhuman and primitive. The smell of burnt ozone filled the air as a blast of potent energy rolled across the floor. It hit the Knights first.

They burst into nothing, disintegrating on the spot.

Skin peeled off the Order members that had betrayed us. Their bones were crushed into dust. The impact was so intense that it burnt their shadows into the floor.

Still flinging off the troll dolls, the Queen spun toward the Prince. Her eyes widened with shock, and then the energy slammed into her. She and the dolls flew off their feet and backward. The Queen hit the wall . . . and crashed through it.

"I think we need to go." Ren grabbed my arm and started backing up. "Like for real."

Pulling my gaze away from the bizarre scene, I turned

and ran down the hall, catching up with the rest of the group.

"What about Fabian?" Tink demanded as the patio doors came into view.

"Forget him," Ren responded.

"What?" Tink launched himself off Ren's shoulder.

"Oh, hell no." I snatched Tink out of mid-air, wrapping my hands around his waist. "You are not going back there."

"But—"

"No." I held tight to Tink as we burst out onto the patio. "And don't you dare bite me or change forms."

Tink's face fell, and I ignored it as I ran across the parking lot. Kalen already had the keys out as he ran to the driver's door. Faye climbed into the front seat as Miles climbed in, heading for the second row. Ren got in and twisted toward me, reaching out a hand. His gaze flicked over my head.

"What the hell?" he demanded, starting to make his way back out.

I turned and my mouth dropped open.

Fabian stormed through the doors, and with him was Drake, his face still bloody. "What the hell are you doing?" I reached for my dagger, but realized I had none left. "What are you doing with Drake?"

"This isn't Drake." Fabian held on to the Prince's arm.

"Bullshit! I know who he is even with the lighter hair."

"You're wrong."

"Fabian, that is the Winter Prince." Faye had rolled down the window. "I saw him every day. That is Drake."

The Winter Prince squinted, shielding his eyes as he swayed unsteadily on his feet. "I am . . ." He trailed off, flinching as if something or someone had gotten near his face.

"That is not the Winter Prince." Tink beat at my fist. "I've seen him before, Ivy. I know what Drake looks like. I saw him in the Otherworld, remember?"

Confused, I shook my head.

"We need to go," Kalen warned. "We need to get the hell out of here."

"Let us in," Fabian demanded.

"No fucking way." Ren pushed me into the seat. "I'm going to kill that son of a bitch. I don't care if he looks like Beach Prince right now."

Ren was out of the SUV before I knew what he was doing. In a heartbeat, his fist slammed into the Prince's jaw, snapping his head back. I shot forward, fear a bitter taste in the back of my throat. The Prince would—

The Prince slowly turned his head back to Ren. His lip was split. He didn't raise his hands or anything as Ren's fist snaked out again, catching him under the chin, knocking his head back.

"Stop!" shouted Tink. "You need to stop, Ren!"

Ren cocked his arm back again, but Fabian caught his fist. "Hit him again, and I will make sure there is nothing left of you."

I snatched the back of Ren's shirt with my free hand and tugged him back. He didn't budge, not until I wrapped my arm around his waist. "That's enough."

"No." Ren shook his head. "That is not nearly enough."

"He's not Drake! Look at him. He's different," Tink shouted, and then the little bastard sunk his teeth into my hand.

"Ouch!" I let go, drawing my hand back and shaking the sting out. Tink flew out of the car, toward the Prince's shoulder. "We don't have time for this, Tink. Get away from—"

"If you don't let both of them into this car, I'm not coming!"

I gaped at the damn brownie. "Are you out of your mind?"

"Are you?" Tink shot back.

"This is not Drake," Fabian said, his voice sounding broken. "This is my brother."

Chapter 31

The ride back to Del Mar was . . . awkward and tense. It probably had to do with the fact that the Prince who kidnapped Ren and me, who had tried to seduce me to bring about a fae apocalypse, and was all-around murderous and psychotic, was sitting in the back seat of the SUV, silent and staring out the window.

Between that, the armies of troll dolls, the betrayal of David, and the appearance of the Queen, it was officially the worst Monday ever.

Ren practically sat facing the back seat the entire ride to the house. So did Miles, and I did the same.

There was something wrong with the Prince.

He didn't speak. He didn't look at any of us. He didn't even respond to any of the terse comments about him. He just sat there, and I couldn't believe I was in a car with him and not trying to murder him.

"He was under an enchantment," Fabian explained, staring at Drake. It was clear they were brothers. I'd seen the similarity before and now, with the change in the hair color, it was obvious. "We believed that he died in the Great War with the Winter Court. I saw him go down, and I couldn't get to him. Queen Morgana took his body. We thought she did so to refuse us our burial tradition. Now I know. She placed him under her spell."

And now we knew what Queen we were dealing with. Of course, it had to be the one who was the boogeyman of all the fae. Great. Just our freaking luck.

"So, are you saying he's not responsible for any of his actions because he was under a spell?" Ren demanded.

"Yes." Fabian looked at Ren. "That is exactly what I'm saying."

"Bullshit," he growled. "That bastard—"

"Was under her spell," Fabian cut in. "Just like a human would be under a glamour. It is a powerful enchantment that only a King or Queen can do. One that is forbidden."

Ren leaned toward the back of the seat. "I. Don't. Care."

"I know it's hard to accept. I'm having a hard time accepting it, too. Trust me," Faye said, having twisted around in her seat. "But when one of our kind is under an enchantment, we cannot control what we do. It would be the same for a mortal."

Miles stiffened. "He killed scores of our members, either by his own hands or on his order."

"And the man you answered to betrayed all of us and his own men," Faye reminded him.

I squeezed my eyes shut against the truth of those words. I couldn't even think about what David had done or that I had ended him.

Miles didn't respond to that, because what could he say? I opened my eyes. "It's not the same thing, though. We didn't know what David was doing or how long he was doing it. We know what *he* was doing."

"But it's not him." Tink landed on the back of our seat.

"It wasn't who he really is. You saw what he did when he came out of the enchantment. He put Queen Bitch through a wall."

"I. Don't. Care."

"This is bullshit," Ren muttered.

"Let me guess. He has no memory of all the horrible shit he's done?" I demanded.

The Prince's head slowly turned, and his eyes met mine. "I remember everything I've done. *Everything.*"

I sucked in a sharp breath as a shiver danced over my skin. He didn't . . . he sounded like the Prince I knew, but at the same time, he didn't. He returned to staring out the window.

"It changes nothing," Ren said.

"It changes everything," Fabian replied. "You'll see. Give him time. You'll understand."

Ren's laugh was harsh. "This is unbelievable."

It really was. All of it, but here we were, and I needed a distraction, because I wanted to whip that thorn stake out of Ren's hand and slam it into the chest of that bastard, enchantment or not.

My gaze shifted to Tink. "You going to explain about the troll dolls?"

He sighed as he walked across the back of our seat, kicking at something none of us could see. "I hate leaving them there. They're my babies."

Babies? They were the stuff of nightmares. "How did you make them move?" I thought about the times I'd find them around the apartment. "Were they always capable of that?"

"Well, I take a drop of my blood and mix it in their hair, so I can reanimate them."

My eyes widened.

"And I tried it out a few times back home." Tink shrugged

as he peered up at me. "Sometimes they got out."

Oh my God.

Those damn dolls had been alive!

"Man, I don't know what about today is more fucked up," Ren muttered.

"The Queen," Faye answered. "That is the most fucked up thing."

"What are we going to do now?" Miles asked.

No one answered.

Because no one had any answers. We spent this entire time believing we were dealing with a psychotic prince, but now we had a Queen to deal with and none of us were prepared for that.

REN CAUGHT MY hand, holding me back on the steps as everyone else made their way into the sprawling home.

"Come here," he said.

I wasn't given much of a choice. Not that I needed one. Holding on to my hand, he pulled me against his chest and folded his arms around me.

Letting out a ragged breath, I closed my eyes and soaked up his closeness and warmth. A long moment passed before he spoke.

"I'm so sorry." Ren kissed my forehead and then each of my eyelids. "I know how you felt about David."

I shuddered. "That was why he was so accepting of me, of what I've changed into. Shit. I thought it was . . ." I couldn't finish that thought. Not right now. "I just can't believe it. Never in a million years would I have ever thought he would turn on us."

"I know." He dragged his hand up the center of my back, threading his fingers through my hair.

"When did this happen? Was he always working with the Queen? Did he know she was here or did she get to him somehow?"

"We're never going to know." The arm at my waist tightened. "But you did the right thing back there."

I had.

That didn't make it any easier.

I swallowed again. "When she grabbed you by the throat, I've never been more afraid in my life."

"Got to admit, I wasn't exactly happy myself." He paused. "But you didn't seem afraid. You were actually pretty badass in your response."

"I would've done it. I swear to—"

"I know," he whispered. "And *that* scares me."

"You were pretty badass, yourself. Punching the Prince and all."

"I want to rip his throat out, Ivy."

I shivered. "He didn't . . . he didn't even try to stop you." Slowly, I lifted my gaze to his. "He didn't retaliate. The Prince I knew would've, Ren. You know that."

Ren looked away, a muscle thumping along his jaw.

"What are we going to do?" I whispered hoarsely. "We have *him* in that house and a crazy, really powerful Queen about to do God knows what. We don't even know how many Order members are left—" My voice cracked. "This is . . . this is terrifying."

He rested his chin on top of my head. "We're going to figure this out," he said after a moment. "We have to."

I didn't see how we could. If we didn't know how to defeat a prince, how in the hell would we defeat the Queen?

The hand in my hair slid to my cheek. Ren tilted my head back, and my eyes drifted shut. He kissed me, and it was gentle and sweet, and somehow it reminded me that there was still good surrounding me. That there was still us in this mess.

Opening my eyes, I pulled back and cupped his cheek, wiping away a smudge of blood. "We better head in there."

"Yeah. We better."

We walked into the house, and both of us stiffened at the sight of the Prince. Fabian placed a hand on his shoulder, steering the silent man away.

"I don't like this." Ren crossed his arms as Fabian led his brother toward the kitchen. "At all."

"Me neither." I watched Tink buzz after them. I couldn't believe that the Prince had been in the car with us and now was in this house with us. There was so much to worry about. Too much. "Are we even safe here?"

"I don't believe David knew where you guys were staying, but that doesn't mean they won't find out." Miles dragged a hand over his head. "Shit. What am I going to tell his wife?"

"Do you think she knew of his actions?" Faye asked.

"I want to say no, but hell, I never saw it coming with David. She could be in on it too." Shoulders tensed, he looked away. "I need to get in contact with someone at the New Orleans branch. I need to . . ."

He needed to make sure they were alive.

God.

I couldn't let myself think of those I knew—those I cared about possibly being dead. If I went down that hellish hole, I would probably never resurface.

Miles turned to me, and for the second time that night, I could see emotion in his expression. It was sorrow this time, deep sorrow. "What you did back there? With David? You had to."

I blinked and swallowed against the sudden burn.

"I just want you to know that." Miles shuddered with

a sigh as he looked at Faye and Kalen. "It's just us now."

Kalen lifted his chin. "We can't stay here long. The Prince might've put her through the wall, but it wouldn't have killed her. Wouldn't have even taken her out of commission for that long."

"The Queen." Faye let out a ragged breath. "I can't believe it. This whole time it was Breena."

"If I didn't need any more reason to hate her." I rubbed at my hip with my palm. "What I don't get is if Breena was always the Queen, then how was I able to overpower her that one time?"

"I think you caught her off-guard." A weak smile graced Faye's lips, but it faded quickly. "I don't think she ever expected you to attack. I thought it was just Breena's arrogance. In reality, it was the Queen's arrogance."

I still couldn't fathom how we didn't know that she was the Queen, but then again, as an Order member, Ren and I were raised and trained to believe that there were no courts, no princes, no queens. We'd been led to believe that they were nothing but dust.

I started to pace.

"We need to address something far more important at the moment," Ren said. "What in the hell are we going to do with him? Are we seriously just going to let him roam around? He—"

"I know, Ren. But I am telling you that man in there is not Drake—not anymore." Faye sat down on one of the thickly cushioned chairs. "That is the older brother of Fabian. The heir to the Summer Court. In all reality, he should be the King."

I gave a curt shake of my head. I didn't even know what to say to all of that. "And where is the real Drake? I'm assuming he was real, wasn't he? Tink saw him once in the

Otherworld."

"He must've died in the war," Kalen answered. "And Queen Morgana instilled Fabian's brother in his place."

"And none of you knew this?" Ren demanded.

"We did not grow up in the Otherworld," Faye said, shaking her head. "We never saw Drake or Fabian's brother. We wouldn't have known. We saw what the Queen wanted us to see. Someone who could pass as Drake. That is how powerful her enchantment is."

If Tink had seen him in the Otherworld before the Great War, then how old was Tink really? Geez. But that wasn't important. "What if this is a trick?"

"Do you not see him?" Faye scooted to the edge of her seat. "He is not the same man I loathed and feared. He didn't strike back when Ren attacked. That alone should be enough evidence."

I met her gaze. "I don't care if he's Team Good Fae now and forever, he's still the man *I* loathe and fear."

Faye pressed her lips together. "I can understand why. I really do. But he attacked the Knights and the Queen. You have to trust me when I say—"

"Trust you?" I laughed as I stopped pacing, standing in front of her. "You all have lied to me since the beginning. You knew that I'd be trapped in the Otherworld and you failed to tell me that."

"That is messed up," Miles chimed in.

I shot him a look.

"I'm glad we've circled back to that little piece of fuckery." Ren's voice hardened to stone. "There is no way in hell Ivy is completing that ritual. No way."

Faye tensed.

"I just want to point out that I didn't know about that." Kalen lifted his hand. "Not at all."

I looked at him.

Kalen shrugged. "Just saying."

"We hoped to have found a way to ensure that you were not trapped," Faye begun. "We—"

"You hoped that you'd find a way to make sure I wasn't trapped? Are you kidding me? What do you think would've happened to me if we completed the ritual and I was trapped with the evil version of the Prince?"

"We didn't have a choice!" Faye shot to her feet, her eyes fierce. "You are the only halfling we know, the only one strong enough to complete the ritual. What other option did we have? Opening the doors would destroy this world. I'm not being dramatic by saying that. It would destroy everything."

"Sacrifice one to save many?" I laughed harshly.

"We hoped it wouldn't come to that."

Ren stepped forward. "Do you know how badly I want to end all of your lives right now?"

"I'm sure you do, Ren, but how is that going to help?" Miles raised his brows. "We're it. And if you don't trust them, I get that. But the last damn thing I ever expected to do was find myself standing with fae and agreeing with them."

"You agree with them about the Prince?" I whirled on Miles. "Seriously?"

"We're going to need him, aren't we?" Miles met my gaze and then Ren's. "If he really isn't Drake and he's that other big blond dude's brother, then we're going to need both of them to defeat her, because what I saw in there—what I saw that she was capable of was nothing like I'd ever seen."

I stepped back, surprised.

"Then what are we going to do?" Faye sat back down. "The Queen is here. Do you have any idea what that means for mortals and fae alike?"

"Oh, I'm guessing the usual bloodbath is in store for everyone," I snapped.

"I know what we need to do."

We all turned at the sound of the voice. It was *him*. The Prince. Formally known as Drake, currently still the guy who holds the number one spot on my to-kill list.

The blood had been washed off his face and his now blond hair was damp and pushed back from his face. "We need to stop the Queen."

Chapter 32

My heart started thumping heavily as I stared at the Prince. I could feel the anger and tension rolling off of Ren, but it was nothing compared to the riot of emotions currently battling inside of me.

Behind him was Fabian and Tink, who was no longer in tiny Tink form. He was full-grown and thankfully dressed.

"You want to know what we need to do," he said, his voice now more like I remembered. Deep. Oddly accented. I wanted to vomit. "We must stop her."

"No shit," I snapped, and his left brow lifted slightly. "There is no 'we' in any of this."

Fabian exhaled roughly. "He's—"

The Prince raised his hand, silencing his brother. "She has every right to be angry. To hate me. As does he."

"Glad we're on the same page," Ren bit out, his jaw tense. "It's literally taking every ounce of my self-control not to take this stake and shove it through your fucking eye."

I sucked in a sharp breath as my gaze darted from Ren to the Prince. The latter's face was impassive, so much so that Miles had to have been impressed by the utter lack of emotion.

"And I would not stop you."

Surprise shot through me. The Prince couldn't be real. There was no way he'd stand there and let Ren kill him.

"Really?" Ren stepped forward. "Let's give that a try."

Fabian stiffened, but it was Tink who spoke up. "Guys, I get that you want to get stabby-stabby, kill-kill with him, but you really need to let that go."

I glared at him. "Easy for you to say."

"It really isn't that easy." Tink met my glare. "I know what he did to you, but who he is now is not the Prince you knew."

My breath caught. "There is no way I could trust anything he has to say. Enchantment or not, he is the Prince. He held me—"

"I know what I've done to you. From the moment I saw you in that hallway, after the enchantment was broken, I remembered. I close my eyes and I see it. When it is silent, I hear your—"

"That's enough." Ren's voice was low with warning.

His gaze slipped from me to Ren. "I recall what I did to you, how I became you—"

"Seriously. Do you have a death wish?" My hands were shaking, so I clasped them together.

"Perhaps," he murmured, and I blinked. "What the Queen wanted is not what I wanted. It never has been. I have no intention of following through with her plan."

"So you don't want to knock me up now?"

His jaw tightened. "No offense, but no."

I lifted my brows. "Relieved."

"I know there is next to nothing that will make you believe me—"

"Actually, there is." An idea occurred to me just then.

"How would we weaken a prince enough to be able to kill them?"

"You have—"

"Brother." Fabian gripped his brother's shoulder. "If you tell them, they will use it against you—against us."

"It's a risk we must bear then," the Prince replied, shaking off his brother's hand. "There are two ways to weaken us. If our magic is turned back on us, it can severely wound us, taking us months to heal. And there is something that is quite poisonous to us if it touches our skin. Worse if it invades our bloodstream. The three of you carry it on your person."

"What?" Miles stepped forward.

"A four-leaf clover," the Prince answered, and Fabian closed his eyes. "It is poisonous not only to us, but to our Knights and other Ancients."

My mouth dropped open as my hand went to the chain around my neck. The encased clover was like a body part, such a part of me that I didn't even think about it. "Are you serious?"

He nodded. "Most of you already carry our greatest weakness. Use that and a thorn stake, and we are not so hard to kill."

Clasping the back of his neck, Fabian looked away.

"And a Queen?" Kalen asked, speaking up for the first time since the Prince had walked out. "Would it weaken a Queen?"

"It would. Normally. Queen Morgana has built up a tolerance to it over the years. It will not affect her."

"Of course not," I muttered, crossing my arms as I glanced over at Ren.

He was still clutching the thorn stake and he hadn't taken his gaze off of the Prince. Not once. I couldn't tell how he felt about any of this beyond the murderous rage clearly etched into his face.

"What does the Queen plan to do?" Faye asked quietly while I was still hung up on the fact that a four-leaf clover could've weakened the damn Ancients and the Prince this entire time.

"She'd want to still open the doorway, right?" Miles sat on the arm of a nearby couch.

"She can't without a prince willing to carry out her demands."

"What if she finds a male halfling and engages in some bow-chicka-bow-wow?" Tink asked.

"The prophecy has never mentioned what would happen if a Queen or King procreated with a halfling, but I imagine it would work," the Prince said.

Fabian faced us. "It would have the same effect. A King or Queen is not of this world, as is a halfling and a child of such a union. It would undo the seals."

I exhaled roughly. "Now we have to worry about the Queen finding someone and getting pregnant?"

"Morgana cannot conceive," the Prince answered.

"And how do you know this?" Ren challenged.

"No. He's right." Hope sparked in Faye's eyes. "Remember? I told you that."

She had. The day I met Fabian.

"The legend we were taught was that Morgana had committed a great misdeed and to escape having her powers stripped, she gave up the ability to create life."

"This sounds like a really bad fantasy novel," Ren muttered, and I blinked slowly.

Everything about this sounded like that, but that was nothing new.

"What great misdeed did she commit?" Tink asked with

interest.

The Prince's jaw hardened and the glint in his eyes mirrored what Ren was giving off. I had a suspicion that whatever thing the Queen had done, it had involved the Prince.

"What will she do now?" I asked, making sure we stayed on topic. "I doubt she's just going to tuck tail and hide."

"If her original plan was to fail, she had a back-up," the Prince explained. "She would go back to the Otherworld, and we must stop her."

My lips parted as I stared at him. There was no way I had heard any of that right.

"If she was to go back to the Otherworld, then why would we stop her?" Kalen frowned.

"You don't understand," Fabian spoke up. "She has the Crystal. If she takes that back to the Otherworld with her, she will be able to reopen the doorways at any time from her side."

"She will come back with whatever army she can gather and there are . . . creatures in our world that would wreak a kind of havoc no mortals have ever seen before," the Prince clipped out. "Out of pure spite and vengeance, she would lay waste to cities. Millions would die."

"Wait." Ren frowned. "The doorways are sealed—"

"They were sealed when *we* came through, were they not?" The Prince met his stare. "They can be reopened again. Not only are there Ancients willing to end their lives to open the doors once more, she wouldn't need them. She could open the door with the Crystal."

I remembered when he'd come through. That was a night I'd never forget. "If she's always been able to open the door to the Otherworld, then why hasn't she before? Why not just bring the army through instead of trying to get a halfling pregnant?"

"Because she can only go through the gateway she came through," he said. "And with the Crystal, she won't need to wait until the Winter Solstice. The Crystal is strong enough to open any gateway."

My shoulders tensed. Nearly all of the doorways in the Otherworld had been destroyed by the brownies—all except the one in New Orleans. The baby apocalypse would've opened all the doorways, whether they were destroyed or not.

"She knows that opening all the doorways would have a greater impact than just one. The Order wouldn't be able to stop whatever comes through all those doors at once."

The Prince nodded.

Understanding crept into Ren's expression. "She's going to try to go through the gateway at the house next to the LaLaurie house."

"We need to get back there before she does." The Prince's gaze flickered over us. "We have to kill her. If we don't, she will take that Crystal with her and she will be back, stronger than before."

"And probably a lot more pissed," Tink guessed.

"How do we kill a Queen? You said yourself she can't be weakened by the clovers," Miles said.

"She'll have what is left of the Knights with her, but if you guys take care of them, my brother and I will take care of the Queen."

I opened my mouth to interrupt.

"Between the two of us, we should be able to take her out." Fabian lifted his chin. "She is the most powerful of our kind, but she is not unstoppable. Not if we all work together."

Glancing over at Ren, I met his gaze. I exhaled slowly. Even though he'd told us what would weaken him, trusting him was still a huge risk.

"You have no reason to trust me and I don't blame you for that," the Prince said, seeming to know my thoughts. "But you have no other option."

And he was right.

We had no other option but to trust him.

WE WERE GOING to leave for New Orleans immediately, so Ren and I went back to the room we spent the night in to grab our bags.

He closed the door behind us. "I don't like this. At all."

I sighed wearily, pushing a strand of hair out of my face. It fell back a second later. "Me neither."

"But that bastard is right." He crossed the room, grabbing one of the bags, practically ripping the zipper open. "We can't let the Queen take the Crystal back to the Otherworld."

Ren was right.

Right now, Faye was getting in contact with Tanner, filling him in on what had gone down and what we'd learned. They were expecting us—all of us—to return to New Orleans.

None of us were sure of who we could contact in the New Orleans branch that wasn't working for the Queen, so at this time we weren't reaching out to them.

I don't think any of us felt comfortable with any of this, but like the Prince had said, we didn't have an option but to keep traveling down the road we were on.

I bit down on my lip. "I just . . ."

Shoving the shirt he'd worn the day before into the bag, Ren looked over his shoulder at me. Whatever he must've seen on my face made him stop and face me. A long moment passed and then he asked, "Where are you at, Ivy?"

I knew what that question meant, and I didn't know how

to answer it. Walking over to the bed, I sat down. "I just don't know about anything anymore." I slowly shook my head. "Every time I think I know something—every time I think I have a handle on what is going on, everything changes. Everything."

Ren was silent as he watched me.

I lifted my hands helplessly. "He is right down the hall. Him. The Prince, but . . . he's not him anymore. At least that's how it seems. But what do we know any more? It could be another trap. Look at David. Never in a million years would I have ever believed for a second he was capable of betraying us. But he did. So what do we know? It could—"

"I don't think it's a trap," he said, surprising me. Ren knelt in front of me, placing his hands on my knees. "I don't care if that bastard had no idea what he was doing while he was under the enchantment. That doesn't mean I don't believe it, but I can't look at him and not see what he did to you, what he wanted to do to you. It doesn't matter that it was the Queen controlling him. I'd rather shove a stake through his chest than work with him."

"Ditto," I murmured.

"But I . . . fuck, I can't believe I'm saying this, but I believe him—believe what he said about the Queen. I don't know what in the hell their history is, but it's evident he hates her as much as we hate him."

That last part brought a wry grin to my lips.

"I still don't like him, but if we're going to stop the Queen, we need him, and we need Fabian." He squeezed my knees. "But we do have a choice."

"How? How do we have any other option?"

Those stunning emerald eyes met and held mine. "We leave."

At first, I didn't think I heard him right. "What?"

"We leave, Sweetness. We get the hell out of here, don't tell anyone what we're doing, and we get as far away as we can. We can even bring Tink, if he wants to go." One side of his lips kicked up. "We could travel, see the world before it inevitably goes to shit. We could live. We've given years of our lives to the Order, to our duties. We don't have to give them a second more."

My breath caught in my throat as a wild yearning sprung to life deep inside me. Could we do that? We'd be wanted by the Order, but what was left of the Order anyway? So many were dead, and the rest we didn't even know if we could trust. Would they even come looking for us while the shit hit the fan and splattered everywhere? Probably not. We could live—live normal lives until we had to face what was happening to the world.

"We have a choice, Ivy." His gaze didn't waver. "Whatever you want to do, I am with you. A hundred percent."

Air lodged in my throat. It was almost too easy to say yes, because saying yes would be better. I wouldn't have to worry about Ren getting hurt or dying, because there was no way we were going to face off with the Queen and not lose someone. It was statistically impossible. I could make Tink leave with us. We'd be safe and happy, at least for a little while.

If I closed my eyes, I could almost see us—the three us traveling the world, visiting places we'd never get the chance to. We wouldn't worry about stopping the Queen or if we could trust the Prince. Like Ren had said, we would live as long as we could.

But I . . . I couldn't say yes.

The word wouldn't even form on the tip of my tongue. It wasn't about duty. It wasn't even about living normal lives. I didn't have it in me to walk away when I knew what was happening—what was going to happen, and I knew Ren would only do that for me, if I chose to walk away.

"I can't," I whispered. "I can't walk away. I'm sorry."

"I didn't think you would." Rising halfway, he cupped my cheeks. "You're too brave to run and hide, but we have that choice and we're making the choice to stay and fight and kick ass."

"Yeah, we are."

Chapter 33

We arrived in New Orleans early Wednesday morning, having driven straight through, only stopping for gas and to grab a quick bite to eat. I didn't know how I fell asleep in that car, sitting between Miles and Ren, but I had with half my upper body in Ren's lap. He'd fallen asleep too, with his head against the window and his hand on my hip. When I woke up, I found Tink twisted around in his seat, staring at me.

"Hi," he whispered.

"Hey." I sat up, waking Ren as I rubbed a hand over my face. "Were you watching me sleep?"

"Maybe."

Ren lifted his arm away from me as he stretched out his neck. "You're such a freak."

"I am." Tink grinned. "We're here, by the way. Just pulling up now."

I glanced over at Miles and saw that he was staring at what appeared to be an abandoned building.

"They told me this was a powerful glamour," he said, his voice hoarse. "I can't believe this has been here this whole time and I had no idea."

"Kind of how I felt." I yawned. "Just wait until you see the inside."

The SUV stopped and the doors swung open. Fabian turned toward Miles before he climbed out. "You're being trusted with something very few people have. You betray the fae here, and I will personally make it so that you wish you were dead."

Miles held Fabian's gaze. "I have no desire to betray these fae if they are what you say they are."

"You will see that I have not lied."

I resisted the urge to point out that he may not be lying about this place, but the fae here were still liar-mc-liar-faces.

Fabian studied Miles for a moment and then stepped out of the SUV. Getting out of the car and sitting after so many hours was painful as all get out as I walked the cramps in my muscles off.

The glamour of the building was still intact as the rusted-over door opened. We hurried inside, out of the dark night. Miles had the same expression on his face that I did the first time I saw the power of the glamour fade away, revealing the luxurious hotel inside.

"Jesus," he muttered, rubbing a hand on his face as he took in the grand lobby.

"It's a lot to take in, isn't it?" I turned to him. "And you had no idea that the fae worked with the Order at one time?"

"I'd heard the stories, but I thought they were rumors. I didn't believe there were fae that didn't feed. Just didn't think it . . ." He trailed off as he watched Tanner approach us.

And I knew why he had been struck silent. Tanner was living and walking proof of a fae who didn't feed. Behind him was Brighton and her mother.

"Merle?" Miles lowered his hand as he stared at the woman.

"You look like a ghost done walked over your grave." Merle lifted her brows, and her daughter seemed to take a deep breath. Brighton's hair was down, and it was probably the first time I'd seen her wear it like that. It fell in soft waves and loose curls, reaching the middle of her back. She gave Ren and I a little smile.

Miles gaped at her. "You knew about this?"

"She has known for some time." Tanner stopped in front of Miles, extending a hand. "I am Tanner."

"Miles." A moment passed and then he shook Tanner's hand. "Uh, nice to meet you."

Tanner started to respond, but his gaze flicked behind us. He dropped Miles' hand and stepped back. "Fabian? Is this . . . ?"

"Yes." Fabian stood beside Tink. "This is my brother."

Tanner paled as he stepped around Kalen and Faye, his eyes wide and full of wonder. "Our King."

"King?" Ren looked down at me, and I shrugged.

The Prince showed no response as Tanner bowed in front of him. "It is an honor," Tanner said. I was waiting for him to kiss the Prince's hand.

"This is weird," I whispered to Ren.

"Everything is weird."

The Prince glanced at us and then spoke. "We should begin to plan."

"Of course." Tanner straightened. "Please come this way. We have refreshments set up."

I arched a brow as Tanner spun on his heel.

Merle eyed the Prince with distaste and a hefty dose of distrust. "An enchantment," she muttered. "How cliché."

The Prince's cool gaze flickered over her. "Agreed."

Merle frowned as she eyed him.

Following Tanner, the Prince passed Brighton. I only knew he'd looked in her direction based on how wide her eyes grew and how she stepped back, bumping into the wall.

Poor Brighton.

We all ended up in one of the large meeting rooms, and there were refreshments. Coffee. Juice. Bagels. Fruit. An entire damn buffet of cold cuts.

I didn't get that treatment when I showed up.

Whatever.

Plopping down on the couch, I stretched my legs out and leaned into the thick cushion. "So, you know what's going on?" I asked as Tink sat down on the arm beside me.

Tanner nodded as he sat in the chair across from us. "I am most sorry to hear about the betrayal of your leader."

Biting down on my lip, I breathed through that sting. "So were we."

Ren sat next to me, his leg pressing against mine. "And we were also sorry to hear that you knew that Ivy would be trapped in the Otherworld if she completed the ritual."

Tanner's cheekbones deepened in color. "As I am sure Faye explained, we hoped to find a way around that."

"Sure," I muttered. It wasn't that I didn't believe them. I just didn't believe there was a way, and they probably knew that deep down. I was the living embodiment of sacrifice the few to the save the many. I could understand that. Didn't mean I was okay with it.

"Doesn't matter now, does it?" Merle said, turning with a cup of coffee in her hands. I looked around, not seeing Brighton. "Our Prince isn't interested in putting a seed in your belly any longer."

I groaned, sinking further into the couch as Tink laughed under his breath. Ren, however, didn't find the comment nearly as amusing.

Neither did the Prince. "No. Instead, we have a powerful Queen that will be close to impossible to kill and we don't nearly have enough time to plan and prepare for her attempt to open the gateway."

Merle smiled at the Prince. "Ah yes, that is a problem, but not nearly as bad as all the gateways springing open all at once."

Ren sighed. "Both sound pretty terrible. We all can agree on that. When do you think she will arrive here?"

The Prince did not sit or eat. He stood behind the chair Fabian sat in, arms folded. "She will most likely make it here by late tonight. She will not waste time, not when she knows that she will face both Fabian and me."

I exhaled roughly. "So, we have what? Twelve hours, give or take a few?"

"That would be correct. It won't be long."

Ren stood. "Then we need to get ready. Rest up as much as we can. All of us."

"And then what?" Tink asked.

"I'll see who is still left in the Order that we can trust," Miles spoke from where he stood by the buffet of food no one was touching. "I'm hoping there are some that are left."

I remembered the look on Dylan's face when Val betrayed us. I hoped he hadn't crossed over to the evil side, but I didn't even know if he was still alive. Or if Jackie was or any of the other Order members I'd known.

"You will have our most skilled warriors," Tanner said. "Some are already at the gateway. She has not shown yet, but they are there and they are ready."

"And you have me," Tink chimed in.

I opened my mouth, but Fabian beat me to it. "You must stay behind."

My brows lifted. "For once, I agree with you."

Tink shot from the arm of the couch. "This is bullshit. I can help."

"I know you can, but if the Queen was to somehow get a hold of you and was able to control you, there would be no hope." Fabian rose. "We need you to stay as far away from her as possible. We also need you here. That is how you help us."

"You know I can help. You know how strong and powerful I am." Tink's jaw was as hard as granite, but for once I kept my mouth shut.

"The Queen was able to control me because I had been wounded in battle. I was weakened and she took full advantage of that." The Prince's voice was heavy as he spoke. "And because of that, I became a monster. She would do the same to you. She knows what it would mean to have a brownie under her control. We cannot risk that. You cannot."

Folding his arms, Tink fell silent.

"Tink," I called out, leaning forward.

He didn't move for a moment and then he turned to me. "I know you want me to stay back."

"I do. We need you to." I met his angry stare. "Because if we fail, we need someone to protect the fae here. They will be the only thing left between the Queen and her destroying the world with her army. You will be our last hope."

Tink stared at me. "Like Obi-Wan?"

My lips twitched. "Yeah, like him."

Tanner twisted in his chair so he could see Tink. "You will defend us. We need you here."

His chest puffed up. "I . . . I will do that. I will make sure nothing happens to those here." He shot to my side and kneeled so we were at eye level. "But you will come back. All of you." He curled his lip in Ren's direction. "Even him."

"We will," I said, making a promise I was going to do every damn thing in my ability to keep. "We will come back."

I CLOSED THE door behind us and leaned against it as Ren walked over to the dresser, unhooking the daggers along his hip. I was quiet as I watched him, but my heart was pounding.

I loved this man.

I loved him because he chased when I ran. I loved him because he never gave up on me, not when I was being held captive and not when I'd closed myself off, shutting everyone out. I loved him because he was a good man, and if I wanted to say screw all of this and leave right now, he'd be right there with me. I loved him because I knew that he would be standing next to me later, ready to fight by my side.

I just loved him.

When he finished unloading what would have been an alarming number of weapons to anyone else, he turned to me.

We needed to sleep the entire day.

We had to, because we needed to be well-rested and then some for what we were going to face tonight.

Neither of us spoke as our gazes collided and connected. There were no words. There didn't need to be. Intent filled those moss-green eyes. My breath caught as raw emotion swelled in my throat. Pushing away from the door, I walked over to him.

Ren gripped my hips, lifting me clean off the floor. I wrapped my legs around his lean waist. His strong hands gripped my rear as he brought my lips to his. There was a wild, out-of-control quality to the way he kissed me. It was needy and demanding, breathtaking and desperate as he rocked me against his hips. I moaned into his kiss as I grabbed at his shirt, wanting it off and wanting it off now.

Ren put me down, bending slightly as I pulled his shirt off. I went for his pants, and he helped, kicking off his shoes and shucking off his pants and briefs in record time.

"Naked," he growled. "Now."

I shuddered and then did as he ordered, stripping out of my clothes. He grew impatient, helping with the shoes and pants, and within minutes, I was naked and on my back, and Ren's mouth was moving over mine once more. His hard length rocked against me, and I clutched his shoulders, moaning as he nipped at my chin and the side of my neck.

What we did in those moments . . .

It was fast and hard and beautiful. He was over me and then inside me. I arched against him, throbbing and aching as he took complete control. Lust and something far more powerful consumed me as his hips moved against mine, deep and slow at first.

His restraint broke and he began to thrust deeper, harder, and I'd never felt fuller, more desperate for more as our bodies moved frantically. Each deep, hard plunge drove up the intensity until it was at a feverish pace. My legs tightened around him, and then that exquisite feeling deep within me coiled and coiled. My head spun as he moved faster, grinding his hips against mine as he gripped my chin, keeping my mouth with his.

And then I broke apart, shattering into a million little pieces as I cried into his kiss. Thrown so high by the tight, mind-numbing waves of pleasure, I didn't think I could take anymore, but I did. Over and over as he rose onto his knees and lifted me up, driving into me with such reckless abandon that I thought I would die. Snaking an arm around my waist, he lifted me onto my knees and into his lips. He thrust once more as his arms folded around me, sealing my body to his as he came, his large body shuddering.

My muscles were limp and useless by the time he lowered me down so I was half spread across his chest, and then neither of us moved for a long time as we struggled to get our breathing under control.

It was me who broke the silence. "That was . . ."

His chest rose with a heavy breath. "I know."

I kissed the slick skin of his chest as I let my eyes drift shut, snuggling close to him.

"Ivy?"

"Mmm?"

"Tonight—once the Queen is gone? I want to go back to my place. I want us to sleep in my bed. I want to wake up tomorrow in my bed with you."

I smiled even though my stomach was filled with knots, chasing away the languid bliss. Planning for later was amazing, but it was also scary as hell. "I'd like that."

"Yeah?"

"Yeah."

Ren pulled me closer to his side. "Good."

I tried to smile again, but I couldn't. Not when balls of dread and unease were piling atop each other in my stomach. Would we have a tonight?

Would we have a tomorrow?

AFTER SLEEPING MOST of the day and resting as much as possible, our crew minus Tink arrived at the house next to the infamous LaLaurie Mansion just after seven. We climbed out on Royal, because there was no way that SUV was going to make it down the narrow road without taking out tourists.

Nervous energy filled me, something I felt many times before, but there was a razor-sharp quality to it this time. Knowing that we were about to face the most dangerous fae known brought the entire world into stark clarity.

Everything had changed since the last time I walked Royal, but in a way, nothing had. I was still the same Ivy who walked this street and entered the house all those weeks ago, prepared to fight and to die to protect the city. I was still her. Yeah, I carried a little more baggage with me. Yeah, I'd been lied to and betrayed, but I was stronger. I was more prepared, and I was ready to protect this city again.

Stepping onto the sidewalk of Royal was like . . . God, it was like finally coming home. It had been so long since I walked these streets. Too long. I glanced down the street, taking in the old buildings and sidewalks crowded with tourists and locals, and I listened to the laughter and shouts, the blaring horns and distant whirling sirens.

Home.

This was home—my home, our home. I wasn't going to let some Queen Bitch bring some kind of army through this gateway, laying waste to this city. Hell no. Resolve filled me.

"I'll be damned if I let her win."

"What?" Ren asked, stepping up on the curb.

Turning to him, I smiled a little. "Just thinking out loud."

He slid me a sidelong glance as the brothers passed us. People stopped and stared as they rounded the corner to what used to be called Hospital Street. Couldn't blame them. The two were well over six feet and looked like Viking conquerors.

Faye and Kalen followed us as we trailed behind the brothers. The house was just as creepy and rundown as I remembered, but a Summer fae stood outside this time, guarding the building.

That was different.

Strange days.

Walking inside, there was no suppressing the shudder the place always brought on, even with the rooms full of people. Miles was already there, as were several Order members.

So relieved to see Jackie, I shot forward and gave her a quick hug. It obviously surprised her, because it took a moment for her to return the gesture.

I turned and looked at Dylan. He stepped back, and I knew he was going to be a no-go on the whole hug thing. "I'm really glad to see you two."

Jackie eyed me intensely while Dylan stared at my ears. "What happened to you, Ivy?"

"Long story," I said, aware that Ren was watching us and definitely listening. "But I'm not—"

"Evil?" Jackie suggested. "Halfling or not, you've always been a little evil."

"No truer words have ever been spoken," Dylan said.

My lips twitched into a small grin. "True."

"Freaking sucks about David though." Jackie shook her head. "I wouldn't have believed it, but . . ."

"But there have been too many unexplained Order deaths in the last couple of weeks, most of them being found dead at home." A muscle ticked along Dylan's jaw. "Skilled members not careless enough to be followed home. Once we talked to Miles, it just started to make sense."

"David's wife?"

Jackie's shoulders tensed. "No one has heard from her in weeks. We don't know if she's dead or not, but we checked out their house after talking to Miles. Her purse was there, so was her phone, but she wasn't."

"That's not a good sign," I said.

"Nope," Dylan agreed. "We don't know if she was aware

of what David was doing or not, but at the end of the day it doesn't really matter. We've lost over half of our active members here."

A ball of emotion filled my throat. Their deaths were so unfair, so freaking senseless. "So, the city is really screwed if the Queen comes back through this gateway with a horde of Otherworld creatures?"

Jackie nodded.

"Hey." Ren nodded at the two as he curled an arm around my shoulders. Dipping his head, he kissed my cheek, and my heart squeezed in the best possible way. I loved all those quick kisses, and I'd never grow tired of them. I just hoped I had a chance to prove that. "I'm going to head upstairs."

"Okay. Be right up."

Ren walked ahead, scoping out the interior. Nothing had changed since the last time we'd been in here. At least as far as I remembered, but the air . . . yeah, the air was heavier. I didn't think it had anything to do with the doorway being here, but more so with all the death that had occurred the first time it had been opened.

I had a horrible feeling tonight we'd be adding to that heaviness.

"Ivy."

Stiffening at the sound of the Prince's voice, I turned. Tension seeped into my muscles as my gaze met his.

He stopped in front of me. "Are you ready for tonight?"

I lifted a shoulder. "As ready as I can be. Are you?"

There was a twitch to his lips, as if he wished to smile but didn't know how. "As ready as I can be."

"Cool." I started to turn away.

"I'm sorry," he said, speaking those two words in a low voice.

My breath caught as I faced him once more. "What?"

"I am sorry. I know my apology means nothing. The things I've done to you, the things I tried to do . . ." He trailed off, his voice hoarse. "I do not ask for your forgiveness for things I could never forgive myself for, but I am sorry for the pain and terror I've caused—"

"Stop," I rasped out, briefly closing my eyes. The bitter tangle of emotions curled around my heart. "I . . . I appreciate the apology. I do, but I . . ." I thought back to what felt like a lifetime ago. "I once was under the compulsion of a fae. How I'd ended up under a compulsion had been my fault. I'd been stupid and I paid for that. Completely under their glamour, I'd let fae into a house where they killed everyone who was important to me. So I know what it feels like to have no control and do things you never would, but I . . ."

"I understand," he simply said after a long moment.

My gaze shot to his, and I thought . . . I thought that maybe he did understand what I couldn't even put into words. It wasn't that I didn't understand he hadn't been in control. He'd even been under a spell, devoid of conscious choice or will, and I guessed that was worse than anything Ren and I had suffered. I understood that, but it was still hard. That I could understand how he became the Prince that terrified me, how he hadn't been responsible, but all that knowledge didn't change the fact that forgiving and forgetting may never be in the cards.

The Prince gave me a curt bow and then he stepped around me, heading upstairs, and I was left standing there, staring at the place where he once was.

Sucking in a sharp breath, I pushed that mess of memories and emotions associated with my capture and headed upstairs. Now was not the time to dwell on any of that. I needed to have a clear head if I had any chance of surviving this night.

Miles followed me up, and I made my way down the narrow, dark hallway. A wave of goosebumps spread over my skin as I neared the entrance to the bedroom.

As I walked through the door and found Ren standing by a boarded-up window near a wooden chair, my heart started kicking around in my chest, doing an erratic dance.

"It's kind of like we came full circle, isn't it?" I said to Ren.

He nodded as he eyed the sealed closet door—the gateway. Right now it just looked like any normal door in an old-as-hell house with a white ceramic handle that most likely jiggled. There was a gap between the top of the door and the frame. It sat slightly crooked.

"It is." Ren paused as a lopsided grin appeared. "In a really messed up way."

Curling an arm around him, I didn't care what it looked like to the others. I wanted to feel his tattooed skin under mine for as long as I could.

I didn't know how much time had passed. Maybe a handful of minutes. Maybe an hour. It felt like time had slowed down to a crawl and also sped up at the same time.

But we didn't have to wait long.

The Prince stiffened and then turned to the doorway. A strange stillness permeated the room. "It's time."

Chapter 34

A shiver snaked its way down my spine, and my hands automatically went to the iron stakes on my thighs. Tiny hairs rose on my body. All around me, people began to react to the peculiar tension seeping into the house.

Dylan blew out a terse breath and it puffed into a misty cloud. "Is it just me or did the temps just drop by twenty degrees?"

"It's not just you," Ren replied.

Ice formed over the doorframe and seeped over the walls as a soft, highly feminine giggle rose from downstairs. A bone-cold wind whipped through the room.

"They're here," Jackie whispered, tendrils of her hair lifting.

A horrible sense of déjà vu slipped over me as I heard the pounding feet and creaking floorboards. We'd been here before. It all started here, and it had been a bloodbath.

I looked at Ren.

His gaze met mine.

He winked.

One side of my lips kicked up. "I love you."

"Prove it to me later."

"I will," I promised as the air caught in my throat.

The Summer fae stepped forward, lifting crossbows as the Queen's fae reached the hallway, and then they were here.

The first through the iced-over doorway was an ordinary fae, and Kalen caught it in the chest with a quick, clean strike. And then there was another, and Jackie took out that one next.

And then they just kept coming, spilling through the open doorway like a plague of locusts. There were so many that they filled the room, and the floor rattled like dry, angry bones under the weight. The wave of Queen's fae swallowed ours, taking them down. Screams ripped through the air as daggers and teeth tore through flesh.

I forced my lungs to inflate and then I let go of the fear and dread that always came with this kind of battle. I sprang into action, like I'd been trained to do—born to do. I caught the nearest fae, slamming the dagger home. Instinct took over. I spun, extending my arm and catching another fae just as Ren launched forward as the first Knight appeared.

They wouldn't be as easy to kill.

Dipping down, he caught the Ancient in the stomach with his shoulder. The force of the broad blow flipped the Ancient over. He landed on his back with a grunt of surprise. Ren spun skillfully, thrusting the thorn stake deep into the Ancient's chest. Ren whirled, shoulders tense, mouth nothing but a slash of a line.

I turned at the sound of pounding feet. An Ancient was gunning for me, eyes full of hatred. My muscles tensed liked they always did before engaging in battle with an enemy that wasn't going to be taken down easily. I waited for the perfect moment, knowing I had to be smart about this. He had a ton more muscle on him than I did, but I was stronger than the last time I stood in this house. He reached for me, and I darted under his arm. Springing up behind him, I slammed my foot into his back. He let out a roar of pain as I dragged the iron dagger along the back of his neck, using everything in me to cut through bone and tissue. Blood sprayed, dotting my chest and face. His roar ended in a gurgle as the dagger punched through the other side. Jerking my arm to the right, I severed his head. His body fell forward and his head went straight down, landing in a splat that turned my stomach.

Gross.

So freaking gross.

A harsh shout drew my attention, and I spun around. My heart dropped like a stone. Ren was surrounded, two Ancients at his back and three fae at his front. Blood trickled from the corner of his mouth as he ducked a blow that would've most likely knocked him out or worse. He was pushed back and a fae jumped on his back. Literally. Like a freaking spider monkey.

I shot forward and gripped the back of the fae's shirt, yanking him off of Ren. I threw it to the floor and swooped down, jabbing the dagger deep into its chest. That fae was no more by the time I straightened and looked over my shoulder.

Ren had taken out one of the Ancients based on the headless body next to him, but he was still surrounded and there was an ugly gash along his forehead that stole my breath. I started toward him just as I caught sight of the Princes. The brothers were tearing through the fae like they were nothing but paper. I couldn't see Kalen or Faye or anyone else in the mess. I hoped that they were still standing.

Grabbing the fae closest to Ren, I spun her around. The

fae's eyes widened in shock as the stake cut through her skin like a hot knife through butter. I jerked the weapon out, my gaze already swinging toward—

A body slammed into me. Knocked off balance, I fell onto my side. A burst of panic hit me as I rolled onto my knees. I started to get up, but pain exploded along my back as a boot came down, knocking my legs and arms out from underneath me. I didn't even know how I managed to hold on to my weapons as my chin knocked off the wood floor.

Grinding my jaw through the pain, I grunted as hard fingers dug into my shoulders, roughly flipping me over. I didn't even have a chance to react. A heartbeat later, an Ancient was on top of me, hands encircling my throat.

My oxygen was cut off as he squeezed down, putting pressure on fragile bones. He was going to snap my neck like a twig! Panic exploded in my stomach. I reacted without thought. Lifting both of my arms, I jabbed the stakes into either side of the Ancient's neck. The fae's hands left my throat, but it was too late to stop me. Screaming, I cut through, severing the spinal cord. Blood spurted as the Ancient trembled and then fell to the side.

Rolling away, I sprang to my feet and spun back to Ren. I came up behind the two fae, slamming my stake into the back of one. The other whirled on me, screeching.

"Hi!" I chirped, dipping down as it swung at me. I launched up, kicking out and swiping the legs out from underneath her. "Bye!"

Thrusting the dagger down, I took out the fae and then popped up. Slipping under Ren's arm, I went straight for the Ancient sneaking up on him. Flipping the stake, I swung my arm out just as the Ancient's body jerked in front of me. His eyes widened and then flames erupted from his sockets. His mouth dropped open and fire crawled out, licking along his cheeks and down his throat. He tipped forward—

I jumped out of the way as he fell and my gaze swung to where he'd once stood. The Prince stood there.

"Fire?" I said stupidly. I'd seen what Fabian had been capable of, but that—that was something else.

The Prince's gaze flickered over me. "You have blood . . . everywhere."

"Yeah," I whispered under my breath, stumbling back a step. "That nifty trick would've been helpful about a minute ago."

"Sorry. Been busy." He spun toward the door.

I turned, finding a female fae charging me, practically impaling herself on my dagger. I blinked as she imploded. "Well then."

Then I spotted Faye.

She sprang onto a chair nimbly and spun like a dancer. Aiming the crossbow, she fired off several shots, one after another. Each arrow found a home, striking down three fae. As they fell, I finally saw Miles. He was bruised and bloody but still standing. Relief filled me.

"Get down!" Fabian shouted.

I whipped around just as Ren popped up beside me. Circling an arm around my waist, he dragged me down to the floor just as the air around us exploded with ragged shards of ice.

"What the hell?" I gasped as what appeared to be icicles shot overhead. They hit the walls, shattering wood. Some hit the flesh of fae and mortal, those who hadn't been fast enough.

I cried out as Kalen went down, a thick icicle embedded in his thigh. Ren cursed as his fingers curled into the back of my shirt.

The soft, almost childish giggle echoed off the walls as

I stared up at the entrance and then there were words, ancient words in a language I had never heard before. They flowed over us like a rush of cold water, sending a chill down my spine.

I twisted, pressing into Ren as a tall, thin shadow appeared in the doorway, and then there she was. The Queen.

She drifted into the room, her sharp eyes darting around and stopping on the Prince. She did not hold the Crystal. The Ancient behind her did.

It was about the size of a basketball, white and frosty looking, but as he stepped into the room, it began to glow an iridescent blue.

Fabian reached the Queen first, his body starting to glow the color of a summer sunrise. The Queen flicked her wrist, and then he was flying backward, pinned to the wall—pinned with jagged icicles, one in each of his shoulders, snagged there like a pinned fly.

"Good God," Ren muttered.

The Prince charged her, but all she did was flick her wrist once more and he was skidding backward across the floor.

"Give up and live," she said, her voice full of smoke and shadows. "Get in my way and die."

Ren and I pushed to our feet as the Prince shoved off the wall.

A low rumble shook the floor, gaining sound and speed. I glanced behind me as Ren did the same thing. A faint blue light appeared at the bottom of the door.

"The door!" I gasped. "She's opening the gateway."

The Queen turned to where we stood and lifted her hand, but Ren and I had already seen what she was capable of. We parted ways, him going in one direction and me in another.

Jumping over fallen bodies, I made it about five paces before I was swept off my feet and sent tumbling backward, ass over head. I slammed into the wall. The impact knocked the air and a stake out of my hands. I was stunned for a moment, unable to move.

The Queen had cleared a path.

That easily.

Even with two princes, an army of Summer fae, and the remaining Order members, she had cleared a pathway.

Fabian and the Prince had seriously overestimated their abilities.

The Queen strode forward, Crystal in her arms. It was glowing intensely now, so bright it was painful to look upon. I bit back a curse, pushing to my feet.

"Help me."

I turned, seeing Fabian. Shooting toward him, I reached for the icicles. They were in deep. "Sorry."

Wincing, I pulled the first one out. His entire body jolted as I dropped the first icicle, but he didn't make a sound until I pulled the second one out. Then he screamed, dropping to his knees. Faye was suddenly at his side, pressing her hand into his wound, stanching the blood flow.

The Prince spun in our direction, and that was when the Ancient who'd entered with the Queen charged the Prince, thrusting his shoulder into the Prince's stomach. They collapsed backward, into the wall. Drywall cracked and gave way as dust filled the air. The wall shook and then half of it shattered apart as they fell through into the other room.

"Use them," Fabian gasped, letting his head fall back. "Use them against her."

My gaze dropped to the thick icicle. It was so cold that it burned my hand. I looked up. The Queen was almost to the door. With my heart in my throat, I pivoted, not giving myself time to think about what I was doing.

Racing across the room, I reached the Queen just as she

turned to me. Surprise flickered over her face as I lifted my arm, swinging the icicle down. She swept to the side, and I missed her chest.

But I didn't miss her.

The icicle cut into her shoulder, sinking deep to the bone. The impact traveled all the way up my arm, jarring my entire body.

Screaming in pain and fury, the Queen lashed out. I didn't even know if she hit me with any part of her or if it was just the might of her fury. Either way, I flew backward, crashing to the floor and rolling several feet. Ears ringing, I came to a stop, slow to realize I was now weaponless.

I pushed up onto my elbows, breathing heavy as I looked across the room. The Queen was also down, on her knees, and tearing at the shoulder of her silvery dress. Dark blood stained the front of it.

The closet door suddenly swung open and intense blue light poured out. She'd opened the gateway. Dammit.

Wind picked up, powerful and fierce. A tremble rattled the floors as my loose curls blew across my face. I pushed myself up to my knees, ignoring the ache in my bones. My stare met the Queen's, and her gaze drifted away from me and to my left. I looked over. The *Crystal.*

The Queen had dropped it.

Rolling over, I scrambled to my feet as my stomach dropped. The Queen was already on her feet and she was closer. My feet slipped over the blood-soaked floorboards.

Ren whipped around and started forward, but it was too late. The Queen reached the Crystal first. I shouted as she wrapped her slender fingers around it. Rising, she clutched it to her chest. She didn't look at me. She didn't look at Ren.

The Queen looked to the Prince, to where he was stumbling back through the wall. "I'll see you again, my love."

His chin jerked up and he roared with fury as he tossed the body of the Knight aside and rushed toward the Queen, but she was as fast as a shadow. She spun on bare feet and ran. I didn't even have a chance to take another breath of air before she went through the doorway, the Crystal in hand. The blue light stretched, forming thick tendrils of light. They touched the Queen and flared intensely.

The blue light expanded and whipped out, circling around my leg. It contracted hard and fast, ripping my leg out from underneath me. I hit the floor and then was slipping across it, toward the door.

Realization slammed into me at the speed of a train. Blood—I was covered in it. Some of it had to be mine, and that meant . . .

My blood must've been on the Crystal.

I was about to be sucked into the Otherworld, along with the Queen.

"Ren!" I screamed, digging into the floor. My nails cracked and broke. Another scream tore through me as I was pulled beyond the opening of the door. Arms flailing, my hands smacked off the door frame. My wide gaze swung around, and there was nothing but darkness beyond the blue light. The force of the Otherworld pulled, stretching my arms until I felt my muscles start to tear. My fingers slipped and I lost my grip.

Hands clamped down on mine, and my gaze flew to Ren's. Oh God, he was there, his feet planted on either side of the door. My body lifted clear off the floor.

"Hold on!" he shouted, his face strained as he tugged.

"Ren, oh God, Ren!" I cried out, panic and terror digging into my bones.

The force grew, lifting Ren up, and I knew it was too powerful. It was going to suck both of us through. Both of us.

No.

I couldn't let that happen to him. I couldn't.

My body twisted so I could see his face. Our gazes collided. "Ren. Let go. Please! Please let go. You've got to let go of me."

Horror filled his expression. "Never—God, never!"

"You need to." Stretched to their limits, my arms and shoulders burned as if they were on fire. "I love you, Ren. I love you so much, but you need to let—"

"Stop!" he shouted, his beautiful face contorting with anguish. "I'm not letting go."

Tears clouded my eyes. "You have to. You—"

Arms circled Ren's waist and then I was being pulled forward, out of the light and beyond the doorway and into Ren's lap as we fell backward. I looked up, over Ren's shoulders as he folded his arms tight around me.

The Prince.

Oh God.

The Prince had pulled me—pulled us—free.

Wind whipped through the room and was ripped out of it, sucking back through the door. Twisting in Ren's arms, my eyes were wide as the bright blue light pulsed once and then twice and then pulled into itself until there was just a dot of light in the never-ending darkness, and then there was nothing but bone-chilling blackness.

The door to the Otherworld swung closed, sealing itself up with the Queen and the Crystal inside.

Chapter 35

Slowly, we picked ourselves up, one at a time. The Prince was helping his brother stand, and Faye was with Kalen, one arm around his shoulders, holding him up. Miles was next to Dylan and Jackie. All of us were still alive, but we . . .

"We failed," I whispered, staring at the sealed doorway. "We actually failed."

Silence greeted me as Ren slipped an arm around my waist, drawing me to his side. I felt his lips brush my temple, but bitter disappointment washed over me, nearly stripping me of whatever strength was left.

We failed.

The Queen was gone, but she was going to come back with a vicious, monstrous army. Probably in days. Hours if we weren't lucky.

I stumbled back.

"But did we really fail?" Dylan asked. "The Queen is gone. So are all the Ancients—"

"We have no idea if all the Ancients are gone, but we had to have taken out nearly all of them." Miles limped forward, picking up a fallen stake. "But the Queen has the Crystal in the Otherworld. She can come back at any time—"

"It won't be for a long time." Fabian's voice was hoarse. "You stabbed her with one of the icicles, right?"

Turning, we looked at him and my mouth dropped open. He was a ghostly color. My gaze shot to Kalen. So was he. Both were barely standing, all of their limbs trembling. "I did. I got her in the shoulder. Pretty deep, too."

The Prince looked at me sharply. "You did? You're sure?"

"Yes. Hit the bone. What?" I pulled away from Ren. "What's going on?"

"If she was wounded with her own magic, her own weapons, she will . . ." The Prince trailed off, and then he did something I hadn't heard from him since the enchantment was broken.

The Prince laughed—a deep, loud laugh.

Ren walked forward, his movements stiff. "Can you fill us in on what's going on? Because I'm not sure what is funny right now."

"Me either," Miles muttered, sheathing the stake at his hip.

"Being wounded by one of those icicles would take any fae time to recover from. It would've killed a mortal." The Prince turned back to his brother, wrapping an arm around his waist. "But for the Queen to be wounded with her own magic is catastrophic. The same for any of us."

"So what does that mean?" Jackie demanded, wiping at the blood along her cheek. "Will it kill her?"

"No." The Prince led Fabian to the door. "But it will greatly weaken her for a very long time."

I didn't dare let any hope grow in me as I limped after them, but I remembered him mentioning this when he'd told us what would weaken them. "How long is a very long time?"

"Months," he answered.

"Months? Are you kidding me? That's not a long time." It was better than weeks or hours, but still not long enough.

He stopped and looked over his shoulder. "Months in the Otherworld are years in the mortal world."

"Years?" Ren repeated. "Like in plural?"

"In plural," the Prince responded. "And while she's weak, she's not going to be able to gather an army. With her powers down and wounded, she won't gain many supporters. Not in the Otherworld, where only the strong and fully powered gain support."

My heart was thundering in my chest. "So, what does this mean exactly?"

"It means we didn't fail," he replied, smiling slightly. It was warm, but didn't reach his eyes. I didn't think any of his smiles did. "We will have years to prepare for her return."

I LIMPED DOWN the steps, my head a mix of conflicting thoughts and emotions. Had we failed? Yes? No? I wasn't sure, and I was too damn tired to really think about it and too freaking ecstatic that we were all alive to beat myself up about not getting the Crystal or killing her.

I'd leave that for tomorrow.

Because we were going to have a tomorrow.

"Ivy!" Tink screeched the moment I reached the bottom of the stairs.

I drew up short as he raced away from Fabian and all but tackled me, wrapping his long arms around me. "You're alive!"

"Yes," I squeaked. "And I thought you were supposed to stay at the hotel."

"I did, but I couldn't wait any longer. I showed up just as everyone was coming down the stairs." He rocked me back and forth. "I went out all by myself and found the place!"

"He wasn't by himself," I heard Tanner say. "He was getting worried, and well, we couldn't stop him."

Squeezing my eyes shut, I hugged him back, too happy to be hugging him again to be mad about him not listening to us.

"What happened?" Tink asked, and I pulled away as Faye began to explain everything.

Ren moved over to the Princes while Tink was given the breakdown, and I saw that Tanner hadn't come alone. Brighton was with him, lingering in the back. She was staring at the two Princes, her pretty face pale.

"We need to get my brother back to the hotel," The Prince said. "He needs to rest, as does Kalen."

Tink moved away from me, hurrying to Fabian's side. "Is he going to be okay?"

"He will be."

"What can we do to help them?" I asked.

"Nothing," he answered. "All we could do is wait for the affects to wear off."

Looking at the pale and drawn faces of Fabian and Kalen, I felt really bad for them. "How long?"

"Too long," grunted Fabian. "We should be fine . . . in a few weeks."

Weeks? My eyes widened.

"I . . . I brought an SUV." Brighton cleared her throat and then spoke up. "I can take them back."

I drew in a shuddering breath and walked over to where the Princes stood. Ren was already there. "Hey," I said, glancing between the two of them. "I just want to thank you for, um, saving us—saving me back there. If you hadn't . . ."

He stared at me. "You do not need to thank me. Ever."

I shifted, uneasy. "But I do. We do."

"She's right." Ren's shoulders tensed as he extended a hand to the Prince. "Thank you, Prince."

The Prince's gaze flickered from Ren's hand to his face, and then after a long moment, he took Ren's hand and shook it. "You're welcome." Releasing Ren's hand, he glanced over at me. And my name is not Prince. It is Caden."

FAINT SUNLIGHT SEEPED under the heavy curtains, slipping its way across the bedroom floor, toward the bed. I had no idea what time it was since Ren apparently didn't believe in bedroom clocks, but I knew it had to be late in the afternoon.

Just like we talked about the day before, we hadn't gone back to Hotel Good Fae last night when everyone left the house on Royal Street. We'd gone back to Ren's, because we . . . because we could, and now it felt like I'd slept forever, but as I stared at the tiny particles of dust dancing in the stream of light, I wasn't sure I was ready to be awake.

Squeezing my eyes shut, I shifted my hips as a wave of unrest swept over me. The arm around my waist tightened, drawing me back against a hard, warm chest. "You should still be asleep," Ren's deep voice rumbled against the skin of my neck.

Reaching down to where his hand rested on my stomach, I threaded my fingers through his. "Shouldn't you be asleep, too?"

"You're awake." He kissed the side of my neck. "So, I'm awake."

Sometimes I wondered if he had an internal Ivy alarm system and if he charged himself a monthly fee for it. I squeezed his hand in return. There was a beat of silence and then he tugged me onto my back, and I found myself staring into sleepy, beautiful green eyes.

Curly brown hair fell forward, brushing against his eyebrows as he rose onto his elbow above me. "I'm not going to ask if you're okay." He swept back a strand of my hair as his gaze searched mine. "Just don't bottle all of this up. A lot has happened, and even though we may have years before we face the Queen again, a lot is still going to happen."

I swallowed razor blades of emotions and whispered, "I promised I wouldn't."

Ren waited as he stared down at me.

Drawing in a shaky breath, I exhaled slowly. "Do you think we really have years before the Queen comes back?"

The tips of Ren's fingers trailed across my cheek, avoiding the deep, purplish bruises and raw cuts that had appeared overnight. "Based on what they said, we have no reason to believe that isn't the case."

"True," I murmured. "But what if they're wrong?"

"What if they're not?" He dragged his thumb under my lip. "What if we have years to live and to make sure we're ready when she comes back? Years, Sweetness. That's a long time. That's a lot of living."

A bit of the knot resting in the pit of my stomach loosened. It didn't go away completely, but it made it easier to breathe. Ren was right. There was no reason that the brothers were wrong. We could have years. "It's over," I said, because I felt like I needed to say it. "It's over for now."

Ren dropped a quick kiss on the tip of my nose. "Yes, it's over for now."

I closed my eyes, letting that really sink in. It still didn't seem real. That we weren't living second to second, day to day.

He kissed my forehead. "You're going to worry about this, but it'll get easier." This time he kissed the corner of my lips and then sighed heavily. "But you already know that."

I did.

Moving on past the fact that the Queen could and most likely would come back wasn't going to be easy. But I couldn't live in fear. A healthy amount of dread was one thing, but we . . .

We really didn't fail last night.

I opened my eyes. "When she does come back, we're going to be ready to kill that bitch."

Ren grinned. "It's so hot when you talk about killing evil fae."

A laugh escaped me, and for the first time in a long time, I let myself really look ahead. I practically had an entire life ahead of me—an entire life with Ren. Of course, we still had our duty. Either of us could die on our next patrol, but with the help of the Summer Court, it wasn't just the Order anymore.

We could have a future.

It may be rough from time to time. Even though I hadn't had a craving since we left California, I knew that it could come back, but if it did, I would deal with it. We had a future—one I wanted to start right now—a hopeful, bright future.

I lifted my chin, and without words, Ren obliged what I was silently seeking. Ren kissed me, and it was deep and consuming and beautiful in all the ways that brought tears to my eyes. Everything Ren felt for me was in that kiss, in *every* kiss, and when he pulled the blanket out from between us, he slipped over me and slid inside me.

The way our bodies joined was nothing like the night before when we returned to Ren's place and immediately raced to the shower, washing off all of the blood. That had been fast and hard, as if it had been the only way to prove that we were still alive—that at the end of it all, we still had each other. This was different. Ren moved painstakingly slow, like it had been the first time for us.

Ren's mouth never left mine. Not as we moved together, our hips pushing and pulling apart. Not once as his hands stayed wrapped around mine, holding them down on either side of my head. Not even as I curled my legs around his waist, taking him as far as we could go. We kissed as if we were drinking from one another, taking sips and then gulping.

There was no room for words. No space left for them as the pace of our hips picked up. There were only soft moans and deeper groans in the brief seconds our mouths were parted. Sweat dampened our bodies, glistened on our skin. Every muscle in my body seemed to tighten and unclench in never-ending waves.

This was . . . this was making love—sweet and steady and soul-scorching. The way he dragged out every kiss, every thrust, absolutely destroyed me in the best possible ways. I never felt closer to Ren, more in love than I did right then.

Ren broke the kiss when he came, speaking my name against my lips in this deep, guttural way that curled my toes and sent me tumbling over the edge into bliss. Tight shivers washed over me. The release flowing throughout my body blew nearly every thought out of my mind, leaving room only for the rolling pleasure.

When it was all over, only when our hearts began to finally slow and I lay curled in his arms, my cheek resting on his chest, did either of us speak.

"What do we do now?" Ren asked as his hand trailed lazily up and down my spine.

That was a loaded question because I knew he wasn't asking about what we were going to do after having mind-blowing sex. He was thinking bigger, long-term. "I don't know," I said after a moment. "I think . . . I think I would want to go back to school."

"Yeah?" His fingers tangled in my hair before slipping free.

I took a shallow breath. "I've missed spring registration, but I could start in the summer or the fall."

"I think that's a good idea."

Excitement blossomed in the center of my chest, unfurling like a rose blooming for the first time. I looked different, but not enough that the mortals would really notice anything. I could easily be in public. No biggie. "I really would like that."

"I can come visit you on campus," he suggested. "You know, just to be distracting."

"That's really helpful."

"I try to be."

Grinning, I trailed my fingers over the taut planes of his stomach. "What about you?"

He didn't even take a second to answer. "Whatever you want to do, where you want to be, that's what I'll do—that's where I'll be."

"Really?" I lifted my chin so I could see his face.

"Really," he repeated. "I thought maybe we could take a vacation, though. I think we earned it."

There was no stopping the smile racing across my face. "A vacation would be awesome."

Those beautiful green eyes were bright. "Where do you want to go?"

"Somewhere cold," I answered immediately. "Somewhere where there will be snow and we can make snowmen and drink hot chocolate and . . . have sex in front of a crackling fireplace."

"I think I know of a few good places back home," he replied. "And I really love your idea of a vacation."

"It was the sex part, wasn't it?"

"Possibly."

I laughed as I settled back down against him. As I lay there, surprise filled me as the realization hit me that there was going to be tomorrow, a week, a month, years to fill up. For some reason, it hadn't struck me until this very moment that we were going to have a real future, barring we didn't get, you know, killed on the job or run over by a speeding trolley. "I guess we really can do that now?"

"Do what?"

"Plan. We can really plan." I bit down on my lip. "For a while there, I really didn't think there was going to be a future. You know? I just kind of stopped thinking about . . . tomorrow."

Ren's hand stilled for a beat and then started moving again. He fell quiet.

"What?" I lifted my head, meeting his gaze.

"You wanted me to let go."

"Ren—"

"You wanted me to let go and if I had you would've been gone."

"I didn't want you to be dragged into the Otherworld with me, Ren. You're angry about that?"

An incredulous look filled his green eyes. "There's a part of me that's pissed about that. Probably going to be a part of me pissed off that you were willing to throw your life away—"

"I wasn't *willing* to throw my life away." I sat up. "It happened so fast, and I realized that you were going to get sucked in, and I—"

"To save me. I know. I understand that." His hand fell to my bare hip. "That doesn't mean I have to like it." His gaze dropped. "But I like *this* right now."

I rolled my eyes. "Stop checking out my breasts."

He arched a brow as he slowly moved his gaze to mine. "Are you seriously telling me not to do that? Do you even know me?"

A reluctant laugh escaped me.

"They're too distracting, Ivy." He brushed his fingers over one breast, causing me to suck in a sharp breath. "They're beautiful and they look so lonely right now. Beautiful breasts should never be lonely."

I smacked his hand away.

A playful grin filled out his lush mouth and then faded away as if it had never been there. His hand fell to his chest, to rest above his heart. "The idea of losing you scares the shit out of me, Ivy. That shock and anger I felt—the shock and anger I still feel and probably always will to some extent was fueled by the terror of knowing you could've been trapped over there, with the Queen and God knows what."

A shudder worked its way through me. The mere thought of being trapped in the Otherworld with the Queen, even a severely wounded Queen, was horrifying because I knew from experience what that would've entailed.

It wouldn't have been pretty.

"We've been through a lot," I whispered. "We both have a lot to deal with."

"Yeah. We do."

And I knew that for years to come I'd still have nightmares. Maybe I would until the day I died. I'd still wake from sleep, full of panic that I was back there, with a chain around my neck, or that I was seconds away from being trapped in the Otherworld. Like grief, that kind of terror wasn't going to go away easily.

I swallowed against the sudden knot in my throat, and he folded one arm behind his head as he stared up at me. "I want you to know I'm not holding that against you. It's not like that. For real."

I knew he wasn't. That wasn't his style. "I don't want you to feel that way anymore."

"And I don't. I really don't." He briefly closed his eyes. "It's just . . . when I think about what could've happened—what almost did—it's a jolt to the system. It takes me back to that very second, but it doesn't hold me there long."

Tucking my hair over one shoulder, I placed my hand on his hard stomach. "I get it. I do. Like I said before, if it had been you asking me to let go, I would've been pissed."

"You would have straight-up punched me in my nuts."

A grin tugged at my lips. I would've. I would've done it until he couldn't walk his fine ass into the Otherworld.

The hand on my hip moved to my back. With the slightest pressure, he brought me back to his chest, to where I was lying before. He kissed the top of my head. "And like *I* said before, I get why you thought that was what needed to happen. I hate saying that, but I get it."

I pressed my lips to his chest and then threw my arm around his waist, squeezing him so tightly that he laughed.

"God," he grunted. "You're unnecessarily strong."

Giggling, I squeezed him again, but this time not as hard.

A few moments passed and then Ren said, "I know I've told you this before, but I need to say it again. Especially now."

"You think my breasts still look lonely?"

Ren laughed. "Believe it or not, that wasn't the direction I was going in."

"Well, that's a shocker."

"I know." He sat up then, bringing me with him, my hair tumbling over my shoulders, and then we were face to face. For a moment, like I did every so often, I got a little-lost staring into those beautiful eyes. "I was scared out of my mind when I thought I was going to lose you, but I was also so fucking blown away by you."

I blinked. "What?"

His eyes searched mine as he reached between us, catching the strands of my hair and tucking them back. "You went after her with that icicle, knowing how dangerous that was. Yet you did it anyway."

"You would've done the same thing," I reasoned.

"That's not the point." Ren cupped my cheek. "You made such a selfless choice. Part of me wants to keep you locked away and preferably chained to a bed because of it, but I don't think I've ever been more awed or impressed by anyone in my life."

Warmth started to invade my cheeks and spread down my throat.

Ren's hand slipped and curled around the nape of my neck. "I love you, Ivy. I think you're beautiful and sexy as hell. You're funny and so damn intelligent that sometimes I don't feel worthy."

"Ren," I whispered, my eyes filling with tears as I placed my hand on his chest.

"And I admire the fuck out of you," Ren continued, his voice thickening. "You are so many amazing things, Ivy, but most of all, you are so damn brave."

Brave.

That word again.

A word that meant so much to me, and I knew Ren was right. He was proud of me, but better yet, I was proud of myself—of what I would've been willing to do and what I had done.

I smiled as I leaned in, pressing my forehead against his. I was *brave*, and I had my entire life to be brave. “I love you,” I whispered.

Ren’s lips curved into a grin against mine. “Prove it.”

The wicked and dangerously seductive world of the fae and the Order continues with *The Prince*, a 1001 Dark Nights novella, coming August 14, 2018.

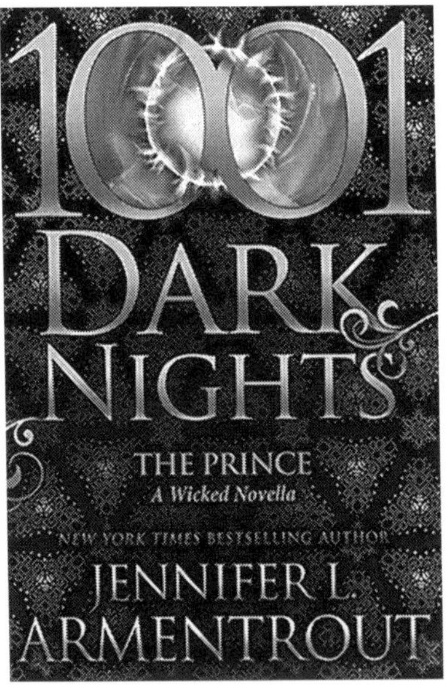

Available for pre-order.

JENNIFER L. ARMENTROUT

1 New York Times and # 1 International Bestselling author Jennifer lives in Martinsburg, West Virginia. All the rumors you've heard about her state aren't true. When she's not hard at work writing. she spends her time reading, watching really bad zombie movies, pretending to write, hanging out with her husband, her Jack Russell Loki and their retired police dog, Diesel. In early 2015, Jennifer was diagnosed with retinitis pigmentosa, a group of rare genetic disorders that involve a breakdown and death of cells in the retina, eventually resulting in loss of vision, among other complications. Due to this diagnosis, educating people on the varying degrees of blindness has become of passion of hers, right alongside writing, which she plans to do as long as she can.

Her dreams of becoming an author started in algebra class, where she spent most of her time writing short stories....which explains her dismal grades in math. Jennifer writes young adult paranormal, science fiction, fantasy, and contemporary romance. She is published with Tor Teen, Entangled Teen, Disney/Hyperion and Harlequin Teen. Her Wicked Series has been optioned by PassionFlix. Jennifer has won numerous awards, including the 2013 Reviewers Choice Award for Wait for You, the 2015 Editor's Pick for Fall With Me, and the 2014/2015 Moerser-Jugendbuch-Jury award for Obsidian. Her young adult romantic suspense novel DON'T LOOK BACK was a 2014 nominated Best in Young Adult Fiction by YALSA. Her adult romantic suspense novel TILL DEATH was an Amazon Editor's Pick and iBook Book of the Month. Her young adult contemporary THE

PROBLEM WITH FOREVER is a 2017 RITA Award Winner in Young Adult Fiction. She also writes Adult and New Adult contemporary and paranormal romance under the name J. Lynn. She is published by Entangled Brazen and HarperCollins.